Vertigo

A Novel

Steven Paul Wilson

Double-D Ranch Books

Double-D Ranch Books —Austin, TX

Printed in the United States of America

Cover Design provided by: Cari Stanhope

Cover Photo by: Heiko Behn @Pixaby.com

ISBN: 13: 978-0-9859434-1-7

Acknowledgments

I'd like to thank the newest members of our small team: Editor and Graphic designer, Cari Stanhope; IT and Web Administrator, Jim F. Zwiener; and General Assistant, Heather Greeson. I'd also like to thank and acknowledge past contributors Brad Kelly, Maria Kennedy, Peter Hughes and Jini Smith. And, finally, I'd like to thank my family for their encouragement and continued support, making all things possible.

Chapter 1

Oh, that smile, that make-a-heart-skip-a-beat smile. Even after so many years, I remember it as if it were yesterday.

Her name was Candy, a lovely and young, green-eyed beauty who radiated health and vitality. She came into my life in the summer of '76. It was a summer of adventure, triumphs and defeats, sadness and joy. And for one Central Texas teen, it was a summer of loves found and lost.

My name is Steven Paul and I'm currently an inmate housed in the Texas Department of Criminal Justice, a place that can truly be defined as hell. And, until, and if and when, my new legal team sorts it out, this place is my home. But, hey, for those who know me, know that I had a life before the steel and concrete concertina that now cages me in prison—a life not void of opportunities. Where did I stray? Sometimes I believe my personal journey on the road to hell began that summer of '76. Maybe? Maybe not? Stick around, decide for yourself, for this is how I remember it...

Vertigo

Chapter 2

I can't help but furtively steal glances at her. Her smile lights the interior of my latest ride—my '69 Pontiac Bonneville with its big block 428 and dual exhaust.

"Hey, you're staring," Candy says and playfully punches me in the arm.

"Technically not, Candy. I'm only furtively stealing glances at you. There's a big difference," I say and smile myself. I'm not sure what it is with women and me, but it seems that I get punched quite regularly by the ones who I meet. "So whatcha smiling about, Candy?"

She shrugs.

"Oh... I don't know. I'm happy that nothing happened to Bonnie for one."

Bonnie's ears perk at the mention of her name and Candy reaches across the front seat to scratch her behind the ear.

"You're a good girl, aren't you Bonnie," she says.

I hardly notice the scent of balsam from Candy's freshly washed hair or the manner in which her T-shirt pulls taut against her small breasts as she twists and stretches from her seat to reach Bonnie. Yeah, right. I confess here and now that I have a real weakness for women and I'm most often guilty of such infractions, supposing such an awareness can be viewed as an infraction.

Anyway, that being said, Bonnie is her dog. A sweet and shy-tempered bull terrier that has been in my care for the past few days due to some very unusual and unfortunate circumstances. I found Bonnie in what remained of Candy's ransacked house—the site of a terrible and horrendous crime. A house from which Candy's friend and dog sitter, a young UT freshman named Kelly Winfield, was abducted, tortured and murdered by a pair of mid-level, Las Vegas mob fuckups. Yeah, I know, deep isn't it? But, that in a nutshell is what brought Candy into my life.

I hang a right on Exposition and head south. "So, other than your relief in finding Bonnie well, nothing else has you smiling? Such as my baby blue eyes? My blond hair? Maybe my dashing good looks?"

She looks over at me. "Nope. Not a thing," she says but continues to smile.

"Not even the obvious fact I routinely workout?"

"Nope, not a thing... Well, maybe your big gun kind of does it for me."

I pat my shoulder-holstered 9mm.

"You mean this little old thing? I bet you'd like to hold it?"

"Umm." She laughs and straightens herself back in her seat. "Maybe later."

You're probably wondering, those of you that don't already know, that is, why exactly am I wearing a holstered 9? Well, it's only a coincidence I have it on me. I was in the process of taking it to my car, for some later beer can killing action, when Candy, bless the Heavens, appeared at my front door. I say "bless the Heavens," for the sight of her mostly vanquished my downtrodden state of mind. It's my 17th birthday. Could she possibly be real, I wondered? Could she be the catalyst that turns my day around? Renews my hope?

So why the blues you ask? Especially in light of the fact it's my 17th, which is a significant age in the great State of Texas, and the age one normally rejoices, for it is the age of consent—an age in which I no longer pose a legal liability for those older, rob-the-cradle women out there who may be otherwise holding back. I mean, someone with my confidence and charm, what other reasons could be holding them back? Could I be wrong? Nah, to know me is to love me, but that's not the point, is it? The point is, why am I still singing the blues this morning?

Just for the record, the morning started off well enough. Actually, quite well. I arose from a deep rejuvenating sleep, feeling spry and thinking what a day to be alive in the big city of Austin. For a June Central-Texas morning, the air was atypically crisp and invigorating. The birds were alive and chattering. The azure sky was dotted with the fluffiest of clouds. Yes, today I believed, as I took a deep breath and filled my lungs with the morning freshness, was poised to be an outstanding day. A continuation of the surreal run-of-luck I'd had the preceding four days, like adding one in the hand and two in the bush to my previously faltering harem of three. Or, luck like a love life that went from Zero to 60 in under four seconds. We're talking about from lights-out missionary style to almost every male's fantasy of lights-on billiard table-top action. And, finally, luck like coming into a sizable fortune (more on that later). A fortune allowing me to retire from the humble position as a busboy at Hansel & Gretel's, a popular eatery right off UT's campus, to become a man about town. Yes, a man about town—a position in which I seem to have been born to excel.

It is for these reasons that my morning, day and future looked promising and bright. I mean what could possibly go wrong?

So, with only Bonnie at my side, I left my sleeping friends at Andy's house feeling on top of the world and we departed for my own house for a much-needed pit stop.

Well, as fate would have it, it was then and there at my house, that, like a house of cards, my world collapsed around me. My new-found fortune mostly is gone, women all but gone and, for the moment, only Bonnie to hear me sing the blues. Thus, my friends, with the wind knocked from my sails, I was left feeling blue.

Anyhow, back to Candy appearing at my front door. She found me through a black, Austin PD detective named Williams with whom I had become acquainted due to some recent excitement in my exclusive West-Austin neighborhood. Upon meeting him, I instantly knew he was not some Mayor's affirmative-action figure placed in Austin's predominantly white police force, but that he had merited his position. What evolved was a strange acquaintance and relationship—to say the least—the parameters of which I myself unsure. Thankfully, Williams, through some keen detecting, learned that Candy's beloved Bonnie was in my possession and passed that information on to Candy. To say the least, I am enthralled by Candy's appearance and presence.

At first, seeing Candy and witnessing her and Bonnie's reunion, it flashed through my mind: "Not you too, Bonnie," but seeing their joy I could not hold the thought. I instantly realized that this reunion was right—that Bonnie was clearly her dog. Bonnie's reaction also told me all that I needed to know about Candy's character—that this is a good woman—for Bonnie is incapable of lies. I have to admit, not only am I enthralled by Candy's presence, but she'd instantly restored my usual optimism and now I can feel at ease in her presence.

Candy reaches forward and sticks a finger through the bullet hole in my windshield.

"So where to first, Steven Paul?"

"Well, high on my priority is getting my windshield replaced before someone cuts themselves and then getting the rear glass replaced which I'm sure you notice is completely missing."

"Yep, I notice. I think that it adds to your mystique."

"More like infamy, you mean?"

I take a left on Lake Austin Blvd.

"Hey, I saw you on the news the other night. It's not every day that there's a shootout in Tarrytown."

"I waited for the news to go live. How did I do in the interview?"

Candy laughs.

"It was pretty funny in a way. Plugging the NRA and all. But, did your friend... What's his name?"

"Andy. "

"Did Andy really cower under his bed? Now, that was funny when you said that and the way the news lady cringed every time you cursed and then innocently asked, 'Am I allowed to say that?'"

"Nah, the cowering part I made up. Andy is part of my crew. He's special in his own sort of way and a major source of entertainment for the rest of the crew and me. You'll meet him soon."

I turn right on South Congress.

"I'll tell you about all the crew while the car's glass is being replaced."

She looks over at me with a curious expression, turns toward me and tucks a leg under.

"So, what was the shootout about anyway? There was nothing on the news the next day but a brief recap and a highly edited clip of your interview."

I meet her eyes.

"If I told you, I'd have to kill you! Just kidding. I'll tell you about it sometime, but first, we're stopping right here at Allens boots..." I turn right on Monroe and pull to the curb. "... and get you that pair of Luccheses and the denim skirt that I promised you since you said you were 'game' earlier."

For those of you who don't know me, I'm right partial to women in short skirts and high-heel cowboy boots. A fetish? Yeah, probably. I'm also big on sayings, adages, clichés and such and employ them every chance I get despite the fact that for most, I don't know their origin. Hey, I watch a lot of TV, okay.

"In all seriousness," Candy says. "I'm game, but confused a bit. I mean you just met me and just like that—" she snaps her fingers. "—you volunteer to take on the responsibility to protect me..."

"Make that 'vow.' Vow to protect you."

"... And now you want to buy me a pair of boots and a skirt? Shouldn't..."

"I have my reasons."

"... Shouldn't I... I mean, shouldn't we discuss the arrangement?"

"All in good time. Now come on. Let's go in. Bonnie, you stay." Candy shrugs, reaches for the door handle, pauses, shakes her head and pushes her door open.

I pull my shoulder holster loose, tuck it and my Beretta under the front seat and exit my car. I take a breath of the still cool air. Is it me, or does the air suddenly smell fresher? Are the birds livelier once more? Is the sky bluer?

I glance over the car at Candy who is patiently watching me and I also wonder if this is the beginning of another run of luck? I smile and decide, here and now, yes, I believe it is.

We enter my favorite Austin boot store. I love the store's ambiance. We're greeted by the smell of new leather and then greeted by the owner himself—a pleasant enough fellow.

"What can I help you young folks with this morning?" he asks. He looks down, checks our feet and notices my ostriches. "Ah." He looks back up at me. "You're the one Cheryl calls Cowboy."

"Yessir, that would be I."

"Son, what in the world did you do to those new ostriches?" He scratches his chin. "Play in the middle of a mud puddle?"

"No, sir. Not on purpose, anyway."

"You called earlier today?"

"Yessir, that would be I." I hike a thumb in Candy's direction. "And this little lady with me is Candy."

Candy blesses us with her pouty look. "Hey, I happen to like my Converses."

"Young lady, I have to side with Cowboy on this one."

He turns and reaches to a lower self, snatches up a can of saddle soap and packet of new polishing rags.

"But first, this will be on the house. It's sacrilege, Son, to treat such a quality boot like that." He hands over the saddle soap and rags. "Now what did the young lady have in mind?"

"I'll field this one, Candy. She would like a pair of size six Luccheses in an iguana, a matching belt and a denim skirt in a..." I stick my head around to check out her rear. "... a size one should work."

She looks at me askance. "How do you know my sizes?"

"The same way that I know your age and weight. Neither of which is anything to be ashamed of, I might add."

"Oh. Okay, I guess," Candy says and bites her lower lip.

"I've got exactly what your young lady is looking for. Follow me."

I must admit I like that thought, "your young lady." Like the quest for the Holy Grail, I shall not be denied.

He leads us into the women's section.

"These tan lizards should be perfect and I do have the matching belt in this color." He picks them up and hands them to Candy. "Try 'em on while I fetch that skirt. Yonder is the mirror, young lady."

I watch Candy as she studies the stitching on the boots' uppers. "These are nice. I'll wait on the skirt and belt and try everything on all at once."

The owner returns with the skirt and belt.

"Here you go, young lady. The dressing room is around the corner in the back. Can I interest y'all in anything else? Shirt perhaps?"

Candy shakes her head no and disappears.

"Yes, sir. How about a pair of boot-cut Wranglers for the lady, as well, and then we'll be set."

Candy returns shortly, hands me her jeans and Converses and spins before me.

"So, what do you think, Steven Paul?"

"Now you're cooking with gas, girl," is what I come up with, but I am also thinking, "good enough to eat." Perhaps something not quite yet appropriate in this developing, one-and-a-half-hour relationship. Take it easy, big boy. All in good time.

She steps before the mirror, twists and checks out her own rear.

"Yeah. I think I like the look," she says as she turns to check out her rear from the other side with a smile.

I've read somewhere, perhaps the informative magazine Playboy, that women's breasts often vary in size, but watching women in the mirror makes me wonder if this is also not true concerning their buns? I read and retain so much useful information.

Candy studies me again: "You sure?"

"Oh. I'm definitely sure." Actually, I'm so sure it hurts, though I'm thinking only the purest of thoughts, you know.

"Perfect then. Let's rock 'n' roll."

I put a finger to my lips. "Shhh. We're in a western-wear store. But, yep, let's roll."

11

We join the owner at the register and the tally comes in under $250. Fuck a 'penny saved is a penny earned.' This is worth every cent. I hand over the cash from the ever-dwindling roll that once made me proud. As Cheryl, a beauty in her own right, so elegantly put it, "a roll that could choke a horse."

"Easy come, easy go," I say.

"Thank y'all for your business," the owner says. "And I almost forgot..."

He reaches under the counter and retrieves an Allens Boots card with a number on it.

"Cheryl called right after you and said should you call again or stop in to give you this number."

I pocket it.

"Thank you, sir. Until next time."

"Y'all come back now and nice meeting you, Candy."

I look at Candy's old jeans and Converse as we begin to exit and wish I could just discard them, but no need in pushing one's luck, right? We step out onto the walk and as the door shuts behind us, the inquisitive Candy must know.

"So, who is this Cheryl? A girlfriend or something?"

Ah. Do I detect a hint of possessiveness? I would like to think so. I inwardly smile.

"Something like that."

"She's not going to try and beat me up if she sees us together, is she?"

"Nah, Probably not." That would be a first, I think. Two women in a little ole catfight over me. In some ways, it almost seems inevitable. Just kidding. But should it ever happen, I would quickly break it up and assure each that there's plenty of me for both of them. I'm always considerate in these types of things. Hey, it's my nature and look, I'm only 17, too. Okay.

I foresee no problems at this time, so no need to cut the old Gordian knot. Besides, Cheryl is now in San Antonio. This I already knew, but the 212 area code confirms it's for me. For those not in the know, Cheryl is a former employee of Allens that I met a few days before and literally charmed out of her pants. Yes, I bought her a skirt too. She, of course, already possessed the boots. She's a tough, witty gal that can hold her own and party hard. She ended up accompanying my crew and me on a celebration limo ride to a Hyde Park titty bar and, not one to kiss-and-tell, she's the one who made my personal, table-top fantasy come true. So, in accordance with my principles, I will not mention this to Candy. Let's keep this between you, me and the bedpost, shall we?

Anyhow, this morning it appeared that I had seen and heard the last of Cheryl, but, lo and behold, I get her number again. Luck? Or could it be fate?

Bonnie is sticking half-out the missing back window as we round the corner and she acknowledges us with a yap.

"Miss us, Bonnie girl, did ya?" I ask. No doubt because you can hear the thump of her tail against the roof of my car emphasized by another yap.

Being the true gentleman and romantic, I open the car door for Candy. She rewards me with the sight of her golden gams as her skirt hikes precariously higher on her thighs before she tucks her legs inside. I feel like a kid in a candy store as I get in on my side and pull the door closed. No pun intended.

Candy reaches over and places a hand on my shoulder.

"Thank you, Steven Paul. That was nice of you."

"You're more than welcome," I say as I crank the car and put her into gear. "Onward through the fog."

"Onward through the fog, huh? Patronize Oat Willie's, do you?"

Oat Willie's is just off UT's drag and Austin's premier head-shop. I back onto Congress and head south again.

"I assumed that you smoked, but didn't notice any roaches in your ashtray so I wasn't going to ask until I knew you better."

"So, my all-American looks didn't fool you?"

"I've seen you a time or two on your motorcycle or in that white Trans Am or whatever is. You're hard to miss. You're preceded by the noise. How come you're not driving your white car? I've heard a few rumors about you, too. You do portray your outlaw persona and air of recklessness quite well."

I look over at her and smile.

"Thank you."

"I'm not sure I meant that as a compliment." She says returning my smile.

"Anyway, it was a Firebird Formula 400 and she's in heaven now. She didn't survive the derby."

"Man, that's a shame. It was a pretty car."

"The new Seville didn't fare any better."

"Not the one involved in the Westover crash the other night?"

"That would be the one," I answer.

"The news said that one driver was arrested on a firearms charge. Now you have bullet holes in this car and a few days back you were in a shootout in my Rockwellian neighborhood. You sure you're not some kind of bullet magnet? You sure I'm safe with you?"

"Hey, let's listen to the radio."

I punch the power and amp buttons on my radio and Van Halen's "Running with the Devil" pumps from the speakers. I quickly punch both off. At least it wasn't Nazareth's "Now your messing with a son-of-a-bitch."

"Tarrytown's very own blue-eyed devil. Am I running with Tarrytown's blue-eyed devil?" Candy asks and laughs.

"Hold that thought. Here's the junkyard." This stretch of South Congress is home to several junkyards. I whip into the dirt drive and pull in front of the shed-style building. "Hold tight. I'll be right back."

I go in and negotiate the price of the glass. They have both of the pieces that I need and can have them installed in 35 to 45 minutes. Luck? Or only a coincidence?

Vertigo

Chapter 3

I open the passenger door.

"Hand me my holster and gun, Candy."

She looks at me with real concern.

"They didn't piss you off in there, did they?"

"No, no." I laugh. "They're going to install the glass and we're going to take a walk."

"You're going to take me for a walk in a junkyard?"

"Hey, I want to show you off in your new duds."

Candy playfully kicks a boot out at me which I easily avoid.

"Thanks," she says.

"Okay. If it makes you feel any better, this walk will not count as our second date. You know, I always get to second base or better on a second date."

Candy reaches and pulls my holster and 9 from its stash spot. I let out an inaudible whistle. I love it when a plan comes together. Yes, our little shopping spree was worth every cent, I'm gleefully reminded.

Candy hands me my gun and offers her other hand so that I can help her from the car.

"Doesn't there have to be a first date first?" she asks.

"Shopping," I reply.

"Oh, shopping. Okay... doesn't there have to be a first base first then?"

"Our kiss."

"I gave you a peck on the cheek."

"Hey, it worked for me." I smile, holding her hand longer than necessary. "Come on, Bonnie. You can come too."

"So, in your way of thinking, by the end of the day, we'll have finished dating and we'll be consummating our marriage?"

"Who says you necessarily have to buy the cow to get the milk?"

Candy drops my hand and I receive my second playful hit to the arm of the day, albeit a mighty hard playful hit.

"Cow! I'll show you cow!"

She adds a painfully playful kick to the shin.

"Whoa, turbo, let's save the foreplay for later."

I slip my arm into my shoulder holster and retake Candy's hand. With a couple of small tugs, we're off.

"Anyway, that's not how the saying goes. I believe it's 'Why buy the cow if the milk's free?' or something like that."

"They'll never accuse me of plagiarism."

"Detective Williams seems to have confidence in your ability to protect me. Why do you guys talk in some kind of code? What's that all about?"

"Some things are better left unsaid. We have some kind of tacit agreement."

"Tacit agreement?"

"Yeah, but I don't actually get it myself. He seems willing to look the other way if I skirt the law somewhat. I can only guess that, in some way, he believes the ends justify the means."

"I'm still not sure why you're willing to protect me. I'm not sure how I stand financially right this minute. That fuckhead excuse of a husband really screwed me over. I don't even know what he did..." Candy stops, takes a deep breath and wipes fresh tears from her eyes. "... but it got Kelly killed."

I drop her hand, put my arm across her shoulders and pull her close.

"I don't know what they're after," Candy says. "But they're serious."

We begin to walk again.

"Now that shithead husband is running scared. Leaves me holding the bag. I mean, it's my house. My late grandmother gave it to me. I want to be able to live safely in my house again."

I feel like shit, listening to her. I know who they were and what they were after, but my crew's lives are at stake and I can't confide in Candy yet.

"My grandparents raised me," she continues. "My parents died in a car crash when I was three. I don't even remember them. No brothers or sisters. My grandparents were all I had."

She wipes at her tears. The only lame thing I can come up with is "Sorry," but then I decide to add: "Candy, you're going to be safe in your home. Whatever dangers there might be, I'll eliminate them."

Candy turns her head into my chest as we silently walk on. I wonder if she can feel my heartbeat. My heart is thumping in my chest and echoing in my ears. Candy's runny nose and tears are dampening my shirt. I wish I could at least lessen her heartache with the knowledge that Kelly's killers are no more. Say something witty like: "They're pushing up daisies now." Or tell her the truth—that they have literally been deep-sixed. The mob pair from Las Vegas known as Tony C and Vinnie are strapped in their Buick Electra, resting at the bottom of a Lake Austin cove. I know this to be true for I put them there. Well, with the help of my crew that is. Will there be more to follow? The stakes are high enough—though it's doubtful. The bottom line is: I don't know.

Candy looks up at me and wipes her nose with the back of her hand.

"Okay. I'm going to quit crying for a while. That's all I've been doing since I learned of Kelly's death. Bonnie and you made me smile again. I don't know if I will ever be able to... let's change the subject, okay?"

"That's a bet. Oops—sorry, Candy. That sounds like a good plan."

I know little of Candy's estranged husband other than what Candy has told me and from what I surmised and deduced. He's apparently a gambling addict and not a good gambler at that. An older man that came into Candy's life at a low point and swept her off her feet. A wannabe high-roller that ran through what he could of Candy's inheritance. A man that then got in with the wrong Vegas crowd and then somehow relieved the wrong people of a half-a-million plus in German bearer bonds—thinking what? That there would be no repercussions.

I know of the bonds' existence because, through a fluke at least, some of them came into my possession—a sequential stack of a hundred. Where are they now? I'm embarrassed to tell those that don't already know. Maybe later. I can't dwell on that for now.

"So, what's your crew like?" Candy asks. "Tell me about them."

"Okay, but let's start heading back." We turn around. A car honks in passing. I flash them a peace sign. Bonnie runs ahead, stops and waits for us. "We're a motley crew for sure. Mostly four of us that hang together. Not much in common other than we like to get together. You know, to drink beer, smoke a little pot and wolf down some pizza or whatever is placed before us.

"Andy's the funniest. Well, let me rephrase that. He's fun to laugh at. The butt of most of our jokes. He keeps us laughing in that respect. Supplies the rest of us with hours of entertainment."

"That sounds mean."

"Oh, it is, but we love him in our own special way. Anyway, he has a metabolism from hell. Andy can eat a horse and never gain and he has the energy to match. He's the war-monger among us, the player of intricate war games which sometimes last for weeks. He spreads big topographical maps that cover entire floors and utilize thousands of tiles representing army units and such. Anyway, none of the rest of us are interested in playing these games.

"Then, there's Jim. Voted most likely to succeed in the real world. A computer programmer who piddles in the stock market. He seems to do well at it, too. Jim's a brawny person but doesn't work out like I do. Apparently, he doesn't need to. That leaves

James. James is small in stature, frail-looking and shy on top of that. I'm working on that. He's starting to break out of his shell. Get a sense of humor. You know, they're all good guys. I trust them all."

"And you?"

"I'm the one parents warn you about," I say and wink.

"I don't believe that. You seem really nice."

"Well, you know what they say?"

"Looks can be deceiving."

"Yes, looks can be deceiving."

"I still don't believe that about you," Candy restates.

"I do have some good qualities."

"Like?"

"I'm fiercely loyal. I'll give you the shirt off my back. And I respect my elders."

"And some negatives?" Candy asks.

"Well, let's see... I like living on the edge. An adrenaline junky. Compulsive. Guilty of wandering eyes at times."

"A womanizer, huh? Have a weakness for women, do you?"

"Yeah," an understatement, I'd say.

"Maybe someday, you'll meet the right one and discover the grass is not always greener on the other side of the fence," Candy says and rests her head back on my chest.

I'm thinking maybe I have, as we leisurely make our way back. I know one thing: Candy feels nice leaning into me. The rest of our walk is in silence. Again, I think of how at ease I feel in Candy's presence.

"Ah, beautiful. They're finished. That was fast, Candy."

I open the passenger door and tilt the seat forward.

"Load up, Bonnie Girl."

Bonnie piles right in and I allow the seat to fall back into place. I bow and offer the open door to Candy.

"Can we go to that German restaurant now? I'm hungry and I feel like drinking my fair share of beer. We can even count it as our third date," she says and adds a smile.

I start to say, "you bet" but catch myself.

"Your wish is my command," I say and close the door for her, round the big Bonneville and let myself in. "Look, they even re-attached the mirror."

I grab the mirror and adjust it the way I like it.

"Onward through the fog."

"Onward through the fog," Candy echoes.

I pull out on South Congress and head north. I punch the radio and amp buttons again. Bob Seger's "Turn the Page" greets us from the rear Jensens. They play a lot of Bob Seger on this station, I realize.

"KLBJ okay?"

"Bob Seger. Cool."

We cross over Ben White and pass a couple of white, working girls. This short stretch of Congress is their haunt.

"That's sad," Candy says noticing the girls. "I wonder sometimes if they can be helped."

Candy starts frantically backhanding me on the shoulder.

"Look! Look! That guy is trying to force the woman into his car!"

We cross Oltorf and I whip into the strip mall's parking lot. "Stay in the car," I say squealing to a stop near the confrontation. I lay on the horn before jumping out and drawing my gun.

They both temporarily stop their struggle. The guy looks rough and tough and even bigger up close. Big in the shoulders and round in the belly. He's sporting a two- or three-day growth and I think to myself, "Oh boy, here we go again." He reminds me of Vinnie and Vinnie was a tough bastard. The muscle of the mob pair. The guy glowers at me.

"This is between my bitch and me."

"Not anymore, Hoss," I say with as much conviction as I can. He laughs.

"What you going to do? Shoot me? When I get done with my bitch, I'm going to stick that gun up your ass."

I take a deep breath and let out a soft whistle.

"Wrong answer."

I step forward and rake the barrel across his face. Blood instantly spews from his broken nose. He let's go of the woman, both hands go to his face and he starts stomping his feet. "Son-of-a-bitch! Son-of-a-bitch! I think you just broke my fucking nose!"

I whack him again and this time good, right in the temple. He crumbles at my feet. Suddenly I get whacked myself from behind.

"Hey, you killed my old man you bastard!"

I raise a hand in defense and turn in time to avoid another whack to the head by the woman's purse. A strap gives this time and the purse's contents scatter.

"Bastard! Now look what you went and done." She yells at me as she drops to all fours and scrambles to gather the spreading crap. Crap that's apparently more important than her old man. A small crowd begins to gather and that is my cue to get out of dodge. I bow to my audience, jump back in my ride and we beat a retreat from the lot.

"Shit. Excuse the French, but that was scary. I can't believe that woman hit you with her purse. Not a very appreciative bitch, was she?" Candy says and we both laugh. Candy continues, "Yes, folks, I've seen it all. Steven Paul with only a gun and a smile saves the day."

We both laugh again. I notice that I'm still holding my gun. I was so into the escape mode that I forgot to put it away. I re-holster my 9 and check my rearview for about the tenth time since leaving the lot. So far, all good—no cops. To the untrained eye, it may seem that I handled the conflict without worry, but my pulse tells a different story.

"Candy, I've got to stop by Austin National Bank for a sec before we go and eat—arrange a couple of things. I'll be in-and-out and after we eat, we can stop back by and I can pick up some cash then."

"Okay, that's cool."

"It will be faster if I jump out, run in and out, while you circle the block."

"No problem."

"You think that you can reach the pedals?" I joke.

"It's seeing over the steering wheel that gives me trouble," she jokes back. "You have something that I can sit on?"

"How about my lap? Let you do a few practice laps. See how you do."

"Right. I bet you'd like that," she smirks good-naturedly.

"Here we are." I pull my holster loose, slide the seat all the way forward, stash my pistol underneath and bail. I enter the spacious lobby and stroll with purpose. I promptly get assistance gaining access to my safety deposit box. The only occupants are two of my remaining bearer bonds. A remaining third bond resides neatly folded and tucked in my rear pocket. Five is all that I managed to retain. Shit, I think, it's a far cry from the original stack of a hundred with which I started. What do some say? "A fool and his money are soon parted." I'd like to think that I only lost them because I was too trusting. Still, no matter how you sugarcoat it, the thing leaves a bitter taste.

You see, I slipped up and I allowed my little South-Austin Jewish girl in on the oh-so-thoughtful stash spot on our house's flat, 20-foot high roof. In my defense, she and I did not know the value of the bonds, if any, at the time of the clever concealment. My additional error was to not foresee her telling her father of my discovery. As a consequence, she and her family absconded to a better life somewhere. As my mother sometimes likes to say, "It is what it is." Anyway, I felt somewhat better when her Dear John letter announced her eternal love for me.

I take the elevator to the second floor where my banker, for all of four days, maintains his plush-leather and oak-paneled digs for an office. Despite being impeccably power-dressed, my banker, an international correspondence banker, is plump, pink-cheeked and easily intimidated.

I drop off the three remaining bonds with him and give specific directions: $5,000 in cash in three individual bank bags, $300 in separate cash and the remainder, minus their nominal fee, to be deposited in my marginal account. Oh, and I let him know that I'd be back after my luncheon to retrieve the cash. They're "luncheons" when dealing with your banker.

Here's a pointer for you: when dealing with bankers, always be assertive. Exactly how long have I been practicing this theory you wonder? Oh, all of four days.

I exit the bank to the noon's brightness. For early June, it's an unseasonably cool day. The second one in the past week. I wade through a score of hopeful pigeons and step to the curb to await my ride. The traffic is lunch-hour, bumper-to-bumper, but it's only a short wait until Candy rounds the corner and I hop in. Getting in on the passenger side, I exaggerate bumping my knees on the dash.

"Damn girl, could you put the seat up any farther?"

She gives me the "yeah, right" look and concentrates again on navigating the boat.

"You know where Hansel & Gretel's is?" I ask.

"Yep, never been there, but I know where it is," she says as she shoots through a small gap in the traffic and just makes the yellow.

I laugh. "You go girl."

"Hey, I'm hungry and thirsty, okay?"

"And sexy."

"Whatever," she says but I can feel her glow and I know that she likes the compliment. I enjoy watching her.

We make it to Hansel & Gretel's in short order. Hansel & Gretel's is housed in an off-white, alpine-looking structure. It features the dark heavy beam look with a tiered steeple roof. It caters to a mostly college crowd and boasts a simple but decent menu, some German ales and lagers, Miller Lite and Lowenbrau Light and Dark, all at reasonable prices.

But my favorite feature is that the Peruvian wife of the owner dotes on me. How this exactly came about I do not know.

We enter through the backdoor and cut through the kitchen with Bonnie tethered to her walking string so that I can see who all is working. I don't see my Peruvian friend. But the kitchen is bustling and full of new faces. I know they had to have hired at least two busboy replacements for Andy and myself. Looking back, I can't see how I ever worked as a lowly busboy. Could my view on life now be distorted having experienced several days of wealth? Do I feel the job is below me? Hell yeah, I'll cop to that. The job was a mere phase and, like I told Andy, "I'm moving on." My new occupation: personal bodyguard to damsels in distress. Yeah, now that sounds more fitting—personal bodyguard. No one seems to be paying us much attention, but several pause briefly enough to coo and pet Bonnie.

We step through the swinging doors into the dining area. The first table before the sole TV is the employee's table and my usual dining spot, but today I prefer only the company of Candy and Bonnie.

Liz, my favorite waitress, spots us.

"Steven Paul, there you are. Everyone has been talking and asking about you." She laughs. "We all saw you on the news. Quite a performance." She laughs some more.

"You liked that, did you?"

Liz is a big-boned, healthy German gal. Not big boned as in "blind-date big-boned," but healthy as in "some fine breeding stock." I've massaged her shoulders many a time and have whispered plenty of dirty nothings in her ear—but to date, to no avail. Still, I'm eternally hopeful and she's still my favorite outside the owner's wife.

"Who's your lady friend?"

"Liz meet Candy."

"Pretty. Candy, you better watch this blue-eyed, split-tongued devil," Liz jokes.

"So where' s Andy? Still cowering under his bed?"

We all laugh.

"Nah, I made that part up. He's probably how I left him: asleep and dreaming of food."

I point to a small vacant table.

"Liz, we'll take that table over there and bring us a cold pitcher of Miller and three of my favorites. Oh, by the way, this is Bonnie. Hold the lettuce and potato salad on her order."

"Should I write this on a ticket? You still a high roller?"

I eternally cringe at the words "high roller," for this is how Candy described her now estranged husband. Actually, it was "no good, wannabe high roller" or something to that effect. I wink at Liz.

"I'll pay as usual."

I show Candy to her seat and take my own. Bonnie does her predictable several spins before plopping to the floor.

"I hope that you didn't mind that I ordered for you?"

"Not at all. I'm starved. This is the first time that I've had an appetite since learning about Kelly."

"I promise you will like it. A grilled roast beef sandwich and I'm not sure of the name of the cheese, but it's delicious. It comes on a sourdough bun with lettuce and ranch dressing."

Liz arrives with the pitcher and expertly fills both frosted mugs.

"There you go. Let me know if I can get you two anything else."

We clink mugs.

"To your safety and to things getting back to normal for you," I toast.

"Amen."

Candy takes a gulp of her beer and wipes the foam from her upper lip with the back of her hand.

"Ahhh... now that's cold," she says.

"You're just as cute as a button, you know that?"

"Thanks."

She sets her mug down.

"Do you really think I'll be safe in my home again?"

"Candy, I told you I would protect you."

"I know, I know. Williams sure seems to think you can protect me and I must say that you handled that big brute earlier like a street punk. It's just that I don't how much I can pay you right now."

"Let's not worry about that right yet. First, we've got to get your house back in order. But not today. Today we're going to have some fun."

"Doing?"

"That I haven't quite figured out yet. I'll study on it while we drink a few pitchers. With the old pumps primed, we'll come up with something."

"If you say so."

Candy knocks back the rest of her beer and I refill her mug.

"You know whatever my stupid husband took must be really valuable. He acted like our ship finally came in. I think I mentioned that before. But the way he acted, it had to be something big. I can't fathom anything worth enough to murder Kelly over. Who did he rip off is what I'd like to know? Maybe they got it back, whatever it was, and headed back to Vegas."

I ignore the speculation knowing what I believe to be the truth.

"One thing we are going to do today is waste some ammo. Get you used to that Smith & Wesson 9 I promised you." I finish my first mug and pour myself a second.

"We'll get you a holster for it too—today or tomorrow."

"Cool, and here comes our food."

Candy rubs her hands together in anticipation. She's fun to watch. Candy takes a healthy bite of her sandwich and smiles as she chews. I tear off a piece of Bonnie's sandwich and feed it to her. She's at full attention now that the food has arrived. I take a bite of my own sandwich and study Candy some more. Did I mention that I think I'm in love? I fall in love easily. I think that's a rule of thumb for most teens, don't you? I'm also in love with my red, one-piece-clad Farrah poster that adorns the wall of my lair and which forever keeps vigil over me, her pert nipples and all.

Candy takes another healthy bite and chases it with her beer.

"William tells me that the insurance company will likely total my Cadillac after what happened to it." She takes another deep draw of beer. "I sure hope so, because I don't think that I could ever ride in it, or even a similar one now."

I get her point, seeing as how Kelly's body was found bound in its trunk and the car itself having been found submerged in 20 feet of water by a young snorkeler at Lake Austin's Tarrytown boat ramps. I refill her mug as Candy continues.

"Since it was only a year old, that will be a chunk of money. But I'll have to buy something to replace it. Maybe something less expensive. A Buick or Olds."

"Both good brands," I remark. Her Cadillac was sweet. A '75 white Eldorado convertible and a mighty big ride for such a petite woman.

Liz replaces our empty pitcher with a fresh one. I feed Bonnie the second half of her sandwich.

"Grandpa also left me his plane..."

"Plane?" Plane, I question, my interest instantly piqued.

"... So, I'll need to find a buyer."

"What kind of plane?"

"Oh, I don't know. I've only seen it once. It's cute though, white with maroon stripes."

"How big?"

"It's small. Maybe big enough for eight or ten plus the pilot."

Her concept of big or small when it comes to planes varies sharply from mine, I think to myself. Big enough for eight or ten passengers. I realize that she's talking about a plane worth a small fortune regardless of the brand and degree of avionics.

"Interesting," I remark.

"It's loud, too. Grampa fired it up. It's got these short chrome pipes coming out of the engines."

Huh, I ponder. Maroon and white with chrome pipes coming off the engines?

"What's its tail look like?"

"Like a big tee. Why? Do you know what kind of plane it is?"

"I'm not sure, but it sounds like one of the new Beechcraft King Air models and if it is, girl, it's worth a small fortune."

"Cool," she says and smiles once again.

We finish our lunch and polish off our second pitcher of beer. Candy has become more animated, talkative, restless in her seat, a real bundle of enthusiasm. Thankfully, she's not the cry in your beer type. I'm captivated as I watch and listen to her morph into a lively, small bundle of joy. Don't they say something like, "dynamite comes in small packages?" Better not give this one a line of coke, I think. Not that I've had much of an experience with it myself. My experience is a one-nighter and perhaps my last. They say it's not addictive, but I have my doubts. My crew and I acquired the coke when shaking down the dagos' ride. Three ounces of quality coke, to be exact, and hundreds of number ten valiums. Most of the coke and all but four of the valiums remain. So, running low on cash, I may turn the stuff over to my Austin High School friend Felix to dispose. Yes, thanks to Congress, the Supreme Court and desegregation, our little world has become much more colorful and interesting.

Watching and listening to Candy, my transformation is all but complete, as well. I feel wonderful about today now and optimistic about the future.

Liz stops by the table one last time. I hand her $20 and also $10 and ask her to call Conan's Pizza for us and order a large and medium supreme pizza, to go, for the boys. If they're up yet, they'll be hungry. Especially Andy, who is always hungry.

Conan's is the finest pizza in town. Unbelievable pizza and for a normal person, one slice will sate their hunger. Candy burps, covers her mouth and giggles. "Oops."

I've got a slight buzz myself.

Vertigo

Chapter 4

I find a lucky spot within a block of Conan's and park.

"Steven Paul, I'm going in with you. I forgot to use the little girl's room before we left."

"Not a problem," I say as we exit the Pontiac and I protectively take her hand. Hey, I am her self-appointed bodyguard, remember?

We stroll off, me as proud as a peacock. The Drag, Guadalupe, is always teeming with UT students and today is no exception. Every make and model can be seen. Lots of summer skin and Farrah 'dos. For now, though, I only have eyes for one. Why did I just think that? Am I running a fever? Could I be that smitten? Probably only a phase, I decide, but perhaps a protracted one.

We enter Conan's, the aromas enough to make one salivate.

"Steven Paul!"

I look to my right. Oops, I think. I forgot about Brandy. I'm in love with Brandy too, a beautiful brunette herself.

"Brandy, I thought you were in West Lake today. Brandy meet Candy."

They curtly nod at each other.

"I was, but I've about had enough of the jerk."

Well, if that's not music to my ears, I think.

I raise a Belushi brow. "Oh?"

"The egotistical shit. I think we're done. Hey, some of the girls at the club swear that they saw you on Channel 7 News."

"That would be I."

"No shit? That's a trip."

"Excuse me, I've got to go visit the little girl's room," Candy interjects.

"Okay, I'll be right here," I say.

"Um... you've got to let go of my hand first."

"Oh yeah. Right."

I release her hand and we watch her walk off.

"Steven Paul, where do you find all of these beautiful cowgirls?"

"Nope. No can tell." I wag a finger at her. "I can't give up all my secrets."

The real secret is that there have only been two, but why disturb Brandy's impression, right?

"Well, I'm impressed. You are an unusual cat. You're not some don's grandson or something like that, are you?"

"Nope, nothing like that."

"Sorry about the sister thing," she says. "You didn't throw my number away, did you?"

I learned this morning, to my dismay, that Brandy had given me her number in hopes of fixing me up with her younger sister when I believed she was interested in me. Imagine the shock.

"Nah, I haven't thrown it away, yet."

"Good. Call it. Here comes your cowgirl... nice meeting you, Candy."

"You too," Candy replies as she reclaims my hand. Is it just me, or does the presence at your side of one beautiful woman make you more attractive and desirable to other beautiful women? In my short years, I believe I'm starting to see a pattern. I mean, my puppy on a string theory proved to be correct.

I pay, pick up my crew's pizzas and we depart.

Out on the walk, Candy stops us for a second.

"How do you know Brandy? Is she a stripper?"

"College student. She works here part-time and part-time as a waitress at the strip joint on 51st Street."

"She's definitely pretty. I bet she said, 'call me' as soon as I was out of earshot."

Is that women's intuition or just a pretty good guess based upon a preponderance of the evidence? I smile but leave her question hanging.

Back to the Bonneville and we're off again. A few more stops and we'll be at Andy's. The first is just blocks away, the "we will sell to anyone with a car" Beer Barn, where we purchase a couple of cases of Bud and a cheap cooler. My normal cooler, Big Blue, is currently at Andy's. We start in on the first case.

Our second stop is Austin National Bank where we do a rerun of our first visit. I jump out, run in and out and we are on our way with Candy behind the wheel.

"What did you do—rob the place?" She jokes as she eyes the three money bags. "Where to now, chief?"

"My house, then Andy's. I want to see if there is anything else at the house that you're interested in shooting."

I take her empty, crunch it, drop it in the floorboard and pull the tab on another one for her. She takes a slug off her fresh Bud. I imagine that she's feeling no pain and I'm feeling better all the time.

"Got any weed at your house?" she asks.

"Yep."

The only thing easier to buy than beer by a minor in the liberal city of Austin is pot—good cheap pot. I'm glad she asked because it reminds me, I have a trash-bag full at the base of the ladder I use to access the roof. Totally disheartened by the discovery of the missing bonds, I unconsciously dropped the bag, my mind solely focused on the missing bonds and my girl Debra's defection.

Fortunately, my crew had no knowledge of the real number of bonds. I had intended today to surprise them by dropping one eighth-mil plus in bonds on each. Instead, now I'll be tossing each of them one of the bank bags. A paltry sum in comparison, but ten times the amount that I have remaining. I will tell them about the rest, but not today. Got to make the best of things, today being my birthday and all. I remember, too, there will be a little more cash coming in. I intend on turning the cocaine and valiums over to Felix and splitting the proceeds with him and among ourselves. That should bring us $1,000 or more apiece. In a bind, I can also liquidate some of our arms, if I decide too. Like the MP-5, a full-auto 9mm, which should bring two grand plus. I'd hate to part with it, but as they say: "easy come, easy go." Though there was nothing easy about obtaining it. It was a going-away present from the recently departed mobster pair.

"Earth to Steven Paul."

I take a sip of my beer and look over.

"Sorry, zoned out there for a second. Park in the drive where I was parked earlier."

"Ten-four."

Candy manages the steep drive with ease. If not one of the best drivers, Candy is one of the cutest for sure.

I open the front door to the house for Candy and Bonnie. Bonnie leads the way. She cuts through the living room, descends the stairs to the communal room and pauses before my lair. Passing through the living room, Candy takes in the 18-foot ceilings, the art displayed from around the world and the giant panes of glass that make up much of the glass, cedar and redwood home.

"Wow, I like your house," she marvels.

"And through these sliding doors is my lair."

I slide open one of the panels and wave her into my small, but well-appointed room.

"Cool. It looks like a bar."

"Well, if you're not old enough to go to the bar, bring the bar to you, I say. I acquired much of this stuff years back."

"Texas flag for a carpet. Where did you get that?"

"My thrifty mother made that for me."

"Cool collection of Lone Star posters. You even have a mini-fridge and a hammock. Looks like you thought of everything. What's up with the three phones? Running a boiler-room operation out of your room, or something?"

"Ever heard of teleconferencing?"

She opens the fridge and looks in.

"Yeah, right. I don't think that's how it works. Yuck. Buckhorn beer."

"Hold that thought, I'll be right back."

I leave her to admire my creativity and head out the rear, sliding-glass doors to retrieve my rather large bag of pot. It lays right where I discarded it. Actually, it looks like a lot more than it is. It's just shy of a pound, but some good and fluffy stuff.

I return to find Candy watching my 25-inch RCA console slowly not come into focus. She laughs as I enter.

"Do you think that you have enough pot there? And what's up with your TV? Probably got high and played with the adjusters."

She laughs once more as I take a seat beside her.

"I think that a tube is going bad," I answer knowing she pegged the problem. Surprisingly, Debra had come to the exact same conclusion. Perhaps I should get high and work on it some more, I decide.

Candy looks up at my Farrah poster.

"Did you ever meet Farrah when she went to UT?"

"Nope, she's slightly older than me." I have yet to cop to my real age. Why let something that trivial hold up this potential relationship, right? With a paper from my pack of Joker's, I twist up a joint like a pro. As they say, "practice makes perfect."

I hand it over.

"Here you go. Ladies first."

I pull one of my many lighters from a front pocket and light the joint for her. One thing that my one day of Cub Scouts taught me is never to leave home without two or more lighters. All that sticks-and-stones, fire-making shit I firmly believe is a product of Hollywood.

We pass the joint around. For Mexican weed, it's a decent grade. I contemplate what to show her first. Hidden under my bed is part of our arsenal. Well, I guess "hidden" is not a very good description. Perhaps "stuffed" paints a clearer picture. Much like my closet, the area beneath my bed is a catch-all for my horde of current gems and artifacts. Even our once-weekly maid draws a line in the sand when it comes to venturing under my bed or in my closet.

I pull out my Colt AR-15 and hand it to her. She passes me the joint in exchange.

"Wow. Nice, it looks like an M-16."

"It's a beauty for sure," I say. "A .223 caliber, fast and accurate. It's only semi-auto, but that's fine when you're talking about quality like this. Conversion kits are not impossible to get either. We'll take it with us."

I next drag out a short-barreled Mossberg 12 gauge.

"This is the Mossberg 12 riot model. Cheap, but effective and dependable."

I lay it on the floor and fish out a canvas-encased shotgun, unzip it and pull it out.

"This here is a Remington 1100 12 gauge. A good reliable gun. These sell by the thousands. Reach under my pillow."

Candy does and pulls out the pistol from beneath.

"Man, it's heavy."

"That's the Colt 1911. Probably the most copied and manufactured pistol in history. It shoots a big .45 round. It's limitation: a seven-round clip." I reach under my bed again and retrieve my MP-5. "This is the cream of the crop when it comes to a light-weight submachine gun, an MP-5."

I pass the joint back.

"Full-auto?"

"Yep, in a 9mm. We'll take it with us, too. The Smith & Wesson that I want to give you is at Andy's."

Candy hands me the roach and I pinch it out and place it on top of the mini-fridge.

"If this is only some of your arsenal, I'd say that you're pretty serious when it comes to protection." She takes a deep breath. "Man, that is some good stuff. I'm stoned."

I grab a good, four-finger lid's worth of pot from the bag, stick it into a baggie and hand it over.

"Here, this is for you. There's plenty of ammo at Andy's. Let's roll."

I stuff the trash bag of pot along with the remaining guns back under my bed, gather up the AR and MP and we're off. Along the short drive, I warn Candy that my crew may stare at first, but otherwise, when it comes to women, they're harmless.

Smokey and Rosie meet us as I turn into Andy's drive. They bark and run alongside us until we come to a stop.

"The little one is Smokey, the other one is Rosie. They're both Andy's dogs and they're spoiled rotten, just like Bonnie. Actually, Andy tries to ignore Rosie, but I make up for it."

"That's mean."

"Yeah, it's not right. Hey, grab a couple of cold ones and the AR and I'll get the pizzas, MP and the money bags."

"So, here we are at the scene of the shootout?"

"Yep, Candy, our current base of operations for the past few days. His parents, you know, have been out of town. I don't think that they've heard anything about the shootout yet, because if they had, they would have called."

We enter the house through the recently replaced rear sliding-glass door. The original fell victim to a burst from the very same MP that I now tote.

"About time, I'm..." Andy stops in mid-sentence at the sight of Candy.

"I know you're starving, Andy," I say.

Jim looks on and can only shake his head in disbelief. I never cease to amaze Jim, I call him Jimbo, when it comes to women. He recently remarked, "Only you can take a girl on a first date to a titty bar," and once he's commented: "You feed them a line of shit and they come out of their panties." I've told him more than once—he needs to listen and learn. My experience is that it doesn't pay to be shy and if you ask ten and only one goes, ask 20. It makes sense, doesn't it? James's mouth drops open and Candy has just met the crew.

"Boys meet Candy. Candy, this one blazing a furrow in the carpet and sweating the pizza is Andy and over here..." I point. "In a state of amazement, is Jim, I call him Jimbo and last but not least..." I nod in James's direction. "This one here in a state of awe is James. Boys, Candy here is Bonnie's owner and our new ward."

I set the pizzas on the coffee table and toss each one of them a bank bag. Despite, I'm sure, dying to know how much money is in the bank bags, they decline to check in front of Candy. But no awkward moment will keep Andy from the pizza. He goes for it, not the medium one, mind you, but the large.

Candy looks all around and sniffs the air.

"Smells like paint and steaks in here."

I point to the freshly painted wall above the couch.

"Had to patch the bullet holes and Andy felt like grilling indoors. Said we might as well enjoy the AC."

"Really?"

Andy almost chokes on his pizza.

"Hey, it was his idea to bring the grill inside."

"Candy, as you can see, Andy has a hard time taking responsibility for his actions."

"No, what I have a hard time doing is not listening to you."

"Andy, go get the extra case of Bud out of the car," I say and then have to add: "It's not a trick."

"Okay."

Candy watches as Andy leaves to fetch the beer. She leans in to whisper, "Is that white streak in the back of Andy's hair natural?"

I laugh.

"Looks kind of like a skunk, doesn't he? But, nah, he tumbled into one of our booby traps and got doused in bleach amongst other things. It was James's idea."

"Don't let him bullshit you, Candy, it was Steve's idea," James says and laughs. Jim joins in. Andy returns with the beer.

"What are you all laughing about?"

Andy is always suspicious when it comes to our laughter and rightfully so.

"Not about Andy, but at—we're laughing at you," I say. "And, I haven't even told Candy yet about how you shot it out with the old TV."

"Hey! You told me to shoot it!"

We all laugh.

"Look, Candy, he's so upset now, he can hardly eat his pizza."

In Andy's defense, I did tell him to shoot out the TV after the house came under automatic gunfire. We were caught off-guard and had to scramble from the living room, leaving behind the spare clips to our weapons and the remainder of our arsenal in the room illuminated only by the TV. But, hey, that's on a need-to-know basis only and for the benefit of a good laugh, Candy need not be enlightened to this fact. We're not mean, we just love Andy in our own special way.

"Aw, fuck you," Andy says between bites and swallows.

"So, he shot it because you told him too? That's strange," Candy says.

"It was in the heat of the battle, Candy. Anyway, that's not important, what is important is that Andy didn't shoot himself in the foot. Boys, tomorrow I volunteered you all to help us get Candy's house back in order. Oh, and I may need y'all to help me protect her too."

"Protect her, but..." Jim starts. I cut him off with a wink.

"But, first, let's teach her how to shoot. I'm going to give her the Smith & Wesson. Y'all eat, then we'll load up Big Blue and go and waste some ammo."

"Works for me," Jim says. Andy and James nod their assent. Behind Andy's house, like a second backyard, is three hundred or so acres believed to be owned by Lady Bird Johnson herself and the perfect place for us to fire our weapons. Candy and I take a seat on the couch. Hogan's Heroes is on the new Curtis Mathis which we bought from Austin's very own charismatic TV and appliance salesman, the "Big O," whose motto is: "You know you paid too much if you didn't buy it from the Big O."

I tear a slice of pizza in half and feed it to the ever-attentive Smokey and Rosie.

"Bonnie, you already had lunch," I tell her, but she licks her snout anyway. I relent and tear her a piece off as well. Maybe she got high from the secondhand smoke, I consider, and now she has the munchies.

I pull the Smith & Wesson from under the couch, eject the clip and hand it to Candy. Safety first, is my belief. Candy turns it back and forth in her hand.

"Nice."

"I thought you would like it. Tomorrow we'll pick you up that extra clip and a holster like I promised you earlier."

I catch Jim shake his head in bewilderment. I can read his thoughts: "You lucky bastard." Not that lucky yet, Jimbo, but I'm working on it.

The pizza goes fast and as good luck would have it, there's still a reasonable amount of ice remaining in Big Blue. Big Blue can swallow a couple of cases of beer easily, but I'm mindful of not overstocking—I don't want Andy straining too much when we make him tote it. Yeah, right.

"If everybody is finished eating, I say let's rock 'n' roll. Andy, add the Bud to the cooler, tote it and Jimbo can carry your AK for you. Oh, and throw our empties in Big Blue for targets. James, you gather up and carry the ammo and I'll carry the MP and the AR. Candy you just bring your pretty self and your new pistol. The dogs we leave behind."

I'm good at giving orders. A born leader, I'd like to believe. It's taking orders where I flounder. I'm not much for law and order either, except when it applies to others, of course. My family hopes it's a phase that I will outgrow, along with my recklessness. Just in case, they hedged their hopes with a double indemnity life insurance policy. Hey, it is what it is.

We exit through the sliding glass door, cross Andy's backyard and enter the woods. It's a beautiful early June afternoon—not the stifling Central Texas norm. I breathe in deep. Yes, the air is fresh once again and my early morning blues are all but gone. Our trek through the woods takes us past the relic that once was my pride and joy, my late '71 Firebird Formula 400, which I decked out in full Trans Am trim. Now, she rests on cinder blocks, what was salvageable salvaged. Candy gawks at it in passing.

"Damn, you weren't kidding when you said it was in a derby."

"Yes, Candy, but she got us out of a bind before she kicked the bucket. Made it right here to her resting spot."

"You sure you're safe to be around?" Candy jokes once again.

"There's a clearing right up here. So far, no one has called the law, so we will set up there," I say.

"Is it legal to shoot out here?"

I wink at Candy.

"It is if you don't get caught." We break through to the clearing. "Andy, set Big Blue here and set us up beer cans in them-there yonder pear cactus," I say with my best southern drawl.

The lingo matches my boots, don't you think?

"Fuck that. You set them up yourself this time."

"You see, Candy, Andy experienced some trauma earlier in his life and it has manifested into a phobia—the fear of setting up beer can targets. I say he should face his fear. You know, dust himself off and get back in the saddle."

Jim and James laugh. Andy pulls the tab on a Bud, downs most of it and belches.

"Candy, the trauma was two days ago and the traumatizer is the one standing next to you. Steve here didn't let me get clear before emptying a 30-round clip in my direction."

"Well, maybe I was a little premature on the trigger, but that's not the point here. The point is, we want Candy to get comfortable and accustomed to her new pistol. Now, face your fear and set up the cans. We're burning daylight here. You're holding up progress."

"I don't think so. It seems like something always bad happens when I listen to you."

"Huh." I rub my chin. "You know, Andy, I can almost see the point you're trying to make. Candy, I bet he will set them up if you ask."

Candy clasps her hands together, scrunches her shoulders and twists a toe into the dirt.

"Will you do it for me? Pretty please."

"Aw, damn. That's not fair."

"Pretty please.'"

"Oh... Okay."

We all laugh. Well, except for Andy, of course. I load him up with the empties.

"Candy, I'm impressed. We make a pretty good team. Stick with me and you'll go places," I say and can't help but smile.

"Like jail," Jim says.

James snickers as Andy trudges off. "I'm glad I'm not in Andy's shoes right about now. "

I pull the tab on a cold Bud, down half and hand it to Candy to hold. I slide the bolt back on the MP chambering a round.

Candy's eyes widen. "You're not."

"Not what? Make you wonder why Andy didn't go out for Special Olympics track and field?"

I flip the safety off. Jim is again watching us. He smiles.

"Andy's quite fast," he says. "And pretty agile when it comes to dodging bullets."

A hundred yards out, Andy props up the last of the cans in the pear cactus and I fire a burst of three into the air.

"And there you go folks, he's off and running."

I lower the barrel and empty the remaining clip, taking out half the cactus and most of the cans. Not bad at 100 yards, I think. I eject the clip, flip the taped clips over, reinsert it, slide the bolt back and chamber another round.

"Man, this is a sweet gun. Not too much recoil. Here you go, Candy, try her out."

I trade her the MP for my beer.

Andy comes to a panting stop beside us, bends at the waist and rests his hands on his knees. "Fucker," he finally manages.

Actually, I was quite easy on him. Didn't kick up any clumps of dirt around him like last time. I *can* play nice.

"What do I do? Just pull the trigger?" Candy asks.

"Point and pull. That's all."

I put a finger in my ear. Candy empties the clip in two bursts.

"Shit! This is badass! Sorry. I guess that wasn't very ladylike, but that was fun."

She didn't actually hit anything but the horizon, but she looked damn hot doing it. I believe we have an NRA member in the making. We spend the next 30 minutes shooting the various weapons before gleefully trekking back. Is it the feeling of power that makes wasting ammo so joyful? Whatever it is, everyone seems happy. Was it just this morning that I was singing the blues? Seems like eons ago. Life, I decide again, is good.

We all enter the living room. Candy and I take our seats back on the couch. Star Trek is on the boob tube, Captain Kirk is standing among a multitude of living furballs. I remember the episode, so adorable until they began breeding like rabbits.

"Steve-O, what are you two going to do for the rest of the day seeing as how it's your birthday?" Jim asks.

I cringe a little inside. I don't want Candy to know my true age. Maybe she won't ask, I hope.

"It's your birthday? Wow. How old are you?"

Shit, how to dodge the question?

"You can count the candles on my cake later." Not great, but workable. "Let's burn one while I think."

Well, if my crew wonders whether Candy smokes pot or not, the cat's now out of the bag. Hope she doesn't mind.

Andy pulls the rolling tray from under his recliner. Several fat doobies are already rolled and Andy passes one to Candy. If nothing else, we have all been raised to be polite. Ladies first, is our golden rule, that and respecting our elders. Candy happens to fall into both categories, but how much older she is I do not know.

Except for the occasional cough or two, we pass the joint in relative silence. Curiosity must finally win out, because Jim picks up his bank bag, unzips it and thumbs the hundred-dollar bills. A smile comes across his face.

"Whatever you decide, I'll buy," Jim says taking a big whiff of the money inside.

I suddenly feel the need for excitement and speed. I realize that I haven't ridden my new Yamaha YZ 250 in a few days and haven't had my usual daily adrenaline fix. I'm an avid motocross rider and have ridden with some of the best. Anybody who knows about the new Yamaha mono-shock knows it's one fast bike. A ride on it would surely fit the bill, but I don't know if Candy has enough faith in me to climb on back. What else exciting can we do? A compulsive thought crosses my mind: Candy's plane. Now that would be a blast, taking it out for a test flight. There's only one drawback: I'm not quite qualified to fly it. Well, maybe two drawbacks: I don't even know what kind of plane it is. I take another hit of the joint and chase it with a gulp of Bud.

"Candy, about your plane?"

"Uh-oh," Jim says.

Andy and James tune in.

"Where exactly is it?"

"It's in a hangar at the airport."

I rub my chin. Why? Hell, I don't know, I'm stoned.

"And you have access to it?"

Jim shakes his head.

"I think I can see where this is going," he says.

"I suppose so," Candy says. "I've only met the owner of the hangar once. Gary. Gary something-or-other at Austin Aviation and Storage."

"He knows it's your plane, though, right?"

"Sure, Grandpa told him that it would be mine someday. Grandpa was fixing to start giving me lessons before he fell ill."

I pull the tab on another Bud and pass it to her.

"How about having Gary pull her out of the hangar, run her through pre-flight and then we take her for a test run. "

"You know how to fly?"

"Does she have wings?"

"Sure."

"Engines?"

"Of course."

"There you go then. I can fly her." That may be stretching my abilities a tad, but one's never too old to learn, right?

"Cool. Sounds fun. Where's the phone and phone book?"

"Kitchen."

"Um, Steve-O, correct me if I'm wrong, but you've never actually flown a plane, have you?" Jim says.

I raise a finger to my lips.

"Shhh. Look, how hard can it possibly be? I'm sure it's like driving a car, only with an added dimension."

"Oookaaay. I'm not sure this is one of your better plans."

"It will be fine, Jimbo. I'm going to wing it."

"Yeah, Jimbo, he's going to wing it. He likes winging things," Andy says with a smirk.

"Steve, I think you've actually lost your mind this time," James says shaking his head.

Candy comes back to the living room.

"All set. This is going to be so much fun. You guys coming? There's plenty of room."

"Um, maybe you and Steve-O better go on," Jim says. "I've got a few things that I need to do."

"Me too," Andy says.

"'James, how about you?"

"Thanks, Candy. It sounds like fun, but I'm afraid of heights. Good luck."

"Good luck?"

"I mean have fun."

"Oh, oh okay."

"If you two make it back..." Jim does the sign of the cross. "How 'bout we all go to Spaghetti Warehouse. I'll buy."

"Candy's call."

"Sure, why not. See you guys later."

I wink.

"Yeah, see you boys later."

Vertigo

Chapter 5

"I like your friends. Jim must be Catholic."

"You noticed that, did you?"

"Yeah. Don't let me smoke any more weed for a while. I've got a hell of a buzz going."

So here we go, airport bound. Not surprisingly, Austin's Municipal Airport is on Airport Road, a small regional airport that is rapidly becoming inadequate for the ever-expanding Austin area.

I pull to the side of the road for a second, in the rearview, my eyes are as red as Candy's.

"Candy, in the dash are Visine and peppermints. It might be a good plan to use both."

I down the remainder of my Bud, crush the can and toss it over my shoulder to the floorboard in back.

"Hand me a couple of extra peppermints if you would and I'll stick them in my pocket."

Candy puts drops in one eye, then the other and passes the bottle and extra peppermints to me.

"There, how do I look?"

"Beautiful."

I blink the drops from my eyes, pop a mint into my mouth and pull back onto the road.

"Hang a left up here," she says. "It's going to be the last hangar on your left."

The hangar and plane slowly come into focus. Holy shit, I think. I recognize it right off: A Super King Air. Now that's a plane.

"Candy, you're sitting on a small fortune here. Maybe we should get our..." I almost slip and say licenses. "Maybe you should consider starting a charter service."

"Really? I told you it was pretty and look, there's Gary."

Taking a second look at the plane, self-doubt starts to rear its ugly head. Maybe this isn't such a good plan. Shake it off, big boy. Probably just the pot talking to you. Remember, I tell myself, that you can ride, drive and fly anything, within reason, of course. Yeah, of course, you can. We exit the Bonneville.

"Candy, good to see you again. And this is?" Gary extends his hand.

"Steven Paul," I say as I take and shake the offered hand.

"Steven Paul? Steven Paul? That name sounds familiar. I think I've seen you somewhere, too."

"Maybe around the airport," I offer knowing there is not a snowball's chance in hell of that.

"Right... It will come to me. You know, Son, you seem awfully young. Not a lot of these planes floating around..."

"Flying around," I correct.

"Okay, flying around. It's still a lot of plane. Do you think you can handle her?"

"Insurance papers in the dash?"

"Seriously, joking aside, are you familiar with this plane? Candy, you sure about this?"

I step forward. "Well, let's see, Gary, you may have me stumped here, but I'll take a stab at your question. What we have here is a Beechcraft twin-turbo propped Super King Air B200—military version introduced late '72, civil early '74. These 200s were developed from the model 100, with the same fuselage, but of course different wings and T-tail. This particular model sports a pair of Pratt & Whitney PT6A-135 engines with 750 hp, or 560 kW, driving four-bladed propellers. Need I say more?"

Gary bows.

"My hat's off to you, sir. It's fueled and ready to go."

As luck would have it, I'm familiar with this model having recently read a brochure on it and was so impressed, I can recall all of its stats. I told you I was feeling lucky again. I have to confess, she's a little more plane then I envisioned, but I'm not totally flying in the dark here—I completed three months of ground school and ended up passing the grueling six-hour FFA exam. Besides, what could possibly go wrong?

Candy smiles.

"Well, we're off then."

"Fly safe."

I wink. I like winking.

"Safety is like second nature to me, Gary."

We enter aft of the wing and work our way to the cockpit. She is a beautiful plane, a perfect executive plane with five rows of plush leather seats, their smell still new. I'd give my left nut for this plane, I think. Not literally, but you know what I mean.

"Candy, this really is a nice plane," I say as I take the pilot's seat and Candy takes the co-pilot's seat. I study the gauges. More than you envisioned, Steven Paul? I ask myself. Simply put, much more. I take a deep breath and exhale. Okay, you can do this.

"Buckle up, Candy."

"Wow, there sure are a lot of gauges." She points to one. "I know what this one is, it's the altimeter and this one here is the airspeed indicator."

"Very good, Candy."

"And this one?" She points.

"Gyrocompass."

"Gyrocompass. How does it work?"

"I don't know how much you know about gyros, but they keep their rigidity in space."

"Oh."

"Well, maybe I can explain it a little better than that. A gyroscope is a device consisting of a spinning mass, typically a disc or wheel, mounted on a base so that its axis can turn freely in any direction and thereby maintain its orientation regardless of any movement of the base."

"Okay. I'm not sure I follow you, but okay."

"So, then a gyrocompass is a compass with a motorized gyroscope whose angular momentum interacts with the force produced by the Earth's rotation to maintain a north-south orientation of the gyroscopic spin axis," I say and smile.

"Thanks, professor and this is the steering wheel of course."

"Essentially. It's called the 'yoke.' It controls the flaps on the tail and if you look out your window, it also controls the outer small flaps, or the 'ailerons.' The pedals here control the tail's rudder and this here controls the wing's big flaps."

"What do they do?"

"Create drag, or lift. Have you ever stuck your hand out the window of your car and played with the wind?"

"Sure."

"Then you noticed that how you held your hand affected how your hand responded to the wind?"

"Sure."

"Okay, then. They're used in takeoffs and landings. Deployed, you have extra lift and drag, which of course affects your stall speed. In short, you can take off and land at a slower speed."

"Okay and this?"

"Inquisitive girl, aren't you? That controls the pitch of the props. The greater the pitch, the bigger bite of air they take and the greater the pull. Take a screw for example. The further the threads are spaced, the faster it will go in, but the harder it is to turn. It serves much like a transmission and before you ask, the rest of the stuff don't worry about. We will not be using the plane's avionics, because we're flying VFR, or visual flight rules."

"Okay."

"Here are the throttles. We'll give her a little throttle, ignition and contact."

The engines fire right off and hum. I throttle her a little bit more and feel her begin to pull against the brakes. I look over at Candy and wink.

"Here's looking at you, kid."

Candy grins like a kid in a candy store. I can't help but grin myself. I watch a Cessna 150 taxi in the distance and decide to follow suit. The moment of truth is rapidly approaching. Surprisingly, I feel suddenly calm and confident. I turn the radio on assuming it's dialed to the right channel, retrieve and key the mike.

"This is King Air GNN 224 to tower. Request permission to take off."

"Roger, King Air. Have visual. The wind's north to northeast at five to ten, barometric pressure 29.92 and holding. Taxi to runway 090 and await go."

"Roger, tower."

I calibrate the altimeter with the current barometric pressure.

"King Air, you're clear for departure. Maintain a 1000, two out."

"Roger that," I say. I bump the throttles and deploy the flaps. We taxi right along.

"Wow, this is exciting." Candy beams.

I pat her on her firm, beautifully tanned leg. "Yes, it is."

I back the throttles and bring our plane to a perpendicular stop to the start of runway 090.

"Tower to King Air, you're clear for departure. The sky's yours."

"Roger that."

I throttle her some more again and pull her around to the start of 090. Here's where I encounter my first true quagmire—at what pitch to set the props? Here we go, I think. The cards are on the table, it's do-or-die time. I could go on forever but realize I'm only stalling. I throttle her up some more and adjust the pitch until she starts to bog some and pull hard against the brakes. I figure I should be alright as long as I don't redline the engines. I mean, there's plenty of runway. I take a deep breath, exhale and push the throttles forward. The engines come to life and the King Air is out of the gate and rocketing down the runway—her thrust pinning us to our seats. Halfway along the runway, I ease back on the yoke and we take to the air. Our shadow precedes us and grows smaller as we gain altitude. At a thousand feet, I retract the flaps, raise the landing gear, back the throttles a tad and adjust the pitch to full. The engines slightly bog again but level out as our airspeed hits 240 knots. I release a sigh and bank sharp to head south. A mile out I bank again and we head west. The cars on the ground look like ants.

"Wow, this is way too cool," Candy says.

I turn off the radio for now and wag the wings a couple of times to test the plane's agility. She's surprisingly responsive.

"Tarrytown at 12:00, prepare to dive," I say.

And dive we do, a thousand feet to a hundred, where I level her out. We buzz Andy's house before I pull back slightly on the yoke to regain some altitude. Candy looks over at me and laughs.

"Whoa, my stomach dropped for a second."

I hold my nose and blow to pop my ears. If she liked that, I wonder how she will react to my next maneuver? I level out and roll the plane. Perfectly executed, I might add.

"Shit! Holy shit!" Candy screams. She puts a hand on her heart. "Oh, I have to catch my breath. I feel like I'm still upside down."

"Vertigo," I say and bank the King Air hard over Lake Austin. I take her down and virtually skim the lake's surface. The props kick up wash behind us.

"Man, I love this plane!"

I pull her into a slight climb—enough to clear the trees to our right and bank hard to take another run over Andy's. I roll her once more, because now I know I can and we buzz Andy's house for the second time. I'd make a fine crop duster, I think.

We can see my crew on the ground waving, no doubt roused by our first pass.

"Too cool!" Candy yells.

"I concur, Candy. Let's pass over West Lake once and then head back."

Candy is glued to her side window as I bank once more to change course. We buzz my friend Alan's Cat Mountain home before turning to head back. So far so good, now we only need to land. I'll wing it again, of course.

As we near the airport, I reduce our airspeed by throttling back and lessening the prop's pitches. I turn the radio back on, retrieve the mike and key it.

"King Air GNN 224 to tower. Approaching from the west. Request permission to land. "

"Roger that, King Air. Hold approach pattern at 500 and await permission to land."

"Huh, that's strange." I scan the horizon all around me. "I don't see any air traffic, do you?"

I drop to 500 feet and bank shy of the airport.

"Nope," Candy says. "There's something going on down there. Did you see all the blue lights on the cars?"

"Unfortunately, yes. Not good, I would speculate."

"What do you mean, not good?"

"They must be securing the runway prior to our landing."

"Securing the runway. Why?"

"My guess is that somebody frowned upon us doing aerials over residential areas."

"That doesn't sound so good," she says looking suddenly pale.

"Yep. It looks like we may be in a little trouble."

"Little trouble. What did I do?"

"Well, it is your plane, you know."

"But you're a pilot, right? I mean, you must be a pilot."

"Funny you should ask..."

"What? What does that mean?"

"Well, I'm almost a pilot. I passed the FAA's exam and all, just lacked some hours, you know... flight hours."

Exacerbated, she asks: "How many hours?"

"Oh, about... about all of them. Well, except for a half-hour."

"Half hour! Are you crazy?"

"Some say it's true. Kind of kills the buzz, doesn't it?"

"Duh. But I didn't know."

"Save it for the jury," I say and laugh. Candy whacks me in the arm.

"It's not funny!"

"Okay, you didn't know, so maybe they'll let you make it. But what about contributing to the delinquency of a minor?"

"Minor! What are you talking about? It's your birthday today, right? How old are you?"

"Seventeen. I'll be in the twelfth grade this year."

Candy smacks herself in the head.

"Seventeen. Well, fuck me running. I think I'm going to be sick."

"Look, I've got a plan..."

"You would."

"We rush your divorce on through, get it annulled or something and claim spousal privileges."

I eternally congratulate myself on my quick thinking.

"Spousal privileges. What the hell is that?"

"The right not to testify against one another. Besides, we're almost at the marriage stage anyway. This flight, you know, counts as another date," I say and smile.

"How can you smile at a time like this?"

"Because I can play my trump card, of course."

"Trump card?"

"My trump card, you know, being a minor and all. Worst case scenario, they have to let me out on my 18th birthday."

"That's great, what a plan. Thank you for sharing that with me."

"Here's something else that I would like to share with you: at least seventeen is the legal age of consent here in Texas, so keep that in mind should I get out early."

She stares out her window. I lay my hand on her leg again. She smacks it, but not too hard.

"Oh, I sure will," she says.

"You're not being facetious here, are you? I've got the feeling your being facetious," I say.

She turns and stares at me.

"I'm fucking with you, girl. They're not going to do anything to you."

"You sure? I don't know if I believe you. I think I know now how Andy must feel most of the time."

"Yeah, I'm sure. We need only to land safely now."

"Wait a minute. Wait, wait, wait a minute. If you have only had a half-hour of flight instructions, then you've never actually landed a plane before, have you?"

"Well, true, I guess technically I've never landed a plane before, but I've fantasized about it more than once."

"Well gee, that sure makes me feel so much better. You probably learned a lot fantasizing about your… your… Farrah poster, too?"

"You would be surprised. She's on my to-do list, too, but of course, the odds are better that we land safely. Besides, don't I look like I know what I'm doing?"

"Right now, you look like a grinning, blue-eyed monster."

"Hey, thanks, that's nice of you to say."

She sighs and looks back out her side window.

"You're welcome. I'm going to cross my fingers and pray for a safe landing."

"That's my girl. That's the spirit. Always think positively, I say. Stick with me kid and you will go places."

I like saying that.

"Tower to King Air, you're now cleared to land on runway 090," comes through the radio's speaker.

I bank back toward the airport and key the mike: "Roger that, tower."

I align up a good mile away on my approach to the runway and drop to 100 feet.

"Oops, I almost forgot to lower the landing gear," I joke. The landing gear locks into place. "That's better. Now we'll give her full flaps."

She slows and rises some with the adjustment. Keeping the RPMs up, I decrease the pitch of the props some more. We slowly descend to the ever-approaching runway. I force her down to ten feet and ease the throttles slowly back—the stall indicator shrieks as we ever-so-lightly touch down on the tarmac.

"Hell yeah. We made it. Thank you, Lord!" Candy yells.

I watch as at least some of the tension drains from Candy's face.

"And Steven Paul," I add.

"What?"

"Thank you, Lord, and Steven Paul."

She unbuckles, leans over and gives me a kiss on the cheek.

"And Steven Paul, Lord... and Steven Paul. Thanks."

Is it my imagination or did she linger on that cheek kiss? Hey, it's a good sign, anyway.

As we taxi off the runway, cop cars box us in.

Vertigo

Chapter 6

A city cop gets out with his bullhorn.

"Pilot there, follow the lead car. That's an order."

I salute the cop.

"Hmm. What do you think Candy? They're coming on kind of strong, wouldn't you say." I smack her hand. "And quit biting your nails."

"Sorry, I'm nervous though."

"And rightfully so. Let me do the talking."

"Maybe we should have headed to Mexico."

"Was that a joke, Candy? I believe I detected a joke here. We make a pretty good pair, I'd say. A right handsome pair I might add, too."

I throttle down and kill the engines. We're surrounded by cops—cops with their guns drawn, that is.

"They do seem pretty serious."

"You think, Candy."

I exit the aft door first, hands raised and yell: "You'll never take me alive, coppers!"

In response, they secure me quite rapidly, face first on the tarmac with my hands cuffed behind my back.

"Leave the girl out of this. She knows nothing," I gallantly yell out.

A pair of cops snatch me up off the ground.

"Don't I at least get a kiss first?" I ask.

"Not today, smart guy," one of the cops says as he removes my wallet from my rear pocket. Maybe they'll mistake my expired library card for a pilot's license, I consider—not.

Another cop leads Candy out of earshot by the elbow. She glances over her shoulder at me with tears in her eyes. I mouth: "Wait for me" and wink before being stuffed in the back of a police car. "Don't forget to write," I yell.

The officer's name tag reads Tom.

"Hang tight, Son, until we sort this mess out," he says.

"Okay, Tom, but don't take too long, I hate suspense."

He slams the door on me in response. Well, that went over well, don't you think? Oh, and for the record, it's hard to get comfortable with your hands cuffed behind your back. I watch a slew of cops form into a huddle. They no doubt are busy discussing my fate. Oh, well, it is what it is. A familiar sedan arrives upon the scene—a nondescript Ford with moon hubcaps. Detective Williams has arrived. What a lovely surprise. This should be interesting, I muse. His eyes grow large as he first spots Candy and then me in the back of a police car. He shakes his head in what I suspect is disbelief. I cannot wave, so, me being me, I improvise and wink. Williams shakes his head once more and joins the huddle. I wonder how this will play out.

Candy stares on from a distance, slump-shouldered and dejected. She's all alone by my car, the police's interest in her apparently having waned. Yep, they got their man, I bet that they are all thinking now.

"The keys are in the ignition," I attempt to mouth to her.

She shrugs and tosses her hands up in frustration. A good ten minutes elapse. The cops look like they're in a heated discussion. Finally, to my relief, Tom the cop breaks from the pack and heads my way, my wallet in his hand. I take that to be a good sign. Tom opens the door.

"All right, Steven Paul, step out, it's your lucky day..."

"Did you miss me, Tom? Say you did."

"Williams has for some reason posted your bond. No telling why. Personally, I don't think I care much for you, but it's not my call." He uncuffs me. "Anyway, there's no telling what the FAA will do, but if I were you, I would expect a very large fine."

I rub some circulation back into my hands and, in a dignified manner, smooth the non-existent wrinkles from my red Izod. I've read somewhere, being an avid reader and all—or did I see it on TV? I watch a lot of TV, too—that women are unconsciously attracted to men wearing red shirts and I tend to believe this, much like I believe my very own puppy-on-the-string theory. Well, maybe it's not my very own theory? Nevertheless, where was I? Oh, yeah.

"Well, Tom, you're not me and I tend to be an optimist. You know, like I see the glass half-full. So, should the FAA choose to impose some arbitrary fine, I will enter into some protracted haggling over the amount, settle for ten cents on the dollar and then, of course, pay none of it. See, the beauty of it, Tom, is that you can't enter into a binding contract with a minor."

"Thanks for the update and as much as I now really hate to say it, you're free to go."

"God speed to you, too, Tom."

I walk over to join Williams and Candy standing beside my Bonneville. Williams, as usual, is impeccably dressed.

"Williams." I blush. "Did you get all decked out for me? You shouldn't have."

"You don't believe in flying under the radar, do you?"

"There you're mistaken, Williams. I've already flown under the radar several times today."

"I don't suppose you're responsible for pistol-whipping a man earlier today? Oh, say, around Oltorf and South Congress?"

"Well, I might have given someone a couple of needed love taps, but I had to get his attention."

"And did you get his attention?"

"I'm not sure, I burned off before he regained consciousness."

Williams chuckles.

"A pilot too, imagine that. Our phones rang off the hook after your aerial display. The tower got suspicious too and phoned in after you departed. Seems that you don't have your radio jargon down quite right."

"Hey, what can I say, I'm a work in progress."

"An understatement, no doubt. You're definitely not afraid of the limelight. Out of curiosity, exactly how long have you been flying?"

"This was my maiden flight."

He smiles and shakes his head.

"Figures. Could you have chosen a more expensive plane?"

"Hey, you got to work with what you got. "

"Right. Listen, there's someone that I want you to meet. Candy, if you will excuse us, I need to speak to Steven in private for a minute."

I follow Williams to his car.

"Anyway, this person who I want you to meet is a good guy. The meeting could be mutually rewarding for both of you. He's at his wits' end right now. He needs help."

"With?"

"I'll leave that up to him to explain. My role here can be an introduction only. Being in my position and all, I'm sure that you can understand. Besides, you owe me one now."

"Yeah, all bullshitting aside, thanks for making my bond. Sure, I'll meet with him, hear him out."

"Where will you be in the morning? Say 9:00 or so?"

"At 10:00 or so, I'll be at Candy's"

"Speaking of Candy, you sure had her scared. A suggestion here and only a suggestion mind you, but in the future, it might serve you well to let someone get to know you and your personality at a somewhat slower pace."

"I feel you."

"Candy seems like a real sweetheart and there's no knocking her looks, but she's really been through a lot these past few days." He pats me on the shoulder. "Try not to hurt her."

Upon my return, Candy hugs and holds on to me for several long seconds.

"You scared me. I thought for sure they were going to haul you away."

She stomps down on my foot.

"Ouch! Shit!"

"That's for not having a freaking pilot's license."

"A slight oversight on my part, but could you hold the foreplay. Hey, I really had you going with the pilot shit, didn't I?"

"Yeah, you had me going alright."

"And, for the record, I wasn't lying about 17 being, you know, the legal age of consent here in Texas."

Candy covers her face suddenly.

"Don't look, but Channel 7 just arrived," Candy says covering her face suddenly.

"Where? Where?"

"I said don't look."

"Uh-oh. Gosh, I think they might have spotted us. Here they come," I gleefully say. I like my moments in the sun.

"Great, I'm getting in the car."

"Suit yourself. I'll cover for you."

"Steven Paul," Channel 7's Stacey Keys says. "FCC nightmare and I assume now an FAA nightmare as well. Any other federal agencies in your sights?"

"Stacey Keys, you assume right. By the way, love your hair."

Yes, it's Stacey Keys, Channel 7's sexy on-the-scene reporter. I've been in love with her forever, it seems.

"Save it, Steven Paul. We're not live this time."

"You really make a statement in that power suit, Stacey."

"Maybe we can get a few workable clips from you today, but I won't hold my breath," she says.

"Why the hostility? Are you trying to rain on my parade, Stacey? I think that maybe you're trying to rain on my parade." I wink at her. I'm good at winking—can do it even with my hands cuffed behind my back. "You know, that standing date to the drive-in is still on the table."

"So, so, so tempting, but let's see..." She scratches a tooth with a fingernail. "How do I put this without hurting your feelings? Let's see. I don't think so."

"Wow, that's great, 'don't think so' is not a no." I smile. "I think you're softening to me, Stacey."

"Actually, I've had a bad day so far and the truth is I find you attractive, amusing and mysterious."

"Wow, really?"

"Not," she says but I glimpse a hint of a smile. "Roll it... This is Stacey Keys on location at Austin Municipal Airport, the scene of some earlier excitement. The information that we have is sketchy at this time, but we do know that it involved this plane..." She points to the background. "A Beechcraft Super King Air and some improper flying over Tarrytown and also parts of West Lake Hills. We've also learned that no arrests have been made at this time, but an investigation is still underway. As you can see, the responders are now wrapping up and leaving the scene. Before me is Austin's very own Steven Paul who many of our viewers will recognize—the alleged pilot."

"Steven Paul, is there anything you can add to enlighten our viewers at this time?"

"Yes, Stacey, scratch the alleged. I am the crack pilot involved. By the way, love Channel 7, keep up the good work guys and gals. Oh, and hi, Jennifer, if you're watching. See you at your big 18th. We'll keep that our little secret for now."

"Steven Paul, the story please."

"Yes, right, sorry. In a nutshell, Stacey, it seems that my style of flying upset some Tarrytown and perhaps West Lake residents today. You see, Stacey, I'm a third-generation crop duster and flying is in my genes—in my blood."

"Now that we have confirmation that you are indeed the pilot, if my information is correct, you buzzed some houses, did a roll or two and skimmed the waters of Lake Austin, scaring some boaters."

"Stacey, I can't speak for the boaters, but that sounds about correct."

"And who is the owner of the plane in question?"

"My friend Candy, the owner, wishes to remain anonymous at this time. You may have noticed her shield her face and duck into my car, but I feel it's safe to say that none of her Tarrytown neighbors will recognize her at this time."

"So, she is in fact one of your Tarrytown neighbors?"

"Sorry Stacey, I decline to either confirm or deny that at this time—no comment."

"Any likely repercussions from today's activities?"

I shrug my shoulders and smile.

"I enlarge my fan base?"

"Thank you, Steven Paul, for yet another interesting interview. This is Stacey Keys, reporting from Austin Municipal Airport."

"See you around, Stacey."

I enter my Bonneville and grin at Candy.

"Well, how did I do? You think I should have shown more profile?"

"I hid my face why?"

"You were overjoyed to be seen with me?"

"Noooo."

"Got me then."

"I was trying to stay anonymous. You know A N O N Y M O U S."

"That's exactly what I told Stacey."

"I think you said, quote..." To emphasize, she does the double-finger quote. "'My friend Candy, the owner, wishes to remain anonymous at this time.' I'd like to emphasize the 'Candy' part for you."

"Hmm, I kind of see your point. Hey, but I hung tough when she tried to pin me down as you being my Tarrytown neighbor. Did you note the sternness in my voice—'No comment?'"

"Yeah, you hung tough on that one. What did Williams want?"

I pull the tab on two cold beers and hand one to Candy.

"I'll tell you tomorrow when I know more." I take a refreshing swallow. "Ah. Onward through the fog, I say."

She takes her own gulp.

"Onward through the fog, then... Who is Jennifer?"

I crank my ride, put her into gear and lay my hand on Candy's leg. A slow smile creases her face. Some pleasant thought must be running through her mind. Probably concerning me. I smile at that thought. Narcissistic? Nah, eternally hopeful.

I punch the power button on the radio. Led Zeppelin's "Stairway to Heaven" cranks from the speakers. It's hard not to sing along, so we both join in: "And she's climbing the stairway to heaven." Well, at least we catch the last line of the lyrics. Candy sticks a hand out the window to play with the wind.

"I bet I could fly, too, now having watched, but I don't think I could ever get up enough nerve. What makes you do the crazy things that you do?"

"Today, I'm trying to impress you."

"Uh-oh, there's still a lot of day left, too... I don't know if it's the same thing, but you did make a lasting impression and now that we're no longer in trouble, I have to admit, that was the bomb. But had I known that you really weren't a pilot, you couldn't have dragged my ass on that plane."

"Would you fly again with me now?"

She takes a drink of her Bud and wipes her mouth with the back of her hand. '

"You're damn right I would."

We both laugh.

"So, your friend Jim really isn't a Catholic, is he?"

"I don't have the slightest idea."

We both laugh some more.

"It really is a beautiful day," Candy says.

"Not as beautiful as you."

"Thank you. You're kind of easy on the eyes yourself."

She lays a hand on top of mine and gets lost in her thoughts. However innocent the gesture may be, it works for me.

Vertigo

Chapter 7

I announce our arrival: "Children of the corn, we're home. Did you miss Daddy?"

I've been trying for what seems like forever to get them to call me the endearing term of "Daddy," but so far, my efforts have born little fruit.

"Steve-O, you're a crazy sonofabitch. I can't believe you didn't get arrested."

"It was a close call, Jimbo, but in the end, they saw things my way."

"Did the police show up?" Andy asks chewing on what looks like a piece of jerky from our stash.

"Seemed liked hundreds," Candy interjects. "Cops and cop cars everywhere, blue lights galore. Hey, how come you guys didn't tell me he's not a pilot?... Gee, don't everyone speak up at once."

"I know why I didn't," Andy says pacing the floor. "Bad things seem to happen to me when I speak up."

"Like your hair?"

"Hair?"

"Oops. Umm... Never mind."

"You fuckers better not have done anything to my hair," Andy says and stomps off toward the bathroom.

"Sorry," Candy says. "I guess he didn't know."

"Fuckers!"

"Well, he knows now," Jim says.

"James did it!" I yell. I look at James. "James I'd hide if I was you and in a hurry."

"But it wasn't my idea."

"I know that, you know that, we all know that, but unfortunately for you, I'll convince Andy otherwise. You hide and I'll distract him with the promise of food. I feel it's the least I can do."

"Yeah, thanks a lot. I'll be outside. Yell at me when you think it's safe to return."

"You got it buddy. What are friends for."

"Fuckers! Okay where is that little shit? Although, Steve, somehow I think that you're responsible."

"Calm down, Andy," I say trying to maintain my composure. "You can touch it up with some hair dye. It's on the same aisle that you frequent so often, you know, the aisle with the douches. He's partial to the strawberry-scented ones," I inform Candy.

"Fuck you. Candy, it's not what you think. I bought one to wash my face with."

"And he's man enough to admit it," I gleefully add.

Jim and I laugh, Candy simply looks confused.

"I'm not sure I want to know," she says.

"It's his fault," Andy says pointing to me. "He convinced me it would get the black shoe polish off my face and it did, well, most of it."

"Shoe polish on your face?"

"You see Candy, I don't always steer him wrong. He douched and smelled strawberry fresh for the rest of the day."

Now we all laugh, well, except Andy, of course. Andy protests.

"It was a night mission. I was in camouflage."

"We had a backup plan, too," I add.

"If the douche didn't work, we were going to dress him in white, deck him in a red jacket and black shoes, give him a cane pole and rent him out as a yard gnome."

"You're just wrong, Steven Paul," Candy says before rejoining Jim and me in laughter.

"Aw, fuck you, guys."

The afternoon flies by with mindless boob-tube viewing, idle chatter and plenty of cold beer consumption. Surprisingly, Candy is at ease among us hormone-crazed male teens, but I wasn't kidding when I told her my crew is harmless. All of them but myself remain bashful when it comes to women and, sadly, I would venture that first base has yet to become a reality for all but Jimbo. I tell them to watch, listen and learn, but as someone once said, "You can lead a horse to water, but you can't make it drink." I personally have come to the conclusion that you only live once and you better grab life by the horns while you can.

We burn another fat one as the Channel 7 news comes on. Our story is at the top of the hour and to my amazement and Candy's dismay, Channel 7 chooses not to edit it.

"See, Candy? You see what I mean? He says whatever he feels like whenever he wants," Andy says with a smirk.

"Well, I get caught up in the moment. You guys don't know what it's like to be in front of the camera, being drilled with question after question."

"Candy, he's a victim of his own circumstances," Jim says laughing. "He's so camera shy, he blurts out any old thing. Now you'll have to live the stigma of being seen with him."

"Is it that bad?"

"You might as well change your name to promiscuous."

"'Loose' is easier to pronounce," Andy says.

Jim continues: "Just look at him. Would you buy a used car from this man?"

We all laugh, except Candy of course. James can even be heard snickering somewhere outside.

"I say, Candy, we should wed right away. Put an end to these rumors."

She laughs with us this time.

"All this laughter makes me hungry."

I'll leave it to you to decide who said that.

"My offer stands. Spaghetti Warehouse. I'll buy," Jim says.

At Jim's insistence, we load up in his '64 Buick Riviera with 430 HO and duals and head to the Spaghetti Warehouse. Even James loads up after a necessary truce and absolution. True to its name, the restaurant is a refurbished warehouse, a low-slung red brick building in the heart of Austin's old warehouse district. It can be found downtown on West 4th & something and serves, among other things, spaghetti. The food is good, the prices fair and it caters to a lively crowd. I'd give you a better address, but it is said, probably by the government originally, that marijuana use affects short-term memory. So, with that in mind, the address is West 4th & something. But, hey, here's something the government doesn't want you to know: smoke a joint and you will have no problems finding the Spaghetti Warehouse or any other eatery for that matter, for your hunger will be your guide.

We dine on spaghetti, of course, salad and garlic sticks and chase it with several pitchers of cold Budweiser Draft. Austin, got to love it and at least one of us is of legal drinking age.

I feel bloated and sated and no one around the table is feeling any pain. As much as I enjoy my crew's company, I'm ready to get Candy alone and ply my trade—seduction. I can only hope that the sight of the interior of her home doesn't dampen her mood.

At Andy's, we gather up Bonnie, a couple of cans of Alpo, our weapons, ammo and take our leave. I decide to try and minimize the blow of seeing her house as-is.

"Candy, don't get too upset about the condition of your house— it's trashed, so expect that. Also, there's no telling if the cops helped matters when they did their search."

"That bad?"

"Yeah, but tomorrow, with the crew's help, we'll get it back in order."

I pull into the short drive fronting her double garage. Her place is a neat '50s-era brick house, much like Andy's, the difference being that Andy's has a long drive and a carport at the rear of the house. Candy's home is simply landscaped and the yard is in desperate need of a cut. Newspapers litter the area around a newer-styled oak and etched-glass entry. Overall, a modest house by Tarrytown standards, but quite livable. When it comes to real estate, it's all about location, location, location and Candy's house is the definition of "location." The land upon which it sets exceeds the value of the house itself. West Austin, especially Tarrytown, has some of the highest real estate values in the state of Texas.

"Candy, you're supposed to suspend your paper subscription when you go out of town, otherwise it's an advertisement for the burglars—'rob me.'"

I slide my holster on and tuck Candy's new Smith into my waistband.

"I know. We forgot," she says as she removes a house key from under a dying potted flower and unlocks her front door.

"Here goes nothing," she says as she inches the door open. She's hesitant to look in or go in. Bonnie likewise seems unsure.

I open the door wider and give Candy a nudge. The living room is not so bad: couch cushions scattered, end-table lamps shattered and hundreds of cassette tapes litter the floor. In addition, all surfaces now are powdered in a layer of fingerprinting dust. Candy sighs.

"Not so bad, so far."

Beyond the living room and to the right is the kitchen. We make our entrance.

"Shit! FUCKERS!" Candy starts to shake. "Sorry, I sound like Andy now."

I put my arm around her shoulders and pull her to me. The kitchen is totally trashed—broken China, pots and pans everywhere and flour blanketing the floor. The fridge door stands ajar.

I check out its contents. The door rests on the open crisper drawer. I push it shut with a toe and close the fridge. We continue through the house. To the left, is a bedroom with a sliding glass door that leads to the side yard. Lingerie and other clothes cover the floor—all the dresser drawers are dumped and haphazardly piled. A large white dildo centers the bed.

I've seen it before laying amongst her lingerie when I passed through this very same room in search of Bonnie. I imagine Candy is somewhat embarrassed in seeing it now. In respect to her fragile feelings, I decide to take it easy on her.

"Damn, girl! You could bust up a concrete sidewalk with that jackhammer!"

Okay, our definition of taking it easy varies, but this is my picnic. Candy noticeably colors.

"It was a gag wedding gift from the girls."

"Gag gift... I'd say so. You could gag Linda Lovelace with that thing. What do you do with it? Store all the household D batteries in it?"

"Noooo."

"Or keep under your pillow for safety, in case of a prowler?"

"Noooo."

"Hey, we can have some fun with this thing."

She stomps on my toe again.

"I don't think so. You're embarrassing me."

My toe throbs slightly.

"Do you always resort to violence? I don't think I want to take you dancing, as light on your feet as you are. What I was thinking is we could have some fun with it by placing it under someone's pillow."

"You're not thinking about doing poor Andy that way, are you?"

"Nah, that wouldn't leave a lasting impression on him."

"Then who?"

"Well, his parents are due to be back..."

She laughs, having forgotten all about her embarrassment.

"You can't. That's... That's just plain wrong. Well, I guess you figured that this is my room, but I don't want to stay in it tonight with the glass door and all. Let's take one of the back rooms."

Hmmm. Let's... Like in, let us? I hope that I heard her right. The back bedrooms are hardly disturbed—being guestrooms, I assume, there was simply not much to disturb. The third room has a TV, so I might as well test the water here. I decide.

"Let's use this room, there being a TV in it."

"Sure, why not."

Bingo. You are a devil after all—a lucky devil, that is. Life is good and looking up more so all the time. Damn, I love it when a plan comes together.

"Hey girl, before we straighten this room up, let's drag the cooler down to the pool and go for a dip."

Candy's house sets on the corner entrance to Reed Park, a little city park with a small, live creek, hundred-year-old oaks, fescue lawns and a public swimming pool. It's a Tarrytown hangout for the beautiful West Austin housewives and their rug rats—women living at least one form of the American Dream: marrying money.

"The pool's closed and locked."

"Do you have a towel and a broom handle?"

Confusion clouds her face.

"Well, sure."

"Then it's not locked and closed to us."

"Okay, I guess, but my bikini is back at the motel."

"And your point is?"

"Umm... No bikini?"

"But you'll fly with someone who has never flown before?"

"I'll get the towels and the broom," she says.

"That's my girl," I say and go out to the car to get the cooler. I shake my head in wonder. I reiterate to the night: "You are a lucky fucker."

The pool itself is 150 yards or so from Candy's side-yard gate. We make our way to the pool, Bonnie in our wake.

"So, now what, chief?"

"Run the towel through the clasp of the lock and tie it tight to the center of the broom."

She does so.

"Like this?"

"Perfect." I open a cold Bud and take a swallow as I look on. "Now twist the broom until the lock pops open."

After about 20 turns the lock pops open.

"Wow, is there anything that you don't know?" Candy jokes.

"Not much, girl. Even a master five can be opened that easily and silently. Let me help you with them boots."

She sits on a lounger and I help her off with her boots. I kick mine off as well, watching as her denim skirt drops to the pavement and gets playfully kicked to the side. I can't help but let out a small whistle and think, there really is a god.

She tosses her Bud cap on the lounger and shucks her T-shirt. Her plain white panties and bra are in sharp contrast to her flawless tan. She dives into the pool as I almost trip over myself coming out of my clothes. She giggles as she surfaces and backstrokes away from me. I dive in after her. The water is still warm from the day's sun and somewhat sobering. I come up in time to catch her by a foot and drag her to me. She struggles and giggles trying to free herself—but not too hard... struggle that is.

I hold her afloat and take in the sight of her. Her whole being appears haloed by the pool's lights. She can only be described as beautiful, the sheer wet cotton leaving little to the imagination.

I kiss her taut belly as she splashes me.

"Girl, you won't deter me like that."

Much like the pool's arduous-to-open lock, Candy's bra strap poses little trouble for me. Folks, it all boils down to finger dexterity and practice and I'm a devout believer in practice.

I spin her in a tight circle, the water frees her small breasts. They're pert and the nipples aroused. I take one in my mouth and she lets go a small gasp, runs her fingers through my hair. I kiss the other and let her feet sink so that I can take her into an embrace.

Candy wraps her legs around me and throws her arms over my shoulders to pull me close. Our lips lock and our tongues tangle in a prolonged kiss. Life is good, runs through my mind once more. I don't know what it's doing for her, but I grow hard and my heart races.

Her hand snakes into my boxers and she grips me.

"Time we go home and consummate our new arrangement," she whispers in my ear.

Can I be so lucky? I smile.

"At least I got a kiss first."

She playfully bites me on the shoulder.

"Let's go now."

Somebody recently did the same thing—bite me on the shoulder—but I'll be damned if I can remember who right now. Must be that short-term memory loss again, but I shan't let that slow me down. Candy taps me on the head.

"Hello in there. Are you listening? I'd like to go now."

"Yes, honey. Don't get your panties in a wad. Do you think we can watch some TV afterward or do we have to cuddle?"

With agility and grace, she lifts herself from the pool and suggestively poses.

"If you don't hurry, I'll start without you."

I need no further encouragement, I'm out of the pool lickety-split. I don't know if "lickety-split" is a real compound word, but you get my meaning, right? Yes, believe it or not, there is some limitation to my stored knowledge. But give me a break, I'm only 17 and that, as you may now guess, is an excuse I intend to keep using. Well, at least for the next year, that is.

With guns, clothes and boots piled on top of the cooler and the cooler in hand, I stroll behind Candy as she sashays toward her house donning only her panties and a towel upon her shoulders— a sight that I'm sure will spawn many wonderful future memories. She's one petite bundle of joy and for now, it looks like my bundle of joy. That thought provokes an involuntary smile.

She dumps the towel at the door and I labor on behind her with my load—well, two loads, if you know what I mean. Loads that I intend to deposit. The first right inside the door and the other... Well, you get the picture.

I set the cooler inside the bedroom door, rub my hands in gleeful anticipation and watch as Candy turns to face me at the foot of the bed. She seductively wiggles out of her panties and allows them to bunch at her feet.

"Is that a pistol in your pocket or are you just glad to see me?" she jokes.

"Actually," I inform her, "The queen of double entendre, Mae West, unleashed that quip and it's 'gun' not 'pistol.'"

"Oh, shut up and get out of those boxers."

I do so and I have to admit, she has my full attention. She pulls me toward her. I lift her out of her panties, lay her on the bed and allow her, without preamble, to guide me in. She wraps her legs around me as well and that surely works for me. I don't think that she could feel any better if she was lined in silk. Her hot breath on my shoulder and soft moans spur me on. Within moments, she kisses me hard, expels her held breath and quakes beneath me. As the last of her tremors subside, her body goes slack, but she maintains her fierce hold on me and soon I too release and collapse upon her. Ah, the definition of heaven, I think.

Between gasps, I manage to eke out: "Damn, girl, you sure didn't last long."

"And you likely set a new world record," she says causing us both to laugh.

If so, oh, the joy in setting records.

"Candy, time is of the essence. It's going on 12:00 and you still haven't given me anything for my birthday."

She pops me in the back of my head.

"How about a black eye?"

"No, something of value," I say and we both laugh some more.

I roll off of her and drag her into the crook of my arm. Her head rests comfortably on my chest and she drapes a leg over me. With the lights still on, my last waking thoughts are: "there is a God," and "you're one lucky bastard."

I sleep the deep sleep of the pure of heart, or is it the sleep of one inebriated, sated and tired? Whichever, I sleep a dreamless sleep.

Chapter 8

I awake somewhat groggy from the previous day of over-imbibing, cottonmouth from hell and a feeling of eyes upon me.

I tentatively open one eye. Candy is on an elbow watching me as her finger lazily plays with my 13 chest hairs. Hey, at least they are easy to count.

"Morning, handsome," she says.

I groan.

"It's morning? Are you sure?"

"Yep," she says as her fingers do the walking, much like the yellow page ads and disappear under the sheet, which we somehow managed to acquire during the night. She innocently finds me and I instantly stiffen at her touch.

"But before we start the day off..." She lifts the sheet and looks under. "We'll start with this little problem first."

"Umm, do you think that you could have come up with a more appropriate adjective and noun as well?"

She gently strokes me and smiles.

"Nope."

"Not even, perhaps, 'hole packing' instead of 'little' and perhaps 'one-eyed monster' instead of 'problem?'"

She straddles me and takes me inside of her.

"Nope, but I will acknowledge it's a tight fit."

"Because?"

"Because of me, of course," she says and we both laugh. She begins working her magic and I'm in bliss, ecstasy—Daddy's home.

"Do you mind if I play with your little titties while you pleasure yourself here?"

"Touché," she says but doesn't miss a stroke.

Her using the word "touché" reminds me of Cheryl. I've read somewhere that if you think of something else while you're doing it, you will last longer. Exactly how you can think of something else, I haven't a clue, but I give it a shot anyway. Cheryl: nope doesn't help. Debra: nope, doesn't help. Brandy: nope doesn't help. My 11th grade science teacher—I'll protect her identity here—but no, it doesn't help.

I circle the wagons, try to think of all of them at once, but nope that doesn't help either. In fact, I think I may have just hurt the situation. One man in an all-women orgy. I smile myself at the thought.

I give up, throw in the towel, shoot from the hip, blow my wad. I guess I'm just trigger happy this morning, it would seem.

Candy pats me on the chest.

"There we go, my three-minute man. All better?" she asks smugly. "Now, maybe we can start the day without you thinking totally about me and my hot, tight, perfectly toned and tanned body."

"You know your bikini trim is slightly off-center. I can help with that. Then we can work on your subservience. You're off to a fair start, but there's room for improvement."

She stands and jumps up and down on the bed a few times before hopping to the floor, narrowly missing Bonnie, who scampers off spooked.

"I've got to get this venom out of me!" Candy yells as she darts from the room.

I yell too: "It's a whole lot less messy if you swallow."

I do my best to always get in the last word. I'm amazed and wonder how they do it. Much like Cheryl, Candy awakes from a previous day of hard-drinking and is bright-eyed and bushy-tailed. More power to them. Got to love them.

Candy returns and bounces a toothbrush off my chest.

"Here, my husband won't be needing this anymore and if it makes you feel any better, you're a better fuck," she says as she spins, giggles and departs again.

I look down at my shriveling member.

"You're damn right," I tell Studly. He likes the attention. We've spent so much quality time together, well him, Farrah and myself, that I'm tempted to buy myself a ring.

I roust myself, stretch and yawn and bend to pat the returned Bonnie on the head.

"Good morning, Bonnie Girl. You know your mama is nuts, don't you?"

She wags her tail in response. I knock everything off the cooler and fish out a couple of cubes of ice.

"Ah, now that's refreshing. Come on, girl. Let's go feed you." Bonnie is all eyes and ears. "Alpo?"

I catch a glimpse of myself in the dresser mirror. My hair sticks out in about ten different places, but I have to concede to the mirror: "You are a handsome devil, aren't you?" Or is that 'conceit' to the mirror? Too early and too much to ponder, I decide.

The aroma of coffee greets me as I enter the trashed kitchen.

Candy cheerfully queries: "Coffee, tea, or me?"

"Well, I've already had you, so how about some coffee."

She laughs and points at my shriveled member.

"How are you going to protect me with that?"

"One stroke at a time, big girl, one stroke at a time." The doorbell rings. "Shit! That must be Williams. Tell him I'll be right with him."

"Like this?" She points to her own nudity.

"Through the door, big girl, through the door."

I'm starting to repeat myself. Better check it now, I tell myself. I rush to put on my clothes, adjust and cover my blond mane with Candy's Bud cap, splash some water on my face and finger-brush my teeth. Fuck the toothbrush.

Back in the kitchen, I knock back my coffee, kiss Candy, inform her that I'll be back shortly and that she should lock the door and keep her pistol handy. She looks at me somewhat disheartened. I hurriedly kiss her again and reassure her that she'll be fine until I get back. I greet Williams at the door. He consults his watch.

"In another six hours, you will have stayed out of trouble and out of the news for 24 hours. What's your secret?"

"Good morning to you, too. Sometimes I even surprise myself, Williams. Let's go meet your friend."

We get in his nondescript Ford with its moon hubcaps.

"This is a new experience for me, Williams."

"What?"

"Riding in the front seat of a police car."

"It's a step up for you then, I guess. Look, as I mentioned..."

"Can we run the siren?"

"As I mentioned, all I can do is make the introduction. Where it goes from there, that will be between you two. I have a good feeling about you and you definitely don't shy away from confrontation. You seem capable enough and I passed all this along."

"Stop. You're going to make me blush."

"I doubt that, but you get my meaning."

We pull into the Holiday House parking lot and park next to a '74 blue Lincoln Continental. The sight of one of West Austin's only eateries reminds me that Candy and I haven't eaten yet this morning. Williams nods toward the Lincoln, extends his hand and we shake.

"Look after Candy, stay out of trouble and good luck on whatever you decide. John will give you a ride back."

"Later, Williams."

I exit the Ford and enter the passenger side of the Lincoln. The driver is a 50ish, weathered gent, in western wear and cowboy hat. My first impression: He's no stranger to the sun or booze. He extends his hand. I shake it.

"John Wallace."

"Steven Paul."

He looks me over.

"I must admit, I'm a little taken back here, Son. I was expecting someone much older."

"Well, Mr. Wallace, as my pappy always says: 'Never judge a book by its cover.' Well that and 'be sure to take your medication, Son.'"

"He really says that?"

"Nah. He mostly tells me to 'be careful, Son.' It's his way of supporting me without condoning my actions."

"Spare the rod and spoil the child?"

"No, I was no stranger to the belt and when I did get a whippin', it was well deserved."

"William tells me you're colorful, creative and capable."

"Like a diamond in the rough, Mr. Wallace. I plan to shine someday. By the way, I like your car. She's got a 460 big block if I'm not mistaken."

"That she does, Son. Anyway, Williams sure speaks highly of you and thinks that you may be able to help me."

"How?"

"In a second..."

"How do you know Williams?"

"Church."

"You don't look like no Baptist." I know, a double negative.

"Well, neither is Williams. Presbyterian when my better half can drag me to church." He pulls a cigar from his shirt pocket, licks it and bites the end off before lighting it. "Mind?"

"Go for it. Again, Mr. Wallace, how do you think I can help?"

"Call me John."

"John."

He pulls an envelope from the car's visor, extracts a picture from it and passes it to me.

"The apple of my eye: Daddy's girl."

"Beautiful."

"Yes, she is—beautiful, intelligent, independent, spirited and, unfortunately, impressionable and hard-headed."

"And the fellow she's with?"

"Dom Pedro, but who really knows."

"I think I'm starting to get the picture. Dom Pedro? Dom Pedro? Wasn't he the first emperor of Brazil, after Brazil declared its independence from Portugal?"

He exhales a cloud of blue smoke, looks over at me and perhaps re-evaluates me.

"Impressed. Who he really is, I do not know. My daughter told me he's a cattle baron and a carioca."

"A resident of Rio de Janeiro."

"Right again. Anyhow, she met this Dom character last summer in Miami. She's a model and an aspiring actress."

"Why not L.A."

"Miami is a major modeling hub. She figured she could get her foot in the door there and later parlay that into an acting career. But that's not important. What's important, as I'm sure you've already guessed, is that my baby is missing. I need you to find my baby and bring her back. What I want you to understand is that money is not a consideration. I'll also sanction any means necessary to find her and get her back.

"As I say, Son, money is no object here. I'm an oilman—a wildcatter. I scraped together everything I could get my hands on, borrowed as much as I could at the age of 20. Put together a crew of roughnecks, purchased a relic of a drilling rig and searched and searched until I found a lease that I could afford, put options on the ones I couldn't.

Like a crap shot, Son. It was all or nothing. Luck, fate, whatever was with me. My first well came in, in a big way. I hit pay dirt, snapped up the surrounding leases and, well, the rest is history. Life's been good to me ever since, but now everything is meaningless without my baby girl. Son, I've got to get her back at all costs."

"I feel you, John, and couldn't agree with you more. And the official channels?"

"At William's suggestion, I contacted the U.S Embassy. They, in turn, contacted the Brazilian Embassy and at first, all was good. The Brazilians were more than willing to help and then suddenly it's as if they were stonewalling me. Nothing, not a word. Don't even bother to return my calls, not even from my attorney."

He pulls a letter from the envelope and passes it too me.

"My one and only communication from Rio. It's postmarked the day following her arrival."

I hold up a finger indicating that I want time to read the letter. The handwriting is loopy and neat.

"Dear Father,

I'm having such fun. The Copacabana Palace is unbelievably jazzy. Today, Dom and I visited Museu Nacional de Belas Artes (National Fine Arts Museum). The array of 18th to 20th Century Brazilian folk art floored me. Then we toured Museu National. It's housed in a place that was donated to the prince regent by the Portuguese trader Ecias Antonio Lopez in 1818. They currently teach social anthropology there and store troves of archaeological finds and skeletons of prehistoric animals from Brazil and all over the world. Afterward, we dined at Adega Da Velha. It specializes in food from northeastern Brazil. I had a famous dish called carne do sol (salted sundried meat, softened in milk and barbecued). Fantastic.

After lunch, we checked out a couple of historic churches. The Catedral Metropolitana de Sao Sebastion (Metropolitan Cathedral of St. Sebastian) and the Igreja do Mostereiro de Sao Bento (St Benedict's Monastery). The gilt!

We dined again at Azumi on the Copacabana with its film noir atmosphere and it's said to be the best sushi place in Rio. The sushi's superb.

Finally, we hit the town and ended up at Bar D'Hotel. Don't let the name fool you, it's one of the hippest nightspots in town and overlooks Leblon Beach.

Oh, I wish you were here. Rio is so, so, exciting! Everyone seems to know and respect Dom. He's very mysterious, though.

No telling what tomorrow will bring!

Give my love to mother.

XOXO Daddy's Girl

"Interesting, quite the aristocrat, isn't he? You do realize that Brazil is still a military regime? That could pose a problem."

"I know. I have to level with you. I've already sent one investigator and haven't heard from him since his initial contact when he arrived in Rio. The hotel says he checked out."

"Hmmm, he probably did—permanently. That doesn't sound good."

"No, not at all," Wallace concedes. "Williams tells me that you fly like a seasoned pilot. Hard to imagine you looking so young and all. If it comes down to it, can you fly a DC-3?"

"Does she have wings and engines?"

"Yep."

"Then I can fly her."

"It's a latter '50s model and has the Pratt & Whitney R-2000 Twin Wasps. A nice old plane. I don't know in what scenario you might need one, but she's available. Do you think you can help, Son? I guess the real question is, will you help me?"

"What's your daughter's name?"

"Melissa."

"Not only am I going to find Melissa, but I'm also going to bring her back. And if God forbid, something has happened to her, I will avenge her."

Wallace lets out the breath he's been holding and pats me on the shoulder. "I like you, Son. You've got moxie. Williams tells me that you and your crew have 'grande cojones,' and I believe him. Open the dash and grab the two money bags. There's $10,000 in cash—start-up money. My phone numbers are there as well. Call me with the names of everyone needing plane and hotel reservations. You do have a passport, don't you?"

"Yes sir, of course. John, I'm going to hold on to this letter for now and as soon as you can get someone to print up 40 of these pictures."

I hand the picture back.

"I'll get them done today, somehow." He reaches under his seat and pulls out an Austin American Statesman—he passes this over to me. "You made the front page this morning. Where do you need me to drop you off and when can I expect to hear from you?"

"Reed Park. I'll call you this evening or no later than lunch tomorrow."

"Fair enough," Wallace says as he cranks the big Lincoln and puts her into gear. "Son, I feel good about this and my wife and I will be praying for you."

We ride in silence the short distance to Candy's. I hope that I'm not biting off more than I can chew. A foray into Rio may well prove to be a foray into the belly of the beast. I don't know much about the military regime there, but I suspect that they like things done their way. I wonder who this character Dom really is— what's his real story? The bottom line, I decide, is that my crew and I are going to find Melissa and bring her back. Assuming she's alive, that is. I need now only convince my crew of this. How it will all come about, I haven't a clue, but my mind is already beginning to churn.

"Turn into the drive with the Bonneville." I turn to shake his hand again. "Later, John."

"Thanks, Son."

I get out money bags in hand and ring the doorbell.

"Who is it?"

"It's me. Open the door."

"What's the password?"

"I brought you a present and an early lunch."

Fact: Women like presents and, if you starve them long enough, they like food, too. A key wouldn't have worked any faster. The lock clicks and Candy opens the door.

"Hey, where's the food? And what about my present?"

"The food's at the Holiday House. I need only call it in. The present... Well... I gave that to you this morning. I need to call the boys and wake their asses up, get this ball rolling."

"What's with the money bags?"

"I've been hired to rescue a damsel in distress. That's who I am— it's what I do." I say with a grin.

"What about me? You vowed to protect me."

"And that I shall do, as well."

"Who is she and where is she?"

"Melissa. Her name is Melissa and she's somewhere in Brazil."

"Brazil! Brazil covers half of South America." She pouts and looks beautiful doing so. "I bet she's pretty." She toys with a strand of hair. "Is she pretty?"

"I'll pick up the trail in Rio... What've her looks got to do with it?"

Candy merely shrugs.

"Look, if it makes you feel any better, on a scale of one to ten, I give her an 11."

"It doesn't. Rio de Janeiro... Fuck it. I'm going with you. You're not leaving me behind." She throws her hands on her sexy hips. "And I mean it!"

"Whoa, hold on turbo. Rio is a dangerous place. Plus, it's ruled by a military regime and there will likely be some shooting."

"Well... Well, I can shoot now, too. You taught me." She pulls her robe open exposing herself. "And what about this?"

She's clearly playing unfairly, but I can play hardball too. I capitulate.

"I'll write you into the script somehow. Hurry, get dressed. People to see, things to do."

I call our order into the Holiday House: Five chicken fried steak dinners and three doggie burgers—they know the routine—hold the lettuce, onions and tomatoes, mayo only. The Holiday House, where I was earlier, is right on Exposition Boulevard and close to the library where I need to stop. Not the expected five-star that would be more at home in the upscale Tarrytown area, but more of a mom-and-pop that features hearty homestyle meals and burgers. Being smokers and being within our limited means, we frequent it often.

I next call the boys. I tell them to gather up trash bags and cleaning supplies and meet us at Candy's. I inform them that I've got lunch covered as an incentive, knowing I need none. The promise of the sight and presence of Candy is enough to spur on any hormone-crazed male teen.

"Candy, bring your library card and let's roll," I yell out.

My library card has expired since the first time and last time I checked out a book. Oh, about four years ago. I checked out a John D. MacDonald "Travis McGee" novel. I returned the book surreptitiously by dropping it in the overnight return box on my only other library visit, four days ago, when I went to the library to learn what I could about German bearer bonds. Somehow, my ferocious appetite for reading doesn't translate into visits to the library. I pick up the tidbits of fact and trivia from more mundane sources and retain enough to get by. Salted enough, almost anything becomes palatable. The library simply is not my haunt. I do, however, devour newspapers and magazines and I am a fan of local and world news. Maybe I should slow down from actually being a part of the news, I consider, but only fleetingly. I was made for the spotlight, an imposing six-foot, 165-pound figure. I know, a legend in my own mind, but, hey, it works for me and at a minimum—one would have to concede—I'm a lucky bastard at times. The proof is in the pudding, I say not knowing exactly what that means.

Candy enters the room sporting her new Wranglers and does a spin for me. A perfect fit and a sight to behold. One couldn't have painted them on any tighter or better. I whistle in appreciation.

We leave Bonnie to guard la casa and take our leave. At the library, we locate and check out a couple of books: a travel guide to Brazil and a history, past and present, of Rio. Luckily, I escape the librarian's keen scrutiny and she doesn't connect me to the MacDonald novel that mysteriously turned up the same day as my last visit. I don't believe in past-due fines—well, as they apply to me, that is.

At the Holiday House, feeling dehydrated, I add five large fountain cokes to our order. Back in the Bonneville, the food's aroma has my stomach growling. I stave off the hunger pains, but succumb to my thirst and end up sucking the bottom out of my coke on our return trip to Candy's. I fret, just a tad, about how things might play out. My crew and I have spent a harrowing past few days and here I seem to be ready for more. No sooner does the danger ebb than I'm willing to plunge right back into the fray. Well, at least my crew has an option of in or out this time, even if I'm locked in. What do they say? "From the pot to the frying pan?" Maybe not too smart, but that's the way it goes. Despite my obvious weaknesses, like beautiful women and such, my word is still my bond and I intend to honor my word. I always do. Well, with the exception of Andy, of course, but Andy and I have this understanding—I build up his expectations only to let him down. I do it for his own good. I believe it builds his character and of course, it does supply the crew and I with limitless laughter. So, we express our love in our own unique way, as I believe I've mentioned before, but to quote mother again: "It is what it is."

The crew awaits us as we pull in. We catch Andy pacing the drive and smoke roiling from Jim's big Buick. I assume Andy is too hungry to think about smoking one with Jim and James. As we exit, he is quick to take the offered box of carryout and Jim requests a minute of alone time with me. He waits for the front door to shut.

"About the money?"

Yes, I've been expecting this, as much as he was expecting more money.

"Funny you should ask," I say as I whip Debra's still-folded Dear John letter from my back pocket and pass it over. "Read it and weep."

He scans over the letter that was left in lieu of the bearer bonds and his mouth drops open.

"Shit, Debra, sweet Debra, ripped you off?"

"No, 'us', Jimbo, she ripped 'us' off." Misery loves company and I'm quick to share 'our' disappointment.

"Un-fucking-believable."

"Didn't see that coming did you, Jimbo?"

He folds the letter, replaces it in the envelope and passes it back.

"No, I didn't, but why did you let her know where they were hidden?"

"Jimbo, have you ever led with your other head? I mean your little head, of course. Oh, right, you haven't started dating yet."

"It's 'lead with your chin,' and you're close to leading with yours," he says but smiles.

"The good news, though, is that I've got us a new gig, a big paying gig." I smile and I place my hand on his shoulder to guide him toward the door. "Have I ever steered you wrong?"

"I can't wait to hear about it."

"Is that cynicism I detect here, Jimbo?" I broaden my smile. "Have I got you killed yet?"

"I guess not," he concedes. "But I'm still not used to getting shot at and if anybody can get us shot at, it's you."

"That's the spirit, Jimbo, give it some time. You'll get used to it."

"That's not necessarily comforting."

We join Candy, James and Andy at the dining table. I rightfully take my place at the head of the table, being the king of my new domain, so to speak. Andy is eyeing the doggie burgers, his meal all but gone. Pot-paranoid James is passively picking at his food, uncomfortable eating before a beautiful woman. Candy sits and casually eats while she flips through the pages of the book on Brazil. My little family, I think. They bring me such joy.

"Honey, these pictures of Brazil are amazing."

Honey? She called me "Honey"—see what I mean about my rightful spot at the head of the table? The prosecution rests. Jim shakes his head and I grin from ear to ear. Not one to kiss and tell.

"Yep, Jimbo, another notch on the old pistol."

"You never cease to amaze me, Steve-O."

"I know, hold the applause please." Yep, a legend in my own mind.

"What are you guys talking about?" Candy asks still flipping pages.

"How radiant you are."

She looks up at me suspiciously before continuing to flip pages.

"Oh, honey." I take my stab at using the term. "Before I send Andy stumbling through the house in search of the beer cooler, did you remember to put your baton away?"

She kicks me under the table and blushes.

"I'll get the cooler," she says.

"It's a big inside joke, Jimbo." I cut him off before he can ask. "A big, big, big inside joke. Hey Andy, how about feeding the dogs their doggie burgers."

"Umm... Don't you think that they would prefer Alpo?"

"Nope, but good try though."

There is simply no way to misinterpret their intense stares and the occasional lick of their snouts. They want burgers.

Candy returns with the cooler and kicks me in the shin again as she takes her seat. I believe this is the type of silent communication that could leave bruises, but easily understood— it means that I'm doing something right.

I grin at her as I dig a cold Bud from the mostly melted ice, pull the tab and take a swallow.

"Ah," I say. "The perfect complement to my lunch. Boys and girls, life is good."

I decide to torture Andy some more. I eat my chicken-fried steak painfully slow.

"If you're just going to play with your food, I'll eat it," Andy says.

"No, no, that's okay."

"So, Steve-O, though I'm afraid to ask, tell me about this new gig."

"The mission, Jim, should you choose to accept it..." Remind you of Mission Impossible, maybe? "Is to assist me—"

"And me," Candy chimes in.

"—in the locating and returning of one missing Melissa Wallace, a right pretty Melissa Wallace, to her Texas oilman father. We'll pick up her spoor in Rio de Janeiro."

"Okay, Steve-O, I might point out that you're really not a detective and you have zero experience in locating or tracking anyone."

"And yesterday I really wasn't a pilot. Your point?"

"And I suppose you have a plan... Or, are you going to wing this one, too?"

"I'm formulating a plan as we speak. You must note that I'm on my first beer of the day and have yet to smoke a morning joint, so I haven't put on my thinking cap yet. Where you all feel nothing but paranoia after a joint, I feel enlightened. The money is going to be right and it is a noble mission. So, boys, I say we get packed and get Brazil-bound."

"Steve, I can't go to Brazil," James says looking uneasy.

"Can't get mama to sign the permission slip? No matter, you'll stay behind to tend to the dogs and monitor Candy's phone. Think you can swing that?" I hand Candy Melissa's letter. "Candy, take notes from this letter and see what you can learn about the locations mentioned.

"So, what do say, boys? We'll blend right in. Fifty-five percent of Brazil is white, plus I intend on recruiting Felix and however many others it might take."

"I'm in," Andy says as he paces and smacks his open hand with a fist. "We'll drop behind enemy lines and..."

"Hold on there, tiger. First, we've got to find her. Huddle up, boys, here's what I know. Melissa meets Dom Pedro in Miami, is impressed and hooks up with him in Rio de Janeiro, is wined and dined that first day and disappears. The Copacabana Palace says she's checked out. The U.S. and Brazilian embassies get involved and something happens—Wallace starts getting stonewalled. No help. Wallace sends an investigator. The investigator reports in the first day and he disappears as well. I've got a letter from Melissa to her father, the one Candy's reading over now, that lists the places that they visited that first day. Apparently, this Dom character is a well-known figure, at least around Rio and claims to be a cattle baron. He also portrays himself as an aristocrat and that, my friends, will be his downfall."

"So, what do you see as the biggest obstacle, Steve-O?"

"Brazil's been a military regime since '64, so that and, of course, arming ourselves could pose a problem. Then we have to locate Melissa, assuming she's alive."

Candy pats me on the shoulder.

"Hey, honey, listen to this, the club Bar D' Hotel is located in Leblon which is only blocks southeast of Copacabana. Ipanema and Leblon beaches are side-by-side. It says here that Garota de Ipanema is where Rio's most lithe and tanned bodies tend to migrate..."

"I'm in!" Jim says.

"It says the area is also known as the Cemeterio de Elefants, I guess I'm pronouncing all of this right, because of the leftist hippies and artists who hang out there. Copacabana and Leme are Rio's most beautiful beaches, it says here, but are no longer a symbol of Rio glam. It says it's still fascinating, but chaotic."

"Very good honey. Keep up the reading. Okay, boys, I guess we might as well hit the hammer and lock it in."

We all bump closed fists, including Candy.

"Hey, Steven Paul, that reminds me that my bikini is still at the motel and my rental car is at your house. I need to gather my stuff, check out and return the rental."

"Right, okay. You guys get started on the house while we do that and go see Felix."

"Conveniently, you'll be getting out of the work," Jim notes.

"Yeah, I'm disappointed, too, but as commander and chief of this operation, commander and chief by my own decree, of course, it's up to me to make these hard decisions. Any input, Candy?"

"Would you do it for me, boys?"

"Not fair, Steve-O," Jim remarks.

We all laugh.

"I know, isn't life grand, though?"

Chapter 9

Candy and I pick up her rental and, ironically, I follow her to the Motel 6, the same motel where the two Guineas that were searching for Candy's estranged husband were staying. What are the odds, I wonder? Two mid-level mobsters staying at a budget motel and then Candy's wannabe high roller picking the very same budget motel. It really is a small world. We stuff a woman's amount of luggage in the Bonneville's massive trunk. How could somebody so small have so much luggage? One consolation: she's already packed. She joins me in the Bonneville.

"So, who is this Felix cat?"

"He's a Mexican friend of mine. I met him back in the ninth grade, thanks to desegregation. He's a pretty diverse fellow. We golf sometimes and our games are about on par with each other. In other words, we both mostly suck and spend time laughing at each other."

"And why do we want to recruit him?"

"It's 'need' to recruit him. He speaks Spanish fluently and he also has a lot of connections that may come in useful. You do know, Candy, that I can't put you on the front line, but somehow, I feel that you will play a contributing role. Exactly what role, I can't say at this stage. What I'd like you to do for now is keep studying the book on Rio, map out the routes of the different locations mentioned in Melissa's letter, or any other place of interest like high-end tourists' locations."

"Okay, I can handle that. Wow, this is exciting. You sure live an exciting life. Are we going to be staying at the Copacabana Palace?"

I feel like warning her that chasing an exciting life is what got her in her past trouble, but I settle for: "That we are, girl."

As noble as I'd like to be, I'm not ready to lose Candy.

"Cool."

Felix lives east of IH 35, off Riverside and Montopolis. His street, Marigold and most of this section of East Austin, is predominately Mexican but I'm accepted here because it's widely known in the area that Felix and I are tight. For the past few years, my crew and I have been buying our pot through him and a few days past he helped me to acquire much of our arsenal. Some, of course, was willed to us by the departing dagos. We also used Felix's uncle to make straw purchases for the additional weapons that Felix couldn't personally locate for us.

Finding Felix in the neighborhood is easy enough. The neighborhood is close-knit and most of the residents in this area are related to each other somehow or another. This visit, again, poses no problem. I find him on his own front porch playing his acoustic guitar. I leave Candy in the car to study the book on Rio.

"Esteban Pablo, good to see you alive. My cousins keep saying that they've been spotting you on the news."

I pull up a chair, dig a Tecate from his cooler and lean back against the house's outer wall.

"That would be I, my friend."

"So, what brings you to the neighborhood? I know you guys haven't smoked all your pot yet."

"Recruitment. I'm here to recruit you on a mission to Rio de Janeiro. I need to locate and bring back a young woman. The pay will be right."

"Rio. I've always wanted to go there. With your newly acquired rep, I imagine we will be shot at?"

"It's highly possible there will be some force involved."

"Is this woman hiding or what?"

"Not likely. She's 100 percent a daddy's girl and she's disappeared. Everyone suspects foul play. I've been assured that money is not an issue in bringing her back."

"Isn't Brazil still under military rule?"

"Yep. We'll have to work within those parameters."

"Fuck it, count me in." We bump cans. "So, when do we leave?"

"Maybe as early as tomorrow. Meet me tonight at the little park in my neighborhood—the house on the corner of the entrance. Don't forget to bring your passport."

We bump cans again.

"Good enough. I'll see you then. Who's that chick in your car?"

"My new girl."

"Another one. She's nice. More power to you, my friend."

"Yeah, I've had a surreal run of luck lately." I dig two more beers from his cooler. "Two for the road—later, my man."

"Later, Esteban."

Back in the Bonneville, I pull the tab on one of the Tecates and pass it to Candy.

"Thanks. Listen to this: botequims are part of the everyday life of a typical carioca. They're eating, drinking and music establishments. The most sophisticated are located in well-to-do neighborhoods. Botequims compete with the beaches as far as recreation. It says they serve as a second home and most cariocas visit on a daily basis. They are part of the cultural core of the city. So, here's my thought: it would seem that if we could locate the botequim that Dom calls home, we'll soon find him." Candy turns toward me, tucks a leg under her, tucks a tuft of hair behind an ear and smiles at me. "So, what do you think?"

"I think we make a hell of a team. How about a kiss?"

"Only if you kiss and tell," she says but smiles.

"Come here then you little tramp," I say as she stretches toward me and gives me a lingering kiss while I drive with one eye on the road.

"Nice, now keep digging girl. We'll need a place to buy arms."

"Ten-four, Captain."

We arrive back at Candy's. The front door is still piled with newspapers and the yard is still in desperate need of mowing. As our new base of operation, having to cede Andy's back to his soon-returning parents, I decide the yard in its shape is unacceptable. Being a good delegator, I delegate a simple job to Candy before we enter the house: have someone pick up the papers and mow the lawn. She gives me her all-knowing smile as we enter the house—the not-even-a-challenge smile.

"Daddy's home," I yell out to announce our return. A quick inspection of the house reveals a marked improvement.

"So, does the house pass your inspection, um... Daddy?" Jim jokes.

"It will do for now, Jimbo. Do we need to shake Andy down to make sure he didn't pilfer anything from Candy's panty drawer?"

"He is predisposed to such things," Jim notes.

"Wearing them, too," James adds. "But I'm not going to be the one to strip-search him."

We all laugh, except Andy of course.

"Aw, fuck you guys."

"So, is Felix in?" Jim asks.

"In like Flynn. Now I need to make a call. Candy get someone to run you to Rylander's for steaks and beer."

"I'll take her if Jim will let me use his car," James volunteers.

"Sure, I don't mind, but the Riviera's a lot of car. Maybe you should let Candy drive."

Andy chuckles.

"He who laughs first doesn't necessarily laugh last," I remind Andy. "Candy, do you have something that you would like to share with Andy?"

"Andy would you mow the lawn for me while I'm gone. The mower's in the shed."

"I guess."

Candy smiles.

"And, oh, gather up all them newspapers while you're at it."

"Candy, grab $100 from one of the money bags. Prime ribs should do and be sure to buy plenty of Bud. Get whatever else you want to go with it. I'll see you, kids, when you get back."

I call Wallace and give him the names of everyone that will be accompanying me. As expected, he's chomping at the bit to get things started. I close the call with an invite to eat steaks and meet the crew.

Upon Candy and James's return, I put the steaks in a beer and Italian dressing marinade. It's a simple, but effective seasoning.

With nothing much left to do or plan, I take the opportunity to make a short trip by my own house to retrieve my previously packed suitcase and to leave a message on the chalkboard that Jim, Andy and I are heading south of the border for a few days. I utilize the board whenever I can. It cuts down on confrontation. Well, at least it delays it some. Although my south of the border destination may be slightly ambiguous and easily misconstrued, it is technically correct. I'm big on technicalities when they benefit me.

Back at Candy's, I'm happy to find her in the kitchen doing whatever it is that women do there. Just kidding. Actually, nothing about the kitchen scares me. I enjoy cooking.

Candy fills me on what we will be having: potato salad, tossed salad, corn on the cob and, for an appetizer, peel-and-eat jumbo shrimp. Works for me. I give her a kiss and a smack on the ass before joining the crew in the living room for some mindless TV.

Candy soon joins us carrying the two library books. She plops down beside me.

"The hillsides north of Copacabana are called favelas and are the high crime areas of Rio. Honey, maybe you can find some weapons there."

"Sounds like a plan. Keep digging and map things out for us. There's a good chance that we will be in Rio tomorrow. Friday night: couldn't have timed it better."

"And as far as picking up Dom's spoor," Candy continues, "since it will be Friday night, we might as well start out by concentrating at the center of Rio's nightlife. According to this, the bars and restaurants of Bazio, which is lower Leblon and not far from where we will be staying looks like the best nightlife. It looks like most of the places are off Av Ataulfo de Paiva and between Rua Aristides Espinola and Rue General Artigas. I have no clue if I'm pronouncing most of this correctly, but I read earlier that if you speak Spanish, most everyone will be able to understand you even if you can't understand them. You would think Portuguese would be closer to Spanish than it is, but what do I know? Hey, honey, check this out."

Candy points to a paragraph in the book on Rio and passes it over. I take a few seconds to scan the paragraph.

"Hey, Andy, you may get lucky yet. On downtime, you can check out the infenihos along Copacabana and Ipanema."

"What the hell are infen... How the hell do you say it?"

"You almost pronounced it right, Andy. They're little hells—nightclubs with prostitutes." I neglect to mention the gays and transvestites that frequent them as well.

"I don't use prostitutes."

"Well, I thought I'd point it out to you as a favor. I imagine someday, you're going to get tired of having sex by yourself."

We all laugh, except Andy of course.

"Ha, ha, Steve. You're too funny."

I ignore Andy's weak jab.

"Jimbo, we need somebody to make a Radio Shack run, buy a dozen of the Realistic walkie-talkies like we bought last time, along with ear-bud attachments and maybe a couple more of the Midland hand-held CBs. The longer-range may come in handy seeing as how we don't know exactly what situations we will encounter."

"Sure, I'll do that myself. May have to go to more than one location for that number of radios. Andy, you want to ride along?"

"Yeah, that would be better than staying here and being the brunt of Steve's jokes."

"It's the 'butt' of my jokes, Andy and that is spelled with a double T," I say being always quick to enlighten him. "You know, Andy, why do you even bother with school when you can learn so much from me? God knows, with your grades you don't go to please your parents."

"Yeah, whatever," Andy says. "Speaking of parents, are you still going to help me explain the bullet holes in our house?"

"Of course. Would I lie to you?"

Jim and James turn to keep from laughing.

"And Andy, keep in mind that lying to you and steering you wrong are two different things."

"I'll keep that in mind, but I'm sure that you will disappoint me again. Come on, Jim, let's go."

"That's the spirit, Andy. Keep that chin up." I grin as I pass the book back to Candy. "And you, big girl, keep digging up all this useful stuff."

"Okay, but the list of places to check out is going to be a long one. Rio's a big place. At least, most of the places to start are concentrated. Hey, now that Andy's gone, do you think that we can change channels?"

I make eye contact with Candy and nod my head side-to-side in James's direction.

"I don't care what we watch," James says.

"I'm just trying to include you, James. We know how sensitive you are."

"I'm not sensitive."

"Okay, defensive."

"I'm not defensive, either."

"Jaaammes."

James blushes under our scrutiny and squirms in his seat.

"Anyone need another beer?" he asks. I guess that's his way of changing the subject.

I get up to change the channel and, with Candy's concurrence, settle on the "Beverly Hillbillies." Doesn't get much funnier than that, and "Green Acres" is in the lineup. God, don't you love it?

I stretch out on the couch and Candy cuddles up beside me. Does it get any better than this? Did I mention the fact that I think I'm in love? Despite the fact that I've seen Candy nude, I bet she looks tight in her bikini. I inwardly smile at the thought.

Chapter 10

I must have dozed because "Green Acres" is going off the air as I open my eyes. Candy is snug as a bug in my arm, breathing through her mouth. Cute as a button. Like most other sayings, where this one originated I haven't a clue and what is exactly cute about a button? One thing I do know, though, is that Candy's small body radiates some pleasant heat.

Candy stirs at Jim and Andy's return. She stifles a yawn and hides her mouth before taking my hand and placing it between her small breasts. I can feel the slow and even tick of her heart. I think that this might be the one to domesticate me but confess to myself that might be a tough row to hoe.

Jim sets his weighted Radio Shack bag to the floor.

"Steve-O, we've got it all, plus extra batteries and chargers. You want Andy to get the fire started?"

Jim is picking up on the art of delegating, I note.

"Yeah. James, you can give him a hand."

"It's not like changing a lightbulb," James jokes.

"True enough, that's why the pair of you should be able to handle it. Besides, you know Andy has a penchant for using gasoline when unsupervised."

"I do not," Andy says. "How come you don't ever have to do anything, Steve?"

"Because there are leaders and there are followers. I'm a born leader and you are a born follower. The Spanish word for follower is 'peon.' Besides, I'm comforting Candy right now."

"I imagine that's very unpleasant," Andy says and smirks.

"And I imagine it may be a feeling that you will never experience, but that's not the point, is it?"

"Whatever. Why do I even bother?"

"So true, Andy." I stick my finger in Candy's mouth as she yawns again and she playfully slaps it away. "Let me up, big girl."

"Oh, fine. But I'm very comfortable. You sure are rough on Andy," Candy says laughing as she rises from the couch. "I know, I know, it's for his own good—it builds character. I have to get up anyway, get the potato salad made and get the corn shucked."

I smack her on the ass as she gets up.

"A woman after my own heart."

"Steve-O, toss me a beer. Any news on when we're leaving?" Jim asks. I toss one over.

"I've invited Wallace over for steaks. We'll find out then."

"You grilling the steaks, Steve-O?" Jim asks.

"Yeah, grilling ours to perfection, converting Andy's to shoe leather. As you know, that's the only way that he will eat them."

"He could fuck up a wet dream," Jim jokes and we both laugh.

I get up to join Candy in the kitchen. I can see Andy and James on the back patio struggling to light the charcoal. The sun is out, but the wind appears to be kicking up. Maybe it will take three to get the grill lit after all. I'll give them a few more minutes, I decide.

I take the time to insert the leaf in Candy's dining table and set the table for seven. We're forced to use paper plates since most of Candy's dinnerware was smashed. Well, there is a consolation, I realize—fewer dishes for Andy to wash, a chore that he's not good at doing anyway. His style of washing usually results in casualties.

The table set, I sip my beer and enjoyably watch over Candy. I can't believe we met only yesterday and, as ironic as it may seem, it's already turning into one of my longer relationships. Just kidding. My relationships tend to be long and enduring. My secret, if I haven't mentioned it before, is to start with a solid foundation. In other words, as someone once said, it's only cheating if you get caught. Okay, you happy? Is that more believable?

Candy waves her potato-encrusted wooden spoon in front of me.

"Earth to Steven Paul. Did you even hear what I just said?"

"Yes, dear."

"Then what did I say?"

"Hey, look, I think they got the fire started."

"That's what I thought," she says as she goes back to stirring.

So, I'm not very good at listening, but I give it a shot anyway. "You said that your secret is the amount of mustard you use."

"No, that's not what I said, but good try. Do you want eggs in here as well?"

"Sure, as long as it doesn't give you gas."

"Ha. Ha. Ladies don't get gas."

"Hmmm. So, that extra hour you women spend in the bathroom has nothing to do with airing it out?"

"Not to change the subject, but would you get me a beer?"

I get up to fetch her a beer.

"It sounds like you're pleading the fifth to me."

I fetch myself another while I'm at it. The doorbell rings as I enter the kitchen. I pull the tab and hand her a beer.

"I'll get it, honey," I say emphasizing "honey." I open the door to Felix. "There goes the neighborhood."

"Don't worry, they'll mistake me as one of your lawn boys. How are you doing, Esteban?"

"Getting by Felix, my man."

Felix follows me into the kitchen toting a small suitcase and a 12-pack of Tecate.

"You staying here?" he says. "I like your new digs, man."

"Felix meet Candy and Candy meet Felix." I wink at her. "He's a Mexican, but he's okay. He has a green card."

Candy reddens a little for him.

"Ignore him, Candy," he says. "Most do when they get to know him and if you keep on feeding him, he'll never leave. That's a word to the wise."

"It's not her cooking that keeps me wrapped around her little finger, it's her..."

"Honey, I think you should put your steaks on now," Candy interrupts.

Felix and I laugh.

"Sorry, Candy. I don't mean to laugh," Felix says. "But I've known this character since the ninth grade."

"It's not a progressive disorder is it?" Candy asks with mock concern.

"If you give him the chance, he'll have you bra-less and shooting pool in short skirts."

That stops Candy in her tracks. She scrunches her nose, pouts her lips and glares at me for a few seconds before she smiles again and goes back to mixing. Felix laughs again.

"I take it he's already got you the skirt," he says.

"And out of one as well I might add," I gleefully say never being one to kiss and tell.

Felix gives me his thumbs up approval and bumps my can.

"Ah, to be young and in love," he says.

"Felix, do you like peel-and-eat shrimp?" Candy asks as she fills a pot with tap water.

"Sure."

"That and burritos, tacos and refried beans and things," I say.

"You sure you like this guy?" Candy asks shaking her head as she turns on the burner.

Andy and James enter from outside. "Hey, Felix," they say simultaneously. I catch a whiff of burnt hair. I look Andy over.

"Andy, you didn't singe your hair by any chance, did you?"

"No."

"He was standing downwind from the grill when he added more fluid," James happily announces as he pulls up a chair. We all laugh, except Andy of course.

"I thought you told me that you were not going to say anything."

"I lied."

"Not bad," I compliment James. "My hard work is finally paying off."

"Did someone burn some hair in here?" Jim asks entering the kitchen. We all point at Andy. Jim shakes his head.

I take Felix's open 12-pack, place it in the fridge and remove the steaks. I take one steak outside and throw it on the grill. Have to give Andy's a big head start. I come back in and retake my seat. Candy sits down beside me.

"Honey, I got the dogs each a pack of hotdogs for the grill. I guess put them on the grill when you put our steaks on."

Felix reaches over and scratches Bonnie behind the ear.

"I haven't seen this one before. Is it yours, Candy?"

"Yep. That's my girl. Her name is Bonnie."

"Bonnie, you're a pretty girl," Felix tells her.

Bonnie licks the underside of Felix's arm in appreciation as Felix continues to scratch her.

Caught in the light just right, Andy's unibrow doesn't seem to be quite as bushy as before and his eyelashes don't look quite right either.

"You know, Andy, Candy can touch up those eyelashes for you with a little of her mascara."

Andy shoots me a bird.

"Touch this up. It only singed the hair on my knuckles and arms."

"Dragging your knuckles the way you do, I'm surprised you had hair on your knuckles as you now claim."

"Well... Well, I did. I'm going to bring the cooler in here."

We all laugh some more, well, except Andy, of course. Got to love him.

We sit and bullshit about high school for a while. All of us but Candy are entering our senior year at Austin High. We're all "Maroons," whatever the hell that is. At least my latest ride sports the school's colors. Jim and Felix advanced with A's, James and I with B's and Andy, well, let's just say that he advanced.

Candy finds her portable radio, brings it into the kitchen and tunes it to KLBJ. Bob Seger's long version of "Beautiful Loser/Ramblin' Man" is playing from his "Live Bullet" album. Somehow, it has me thinking that it doesn't get much better than this. A beautiful new girlfriend and surrounded by my good friends. Of course, there's also Bonnie, Rosie and Smokey—can't forget about them.

I go out to flip Andy's soon-to-be shoe leather. We want the texture to be consistent. I intend to slightly sear ours when Wallace arrives. I don't go for outright rare, but it's a close call.

Everyone else's I'll grill to order. I leave the patio door open, deciding we should smoke one before Wallace's arrival—just for the hell of it—just because we can. Life is good. I don't know Wallace's feelings concerning pot, but I want him to leave here this evening optimistic about our chances of success. I know that I intend to give it my all, but realistically, I realize that this may well be the biggest challenge of my life. The pot leaves a shadow of a doubt, but I hope that it fades along with the weed's high.

Bonnie barks—jumps to attention. Smokey and Rosie join in seconds before the doorbell announces Wallace's arrival. I turn down Creedence's "Down on the Corner" and answer the door.

I greet Wallace with a firm shake. He's carrying an attaché case and is attired much the same as before. I realize now that he's shorter than my initial impression. That aside, there's nothing lacking in his firm, callused grip or his imposing good-old-boy aura.

Showing respect, I seat Wallace at the head of the table and take my seat at the other end—the other head of the table. Who's to say that there can't be two heads to a table? I choose to view it as such.

"Wallace, I'd like you..."

"John."

"John, I'd like you to meet Jim here." They shake hands. "Andy." They shake. "James." They shake. "Felix." They shake. "And, last but not least, the lovely Candy." Wallace bows slightly and shakes her hand as well.

"John, if you will give me a second, I'm going to throw our steaks on before we get down to business. Andy, get John a beer."

I slice the hotdog packs open with my trusty Uncle Henry and toss them on the grill along with our steaks. Back in the kitchen, I retake my seat.

"They'll be medium rare unless someone tells me otherwise. Okay, medium rare, it is. John, I cede the floor to you. What do you have for us?"

He opens his attaché case and removes a stack of photos. He hands the stack to Felix to pass around.

"There's 40 of these prints, Steven, as you requested." He removes another stack and passes them along. "And here are 40 more of Melissa alone. A profile shot. I thought it could help."

There is silence all around as the pictures are passed. There's no denying Melissa's beauty. Although her beauty should not be relevant, her pictures seem to have a profound effect on everyone. As superficial as it may be, her beauty, at least for me, makes my resolve to rescue her that much more tangible. Is it easier to rescue someone if they're beautiful? Something to ponder.

Wallace picks out a stack of airline tickets from his case.

"I got the earliest smoking flight out of Austin—a 1:00 p.m. departure on Delta with a short stopover in Houston—don't even have to change planes. Then it's off to Miami with an ETA of 5:15 p.m. There will be a two-hour layover there and then it will be TWA for a direct flight to Rio's international airport, Aeroporto Galeao. The ETA there is 2:00 a.m. Is anyone here 21?"

Candy tentatively raises her hand.

"Okay, I'll rent the car in your name. They have a Hertz right there at the airport. Let me call that in and get it arranged."

Candy points to the kitchen phone.

"I'll check on the steaks while you do that," I say.

I go out to flip them over and, oh, do they smell good. Back in the kitchen, Wallace is hanging up the phone.

"Okay, that was easy enough," he says. "Earlier, I booked two suites at the Palace, one in your name, Steven and one in Felix's. They're not adjoining, but they are on the same floor. The Palace is on Copacabana Beach. It's where my daughter briefly stayed before she disappeared."

"Mr. Wallace..."

"Call me John, Candy."

"Okay, John we've been doing some research and I think we have a pretty good game plan in the works."

"No offense, Candy, but I'm not real comfortable with you being involved in this matter, being a woman and all, but I'm going to bow to Steven's judgment on this. Not that I believe that a woman's place is in the kitchen, barefoot and pregnant. I just fear for your safety, young lady. If you ever met my wife, you'd know I could never think like that."

Bow to my judgment? My judgment? Don't hear that often. Even though I suspect my own judgment on this call, I sit a little taller in my chair. The sad fact is that I bowed to Candy's female persuasion, but who in my young position wouldn't? I'll keep this little fact to myself.

"I appreciate your concern, Mr.—um, John, but I know how to shoot."

"Whoa." Wallace throws up his hands. "Don't have to convince me, young lady, but please, please, be careful."

"With that said, I'm going to gather the steaks," I say

"Amen, Son."

John's amen is followed by a chorus of amens around the table. Candy serves the potato salad and corn as I serve the steaks. All but Andy's are succulent and tender enough that they can be cut with a butter knife. Andy almost loses his knife several times trying to saw through his. I'm tempted to lend him my Uncle Henry but decide I spend too much time keeping it honed to do that.

Although clearly not intended to be a memorable event, under the circumstances, the dinner goes over well. After dinner, Wallace retrieves a 25-year-old Scotch from his Lincoln and fires up one of his aromatic cigars. He takes a pull right from the expensive bottle and passes it around.

"To a successful mission and a safe return."

The Scotch is smooth and warms all the way down. John tosses a pad of traveler's checks on the table.

"There's $2,000 more, in case of emergencies. Not everyone down there takes them, but everybody takes God's good old U.S. greenbacks. One last thing." He reaches into his case again and smiles. "Visas in everyone's names except James's. James, I take it you're not going since I wasn't given your name."

"Yes, sir, they need me to stay behind and monitor Candy's phone."

"Right," Wallace continues. "Finding the Palace is a breeze. Every other cab is headed to Copacabana beach, Ipanema and Leblon. Well, people, that's it. I guess I'll take my leave. My better half is probably pacing the floor. Can't keep the little woman waiting. God bless you all and keep you safe. We'll be praying for you."

He shakes hands all the way around again and takes one last look at us.

"I feel good about this. Yep, I feel good about this. Oh," Wallace turns one last time before exiting the kitchen. "Can anyone spare a joint? I need to unwind." He laughs. "I'm joking. I smelled the pot earlier. See you guys and gal when you get back. I'll see my way out."

Candy clears the table. Andy passes out a fresh round of Buds and one Tecate. Frampton's "Do You Feel Like We Do" comes on the small radio. I turn it up. Man, you can get lost in this song, I think to myself. I still feel the glow from the Scotch. If I could sing, I'd sing along. Only Peter Frampton and Bob Seger can pull off a song this long and get the stations to play it.

"Well, boys and girls," I say. "It looks like we're all set. Everyone pack your camo in case we need them and Andy, no, you can't bring your machete. You can bring your canteen if you have to. I'm taking my Uncle Henry."

I get up and grab one of the money bags, count out $1100 and pass it to James.

"Your job, as you know, is to monitor Candy's phone and take care of the dogs and anything else on this end. If you can't handle it, give Wallace a call."

I give everybody else $1300 apiece.

"Some pocket money and some flash money, should you need it."

"Steve-O, how are you coming along with that plan of yours?"

"Well, Jimbo, it's like this... We'll play it by ear—play the cards as they're dealt."

"In other words, Steve-O, our usual plan. We're going to wing it."

We all laugh.

The evening winds down and after another joint, just because we can, everyone but Felix takes off. The crew agrees to meet back at Candy's by 11:00 a.m. Felix, Candy and I retire to the living room. Tonight's TV lineup: Charlie's Angels without Farrah. I mean, what the fuck is up with that? Has her husband lost his friggin' mind? He can't handle Fawcett's success. Prediction: the marriage is never going to last. Second in the lineup: Columbo. Then it's The Carol Burnett Show, love that Tim Conway, followed by Channel 7 News. Probably will be dull, seeing as how I didn't make the evening cut. I mean, what is news without me? I hate to disappoint my fan base, but hey, it is what it is. Life goes on. And, finally, we plan to watch The Johnny Carson Show. I like the way McMann says: "Here's Johnny." I make it a point to store that phrase in the back of my mind for future use. Yes, there's a time and place for everything.

At the end of Carson, Candy leaves the room and comes back with a pillow and blanket for Felix. She tugs at my hand.

"Felix." I wink. "I think this is my cue that I'm needed in the bedroom."

Felix gives me thumbs up. Candy throws her hands on her hips.

"Keep it up, Big Boy and you're going to talk yourself right out of a job."

Hmm, can't have that. But for the record, it's tough at times being treated as an object. Aren't there laws against things like this? If not, there should be. I decide to grin and bear it. Yeah, right... I can't help but grin.

Before we pass, Candy pulls me into the bathroom. "I think we'll have a shower first, Big Boy."

"It's Sunday already? The first of the month? What's the deal?"

"Close enough. Hurry up, get out of them duds, Cowboy. I need my back washed."

So, I was right about the servicing part after all. She raises a foot and I tug her boot loose, then the other. She wiggles out of her jeans and panties.

"Isn't that what Cheryl, whatever her name is, from Allens boots calls you? 'Cowboy?'"

"Yep."

"Why?"

"Because I ride them hard and put them away wet. "

"Yeah, right," she says tugging at the button on my jeans. "Could you hurry up."

Pertinacious, isn't she? Got to love her. I toe my boots off one at a time and kick them to the side. The rest of my clothes disappear before she even has the water adjusted. Her bending at the waist has its effect on me. I part the shower curtain without any hands. Please don't try this at home. Whether I can repeat this feat on the way out of the shower is yet to be seen. I'm here to tell you, showering takes on a whole new meaning when showering with Candy. "Overriding joy" would sum it up perfectly.

I trail the nude and giggling Candy into the bedroom. Bonnie is curled and centered in our bed.

"Sorry, Bonnie," I have to tell her. "Not tonight."

With the snap of fingers and a point, she hops to the floor. She does her customary spin and yawn before settling at the foot of the bed.

I yank the spread aside, Candy climbs aboard and I do a playful dive onto the bed, bouncing Candy to the floor.

"Hey!" she yells and giggles. "I landed right on my ass."

The foot of the bed collapses with a bang, sending Bonnie scampering from the room with a yelp.

"Oops," I say. Still giggling, Candy crawls back onto the sloping bed.

"Shit!" She laughs. "I think you broke the fucking bed."

I roll her on top of me. The head of the bed crashes to the floor and the headboard bonks Candy on the head.

"Ow, that smarts," she says rubbing her head and giggling all the while.

I laugh so hard that I almost lose my erection. Almost. She roughly guides me in. I take it that she likes it on top. In the lee of the headboard, I let her do her magic. One of my last thoughts of the evening is: it doesn't get any better than this.

Chapter 11

As my eyes slowly open, I notice that the sunshine coming through the east window casts a strange shadow over our torsos. Oh, the headboard, I realize. I remember now that the bed had a slight accident last night. I inwardly smile at the thought. Candy is still down for the count and sleeping soundly. Her cheek rests on my chest. Her leg is draped across me. She looks so peaceful in her sleep.

Sometime during the night, Bonnie braved a return. She sleeps curled at the corner of the bed. Looking at them, I sure hate to disturb their tranquility, but I've got to piss like a Russian racehorse.

I tuck the hair covering Candy's forehead behind her ear and kiss her there. She sleepily smiles, but only snuggles even closer. I truly hate to disturb her, but hey, my back teeth are floating. I tickle her nose with a few strands of her hair. She rubs her nose several times before finally waking with a big yawn.

"Good morning, sunshine. Hey, you have a gold tooth back there, girl." She twirls a finger in my embarrassingly sparse chest hair. Well, embarrassing if I embarrassed easily, that is. I look into her dazzling and mesmerizing eyes.

"Was I good last night," I joke.

"You fell asleep on me, but otherwise you were great."

"Yep, I do some of my best work when I'm asleep. Let me up, girl, I've got to water the horse. I mean, like right now, girl."

"Oh, okay, but hurry back. I have something to show you," she says as she stretches.

I drain the lizard and brush my teeth before returning to the bedroom. She grins up at me.

"Hey, look what I can do," she says lifting her legs and tucking her ankles behind her arms.

I gulp and gape. I mean, I really gulp and gape. I wipe the fresh sheen of sweat from my upper lip and brow. I'm thinking not even Wonder Woman—what's her name? Something Carter—can do this. I'm temporarily at a loss for words.

She lets loose her ankles and laughs up at me as she stretches back out.

"Too bad it's so uncomfortable." She laughs some more. "I wish I had a camera just now."

"I wish I had one too. The boys will never believe me."

Candy leans forward, grabs me by my member and pulls me toward her.

"Your turn to do the work, big boy. Maybe this way you won't fall asleep."

Unable to think of anything else but her former amazingly agile position, I make quick work of it. Hey, in my defense, this one's on her. And, hey, I'm only 17, okay? There're still a few issues with the hair trigger to iron out, but I'll work on it. She kisses me anyway and pats me on the shoulder.

"That's okay, stud. You'll do better next time."

"You know it's your fault, don't you?" I'm quick to point out. She gives me her smug look.

"I know. I'm just too good."

We both laugh.

"Come on, sport," Candy says. "It's time to get up anyway. I'm excited. We're going to have some fun."

I hate to remind her, but I do.

"We're not actually going on a vacation, you know."

"I know, I know." She whacks me with her pillow. "But it's still exciting. Can't a girl get excited? I've got to unpack and repack. I've got to get busy. Lots to do. Oh, and what does a girl have to do to get breakfast around here?"

I resign myself to making breakfast, but mostly because we have company. I mean, she's already fired off some of her best morning ammo.

I check the fridge for whatever else Andy might have picked up the day before. Perfect, I think. There're breakfast chops, a second carton of eggs, some ripe tomatoes and a loaf of bread. I tell Felix he's on his own if he wants to brew some coffee. My worldly knowledge doesn't include the art of brewing a simple pot of coffee. Yes, as inconceivable as it may seem and as well-rounded as I am, it's true.

Felix sits down with his coffee cup.

"Esteban, it sounded like you two were tearing the house down last night. Bonnie spent most of the night at the foot of the couch."

"Bed gave out," I say leaving lots of room for interpretation.

"More power to you, man."

Candy comes bouncing in with her cute little self.

"Perfect. Right on time. Morning, Felix."

"Candy."

"Felix, note Candy's healthy glow."

"Yep. Noted. I see it all right."

"It's the sign of a truly contented woman—sated, she is."

"That's what I was thinking," Felix says and we all laugh, Candy included.

We shoot the breeze while we eat our breakfast. I give Bonnie her chop and let her out the back for her morning constitutional. Shortly, the crew arrives. Nothing left to do or plan. We smoke one just because we can. Everyone has a single suitcase but Candy, of course. She has no less than three to be checked and one to carry on. We distribute our electronics amongst the cases. I imagine that our gear will raise some red flags getting through customs, but none of it is hi-tech, or illegal for that matter. We'll cross that bridge if it becomes an issue.

We load our luggage in the trunk of Jim's big Buick and bid James and the mutts adieu. I have to admit that it is pretty exciting and perhaps a wee bit scary, as well. But, the secret to being a true leader is to never show any fear. So, I decide to keep the wee-bit-scared part to myself.

The airport is a 15-minute ride. We park in long-term parking. The day is picture perfect. I imagine that Rio is about the same distance from the equator as we are now, only on the other side. This is mere speculation on my part, but if it's true, then they should be experiencing mirror weather. Time will tell.

We all carry two suitcases a piece but you know who. As she strolls along, she looks good enough to eat and garners plenty of attention. She donned her boots and denim skirt—to please me, I'd like to think—and now she swishes her tight little ass right along. Once again, I'm proud as a peacock and six-feet tall and bulletproof.

We enter the coolness of the airport's concourse. Candy clops right along. It makes me wonder why my boots don't make the same noise? We check our baggage and gather our boarding passes. We're directed to gate 10A.

"Hey, cool," Candy says. "Wallace bought us first-class tickets."

"Well, in that case, the drinks are on me," I say.

We're early but are allowed to board anyway. Half the fun of flying first class is to board early and watch the disappointment of all those less fortunate as they pass. Exactly how long have I known this, you wonder? Oh, about one minute. Anyway, the world is made of winners and losers and at the moment I just happen to be riding a winning wave. There will be no raining on my parade, at least for now.

We're greeted by a pair of friendly and pleasant-looking stewardesses. Oh, and they smell good, too. The taller of the two, a leggy 30ish brunette, shows us to our seats. She sports a Farrah cut and white even teeth. Oops, I almost forgot. She also sports a nice set of knockers. These are things on which an untrained eye might not pick up. Therefore, I feel duty-bound to share my observations.

If I'm not mistaken, I'm picking up a vibe here. I think she has made me the leader of our little group. Perhaps my striking handsomeness gives me up. I amuse myself with the thought. She's naturally drawn to me, like a moth to a flame.

"Can I get you two anything while we wait for departure?" she offers.

"Your phone number, port of call and itinerary, Jane," I say.

Her nametag reads Jane. Candy elbows me in the ribs.

"She means drinks, silly. Jane, you'll have to excuse him. He's never been quite right again since his bout with malaria and, well, unfortunately, he didn't make it very far in school. I'll have a gin and tonic, please."

"Jane, what the little lady is really trying to say is that she doesn't like sharing. For the record, that's her hang-up not mine. I have no such qualms sharing me. And, thank you for asking. I'll have a Jack and Coke."

Jane does a double-take, no doubt assessing my age, but finally assents.

"Yes, sir, Jack and Coke it is."

"Jane, if you'd be so kind, bring my crew whatever they wish," I say with a smile.

I fold $20 and try to pass it to her. Candy smiles but elbows me again anyway.

"Thank you, sir, but gratuities are not necessary."

Candy snatches the money from my grip and tucks it in her bra.

"I'll just hold that for you, honey." We all laugh. Jane reddens. I dazzle her with a smile as she turns to the others. Isn't life grand? Making life easier on Jane, the rest of the crew order Buds. Out of Jane's earshot, Candy has to know.

"You're really trying to get her number, aren't you?"

"Candy, Candy, to be so old and yet so insecure. Ask yourself this: 'What in the world can I do with a woman with legs that long?'"

"Right." She pouts. I grab her bare thigh and give her a good shake.

"But it's you that I'm crazy about, you little tart."

"Thanks, I guess. But I think I better keep my eye on you."

She pulls the book about Rio from her satchel/purse.

"Hey, while we're in the air, we might as well study up on some of the key phrases. Much of it is similar, or even the same, as Spanish."

I wink at her.

"See, moments like this are why I love you."

She points a finger and shoots me. Oops, I let that slip. I better be more careful. I don't want to over-empower her. "Give them an inch and they'll take a mile," my pappy always says. Just kidding, but if he was here, I bet he'd give me a thumbs up when it comes to Candy. This I can hear him saying, though: "That one's a keeper." In reality, my dad and I are as close as father and son can be. To my mom's dismay, I've taken after him in ways that made their marriage unworkable. Yep, there better be room for understanding when it comes to relationships and me. See that now?

The whiskey's smooth, but it's really not me. I decide it must be one of those acquired tastes. I'll stick to my beer from here on out.

Jane goes through the in-flight safety instructions. I've always thought that they should add to the instructions: "In case of an emergency, kiss your ass goodbye." The truth, however, is that flying is safer than crossing the street, but It's also true that when a plane goes down, there are most often no survivors.

The engines rev and the thrust pins us to our seats. Candy grips the armrest in one death-grip and my hand with the other. I marvel again how small her hand is in mine and am surprised by her reaction to take-off.

Safely off the ground, Candy emits an audible sigh of relief.

"Damn, girl, what's up with that?"

"I don't like taking off or landing."

"That I can see, but you didn't react like that when you flew with me."

"I had a couple pitchers of beer in me then." She smiles. "I intend to be in much better shape by the time we land."

I like her resolve and order another round, though I make mine a Bud now. We decide to study on the long leg of our trip—Miami to Rio.

It seems as though we're barely airborne before we begin our descent. We arrive safely at Houston's Intercontinental Airport. Another round and we're soon airborne again. This a slightly longer leg, but as they say, "time flies when you're having fun," and we're in a festive mood. A moment of temporary insanity may be a better way of looking at it.

We make another safe landing at Miami International Airport, Candy's fear of take-offs and landings all but gone.

The sprawling airport is bustling and is awash with every year, make and model of a person known to man. As a major port of entry, people from all corners of the world can be witnessed here.

We take a shuttle to a distant TWA terminal and then a moving sidewalk to our departure gate. Having time to kill, we zero in on an open-air kiosk that serves beer in plastic cups. We watch the masses of every walk of life come and go. To say it's amazing is an understatement. As I watch the menagerie, I'm stuck with a prevailing thought: "Where do they find all these beautiful stewardesses?" Like watching a tennis match, I'm really getting into it. As you know, I'm not one to let such things go unnoticed.

"Man, where did they find all these beautiful stewardesses?" I catch an elbow to the ribs. Oops, I realize that I must have shared my thoughts out loud. To live is to learn.

Of course, we board early again at my suggestion. In the upswing of the alcohol's buzz, we've taken on a boisterous air. I think Newton had some laws along these lines: "A party in motion tends to stay in motion unless enacted upon by an... Sorry, forgot the rest of it, but how about this one: "What goes up must come down." Well, that one might not be Newton's, but you get the point and if not, the point is: we're feeling no pain, um, for now.

We're greeted by another pair of lovelies. Another Jane, what are the odds? Well, apparently pretty good. I present my boarding pass with a wink and a flourish. I hold on to it a few seconds longer than necessary. Jane handles the extra awkward seconds like a pro—she pulls me with it in the desired direction. Candy supplements Jane's effort with a kickstart of her own. How nice of her to lend a boot.

I placate Candy and restore her confidence with a kiss, but I believe I'm starting to see a pattern here—Candy is not shy about expressing herself physically. Ah, to be young and in love.

After a fresh round of drinks, including a fortifying departure gin and tonic for Candy, we are buckled and screaming down the tarmac.

As we level off, the "fasten your seatbelts" and "no smoking" signs extinguish and we're notified, via our pilot, that we're now free to move about the cabin. Man, I'm glad that he shared that with us.

Candy takes my hand, gives it a little squeeze and smiles as she turns to focus on the cumulus clouds through the cabin's window. She really is sweet, beautiful and sexy. Another thought, a delicious one, also runs through my mind—joining the mile-high club. I berate myself for not thinking of it sooner.

I lean over, kiss Candy on her exposed neck and whisper in her ear. "Ever heard of the mile-high club?"

Candy focuses on me again and a smile returns to her face. Hmm, maybe being so sweet to her really does pay off, I think. She hikes her skirt, exposing more thigh, does a lazy-eight on my chest with a finger and leans into me to whisper. I can feel the heat of her breath on my neck. I gleefully wring my hands in anticipation.

"Nope," she says. "Ask the stewardess. She probably has."

She winks at me and readjusts her skirt. Dammit. Sure didn't see that coming.

"Touché," I say. We both laugh.

It's a long flight. I hear dad tell me, "Go with plan B, Son." Plan B? Oh, ply her with my charm and, oh, more gin and tonics. Now, that sounds like a good plan. I decide to get right on top of that. Jane arrives pushing her service cart.

"Would you and your wife care for something to eat?"

I chuckle. "Oh, she's not my wife. She's my sister." Oops, dammit. That small slip probably doesn't help plan B. Focus on plan B, you idiot.

"Oh, I'm sorry. I assumed..."

"Save the apology, honey," Candy says. "I'm not his sister. I'm his soon to be ex-wife, but we're going to skip the wedding first and, oh, let's see, the honeymoon, too."

"Oh... Okay."

"But I am hungry. Hook us up."

Okay, that went over well. Back to plan B, Steven Paul.

"And another round when you get a chance, Jane," I say.

Jane places our TV dinner meals on our extended trays.

"Yes, sir. Enjoy your meal."

I look over my food. Hmm, maybe a five-ounce filet mignon, some kind of diminutive looking potatoes, something that I don't recognize and a sprig of parsley. I'll give them an A for presentation, but I'd hate to see what the less-fortunate, lower-class are served. Yep, I'm part of the elite now based upon seating alone. Well, maybe not seating alone. There's also my fine handstitched Nocona ostriches to consider and my genetically blessed good looks. Oh, and my girlfriend's pretty tight, too.

The steak is actually quite palatable. I look over at Andy. His meal is all but gone and he's fidgeting in his seat. I give him hope. I feel duty-bound to give him hope.

"Andy, that's only the first course. There's still the second, third and the main entree to come."

Candy giggles. She either thinks that's funny or the gin and tonics are starting to talk to her. Or, wait, maybe she's thinking of joining the mile-high club after all. Yep, that's probably it. I smile at the thought.

Jane returns to remove our meal trays and replaces them with our drinks. I remember I'm working on plan B. I keep my thoughts to myself. I hope Candy notices my self-control. She should. It comes naturally to me.

Candy pulls out the book on Rio again. I guess it's time to learn. "Okay, listen up, boys. We might as well use some of this time to learn some keywords and phrases."

Everyone tunes in, or at least pretends to. I wonder if Andy can concentrate on anything other than his hunger pains.

"Felix, some of these you'll know," Candy says.

"Being Mexican and all," I help out.

"Remember, he's your friend," Candy continues. "We won't worry about their spelling, only their pronunciation. Okay, repeat after me:

"Hello—O-la."

"O-la."

"Hi—Oy."

"Oy."

"Good day—Bong dee-a."

"Bong dee-a."

"Good evening—Bo-a noy-te."

"Bo-a noy-te."

"See you later—A-te mais tarr-de."

"A-te mais tarr de."

"Goodbye—Chay."

"Chay."

"How are you—Ko-mo vai"

"Ko-mo vai?"

"Yes—Seem."

"Seem."

"No—Nowng."

"Nowng."

"Okay, here's a big one: 'Does anyone around here speak english?'—Vo-se fo la eengles?"

"Vo-se fo la eengles?"

I raise my hand.

"Okay, hold up a second. Let me see that book. I'm going to tailor a couple specifically for Andy." I take the book and scan it for a few seconds. "Okay, listen up Andy: Gos-ta-ree-a de kom prarrgarota."

"I'm not repeating it until I know what it means."

"I'd like to buy girl."

We all laugh, including Jane as she approaches, who apparently overheard me and apparently understands Portuguese.

"Aw, fuck you," Andy says.

"Or how about this one, Andy? I'll simulate your side of the conversation—Po-so verr?... kwan-to?... es-ta mweeng to ka-ro... ten oo-ma koy-za mais ba-ra-ta? Or 'may I look at girl, how much, that's too expensive, do you have something cheaper?'"

We all laugh some more.

"Whatever, Steve."

"I know, I know," I say. "It's too much for you to remember. Like for school, I'll make you out a cheat sheet. You are familiar with cheat sheets aren't you, Andy?"

"Yeah, you taught me all about them."

"Good one, Andy," Candy says but not meaning it. She snatches the book from my hands. "That's enough studying for now, but I think that you may be onto something here. Everybody makes out their own cheat sheets."

"Or how about we just stick with the Mexican?" I say.

Candy shakes her head.

"Felix, you choose to hang out with this guy?"

"Si, as long as he's buying the cervesa."

Candy giggles looking back at the book.

"Here's a couple that might come in handy." She points to two. The first one: "Do you have a baby change room?" And the second: "Are children allowed?"

I look over.

"I like this one better." It's "Do you mind if I breastfeed here?" I try saying it the best that I can. "Voce se importa se eu amamentar aqui? I'll ask Jane."

Candy playfully smacks my arm.

"If you're planning on any breastfeeding, Mister, you better be talking about mine."

"But hers look like they have more storage capacity," I say a most valid argument in a beer drinker's mind.

She twists my ear.

"Ow, dammit, girl."

"It's not always the quantity of milk that matters, but the quality. Besides, more than a mouthful is a waste."

Hmm, another valid argument to a beer drinker, I think.

"And, girl, that's why I love you." Oops, remember Esteban: "Loose lips sink ships." But, hey, to know Candy is sure to love Candy. I lean over and kiss her exposed neck. I whisper in her ear: "Should I call for a couple of pillows and a blanket?"

"Hmm, okay, but only if you promise to fondle me. Let's have a couple more rounds first."

"Okay, I'll acquiesce to your whims." I'd tell her with a smile, but that would be forking over too much power.

Jane stops by again

"Would you two care to watch a movie? We have Taxi Driver with Jodie Foster and Robert De Niro. It's a controversial movie, but a good one."

"Seem," I say almost the only word from the lesson I remember, contrary to my usual ability to recall most everything from my crowded memory banks. Could the beer be dulling my senses? Nah, I'm just overly focused on plan B.

"Can I get you two anything else?"

Got to stay focused, got to stay focused, I tell myself for what seems the umpteenth time.

"Another round for the little woman and I."

I bet she didn't see that coming. Yeah, right. If nothing else, I'm sure she's noticed that I'm consistent when it comes to ordering rounds. I look over at Jim.

"You sure are being quiet today."

"Catching up on some of these Wall Street Journals. Deciding whether I want to alter my portfolio."

"Any interesting IPO's on the horizon?"

"Not that I'm interested in, Steve-O."

"Well, Jimbo, historically the market fares well in an election year—with the exception of the Depression Era, that is. Maybe just stick with the blue chips and see how the third and fourth quarters play out. GE, IBM and hell, maybe even TI. By the way, how is Gate's and Allen's stock doing? What's the company's name, Microsoft or something?"

"Yeah, Microsoft. It's up. I like them for the long haul. My bet: buy and hold. Plus, I need to defer some capital gains this year."

Felix pipes in.

"I'd keep an eye on Steve Jobs and Apple computer. I think it's poised to go heads up with IBM and Microsoft. Jobs and his partner are no dummies."

"I'm watching what they do, but I think that you hit the nail on the head, Felix," Jim says.

"You don't fuck with futures at all. Do you, Jimbo?" I ask.

"Too volatile for my blood right now."

"I predict the economy will begin to accelerate," I say. "Consumer confidence is up. Hiring has picked up. Everything looks good. I believe the GDP will continue to expand at a rapid clip—five, six, maybe even seven percent. Oil might spike again some, but coming off the heels of OPEC's embargo, I don't think OPEC will bust a grape again any time soon. Personally, I'd bet against gold. I think the fed will keep inflation in check."

"I feel you, Steve-O, but I think I'll let things ride as-is for the remainder of the year."

"No need to rock the boat then, huh Jim?" Felix says.

Leaving the projector that she was setting up, Jane approaches with a confused look.

"Excuse me, I don't mean to interrupt, but I couldn't help overhearing. It's got me wondering exactly what you guys do?"

"I'll field this one," I say. "If I told you, Jane, I'd have to kill you."

We all laugh.

"Just kidding, Jane. We're just a small youth think-tank that believes in capitalism and the beauty of insider trading."

"Oh, okay. Any tips that you guys can give me?"

Candy raises her hand.

"I'll field this one guys." She points at me. "Don't listen to this blue-eyed, split-tongued devil. Don't walk—run."

Everyone laughs. Jane remains confused. Candy continues.

"Talk to one of these two," she says pointing in Jim and Felix's direction. "They're too much like gentlemen to steer you wrong."

Is that some kind of back-door jab at me, I wonder? Nah, can't be. I'm a gentleman, too. Well, in my own special way that is.

"Well, the movie's ready. I'll just go and turn the projector on. Enjoy."

For the next couple hours, we're engrossed in what turns out to be a pretty damn good movie. I find nothing controversial about it. Where were all these critics during the 60s, I wonder? Besides, I read that they used Jodie's older sister as a body double in a lot of the scenes. In my opinion, of which I have many, Foster is a fine actress and she's going to grow up to be a looker.

I catch Candy yawning and fighting to remain alert. Conclusion: she may be on the downside of the gin and tonics. I call for a blanket and pillows. With the seats reclined and the lights dimmed, Candy curls into me. To my dismay, she's asleep before I can even ask if she's comfortable. I kiss her forehead. So much for plan B. If you can't beat 'em, join 'em, someone once said. I decide to close my eyes for just a minute.

Vertigo

Chapter 12

"Sir. Sir, wake up."

My eye-lids are slow to open. They feel like they are weighted in lead.

"Huh? What? Oh, Jane, what's up?"

"We're minutes from final approach. I need everyone to put their seats in the upright position and to fasten their seatbelts."

"Yes ma'am. Anything for you, Jane."

See, I told you I'm a gentleman. My actions don't lie.

Candy is slow to wake, but perks at the news that we're nearing final approach. I have to swallow a couple of times to make my ears pop. The plane's PA system comes to life.

"Ladies and Gentlemen, this is your captain. We are now on final approach. Our ETA is 1:45 a.m. Rio time. The airport's weather is a balmy 75. Enjoy your stay in Rio and thank you for flying TWA."

With a ding, the fasten seatbelt and no smoking signs light up. Candy is glued to her window.

"Wow! Look at all those lights. Look out, Rio de Janeiro, here we come."

I feel her. This is exciting. We arrive with another smooth landing. Here we are in big Rio, would have never expected this only a few days back. I slightly fret. Hope things work out. Too late to second guess your decision now, big boy.

We soon deplane and follow the arrows. For a country ruled by a military regime, customs seems lax on security and are overly friendly. I suspect that tourism still plays a major role in the economy here. Customs check our visas, stamp our passports and wave us on through. Only a few military personnel appear to be present throughout the airport. I take that as a good sign.

Thirty minutes later, apparently posing no trouble, we are allowed to retrieve our luggage and make our way to the Hertz counter. Candy presents her license and passport and, after signing a number of papers, she's given the keys to a '76 Chevy Monte Carlo. It'll work and the car is on site.

We step out of the airport and into a different world.

"Um carro? Um carro? Taxi? Um carro?"

I raise my hand to quell the onslaught.

"Não." I look over at my crew. "Candy and I will get the car. Watch the luggage and we'll pick you up here. Also, keep an eye out for anyone heading to the beach. And, oh Andy, no wandering off."

The Hertz lot is maybe a quarter of a mile off, but it feels good to stretch the legs. Candy waves the numbered key to the attendant and flashes her copy of the contract.

"Por favor," she says.

I snatch the keys from her hand.

"I'll take that, honey."

"Como vail?" the attendant asks.

I scan my memory banks for "fine and you?"

"Bemi e voce?" I manage.

"Ta o' timo."

I scratch my head on that one.

"Great," he helps out. "De onde voce? Desculpa. Sorry, where you from?"

"Texas," Candy says.

"Oba! Chocante. Cool. Aqui. Here's your car."

"Thanks."

Gentleman to the core, I unlock the passenger door for Candy.

"People sure seem friendly here," Candy notes. "Don't they?"

We circle around to where the boys await.

"Well, lookie there, Candy. If I'm not mistaken, that's Jane there with the boys. Huh, imagine that."

"Yeah, imagine that. I wonder what she wants?"

"Candy, Candy. That's not very Christian like. I imagine that she only wants to help out." I grin.

"I don't think that we have room in the car for her and her long legs," she says with the finger quotes.

"Well, Candy, I see your point. Hmm. Well, we could always have you drive and she can sit in my lap."

"I don't think so."

I pinch Candy's cheek and give it a little shake. "Ain't you the cat's meow." I put the Chevy in park, kill the engine and pop the trunk.

"Jane, fancy meeting you here."

"She's heading to the Rio Hostel in Ipanema," Jim says. "She can show us the way to the Palace and save herself a taxi fare as well."

"Great. That is exactly what Candy was saying when she saw you standing here."

"That's very sweet of her."

I smile.

"Isn't it? She's very, very understanding in so many ways."

Jim shakes his head as he looks on. "Jane, let me help you with your luggage."

"Thank you. Is it Jim or Jimbo?"

"Either is fine."

Luggage loaded, we all pile into the brand-new, white Monte Carlo. Felix takes shotgun and Jane gets sandwiched between Jim and Andy in the back. I adjust my rearview mirror so it frames Jane's animated face perfectly. Our eyes briefly meet. I wonder what Jane looks like with those long legs in a bikini? I crank the car and put her into gear. You never know, big boy, I tell myself. Stranger things have happened. We bump into her at the beach, soak up some sun and drinks and Candy and I invite her up to the suite...

Candy taps me on the head. "Esteban, are we going to go or not?"

I pull out into the departing traffic. Jane leans forward to speak to Candy. I'm conscious of Jane's fingertips lightly touching my shoulder.

"Candy, I love your tan. You must spend a lot of time in the sun. I have 72 hours off and I plan to catch some rays."

Hmm... In town for 72 hours. Who is she really telling that to? I would wonder, wouldn't I?

"Thanks. I hope to catch some rays while I'm here too."

"You'll love the Palace and the beach there, but if you get a chance, you have to check out Ipanema Beach. The name of the place I stay is the Rio Hostel. It's budget, but the airline only allows so much. Anyway, it's neat. You'll see. It's like a little villa and there's an airy top deck with hammocks and a small veranda. Hey, I'm in room 12. Give me a call if you want to hang out."

Hmm, room 12, huh? Duly noted.

"Sure, I might just do that," Candy says and nods her head in my direction. "Dodge silver-tongue for an afternoon."

"Hey, earlier, I was a split-tongued devil."

"Oh, they're pretty much interchangeable," Candy assures me while patting my leg.

Jane slightly scratches my shoulder before leaning back in her seat. For a moment, I catch her eyes again in the rearview. There's a hint of a smile on her face before she averts her eyes. Could I be reading more into this than there actually is?

I sigh. If so, too bad, I tell myself, because you're not about to do anything to endanger your budding relationship with Candy. As much as I joke and tease, I realize that I really am crazy about the girl and would never want to hurt her. See, and here you were eager to think the worst of me. Yeah, you're right. I haven't been put to the real test yet. Uh-oh, could I be pussy whipped? Until now, I believed that to be only a myth. I check my forehead to see if I'm running a fever. Nope. Maybe you're just infatuated. Yeah, now that sounds more reasonable. Then again, should Candy invite Jane to our suite, well...

Jane interrupts my thoughts. "Take a left at the airport exit. It's mostly due south from here. Maybe ten miles or so. For now, follow the coast. We'll pass through Flamingo and when we get to Bota Fogo, you'll see the sign to Copacabana. Leme is to the left, we'll by-pass that all together."

"So, where are you from, Jane?" Jim asks.

"From North Miami Beach. For now, I do the Miami/Rio flights only. If I ever tire of Rio, which I seriously doubt, I might change it up."

"Maybe we'll see you around," Jim says. I'll have to remind Jimbo to not be so aggressive in the future. I inwardly smile. Jimbo, it's going to work out for you yet. Voted most likely to succeed in the real world, it's only a matter of time, for as we know, success attracts beauty, which is another one of Newton's laws that currently eludes me. But I do realize that the realism of success attracts beauty is dictated by more than mere chance or coincidence. One only need to hang out in Tarrytown for a while to know how true this is. The fruits of one's labor is a good way to look at it, I decide.

Candy runs her fingers through my hair.

"I wonder what's running through that cranium of yours right now," she softly says. I glance down at her legs and back up at her.

"You, our suite and my continued education."

I see the sign for Copacabana Beach and continue on.

"Just keep following the signs and we will eventually come out on Av Atlantica. The Palace is on the corner there and I'm maybe a mile beyond that," Jane says.

The Monte Carlo has an AM/FM cassette—makes me wish that I owned some cassettes. I've yet to upgrade from my 8-track collection. Hmm, maybe it's time to join the '70s tech wise? Well, format wise that is, for I own some bad-ass 8-tracks.

"We're coming up on the Palace now. In many ways, it's still the place to stay. Do you have your room numbers yet?" Jane asks no one in particular.

"We have a couple of suites, but don't know the suite numbers yet," Candy says. "Mine and devil boy's here are registered under Steven Paul."

She ruffles my hair. I turn right on Av Atlantica. We take in the Palace as we slowly pass by. Not as regal looking or imposing as I imagined, but still rather spectacular considering that it was built in '23.

I read that it was really hopping in the 50's and 60's and that it has had many distinguished visitors including Ava Gardner and Orson Welles.

"Suites. Cool." Jane pulls herself close and again I feel her fingers brush my shoulder. "You're going to love the views. The suites are on the top floor facing the beach and have terraces where you can dine. The Palace also has a large swimming pool should you wish to forgo the beach, but all the interesting crowds are on the beach—that's where you really want to sun."

"What I need to know is, do they have food service at this joint?" Andy asks in all seriousness. "I could go for some triple burgers and fries."

"I'll field this one, Jane," I say. "Andy, it's called room service and of course they have it, but I doubt seriously that they have burgers and fries. I'll tell you what..."

"What?"

"Since you don't speak Portuguese, Candy and I will order up the food for you."

"You don't speak Portuguese either."

"That's true, but we have the book."

"Yeah, well then, make it a lot of food. I'm starving. And don't forget the beer."

I wink at Candy. "I wouldn't dream of it. Wouldn't have it any other way."

Jane taps my shoulder. This time there's no mistaking it.

"Okay, slow down," she says. "Take the road coming up, Av Rainha Elizabeth and then turn right on the fifth road to the right. It's a half block up on your right."

I make the right turn, cross four intersecting roads, turn right again and stop before the Rio Hostel.

"I wouldn't mind staying here myself," Candy says. "It's quaint."

I throw the Chevy into park, kill the engine and pop the trunk. "Felix, help Jane with her bags. Jane, nice meeting you. Maybe we'll see you around."

Everyone says their goodbyes. She seems pretty cool, I think. I wonder how old she is? Maybe 30, I'd guess.

We make the return trip to the Palace and find a place to park out front. For going on 3:00 a.m., there's still a lot of activity along the beach along with people entering and exiting the Palace.

We exit our ride, gather up our bags and make our way toward the entrance where we are quickly swooped upon and relieved of our luggage.

Candy takes my hand and gives it a good squeeze. We pull up short just inside the entrance. Candy gives my hand another squeeze.

"Wow! Check it out! Look at those chandeliers. Shit, oops sorry. This is really exciting. Imagine this place in its heyday."

I take an appraising look around. It's hard to imagine this trip as anything other than a vacation, but the fact is, it's not a vacation. It's a serious, serious mission.

"Candy, it's really elegant, but keep in mind that we're here for a purpose. Tomorrow we have to get busy."

She looks up at me and her eyes grow large. "I know, I know. But, for the rest of the night, or for at least a few hours, can we pretend otherwise?"

Not fair. Not fair, I tell myself. I swallow hard at the implicit suggestion her pretty eyes convey. I throw in the towel.

"You win, girl."

Checking in is less than a formality. The bellhops are quick to show us to our suites. Candy is feeling generous as she tips our bellhop from her bra. Not a bad way to make an impression, I suppose, with my $20.

The boys ended up in suite 701 and Candy and I, 704. I don't know much about interior design. I know... Imagine that. And, it's hard for me to believe as well. So, I'll throw some generics out there: ritzy, lavish, posh, or how about this catchall: Portuguese baroque. Yeah, that sounds good—Portuguese baroque with ornate crown molding and a large-gilded mirror. All of this is around the centerpiece, a smaller version of the chandelier that first catches your eye when you enter the Palace. Well, to say the least, our suite is nice and I can only imagine how much it set Wallace back.

I follow Candy onto the terrace, put my arms around her from behind for a minute and just enjoy her being, the view of the beach and the breeze coming off the ocean.

Candy turns in my arms, tip toes and kisses me long and deep.

"Let's order room service and get naked," she says. She squeezes me through my jeans to emphasize her words.

"With your magic touch, how could I possibly refuse." I smile. "No need for the book. I spotted a couple of menus, so as long as they're in English, we're good to go."

I lead her back through the terrace doors, leaving them open so that we can continue to enjoy some of the ocean's breeze and catch the night noises from seven stories below. We share a menu. Everything—appetizers, entrees, sides, drinks and desserts—is translated into English. Candy points to an entree.

"How about this one: pato no tucuppi? Looks good. It's roast duck flavored with garlic, juice of the manioc plant, whatever that is, and jumbu."

Hmm, now that sounds promising. Might get the juices flowing.

"Okay, sounds like a winner. Let's add two pitchers of iced caipirinha, which is a drink made of cachaça and fruit."

"What's cachaça?" Candy asks.

"It says here that it's a sugar cane spirit."

"Okay, but in case that doesn't sit well, let's get a bucket of beer, too. Cerveja Antarctica bem gelada or 'icy cold long-necks.'"

"Call her in, big girl."

"What about the boys?"

"I don't need them to watch. I can tell them all about my night's performance in the morning." I grin.

"You and your grin. You know it's not going to always get you out of trouble."

"But you do recognize it as one of my best weapons? Anyway, they'll figure it out. Bill ours to our room."

Candy calls in our order. Thirty minutes, she informs me. That's enough time to do a lot of things, but we opt for a long leisurely shower together. Afterward, we don a pair of the Palace's robes. Candy's engulfs her, but somehow it makes her all the more appealing.

There comes a knock on our door. Room service has arrived. I dig $20 from my jeans. I'm greeted by the same bellhop. His smile says he's in for the long haul. Candy's either made a lasting impression or the earlier tip made a new friend.

We have him set up on the terrace. Just like the movies, the duck is presented as a silver-covered dish. I note that the silverware is actual sterling as well. The bellhop tells us that the Palace's chef has sent up a complimentary dessert. A simple pave—a creamy cake—along with an aba caxi sorvete—pineapple ice cream. Conclusion: the chef wants in on some of the action. Well, that's what makes the world go around. I retrieve another $20 from my jeans and slap both into the bellhop's outstretched hand. "One for the chef," I remind him. With a bow and the tips safely ensconced in his firm grip, he takes his leave.

Candy and I dig In. The duck is, here's a word that I use sparingly, "delightful," and the caipirinha—well, fruity. Imagine that and "bem gelada," my new word for the day. Yes, the caipirinha is "icy cold." The cachaça gives it a pleasant bite. Conclusion: tasty, but not something that I'll get addicted to.

The ocean breeze is refreshing. Sated in all ways but one, I turn my focus to Candy. There's a mischievous look in her eyes as she stands and turns to face the terrace railing. She lets her robe drop to the floor as she studies the nightlife below.

I turn my chair to face her and to get a better, admiring view from behind. My prevailing thought: you are one lucky fucker at times, you know. Looking on, I have only one wish for the moment: I wish that Candy stays in my life a long, long time.

I hand her the caipirinha as she turns back to face me. She takes a casual sip and then allows some to provocatively drip on each of her breasts as she steps toward me. She keeps me from rising with a hand on my shoulder. She leans in offering me a taste. I happily oblige while her fingers work the belt of my robe loose. She straddles me and takes me inside her.

"Oi!" she says as she begins her sensuous motions atop me.

With hands to her hips, I slow her motions even more. I want to savor every movement of our union together and for as long as possible. She intermittently kisses me. She too seems to be savoring our time together. The near-full moon and the ambient light from our suite illuminate her face, shoulders and breasts. I think to myself that it doesn't get any better than this. A thought that seems to pop up often in Candy's presence.

She sucks on my neck and finally I can hold back no longer. I pull her tight and release with a gush. Candy trembles slightly in my lap. She holds me tight and remains in my lap as I slowly grow soft inside her. Her breath is hot on my neck and for a time, I can't tell whose heart beats the fastest.

"Oba," she hoarsely whispers.

"Oba?"

She playfully bites my shoulder. "Yes oba. Wow."

A thousand things to say, but for once I let things ride as is.

Mutually sated, she leads me to the king-size poster bed. As the eastern sky lightens, we lay entwined and catch a few more hours of needed sleep.

Vertigo

Chapter 13

A steady rap on the door and the repeated sound of "room service," finally gets us to stir. We both wearily open our eyes and let out a moan in unison. I laugh to mask the pain and Candy follows suit.

"Hold on a moment!" I yell. And, oh does it hurt to yell. "I'm coming," I add.

I laugh some more as Candy rubs her eyes and tentatively sits up.

"Candy, what the fuck do they put in the drinks?"

Candy snatches her pillow, buries her face in it and flops back to the bed. I catch a muffled "my fucking head" through the pillow.

I give her pillow a healthy tug. She maintains her death grip and kicks her feet like a bad-tempered child. I can hear her pained giggles through the pillow.

I get off the oversized bed and search the immediate area for my robe before realizing it's on the terrace along with everything else from earlier. I gather the robe and slip into it. From the mostly melted ice, I grab an Antarctica: hair of the dog. I snag the beer cap against the edge of the iron-rimmed table and give it a good smack. The lid flips to the floor. You know what they say: "When thrown, you're supposed to dust yourself off and get back on." Yeah, I know that's not how it goes, but with my head pounding, that's as close as I'm going to get. Besides, you get the point. I take a test swig. Hmm, not bad. I take another sip. Yes, they brew a decent beer.

I answer our door to our grinning bellhop. This guy must not sleep.

"Bom dia amigo. Compliments of suite 701."

"Thanks. How thoughtful of them."

"The terrace, sir?"

I nod my consent as I dig another $20 from my rumpled jeans. As I turn, I catch a glimpse of myself in one of the gilded mirrors. I have to do a double take. Ah-ha, that might be another reason the bellhop's grinning. I have a fucking hickey on my neck and get this—it's my first and, until earlier, something I've always managed to avoid. I sigh and muse: there goes my angelical image.

I gather Candy's robe from the terrace and take it to her. She's still hiding under her pillow and still nude.

"Honey, you don't have to keep your face covered like that. I'll still do you." I dodge the pillow and toss her the robe. "Breakfast on the terrace."

She sits up and laughs at the sight of me.

"Yes, I've seen it. You went and marked your territory."

I salute her with my half-finished beer.

"Enjoy," the bellhop tells me. "Manhã. I brought you some fruits: Abacaxi, fruta do conde, jaca, graviola, laranga, mamão and manga. Many of the fruits of Brazil. There's pineapple, sugar-apple, jack fruit, orange, apple, papaya and mango. Also, you'll find ovos or eggs, porco or pork and queijo or cheese." He nods at my beer. "I see you already have your coffee, but there is also some of our house blend. Ring if I can be of any further service."

"Thanks." I hand him $20. "Adieu."

I know it's French, but it's close enough for comfort.

He hauls the earlier debris away with the exception of the Antarctica, which is now freshly iced. I look up at the noon sun and then the crowded beach below. Other than the pulse in my head, I decide that life is good.

Candy joins me on the terrace for a leisurely breakfast. Finishing up, I realize it's time to come up with a game plan. I stare at a picture of Melissa and tell her: "We're going to get you back girl. That's a promise."

Another shower sparks additional life into us. I dress and thread my belt through the sheath of my Uncle Henry.

"Candy, buzz the boy's suite and tell them to come on over. It's time to get started."

I open the book on Rio, pull the tab on another beer and, as I scan the pages, I begin to formulate a plan. The crew arrives looking spryer than I feel. They gather around the table.

"Okay boys, time to get this show on the road. Rio's spread out and there are places from Leblon to Centro to check out. Most every place that we need to check doesn't come alive until evening and night. That gives us some hours still. Since we don't know yet what we're up against, I believe the first course of action is to acquire some weapons. Candy says that the crime in the favelas is rampant, so that's where we shall start our search. The favelas are throughout the hillsides surrounding Rio. One place the book specifically mentions is Rocina, but I can't find it referenced anywhere on the map. That being said, we'll go with plan B."

I smile.

"And plan B, Steve-O, is to wing it?"

"That's correct, Jimbo, we're going to wing it." There are chuckles all around the table. "Most of the favelas are accessible by motorcycle or on foot only. So, Felix, you see about renting us four motorcycles, but keep in mind that if we have to, we'll buy a couple outright. Andy, while Felix is doing that, I need you to go down to the lobby and break down some hundreds. We'll need graft money."

I drum my fingers on the table as I think.

"What else needs done right now, Steve-O?" Jim asks.

"Until we get the bikes, nothing."

"What about me? I want to go, too."

"Not to the favelas, Candy. You can come along this evening when we begin our search for this Dom character."

Candy blows the bangs from her forehead and eyes. "I don't want to be stuck in this suite all afternoon alone."

I drum my fingers some more. "Tell you what. Go get you some sun. Take the book on Rio and Melissa's letter and plot out the places to be searched. Start with the most expensive and go from there. Hell, give Jane a call. Maybe she would like to hang out with you for a few hours. Plus, you can pick her brain on Rio. Take a picture of Dom and Melissa as well..."

The phone rings interrupting me. I rise from the table.

"I'll get it. It's probably Wallace checking in," I say and then into the phone: "Hello?"

"Afternoon, handsome."

"Ah, Jane, speak of the devil."

"I heard *you* were the devil."

"Only in the bedroom, Jane. We were just talking about you."

"Oh, really. I thought I'd call and see if Candy wanted to catch some rays with me. I thought that I'd try out my new fio dental and see what kind of reaction I get."

"Stiff ones, likely," I say.

She laughs. "I bet you are the devil when you want to be."

"Hold that thought. I'll get Candy. Candy, it's for you!"

Candy enters the room sporting a puzzled look.

I wink and mouth "Jane" as I hand her the phone.

I rejoin Jim on the terrace. "It's Jane. She wants to see what kind of reactions her new fio dental gets. I told her a 'stiff one, likely.'"

Jim laughs as he reaches for a beer. "She's nice looking. I'd like to see her in any kind of bikini myself. Wonder how old she is... 30? Where's the opener?"

"Probably." I take the beer from him, pop the lid and pass it back. "You sure were coming on pretty strong last night in the car, you know."

"Yeah, right," he says and we both laugh.

"Steve-O, don't fuck up your relationship with Candy over a woman who lives in Miami. It appears from your neck that Candy is really into you. I see you scheming over there."

I unconsciously rub my neck, pop the cap on another beer and take a big pull.

"Not a chance, Jimbo. Not a chance." I grin then add, "But what if Candy brings her back here?"

"You're the only one that I know who can piss into the wind and not get wet," Jim says. We bump long-necks on that one.

"Life is full of surprises ain't it, Jimbo?" I like the word ain't, don't you? Keeps your parents cringing.

We both step to the terrace railing to watch the activity below.

"Fucking Rio… Who would have thought, Steve-O?"

"Yeah. Fucking Rio, man."

"Steve-O, do you really think that the economy will expand at a rapid clip next year?"

I laugh. "I don't have a fucking clue, Jimbo."

"Yeah, that's what I figured."

We bump long-necks again. Andy returns.

"I got $1,000 in $20s. Well, minus the $20 that they charged me because of the exchange rate."

I wrap my arm around his shoulders. "You might not win many races, but you're still my dog, Andy."

"I'm out of here. Going to take the car." Candy does a spin at the terrace doors. "What do you think of my sundress?"

"Beautiful, like you. Hey, take one of the walkie-talkies in case we need to find you. Be sure to put batteries in it."

She blows me a kiss and spins. "Yes, honey."

"Andy, we're going to be taking walkie-talkies, too. Put batteries in some."

Andy clicks his heels and salutes, "Ya volt, Herr Commandant."

Felix returns and joins us on the terrace.

"Got 'em. Kawasaki 175 Enduros. Fifty a piece for half a day, which is four hours. They'll be out front in ten minutes. The way it works around here is that they come with a rider. They call them 'uma motocicleta.'"

"Fuck that," I say.

"That's what I said," Felix continues. "Fuck that. That's why they cost so much. They didn't want to rent them to us at all until I told them that we're staying at the Palace."

"Well, all right then. We'll start with the favelas west of here," I say. "If anyone gets lost, head east. Can't miss the ocean."

"My survival knife has a compass in the handle."

I shake my head in amazement. "It would, Andy. By all means, bring it along."

"Also matches, fishing line and a hook."

Also, to my amazement, Jim and Felix manage to maintain their stoic expressions. The phone rings again.

"I'll get it," I offer. "Probably Jane wanting me know that her new fio dental is a momo bikini as well."

I answer the phone. "Hello?"

"Steven Paul! Thank God I caught you!"

"Wallace slow down. Are you alright, man?"

"No! Listen! I just received a call—a ransom demand. Said he wanted $1 million U.S. within 48 hours if I ever wanted to see my daughter again. Said that they would start sending body parts until I did."

"Shit! 48 hours."

"Bastards. I told the caller that I needed more time—that not all my assets are liquid. They agreed to a week."

"What else? Anything that might help us? You said 'he.' You said 'they.' Which is it?"

"Hell, I only heard one person. Sounded South American, but it also sounded like he had mothballs in his mouth. Listen, I talked to Williams. He said the chances of getting her back after a ransom is paid are about nil. Son, dammit! You boys got to find her and get her back. If they hurt her, so help me, I'll hound whoever is responsible to the far corners of the earth."

"Okay, Wallace... John. We're headed out now on motorcycles in search of weapons. We'll begin a systematic search for this Dom fucker and your daughter this evening. If you can't get ahold of us, don't panic. It means that we're on the job. I'll report when I can."

"I'm coming to Rio."

"No, John, hang tight. We may need you there. John, we're going to get her back."

"Thank you, Son. Thank you."

"John, try to relax. Stay calm. If you need to, take a valium. If you don't have any, go by Candy's and get some from James. Okay, I'll talk to you later."

I step back out onto the terrace. All eyes are expectantly on me.

"Not good boys, John got a ransom demand. One million dollars by week's end or they are going to start sending body parts. At this point, we don't know how many people are involved."

There's a collective "Shit!"

"Let's get her back, boys."

"Fucking A. Let's roll," Felix says. We all hit the hammer. The crew is back in action, albeit with a new player—Felix. We find the Kawasakis waiting for us out front. A picture of my Mexican ex-gal, Angie, flashes through my mind. She rides a Kawasaki much like the ones that we are now about to ride. She left me satisfied but confused. The memory prompts a shake of the head and a smile. You lose some and you win some. Isn't that how it goes?

The early afternoon sun beams, but is offset by the ocean's breeze. The Kawasakis look new. Business for this mode of transportation must be good. My bike kicks right over. I wait for the boys to fire up and we're off.

I pull a small wheelie as I catch second out on Av Atlantica and immediately set her back down as I lay into the turn to my left. Slow down, turbo, I tell myself and remind myself to remember that I'm not in a motocross race. I temper things down a notch and work my way northwest retracing our route from the airport. At the first opportunity, I change course to maintain the westward direction that I wish. To do so, we have to do a number of zig-zags, but eventually we end up in the hills. At the onset of the hills, the lanes begin to narrow and the area starts to take on a desperate feel—the sparse characters become more prolific and shadier in appearance. We have found the favelas.

I find what I believe to be a corner neighborhood botequim and bring us to a stop. The few people outside eye us wearily as we dismount. Might as well break the ice, I decide. Inside there's a hodgepodge of articles for sale, indicating that this is also the home to a secondhand shop. I recall now reading this is a common trait among Rio's botequims.

I pull out a pair of $20s and hold them before the proprietor.

"U.S., seem?"

He nods as he dries an ear-less beer mug. "Seem."

I raise a finger and do a circle in the air indicating a round for the house. I toss the money on the counter.

"De onde vove e'? He asks. I remember this one.

"Eu sou Texas."

"Nossa!" He busies himself handing out long-necks. Done, he pulls a bottle from beneath the counter along with a shot glass. It's cachaça and the sight of it is almost enough to make me break into a sweat. He pours a shot.

"Por favor," he says and slides the shot toward me. I down it in one swallow and wipe my mouth with the back of my hand.

"Muito." He grins. His grill is missing a couple teeth.

I pull one of Melissa's and Dom's pictures from my back pocket and show it to him. I point to Dom.

He shakes his head. "Não."

I take another $20 and hold it with the picture. He regrettably shakes his head no again.

I take my beer and step back into the afternoon heat. Felix makes a round with a picture as I contemplate our next move. I take a big pull of the icy beer. It causes my brain to freeze for a second. I hand the remainder to a bum who has already polished off his free beer.

"Fuma?" I ask him.

"Seem, 10 perto em frente." He indicates up the street and a block over and up the street again. I drop a $20 into his outstretched hands.

"Muito obrigada."

I'm rewarded with a toothless smile that halves his face. I point to both my eyes, the bikes, then him. He vigorously nods. "Seem, seem."

Felix comes up dry—no hits on the picture. I look at my crew.

"Boys let's go fishing and see if my all-American good looks can draw out any undesirables."

"You're fucking kidding, right, Steve-O?"

"Nope, Jimbo. Andy, you and Felix go a block over and head up. I'll give you all a head start. From two blocks up, cut across and check on me. Then every block thereafter. Jimbo, you follow behind me a block back. Try to keep me in sight in case I need help."

"Shit, Esteban, I don't think that's a very good plan," Felix says. "This looks like a rough area."

I tuck my Izod behind the Uncle Henry's sheath and snap open its cover.

"There, that's better." I smile. "That's the beauty of the plan. Boys, take off."

"Shit, Esteban. I sure hope you know what you're doing," Felix says.

I smile to myself as I take in my surrounding environment. I hear my dad's voice: "Boy, I don't know about this one."

The bum steps back out of the botequim and hands me another sweltering long-neck. I roll it across my forehead before taking a swallow. I salute the bum with it and start my trek up the hillside. I whistle The Andy Griffith Show's tune as I leisurely stroll along. I wonder if they've got the show dubbed in Portuguese?

No bites on the first block. I continue on. There's a couple of thuggish looking characters ahead. They're grungy and trying to look menacing. Menacing or not, I could not have asked for better odds—two against one. Yeah, right.

"So, what's your plan?" I hear my dad ask.

"Oh, to have a civilized conversation with them, of course." Oops, I think that I thought that out loud. I start back with my whistling. Mutt and Jeff move to partially block my path. Yep, they must want to talk. I dazzle them with a smile as I pull up short.

"Cara, grana, the shorter one says and motions with his hands to give it up. "Eu fico com ele!"

Hmm, I assume he wants my money. I raise my left hand.

"Hold on there, Hoss. I've got a proposition for you two. I need to buy some pistols, you know, pistolas?" Hmm, they stare on. Let me try another approach. "How are you? Como Vai?"

Okay, that one didn't go over so well either. I decide that I'll try 'pleased to meet you.' "Umm... Prazen em conhecê-lo."

The taller of the two laughs.

"Andre, ta luco," he says and nods in my direction.

Andre, well I know one of their names now. That's progress, isn't it? Andre pulls a switchblade and flicks it open within the blink of an eye. Equally fast, I pull my Uncle Henry and, with the flip of my wrist, it locks in place. I grin. I pride myself on my speed.

"Aw, you want to compare knives, do you Andre? Andre sounds French. Oui, oui," I say and laugh.

Andre switches his blade from hand-to-hand.

"Is this guy for real?" I say. "Andre, you've been watching way too much TV."

He takes a swipe at me which I easily avoid.

I throw my left hand high in the air behind me, take a couple toe-to-heel hops toward him and thrust my trusty Uncle Henry at Andre like my blade is an épée.

"En garde!"

Dramatically, theatrically, or comically, however you want to view my move, it causes an unexpected reaction—Andre staggers back and almost trips over himself.

His partner joins me in laughter.

"Enough of this play, gringo," he says as I notice Felix and Andy round the corner a half block up.

The tall one goes for a pistol tucked in his jeans. It snags for a second before coming clear. I take the split-second opportunity to step in and plant a boot square to his nuts. Folks, I'm here to tell you, I score a goal, he grabs his crotch and screams, "Mother Fucker!"—drops to his knees and in what seems like slow motion, topples over.

I relock and reload and drop-kick him in the jaw like I want to send his head into the stratosphere. A sickening crunch reverberates in my ears. An involuntary shudder passes through me. I can still feel the bone giving.

The gun skidders to a stop before me. I casually place my foot on it.

With the pattering sound of approaching feet, Andre looks like a deer caught in headlights. He throws his knife down, but can't decide which way to run. With a full head of steam and a banshee wail, Andy slams into Andre sending them sprawling. The tackle sends them a good five yards beyond me.

Nice move Andy, I think. I throw an imaginary flag. "Personal foul. Unnecessary roughness." I yell.

Felix laughs as he tries to catch his breath. "You're fucking wrong, Esteban," he says reminding me of Candy uttering the exact same words.

I pick the pistol off the ground. "Don't you love it when a plan comes together?"

The pistol's a grimy looking Colt 1911, .45 caliber. I imagine that there are millions of these around, the country being under military rule and all. I drop the clip. The clip's heavy—it no doubt holds its seven-round capacity. I jack the slide slightly and note that there's a round chambered.

"Good deal. One down, three to go. Andy, help Andre up." I reinsert the clip and cock the hammer.

"Steve-O, who taught you to kick like that, the Rockettes?"

"Kick and a grin, Jimbo—both disarming tools when utilized properly."

Andy throws Andre up against the nearest hovel. I step up and lightly tap Andre on the temple a couple of times with the barrel of the gun.

"Ain't no fun when the rabbit's got the gun."

My crew laughs. It's not every day that you get to say that.

"Por favor! I have no money—please let me go!"

"Andre, Andre, now you speak English, seem?" I let the hammer down, smile at him and put my arm around his shoulder. "Can't we just all get along? Lighten up, Andre, I'm only fucking with you. How about I buy you a beer? I want to run something by you." I ruffle his greasy hair. "Maybe we can turn things around here for you, Andre. You would like that, wouldn't you?"

"Seem. Seem. Whatever you say, man."

"Now that's the spirit, Andre. That's really great. I think we're going to be really good friends." I dust some debris from his shirt, straighten his collar. "There, that's better. By the way, Andre, I'm Steven Paul. My friends and I, well, we're from Texas. You probably noticed the fine ostriches I'm wearing." I toe his partner who is still out cold. "Hmm, sorry about your partner, Andre. It seems that we got off on the wrong boot." I chuckle at my cleverness. "The wrong boot, get it? Boot? Foot? Boot? Never mind. Anyway, your partner doesn't seem to be faring so well."

Surrounding Andre, we start on our trek back down the hill. I tuck the pistol into my waistband. Andy plays with Andre's switchblade along the way.

"You know, Andre, we've got a slightly used switchblade for sale if you're interested. Andre, Andre. I'm fucking with you again. You know, you're quiet, but you're a likeable kind of guy. Andy, give him his knife back."

"Shit, but... all right." Andy hands Andre his knife. Andre's hesitant to take it—his hand shakes as it does so.

My heartbeat has returned to normal. It usually elevates when I'm confronted with a knife. Oh, that's right, this is the first time I've been confronted with a knife. I'm here to tell you, it's quite frightening. The key, yep, I've said it before: never let them see your fear.

We step back into the botequim with our new friend. The proprietor lights up. I toss another pair of $20s to the counter.

"Por Favor. Another round for the house, amigo."

"Seem."

We take one of the few tables. I direct Andre to the corner chair and take the seat next to him. I wait on the proprietor to bring us our beer.

I take a swallow. "Ah, now that's refreshing. See, now isn't this nice, Andre? A bunch of friends sitting around sharing a beer and a laugh."

He remains mute, but finally nods.

"Good. I want you to make some money. You want to make some money, don't you?"

"Seem. Okay... I guess so."

"Now we're seeing eye-to-eye. Here's the deal Andre... How's the beer by the way?"

He takes a nervous sip in response.

"Good. Here's the deal Andre—we need five, oh my bad, four pistols. Nines preferably, but .45s will do, if necessary. We'll pay you, say, $500 U.S. above cost and let's say... another $500 bonus if you deliver within 24 hours. So, what do you say there, Andre?"

He squirms in his seat. "I... I... I don't know. Maybe. Um, I suppose... I suppose I could find four..."

"So..." I prompt.

"Well, I need... I need some of the cash up front."

"Well, I guess that's fair enough since we're amongst friends here. We are amongst friends, aren't we, Andre?"

"Ye... Yeah."

I peel off five crisp hundreds, fold them and stuff them inside his shirt pocket.

"There's only one slight catch, Andre—if you fuck us, I'll personally hunt you down and kill you. Capisce?"

"Capisce?"

"You understand?"

"Ye... Yeah."

I slap the table hard, jarring the beer bottles. Andre nearly jumps out of his chair.

"Great. We'll see you here, tomorrow, at this time. Now finish your beer and run along." I pull my chair aside to let him pass. "Well boys, that's settled. Same time, same place, same bat station. We should have our weapons tomorrow."

"Steve-O, I don't know. I think that you just gave away $500."

"I don't know either, Jim," Felix says. "But that was one scared fucker."

We all laugh.

"How'd you like my tackle, Steve?"

"Andy, as much as I hate to compliment you, that was one fine tackle. Let's drink one more round, and hit the road. Tomorrow, we'll come back in the car. I'm sure that I can find this place again."

We bump bottles on the last round. I salute the bum as well, who has seemingly grown in stature and is now allowed to stand within the structure. I'm sure that will remain true until the last of his money is gone. I decide to bless his game again tomorrow.

There's a lot of back slapping as we take our leave. Buying a round of beer is more effective and more practical than offering an olive branch any day. Yep, I muse, the universal gesture of peace—a round for the house.

Feeling good, I ride a decent wheelie leaving out. Not an easy feat on a bike with half the power that you're used to. Man, it makes me miss my YZ.

We reconvene on the terrace of my suite and order up a couple of buckets of Antarctica. If it isn't evident by now, we're real partial to our beer. Perhaps it's only because we haven't yet had a reason to get on the wagon.

"Now what, Steve-O?"

"Well, Candy's not back and she's got the book. Hopefully, she's in range. Let me see if I can catch her on the walkie-talkie. Base to Candy, come in girl."

There's some static and giggling. "This is Candy."

"We need your tight little ass back at camp."

"Tell him I'm coming, too. Hush... Candy en route."

"Ten-four."

Jim grins. "Steve-O, it looks like we're going to have some company. If you somehow pull off what I can see in your eyes, I'll bow at your feet for the rest of the year."

I smile. "Yeah, damn the luck." We all laugh. "Boys, I like to say that in the bedroom, two's company and three's a blast."

Felix throws a wadded napkin at me. "Dream on."

"Well, Felix, it's like this: if I get them both in the bedroom, there won't be any Mexican standoff."

Andy moves to the railing. "Things are starting to hop down there. Hardly ever see any military either."

"Well, let's look at that as a blessing," I say and drift off into my own little world.

Vertigo

Chapter 14

Candy returns with Jane in tow. It looks like we may have a new friend. Both glow from the day's sun. Jane carries a small suitcase in her hand. Clearly in a festive mood, Candy leans in to give me a kiss.

"Hi honey, we're home."

"Yes, I can see that and I see that you brought the lovely Jane with you. Jane, how are you?"

"Well, I think that I might be sunburned in places that are not used to the sun."

"I'll get my medical bag and get right on top of that, Jane."

"I bet you'd like that, honey. Jane, come on. We have to get ready. Jane's going to dinner with us."

And I bet you would win that bet, I say to myself. "Oh, ookaay."

"You said to make a list and we have to eat. Jane says one of the nicest places to dine is the Confeitaria Colombo in Centro."

"You'll love it," Jane helps out. "It's one of Rio's most beautiful examples of belle e'pogue architecture. It's also one of the most elegant places to dine in the city. There's also a smaller version, a deli, right here on Copacabana."

"Well, Jane, that sure makes me feel better," I say.

She smiles and momentarily rests her hand on my shoulder. "Yes, I thought it would. Well, us girls have got to get ready."

201

They turn to leave.

"Oh Jane, one second." I pull a picture of Dom and Melissa from my back pocket and hold it before her. "Ever seen either of these two?"

She stabs the picture with a finger. "Yeah, I've seen this guy on my flight several times. Goes by the name of Dom Pedro. How original. Always acts so proper, so sophisticated. Hits on me every time. Something about him always gives me the creeps—bad vibes. I wouldn't touch him with a ten-foot pole."

"And the woman?"

"She's gorgeous. No, I'd remember her."

"Anything else that you can tell me about him?"

"No, but having seen him several times on my flight, he must be a frequent flier. Why? What's up? Who's the girl?"

"Go get ready, Jane."

Candy sets the Rio book and a small spiral notebook on the table.

"Give us 30 minutes." She leans in and gives me another kiss before hurrying off.

I open the spiral.

"She has other top-end restaurants in Centro listed and plotted on a map," I say to Felix. "Da Silva, Cais do Oriente and Alba Mar. For drinking, she also has some places in the area listed. A place called Amarelinho and Boyeco Casual." I flip through additional pages. "It looks like most of the live music, dancing and the samba clubs, however, are in Lapa. If we don't get lucky tonight, that will be on our agenda tomorrow evening. The nightclubs Candy listed all seem to be back this way, so we'll hit them tonight. First and foremost is Bar D'Hotel, since from Melissa's letter, we know that he took her there. There's Barronti in Ipanema, Melt in Lablon and Clandestino and Fosfo Box right here in Copacabana. Rio's big. There may be others we have to check, too."

"So, we're showing the pictures too, I suppose?" Felix asks.

"Yeah, that and greasing palms. We need a regular at each joint. Pay them and promise them more if they help us locate Dom."

"Steve-O, what if he catches wind that people are looking for him? We may spook him and cause him to go underground."

"Well, Jimbo, nothing we can do about that, but I bet you the guy is too arrogant to spook. Since there are four places in Centro where he might dine, I say that we split into two groups and take our walkie-talkies and ear pieces so that we can communicate."

"I imagine our teams will be equitably split, as in me with the hard-tails and you with the split-tails," Jim says.

"Can't get anything by you, Jimbo," I say with a smile.

We all laugh.

"It doesn't matter how we split up as long as there is plenty of food involved," Andy says.

"See, Jimbo, there you go. You heard it straight from the horse's mouth."

We bump bottles on that one.

Candy and Jane step out onto the terrace. There's a collective quiet approval. I break the ice with a whistle. Both are dressed in sleek, form-fitting evening gowns and high-heels—both look stunning.

"Ladies, you two look good enough to eat," I say in all sincerity and as fate would have it, it's still something on this 17-year-old's to-do list. I know, I can hardly believe it myself.

Candy sits in my lap and drapes her arms over my shoulders. She whispers in my ear, "Promises, promises."

I inhale deeply. Her fragrance is intoxicating. I almost lose my train of thought.

"I really love the way you did your hair," I tell her and I do. She's wearing it up and coifed glamorously. Note: women love compliments, especially on their hair and their asses.

Jane looks very enticing as well. Lots of tan legs and cleavage—her longer hair is styled to rest on her right shoulder. She wears simple jewelry—a choker of pearls and matching pearl studs in her ears.

The cat has definitely got the boy's tongues and if Candy doesn't quit wiggling in my lap, I'll soon lose my composure. Oh, the woes of youth. Sometimes I hate to be in my position, but hey, this isn't one of them.

Candy stands and drops the car keys into my lap. "Are we ready to go, Big Boy?"

"Yeah, are we ready to go, Big Boy?" Jane echoes.

I down my beer and slap my thighs.

"Fuck it! Let's roll! Candy, do you have your walkie-talkie?"

"It won't fit in my clutch purse."

I smack myself in the forehead. "Of course, what was I thinking. I'll carry one. Andy, you carry one, too."

We hit the road with Jane giving directions. We drop the dejected boys at Da Silva and continue the short drive to Confeitaria Colombo.

Entering the place is awe inspiring. Jane explains that the place was founded in 1894, remodeled in 1914 and enlarged in 1920. It's very impressive with its stained-glass Louis XVI style windows, its gigantic Belgian brocaded mirrors, jacaranda wood furniture and marble countertops. I feel pretty impressive, too, with a long-legged blonde on one arm and a petite brunette on the other. Life is good.

The Colombo's ground floor has two large deli counters and a tea room. The Colombo also features an upper balcony area overlooking the extravagant seating area below. This section of the Colombo is reserved for more traditional dining.

We are greeted by a black Brazilian hostess dressed in a formal black pleated midi, a white collared blouse and black bowtie. The ladies want to dine and be seen so we opt for the upper level. They garner their fair share of attention along the way. I catch a few of the lady diners looking, too. I bestow upon them my most dazzling smile regardless of at whom they may be looking. I'm mean, who's to say that they are not taken in by my rugged, wind-blown good looks and my red Izod and ostriches—a stylish contrast to the rampant suit-and-tie-wearing male diners.

I ask the hostess if she speaks English. "Voce fola inglés?"

"Não desculpa," she answers.

Okay, I decide on another tack and ask her if anyone here speaks English.

"Alque aqui fola inglés?"

She raises a finger. "Seem, com liceca."

Jane translates. "She said 'yes, excuse me.' You know, Steven Paul, for a white boy, your Portuguese is coming along."

"Some say it is true, Jane. Some say it is true. How about you order for me, you being a woman about town and all."

"Order for me, too," Candy echoes.

"I'll ask her what she recommends," Jane says.

Our new waitress approaches our table. She's similarly attired. Another black Brazilian, albeit green-eyed. 'Exotic,' comes to mind. I've read that the black Brazilians are often discriminated against. If so, it's not evident here.

"May I get you something to drink while you look over the menu or are you ready to order?"

"Oque voce' recommenda?" Jane asks.

"The vatapá is especially good tonight. It's a seafood dish in a manioc sauce and dendê oil. And I would recommend to go with that the casquinha de siri, or our stuffed crab."

We all agree with her recommendation.

"And to drink?"

"Bring us girls a chope. Candy, it's a pale blonde pilsner draft and it's light and tasty," Jane says.

"Antarctica will be fine with me," I say.

"Anything else?"

"Yes." I pull the picture of Dom and Melissa from my back pocket and set it on the edge of the table. "Have you ever seen either of these two here before?"

I see an immediate reaction in her eyes.

"I'm sorry... I... I can't help you."

"Can't or won't?" I push.

"If there's nothing else, I'll..."

I fold and place a crisp $100 on top of the picture.

"It's very important that we locate them. We're staying at the Palace, suite 704. A simple call if he shows up, nothing more. No one will know the difference. One call equals $400 more."

She takes a nervous look around. "You... You have to promise no one will know."

"That's a promise."

The money disappears with her.

"Wow, I wish that I knew something. I'd sell the pervert right out in a flash. You never did tell me what this is all about, but it must be serious if you're about to start handing out hundreds like that."

"Jane, all bullshit aside, it may be deadly serious."

"If you're trying to be melodramatic, it's working. You're starting to scare me."

"Not my intention, Jane, but we need to find this Dom character really fast."

"It's important, Jane. I promise," Candy adds.

"Well okay, I think I get the picture—that's your real reason for being in Rio. Shit, if that's the case, count me in. I want to help. I know enough Portuguese to get by. Give me some $20s and I'll snoop around some while we wait on our food."

I dig out five $20s for her. As she heads off, I notice there are no panty lines. Naturally, I notice things like this. It's my job—it's what I do. Well, that along with protecting and rescuing damsels in distress, that is.

"Did you get an eye-full?" Candy jokes.

"Hey, honey, here comes our beer."

Our beer arrives bem gelada. Jane rejoins us and takes a swig of her pale blonde pilsner draft. Said like that, it does sound appealing, don't you think?

"I chummed the water. Look for some bites soon." She smiles with self-assurance.

"Any strange reactions like the one we got from our waitress?"

"A couple looked wary and a few refused to take any money altogether. Something about this guy must scare them. Even pushed, no one would say what though. I sure hope you guys know what you're doing."

We set the case aside long enough to eat our meal and drink another round. The waitress's recommendation is right on target. The meal is exquisite, another word that I use sparingly and I tip our waitress accordingly. We decline dessert.

I radio Andy. Andy says that they are also ready to roll onto the next "eating joint," as Andy so articulately puts it. I tell him "hold that thought. We're en route."

They're waiting for us in front of the Da Silva when we arrive. We park for a minute to compare notes. The consensus is that we ended up with similar results—no one is eager to help and some just outright refused. Such is life.

Since I'm not overly crazy about Chinese food, we drop the boys at Cais do Oriente and we move onto the Alaba Mar. The building itself is a unique green gazebo-style structure which offers superb views of Nitero'i and Baia de Guanabara.

The girls switch to the heavy stuff and decide to drink Antarctica along with me. We order a couple dozen oysters on the half shell and Candy and I start on them while Jane, the new sleuth, passes out $20s getting, once again, mixed results. It's becoming clearly evident that most everyone recognizes Dom Pedro, but it's also becoming equally evident that everyone is leery about getting involved and that some are just going to downright refuse to take the money.

I take the results with a grain of salt. One thing on which I can count is that greed will prevail. And, since we're saturating the right places with $20s and the promise of a fat paycheck, it's only a matter of time before a call will come in. With that in mind, I realize that after tonight, we'll have to leave someone at the suite to monitor the phone.

I radio Andy that we're on the way. I feel like a member of the Secret Service with my earbud and I do catch the occasional stare.

We pick the boys up at the Cais do Oriente. They're singing the same tune once again: some leery takers.

We head back toward our base to continue our search. We drop the boys off at D'Hotel and the girls and I continue the few blocks to the Baronneti. The Baronneti has a sleek and trim interior and, despite the still relatively early hour, the place is hopping. The two dance floors are nearly full. It's mostly a young crowd and I think to myself that this is the place to party and get lucky if you're single. Damn the luck. Just kidding. I already feel like the luckiest man in Rio. And, I mean, who knows how the night will pan out? Aw, to be young and ever-hopeful—a curse and a blessing.

Jane orders some kind of fruity concoction that seems to be prevalent among the party goers. One sip and there's no mistaking the taste of high-octane cachaça. Well, I tell myself, when in Brazil, do as the Brazilians do. Anyhow, my resolve is consistent with any successful undercover operation—the key to success is to blend in. I down my drink in furtherance of my grand plan and flag a passing waitress. She's a brown-haired, brown-eyed cutie clad in some short-shorts and a push-up bra. Nice.

I pull the picture and $20 from my pocket. She plucks the money from my hand even before I have time to open my mouth.

"Yeah, I know him. Dom fucking Pedro."

Could this be a woman scorned? If so, what a lucky find.

"What do you want to know about him? I sure would like to help."

"Your English is pretty good. You're not from around here, are you?" I ask.

"Nope, Texas—Laredo. And listen, your $20 just bought me a break. Follow me, so that we can talk."

Over the din, I tell the girls that I'll be right back. Jane takes Candy's drink and places both their drinks on the waitress's tray. I watch as Jane drags Candy toward the dance floor. A Bob Seger song flashes through my mind: "Oh, they love to watch them strut."

I follow the waitress through a side door and into what appears to be a breakroom. I take a seat opposite of her. The top of her breasts glisten with a sheen of perspiration. Yes, I know, guilty again. Much like Candy, she blows the bangs from her eyes.

"I suppose you're looking for the bum. What did he do? Cheat you out of some money?"

"Nope. You don't recognize the girl, do you?"

"Nope, never seen her before."

"By the way, we're from Texas, too."

"No way! Far fucking out! I'm trying to earn enough money to get back. It was hard to even find a job, because I speak almost zero Portuguese."

"Then we may be in business. You help us find him and I'll get you back, plus."

She smiles and sticks out her hand. "Bet. Sandra by the way."

The thought goes through my mind that I'd rather consummate the deal, but I settle for the shake. "Steven Paul."

"I don't know exactly where to find him, but I'll put some feelers out. I've made a number of friends who work around town. Where are you staying?

"Palace, suite 704"

"Suite, neat. A high roller, huh?"

"I take it that you don't care for the guy?"

"That's an understatement—I can't stand the guy. He's the reason why I'm stranded here. He bought my plane fare here and assumed that would entitle him to the pussy. It doesn't work that way with me. If everything clicked, maybe."

Hmm, a real straight shooter. I like this girl, I decide.

"Anyway, I start to get these creepy feelings, you know, like something isn't right. He kept trying to get me to go to his ranch somewhere beyond the hills and when I refused, he stormed out and left me hanging."

"What else do you know about him?"

"He's rumored to be a leftist, but the military doesn't seem to fuck with him. Hey, I like your boots."

I can see the laughter in her eyes.

"Ever consider cleaning them?"

I smile. "Not much time in between rodeos."

This time she does laugh.

"Sure. Are you with both women?"

"My sisters, you mean?"

"Good one. You have a hard time staying focused, don't you?" She smiles. "Try not to spread yourself too thin. I better get back to work, but you'll be hearing from me."

I follow her back out the door. Her short-shorts are a mite shy of covering her firm buns. Not an unpleasant sight, I might add. She leads me back to where she found me.

I order us another round and one for her.

"Be right back, handsome," she says.

Okay, I might have only imagined she said that, but that's not the point. The point is... Well, I forgot the point. The ladies rejoin me, giggling.

"That was fun," Candy says. "Make another girlfriend did you, Big Boy?"

"No, Sandra only wanted me to see the V.I.P. lounge and all that entails. She's very friendly."

"That's nice. What did she have to say? She didn't hesitate snatching up your $20."

"Well, girls, we may be in luck. She's not actually a woman scorned, but she can't stand the fucker and she's more than willing to help us find him."

"That's a pleasant surprise," Jane says. "Give me some more $20s anyway. Let me do a little more chumming."

I hand Jane some more and she's off and running.

"So, what else did she say? You were gone for a good minute."

"Oh, that Dom paid her fare here and when she wouldn't give up the quote 'pussy,' he left her hanging. Now she's trying to save the money to get back to Laredo."

"Laredo, you're fucking kidding."

"I kid you not. So naturally, she's very enthusiastic in helping us."

"What a deal. She's a cutie. Did you notice?"

I grab Candy and kiss her on the forehead.

"I have eyes for you only, honey."

"Good answer. But you really would benefit from a pair of mirrored glasses."

Candy hooks her arm through mine at the sight of Sandra's approach.

"So, you're Steven Paul's sister from Texas?... I'm joking." She sticks out her hand. "Hi, I'm Sandra."

Candy takes the offered hand. "Candy, nice to meet you. I hear that you want to help."

"More than you might imagine."

Jane returns and offers her hand. "Jane."

They shake.

"Sandra," Sandra says. "Nice meeting you both. I love your outfits. You both look like a million dollars."

Candy and Jane thank her for the compliments. Sandra passes out our drinks.

"I hope I'm the one that helps find the scumbag."

"I hope you are, too," I say as I hand her a $20 for the drinks. "After these drinks, we're going to check out a couple more places on Copacabana. I hope we hear from you."

"Neat, I'll be in touch... Later."

We say our goodbyes.

"She seems nice enough," Jane comments. "Cute, too."

We watch as Sandra weaves through the crowd and disappears.

"Yes, gives the short-shorts a whole new meaning," I can't help but say.

We watch the dancers while we finish off our drinks. Time to move onto our final destination of the night. I radio Andy and tell him that we're on our way.

We arrive to find the boys waiting outside the D'Hotel. It appears that Andy has made a new friend. Jim and Felix stand apart from Andy, grinning ear-to-ear.

I roll down my window. "What's up, Andy?"

"Maria wants to ride with us to our next stop."

Maria, huh?

"Maria, those are awful large eyes you have there and hands and feet."

Andy still manages to grow pale in the dim light.

"Sure, why not," I say. "We don't have much room, though. You'll have to sit on Andy's lap."

We all break into laughter, except Andy and Maria, of course.

"Fuck that! Let me in!" Andy screams.

I open the door to let them all pile in. "Well, Andy, you going to kiss and tell?"

We all laugh some more.

"I didn't make it that far."

"Well, that sure takes a load off my mind," I say. "Boys, we're off to our last stop of the evening. We'll drop you all off at Clandestino. Stay as long as you like. It's only four blocks northwest of the Palace. Andy, a rule of thumb, if their handshake takes you to your knees, steer clear."

"Whatever."

We drop them off and head to our destination, the Fosfobox. Turns out it's a subterranean club tucked away beneath a shopping center close to the metro station. We find the place literally rocking out as we enter. The crowd is alive—eclectic.

After we pass out the last of the $20s for the night, I decide that I'm going to hit the dance floor with the girls. What I lack in rhythm, I make up for with a lack of inhibition and, not to mention, the drinks are starting to kick in. The girls are animated and I suspect are also feeling no pain. I further decide that it's okay to mix a little pleasure with business. I mean, wouldn't you too if you were a 17-year-old heterosexual accompanied by two sexy, scantily clad women? Yep, that's what I thought. The prosecution rests. For the next two hours, we drink, dance and laugh. Life is surely good. With a girl on both arms, we finally drag ass from the club. Outside, the night is cool and fresh—a break from the smoky club below. I feel optimistic that the evening's activities will produce results and that tomorrow we'll get at least one call. Now that I think about it, I hope the call's from Sandra. But even if not, I'm going to help her get back to Texas.

The girls and I arrive back at the Palace in high spirits. Passing through the lobby, I espy—who else—our trusted bellhop. He's eager to please. I order up a bucket of Antarctica, eternally hopeful. I wonder if this final round of beer will prove to be the last stimulus needed to make at least one young man's fantasy come true. Hey, crazier things have happened and, I mean, we're all potentially consenting adults here—well, at least I think so, being 17 and all. As posh as our suite is, we opt for the terrace again anyway. Our bucket of beer is soon to follow. I send the grinning bellhop on his way with another of my ever-dwindling $20s. The few remaining $20s makes me realize that there's a hell of a lot of overhead running the tight ship that I do.

I kick back, put my feet up on the table, sip my beer and contentedly listen to the girls chatter about the evening, Miami, Austin and this and that.

"Honey, Jane is going to borrow one of my teddies and spend the night here with us."

Hmm, okay. "Won't your teddy be too short? Won't Jane's panties show?"

I grin at the thought.

"Oh, she doesn't wear panties," Candy says with a smile.

I swallow on that one. "Okay, I guess I'll still feel safe sleeping between you two."

Candy smiles again. "You mean after we compare techniques?"

I swallow again and wipe the sheen from my brow.

"Techniques?" I squeak. They both lick their lips.

"You know, techniques on giving head, or as you boys like to say 'blowjobs,'" they say in unison.

Have I died and gone to heaven?

"Honey! Honey! Honey! Wake up."

I feel somebody shaking my shoulder. The last thing that I want to do is open my eyes, but I do so begrudgingly.

"Honey, you feel asleep. You must have been dreaming. You were mumbling something about techniques."

"Of course. I didn't die and go to heaven. I fell asleep."

"What? Never mind. I'm going to run Jane back to her hotel."

"Okay, I guess," I say sure that my voice betrays my disappointment. I reach for a beer, but the bucket has runneth dry. I let out an audible sigh.

"Oh, we polished off the beer."

The girls giggle as they take their leave. I close my eyes again. Okay, where was I? Oh yeah, wishful dreaming. I'm awakened again by the ruffling of my hair.

"Come on, Big Boy, let's go to bed. Aw, don't look so sad." She laughs. "You still have me."

"Okay, but you're not going to pour salt in my wound, are you?"

She leans in and gives me a deep kiss. I feel much better. Candy is a passionate kisser. I follow her into the bedroom. We undress and climb into the spacious bed. Candy makes me remember that I'm one lucky fucker. Hell, I may even be the luckiest man in Rio, I realize.

Chapter 15

I awake to another realization that I'm alone in the bed and the room. Candy must sense that I've awaken for she yells out to me.

"I'm in here. I ordered breakfast. I talked to Wallace, too—told him we were making progress. I told him you were in the shower."

"Okay," I holler back. "Do we have time to take a shower?"

"You do. I already have."

Okay, I think, that takes the fun out of my shower. I shower and dress anyway. As I tuck my .45 in my waistband, I catch sight of myself in the mirror. My reflection reminds me of Bickle, or De Niro, in Taxi Driver.

"You talking to me? You talking to me? Then who the hell else you talking to? You talking to me? Well, I'm the only one here," I tell the mirror and smile.

"Are you talking to the mirror again?" Candy yells from another room.

"Nooo." I take one last look and mouth to the mirror: "You are a handsome devil, aren't you?"

I find Candy on the terrace looking spry and beautiful. She's wearing her bikini, which I haven't seen before and a sheer wrap.

"Morning, beautiful," I say and give her a kiss.

"The boys are on the way over. Jane said that she would catch a cab and be over later."

"You know that I have to go check on the guns in a little bit and we're going to have to have someone here to monitor the phone around the clock now?"

"I know. If we have to, Jane and I might tan right here on the terrace. Oh, and in the nude—eliminate those unsightly tan lines."

"Well, I guess the three of us should have no problem monitoring the phone then."

"Right, good try. If nothing else, you're persistent. I can read your devious little thoughts like a book."

"That transparent, huh?"

We both laugh. I like the sound of her laughter.

"I ordered a good homestyle breakfast—enough for eight. Eggs scrambled and fried, tons of bacon, hash browns, toast and orange juice and coffee."

"Not only beautiful, but smart."

She does a spin so that I can admire her. "That's what I was thinking."

There's a knock on the door.

"I'll get it," she announces.

It's our 24/7 bellhop and he's beaming like usual. I dig one of my last crumpled $20s from my pocket and slap it in his outstretched hand. I point to the terrace—he knows the routine.

A second knock announces the crew's arrival. We all take our customary places around the table and dig in. The food is devoured within minutes.

"Once we check on the guns, then what, Steve-O?" Jim asks.

"Maybe we will check a few of the higher-end lunch places, assuming all goes well with the firearm acquisition. Candy, what's the name of the place where they ate lunch that was written in the letter?"

"Adega da Velha and it's on Rua Paulo Barreto in Botofoga. I'll draw you a map. It's on the way to the airport."

"Yeah, I remember—it's right before you get to Flamingo. I can find that. So, until this evening, not much else we can do absent a call here. Andy, go break some more $100. If you run into our bellhop, he's got a pocket full of $20."

"Ten four."

Felix smiles. "I take it the lovely Jane went back to her hotel last night. And to think you seemed to be doing so well."

"Don't look so smug, my friend." I also smile. "She didn't go until she had some nightcaps here first."

I reassert my winning smile—the kind of smile that leaves a lot of room for interpretation, or should I say "misinterpretation?"

Cool as a cucumber, Candy opts not to blow my cover.

As usual, Jim merely chooses to shake his head. Well, I did get quite close, you know, in my dream at least. Still upbeat and optimistic, I think to myself. You may have lost that battle, but not the war, big boy. The thought reminds me of a recent study about which I read. The study claimed that the average male thinks about sex every eight seconds. I wonder how true that is? I know had I participated, I would have skewed the results.

Andy returns with a stack of $20s. I decide to forgo the question of how much the latest transaction set us back. Again, someone once said, "you can lead a horse to water, but you can't necessarily get him to drink." Well, something like that. You get the point. Someday, I might get the saying right.

"Well, boys, let's rock 'n' roll." I lean in to give Candy a kiss. "Later, honey."

We're off again in the mighty Chevy. Finding the neighborhood botequim again turns out to be a breeze. The bum is present and he has been relegated to the outdoors once more. He breaks into a grin as he recognizes we're the occupants of the new Monte Carlo.

Things from the outside look the same as they did the day before. I expect one of three things. One: Andre and his friend want payback and this is an ambush. Two: Andre is a no-show and he has beat me for the money. Or three: Andre has come through and all is well. Naturally, I hope for the latter, that my idle threat has been heeded and that Andre has come through for us.

I leave the car running. "Hold on. Let me check it out." I exit the car and prepare for the worst. I cautiously approach the entrance and indicate to the bum to give me a minute. I mentally and physically prepare myself to cross the threshold. I hold the front of my Izod in preparation for a quick snatch of my pistol. Reality sets in. My tumultuous heart skips a beat. I have one pistol and eight rounds. Not good, big boy, I tell myself. I hear my dad tell me, "go with the plan, Son." Plan?

My plan was to get Jane and Candy in bed at the same time. "Not that plan, Son." Fuck it. I take a deep breath and step into the gloom. The clamor dies upon my entrance, but hmm, no bullets. The proprietor smiles and to the right, in the same chair as before, sits Andre.

I let out my breath and smile. Don't you love it when a plan comes together?

"Por favor." I indicate a round for the house. I dig out my fold of $20s, pass one back through the door to the bum and motion for my crew to come in.

I join Andre at the table. He's on his way to being three sheets to wind, but he's here—no small miracle, I'm sure. There's a small cardboard box at his feet.

"Andre, Andre, my friend. Good to see you."

"Steven Paul." He feebly attempts a smile. "I almost took the money and ran, but as my friend Alfredo said before you shattered his jaw: 'Ta louco.' I no want to fuck you over, man."

The crew and the beer arrive at the table.

"Some say it is true, Andre. You made a wise decision."

I toast him with my first beer of the day. Yep, I practice self-control from time to time.

"So, Andre, whatcha got for us?"

He wipes his face on his sleeve. "Man, you got to understand. I did my best. You bustin' up Alfredo's jaw and takin' his gun got people talkin' a ta louco gringo. It makes me nervous to be here, man."

"I feel you, Andre. What do you got?"

Andre picks the small box from the floor and places it before me. I don't know whether to be happy or sad as I look in on its contents. Three of the weapons instantly register. Three more Colt 1911s. For these, there's a couple spare clips and a box of .45s. The fourth pistol, to my dismay, is a small caliber, possibly a 22 or 25. I pick it up and take a closer look. I'm surprised to see that it's at least a quality gun, a Beretta 25 automatic. Cute, but not very effective.

I eye a nervous Andre before smiling and slapping him on his back.

"Close enough for comfort, Andre. You did all right."

I down my beer, wipe my mouth with the back of my hand and indicate another round for the house. I pocket the 25 and one of the clips and push the box across to Jim and Felix. I leave it to them to decide on who gets the odd clip.

I peel off five, crisp $100s and, after a thought, I peel off a sixth. I place the five bills before him.

"Andre, there may come a time in the next few days where we might need some hired muscle—interested?"

He nervously eyes the bills before him.

"No catch, man," I say. "The bills are yours—the whole kit and caboodle. Again, you interested?"

"Shh... Sure."

I slap the table, jarring the bottles and almost causing Andre to jump from his seat. Slow learner, I think to myself. And, though not one to admit it, my hand stings like hell.

"Great! That's fucking great, Andre. I like your spirit, gung ho and all." I set the sixth bill down before him. "I want you here every day for a week, right here, same time, every day. Can you do that for me, Andre?"

"Shh... Sure."

"Well, boys, I guess that settles that," I say and wave the proprietor over. "Andre, translate for me."

I dig another $120 from my pocket and hand it to the proprietor.

"Tell him the $20 is for him and the $100 is to buy the bum lunch every day until the money is gone. Got that, Andre?"

The proprietor grins and nods at the translation.

"Okay, that's settled," I say. "Grab your beers, boys. Let's rock 'n' roll."

We step back into the day's brightness. The air is still and somewhat stagnant this far inland, something I hadn't noticed earlier. Or it may be only a feeling that I'm getting from the decrepit neighborhood. A rumbling motor draws my attention up the block. Idling at the curb is a late '60s Cadillac in need of a new muffler. The vehicle, at this distance, seems fully occupied.

Felix notices too. "Looks like we may have company."

Jim and Andy turn to follow our stare.

"Curious, could be trouble," Jim says.

"Trouble is as trouble does, Jimbo," I say not exactly sure what that means. "Hang tight, boys. I'll check it out." I pull my shirt up to reveal my pistol and start my trek toward the Caddy. Half a block shy, the Caddy's engine revs and the back tires begin to spin, scream and smoke in reverse. I watch as the Caddy clears the nearest intersection, reverses course and, in another scream of rubber and smog, disappears from view. I'm not sure, but I think that, for a second, I caught sight of a bandaged face.

I walk the short distance to rejoin my crew.

"I guess they weren't interested in sharing their feelings today."

Felix chuckles. "You sure have an interesting way of going about things, Esteban. As unorthodox as you may be, you seem to get results."

"Maybe they thought he was a tire kicker and they got scared," Jim adds

"Something to ponder, Jimbo," I say as we load up.

"Why did you give $100 to feed some bum?" Andy asks like it is some kind of personal affront. "You've never given more than a few dollars to me at one time."

"But Andy, you're a busboy, remember?"

"You were a busboy, too, a week ago."

"Why rehash my sordid past. I've told you that I've matured and moved on. And besides, I see potential in the bum."

I crank our ride.

"Well, I quit, too," Andy says.

"Yes, but you'll ultimately go back. I mean you drive a Pinto for Christ sakes."

I put the car in gear and pull away from the curb.

"And, Andy, as for the bum, there's GP, QP and just plain old PR for helping the bum out—take your pick."

"How about I pick stupid—just plain old stupid."

I adjust my rearview.

"People who live in glass houses," I remind Andy.

Jim laughs. "Actually, Steve-O, you do live in a glass house."

Hmm, good point.

"Let's check out the Adega da Velha."

"Can we order something to eat while we're at it?"

We all laugh, except Andy of course.

Just for the hell of it, I tromp down on the Chevy. Hmm, not what I'm used to, but not bad for a 350. Personally, though, I like the throaty sound of a bigger bore and duals, be it a small block or big block.

Following Candy's road maps is easy enough. Our return trip takes us along R. General Poliadoro and the street that we're seeking, Rea Paulo Barreto, tees into it. The restaurant is smaller than I envisioned and is rather reminiscent, but nicer than, the botequim we just left. The place also has much more of an informal feel to it then I was expecting.

The waitress who greets us is a cute little blond number, colorfully clad. She greets us in English. I wonder what gave us away? I recall from Melissa's letter that the place specializes in food from northeastern Brazil and she had dined here on some sort of dried, then softened, then barbequed meat.

I order us a large platter along with a round of Antarctica, of course. Who would have thought?

"Can I get you boys anything else, Steven Paul? Don't look so surprised. I know exactly who you are. Sandra called me this morning and woke my skinny ass up." She smiles. "Yes, Dom Pedro dines here quite often and I hope you guys are extremely careful. I don't know the story on this cat, but the rumor is that he is some kind of rich leftist. Why the army lets him make it around Rio, I'm not sure. Dissidence is frowned upon. People sometimes disappear. Suite 704—I'll call if he shows up. Sandra's a cool chick. I'll miss her, but I hope you guys help her get home."

"How did you make me? I was with two women when I met Sandra."

"Blond hair, blue eyes, an Izod shirt and ostrich boots." She smiles again. "You're easy to pick out in a crowd. Plus, she said you were handsome for a youngster."

Yes, I can see her point—it's hard to mistake these good looks. I inwardly smile.

"Well, she's right easy on the eyes herself, as are you, by the way."

She laughs. "She said you distract easily, too. I'll be right back with you boys' beer."

"Good news spreads fast, huh, Steve-O? Who's this Sandra chick? You never mentioned her," Jim says.

"Yeah, I got sidetracked when I saw Andy with his new friend."

"She... He wasn't my friend."

"Anyway, we met her at the Baronneti in Ipanema. She's a waitress there. Get this... She's from Laredo and Dom fucking Pedro left her hanging."

"You're shitting us," Felix says.

"I shit you not. So, as you can imagine, she's more than eager to help. She said she would make some calls and apparently she did."

The waitress returns with our beer. She's pretty, smells nice and displays a lovely cleavage which I can't help but notice as she bends to pass out the beer.

"Here you go, boys. By the way, I'm Heidi."

"Nice," I say meaning the complete package. "You German?"

"Half and half. Dad's German. Mom's Portuguese. I'll be back with your food order shortly."

Out of earshot, I ask Andy, "What do you think, Andy?"

"She's a woman."

We all laugh.

"That's not what I meant, but at least your batting 500 now."

We shoot the shit and sip our beer until the food arrives. Heidi talks us into trying Brahma, another popular brand of national beer. The barbecue is different, but good. The beer full and stout. I tip Heidi handsomely. I'm a big tipper by nature, you know. It's also easier when it's part of the 'budget.'

"So, what now, Steve-O?" Jim asks as we make our way back to the car.

"Unless Andy wants to stop and eat again, I guess it's back to the Palace. Then you can take a walkie-talkie and check out the beach, or whatever, as long as you stay in range."

Felix taps me on the shoulder as I go to open the door of the Chevy.

"Don't look now, but I'm sure that we've got company this time."

I don't take him literally and look. "Yep, the old Caddy. Hmm, wonder how they found us?"

A quarter mile up and to the right of the tee sits the Caddy, the front end and windshield exposed.

"Well, I do believe we have piqued their interest for some reason," Jim says. "What now?"

"Lock and load," Andy says.

I open the Chevy's door. "Well boys, you heard it straight from the horse's mouth. Let's lock, load and rock 'n' roll."

As we pull onto the street, the Caddy reverses from sight. That's strange, I think, for I'm sure they know we spotted them.

I smile. "Boys, you may find it prudent to buckle up."

Jim, who's riding shotgun, turns to Felix in the back. "I know the look. This may not be pretty."

I tromp down hard on the Chevy's gas pedal and she quickly eats up the quarter mile. In my periphery, Jim grabs the dash.

"Shit! Hold on! Here we go!" he yells. Coming up fast on the tee, I lay hard on the brakes, steer into a squealing slide and get back hard on the gas pedal. The inside tire spins for a second before gaining traction.

We blow past the Caddy. Its passengers wide-eyed and open-mouthed.

"Shit!" Jim yells again as I lock the tires, putting the Chevy into a 180. The heavy car screams in protesting rubber and shudders to a stop. We're now officially behind the Caddy.

I grin, holding the brakes and the gas. The rear tires roil and the interior begins to fill with smoke. The Caddy comes to life in its own cloud of blue smoke. As I let off the brakes, I notice Jim reassert his grip on the dash.

"Shit! Here we go again!" he yells once more.

Passing through the Caddy's smoke, we come up hard on its ass. I'm eating up his bumper waiting for an opportunity to pit the heavier car. We make some incidental contact coming into an S curve. I resolve to not let them shake us.

"Hell yeah!" Andy screams in my ear.

Coming out of the second half of the S curve, we make jarring contact with the rear bumper on the Caddy's driver's side. The Caddy spins and disappears before us.

"Fucking A!" Felix yells as he maintains a death grip on the seat before him.

I catch the tail end of the Caddy's demise in my rearview. The Caddy's down for the count. I watch as it comes to a crumpling rest among the last half-dozen cars or so that it struck.

"Fuck! That was exhilarating!" I yell as I slam the center of the steering wheel, blowing the horn. "Man, did you guys see that? We better get the fuck out of dodge."

I hightail it for another mile, but dial her down as the adrenaline begins to dissipate.

"Did you see the eyes on those fuckers as we blew by them, Steve-O?"

We all laugh, a big part of it in relief.

"Yeah, I saw them, but more than that, it's what I didn't see that has me wondering. I didn't see anyone with a bandaged face."

"So, we know that the one you drop-kicked wasn't likely in the car," Felix concludes.

I nod my head in agreement. "That's what I'm thinking, too, but there's something else to consider. I didn't notice anyone following us from the Palace and I would have noticed. I'm always on the lookout for cops."

"You're definitely diligent in that respect, Steve-O. Well, I don't know about the rest of you, but now that that's over, I think I'm going to unwind on the beach for a little while," Jim says.

"You going to take your chick repellant with you?" I ask.

"Chick repellant?"

"Yeah, Andy."

We all laugh, except Andy of course.

"Aw, fuck you."

Isn't life grand? I wonder if I can sneak up on the girls tanning on the terrace. Wouldn't that be a pleasant surprise? A pleasant surprise for me, that is. The thought makes me smile. I think I've mentioned this before, but if not, I'm here to tell you that I easily amuse myself at times.

We arrive safely back at the Palace. On close inspection, the Chevy fared pretty well. I like the word "fared" paired with the word "pretty." Pretty is subjective in that light, wouldn't you say? I mean beauty is in the eyes of the beholder, right? How is that relevant, you ask? It isn't, I'm just throwing it out there. The point is, the Chevy survived virtually unscathed, the rubber bumper trim only somewhat abraded. Makes you proud to be an American. There's no sign of our bellhop as we pass through the lobby. I'll have to phone up a bucket of beer to keep the old psyche lubricated. I part company with my crew on our floor to quietly and furtively enter my suite. I can be quiet and furtive when the need arises—like the need to catch the girls tanning topless. Yes, I'm sure you feel my glee, but to my dismay the girls are sunning on their stomachs. As a consolation prize, Jane's wearing her fio dental. Hmm, so the old girl wasn't lying about that. I announce my presence. "Daddy's home." I can hardly conceal my joy. They both turn in surprise.

"Shit, you scared the shit out of me," Candy says. She raises and places a hand over her heart. Jane simply returns my smile.

"How unexpected of you, Steven Paul," she says good-naturedly.

"Isn't it?" I reply. I grab a beer from their bucket, pull the tab off and take a contemplative swig. "If either of you girls decide to tan the other side, I guess y'all can subject me to the displeasure of applying the lotion."

"Candy, how did you find such a helpful young man?"

"They broke the mold with this one," Candy says and smiles.

Oh yeah, if that's the case, Candy, it's only right that you should share, I think. "Always willing to lend a hand," is what comes out.

I put forth my best innocent shrug while thinking to myself that at this stage of the game, I'm willing to lend a tongue, too. Got to break it in someday, right? Fertilize the old 'stache, so to speak. I toe my boots off and shuck my clothes down to my boxers. I'm good at shucking clothes.

"Might as well catch some rays with you girls."

Candy gets up, gives me a kiss and pinches my side. "Aren't you a tad young to be getting love handles?"

I look to see what she's talking about. Hmm, could it be true? Nah, it's only the angle of the sun playing tricks on the mind. Well, that and possibly the lack of discipline lately. I've really been floundering when it comes to working out. Well, nothing else much to do, but up my sexual output. What better way to burn a quick 300 calories, I ask you? Ah, to be so young and optimistic.

I look over my current stable of girls and think to myself: you could bounce a quarter off either one of these two girls' asses.

"A penny for your thoughts," Jane says.

"I'm thinking about quarters."

"Quarters? Okay, I guess."

"Ten-to-one, it has some kind of sexual connotation to it," Candy says.

"You two make an unusual pair. Exactly how long have you been together?"

"Oh, about four days," Candy says and we both laugh.

The beer is good—the view even better. Fio dental... I wonder when the custom will hit our shores? Although, one need give

Austin credit where credit is due. Austin's Barton Springs in Zilker Park has been open for topless swimmers and sun bathers for as long as I can remember. And, one mustn't overlook Lake Travis, which is home to Hippy Hollow, a totally nude swimming spot. It's only a matter of time, I think, before the fio dental will be the norm, if nowhere else, in the greater Central Texas region. And, not a minute too soon, I might add.

I kick back and prop my feet on the terrace railing. "Patience is a virtue, Son," I hear my dad say. Yep Dad, I think I'll sit right here, sip my beer, enjoy the current view and patiently wait Jane out. I'll just close my eyes for a minute first.

Vertigo

Chapter 16

I feel someone straddle me and run their fingers through my hair. "Wake up honey." I open my eyes to find Candy's captivating green eyes staring into mine. A smile so wide and devious looking that her right cheek dimples.

"We're done tanning," she gleefully announces.

"Of course. Where' s Jane?" I ask in a voice thick with disappointment.

"Why, she's in the bedroom waiting on us, of course."

I swallow and I hear "Us?" squeak out.

She flicks the tip of my nose. "Just kidding, honey. She's ordering room service and another bucket of beer. We drank all the beer while you slept."

I sigh. "Of course."

She pinches both my cheeks, pulls my face into a smile and gives me a quick smack on the lips.

"There, don't you feel better now?"

"I suppose."

"You know, I really should have woken you earlier. You really caught a lot of sun sitting here."

Jane rejoins us on the terrace.

"Oh, I see you woke up devil boy. It's a shame, Steven Paul, that you slept through my entire gravity defying act."

"Gravity defying act?"

"She means tanning on her back and boy are they ever gravity defying."

They both laugh.

I'm tempted to say, "At your age," but settle for "Thanks for sharing that information with me, but you know as they say 'seeing is believing.' I'm sorry but I just can't take your word on that."

I shrug and reach for a beer that isn't there. Damn, I'm starting to think the girls are conspiring against me.

Jane shrugs back. "Well, suit yourself. I ordered some tagliatelle with Italian sausage ragout. And, because of the girl talk, I decided to order you a couple dozen oysters. Maybe the vitamin E will help you, you know, with your little performance problem."

They both giggle like school girls. I hope Jane realizes that this means war. No holds barred, girls.

"You know what they say Jane, 'practice makes perfect,' and oh, Candy, variety is the spice of life."

Candy smiles. "That's why I keep some positions in reserve."

The vision of her agility pops to mind. She's got you there, big boy, I concede to myself. I'll bide my time for now. There's a knock at our door. After another quick smack to my lips, Candy hops from my lap to answer.

Having Jane alone for a second, I'd lick my brows at the opportunity if I could, but dammit, I can't. I wink instead. She in turn flashes me with her breasts. The girls are right, they sure appear gravity defying to me. I humbly grant her a point and acknowledge it with a thumbs up. A nice healthy 36C, I suspect. I, however, now have a new concern—are they real? I wonder if a taste test can establish that? I adjust my boxers.

Candy directs the bellhop to set up on the terrace. He's a fresh face. I guess our guy had to finally cop some Zzzs. I tip him and send him on his way. I pop the caps on three beers and pass two to the girls as they join me at the table. We bump bottles before digging into the grub. Not suspicious, mind you, but not willing to take chances either, I eat more than my share of the oysters.

Jane rubs my inner thigh with her foot under the table, almost reaching my crotch. She's not really playing fair, is she? I readjust my boxers yet again.

The ringing phone breaks my reverie. Candy jumps up to get it. Jane licks her lips as her foot finally makes contact. Reluctantly, I disengage her foot. In all likelihood, the call's for me and I'm not quite up to answering it with a limp.

"Steve, it's Heidi!" Candy yells.

Bingo, I think, our diligence has paid off. I hurry to the phone.

"Hello."

"It's Heidi... He's here."

"Shit, how long do you think he'll be there?" I ask knowing I have to round up my crew.

"A short while, but it doesn't matter, I overheard where he's going."

"Where?"

"You going to help Sandra?"

"Of course, and I'm going to give you a big hug and a kiss as well."

"Okay, he's going to a place called Bilhares Guanabara. It's a combination bar and pool hall. I hear he's big on pool and gambling. I don't know the address, but it overlooks Praça Tiradentes. Know where it is?"

"Praça Tiradentes. Praça Tiradentes. Yeah, I think I know, I think I can find it."

"Good, but if you can't, stop by here and I'll leave to show you. I'll tell them here that I'm not feeling well."

"You're a sweetheart, Heidi."

"And, Steven Paul, please be careful."

"Thanks, Heidi. Later."

I step back out on the terrace.

"Found him, I need to radio the boys."

"We're going, too," Candy stubbornly announces.

"Shit, let me think, let me think... Okay, dress nice like last night. Hell, wear the same thing if need be."

I radio the boys and tell them to get back to headquarters ASAP. I pace the terrace as I think. Maybe I can use his grandiosity against him somehow? Ultimate objective: find where he's keeping

Melissa, assuming she's alive, that is. Conclusion: wing it, big boy, just wing it. Well, it's sort of a plan, I guess.

I dress, wishing that I had more jewelry. I have a lone silver bracelet that my uncle got somewhere in the Philippines. It's nice and heavy, fat in the middle and tapers toward each end before budding into snake heads. With the boots, it will have to do. I pop the top off another beer and pace. I check to make sure that my .45 has a round chambered, despite the fact that I know it does. I snap and realize that Dom will recognize Jane, but then decide that that might work to our advantage. He likely won't suspect our presence, assuming that he hasn't already been tipped that people are looking for him. Even so, I consider, he might find it amusing, like a cat playing with a mouse. Well, I think, never underestimate Steven Paul and his crew of merry men—and oh, his lovely ladies.

The girls reappear on the terrace looking... Well, looking fine, or even "edible" for those that prefer that term. I dig in my back pocket and remove the Beretta.

"Here's a little something for you, honey," I say to Candy as I pass it over. "There's a round in the chamber, the safety is off, so all you need to do is cock the hammer, point and pull the trigger. Oh, preferably at close range. And as luck would have it, it will fit nicely in your clutch purse."

Candy eyes her new pistol like it's a toy, turning it this way and that, pointing it this way and that.

"It's really cute. What do you think, Jane?"

"Cute as can be."

"Maybe you should try it on in front of the mirror," I say.

Candy playfully gives me the evil eye.

"I think that I make quite the fashion statement with this jewel," she says smugly.

"I have to agree. It matches your shoes. You go, girl," her confederate says.

A knock announces the crew's arrival. Fashion statement herself gets the door.

"You're playing with fire," I warn Jane.

"You or Candy?"

"In my adolescent dreamworld, I'd like to believe it's with Candy and me."

"Sometimes, one's rewarded for their patience," she says.

"I hope you're right," I tell her and dad alike.

The boys look and sound winded. Jim catches his breath long enough to speak.

"We were all the way down in Leblon. A place called Academia da Cachaça or something like that. The place is bad ass."

"So, where is he? What's the plan?" Felix asks.

"He's headed to a pool hall. I've studied on this long and hard..."

"So, we wing it, right?" Felix says.

We all laugh. Felix is a quick study.

"Some of my best laid plans are when I wing it."

"We taking the girls, too?" Andy asks.

"They really don't have as much BB gun experience as you, Andy, but they sure do make for some fine eye candy. No pun intended, Candy. Can I get an 'Amen?'"

"Amen!" Jim and Felix echo.

I take the last swallow of my beer, set the bottle down and stick out my fist. Ladies and gentlemen, let's hit the hammer and then rock 'n' roll."

We all hit the hammer, the girls included.

We file out of the Palace and pile into the Chevy.

"Know where the place is, Steve-O?"

"Sort of. It's somewhere near the coast, close to Cinelandia. It overlooks Praça something or other. Worst case scenario, Heidi offered to show us if need be."

"Works for me," Jim says.

"We going to take him hostage and force him to give up John's daughter?" Andy asks.

I crank our ride and put her in gear while I think it over. "Let's play it by ear for now, shall we?"

Finding the first of the Praças proves to be easy. The area is alive with pedestrian traffic. I pull to the side, roll down my window and flag over an older, sandaled woman.

"Bilharess Guanabara por favor?" I ask her.

She points west. "Em frente vire a directa."

"She says straight ahead, turn right. Thanks, Obrigado," Jane says. I nod my thanks, roll up my window and make the left.

"Okay, we're going to pretend that we're not together. We'll stagger our entrances. Andy and Jim, you two go in first and get a table if one's available. Felix, you'll follow a few minutes later. Take a position at the bar. The girls and I will follow ten minutes later. Each of you give me some hundreds. I need a decent roll to play my part. I'm willing to bet his weakness lies in his arrogance."

They all give me several hundred a piece, except Candy, who prefers to keep back-up in her dainty purse.

"Hit him where he's weak then, Steve-O. Let us out, Andy. Come on, let's go."

I let Andy and Jim out on my side.

"Well, Esteban, let's see you work your magic again."

"How can I fail with one on each arm like these two?"

"Don't worry, Felix. I have his back, too." Candy says.

"Well, Jane," I say. "As revolting as it may be, you'll need to show me lots of attention in there so that we can pull this off." I inwardly smile at my cleverness. I put a lot of emphasis on the word "We." I believe in being a team player and, who knows, it may produce a cheap thrill.

"Maybe y'all should practice some in the car first," Candy says with mock sarcasm.

I pat Candy's leg. "I'm only worried about results, honey, not protocol or political correctness."

"What's that supposed to mean?"

I shrug. "Nothing, honey. I just liked the way it sounded. Ladies, if you're ready. Remember we need to be believable. We mustn't spare the affection."

Damn you're good, I tell myself. I'm close to patting myself on the back. We exit our ride and they each take an arm. I goose Jane a good one causing her to misstep in her high heels. She recovers her step and composure grandly. The fact she's quite firm down there pleasantly registers.

With one on each arm and a smile on my face like there's no tomorrow, we make our grand entrance. The place is spacious and well lit, the high ceiling supported by heavy columns throughout and the nine-foot regulation tables are amply spaced.

We come to the immediate attention of the patrons. I spot Dom and watch his startled expression as he recognizes Jane. We make our way to the bar.

I pull a roll from my front pocket big enough to choke a horse and peel off a crisp hundred. I hold it up before the bartender. "Seem?"

He nods and continues to polish the spotless mahogany bar-top. I indicate a round for the house with an upraised finger and a circular motion. "Por favor." I'm getting good at this.

He nods again as he picks up the bill.

"De on de voce' e?" he asks. Ah, a familiar question.

"Eu soy do States," I answer. He nods once more as he starts to pull different brands of beer from the cooler below the counter. He pops the caps as the patrons start amassing to claim their free beer. There's a fair amount of good cheer in the process.

Like a shepherd over his new flock, I return the gracious smiles. I watch Dom out of the corner of my eye. He's yet to make his approach, but I'm confident that he will. He's in the company of an appealing older lady, very prim and proper. A classic beauty, some would say. Dom is in the process of giving her billiards pointers. A moment of watching him convinces me she will not be getting better and that his game is not on par with mine. His stance, bridge, cue-grip and stroke give him away.

I personally conform to the style of 80 percent of the world's top players, Willie Mosconi and Minnesota Fats among them. I decide that playing him will be like taking candy from a baby. I could probably beat him with broom stick. I chuckle at the thought.

Jane leans in and runs her tongue up the side of my neck, stopping just short of my ear. I can feel her hot breath as she whispers: "Here he comes, Steven Paul. How am I doing so far?"

Stirring, Jane's role-playing is off to a damn good start. I almost wonder if this is the same Jane we met on the plane.

Dom and his lady friend, out of politeness I'm sure, retrieve their free round. "Ah, TWA Jane, if I'm not mistaken. I'm surprised to see you here."

He partially extends his hand and Jane reluctantly extends hers. He bows and kisses the top of her hand. Presumptuous, I think. I can almost feel Jane cringe.

He leers. "It's always a pleasure."

"Dom," is all she says.

"This is Rosanne and your young companions, Jane?"

I field the question. "Esteban Pablo and this lovely lady on my right is Candy."

"True, quite lovely. It's a pleasure to make both your acquaintances," he says but doesn't offer his hand.

"If it's not too presumptuous of me, what brings you to my neck of the woods, Jane?"

"Esteban has agreed to give us girls some billiard tips."

"Ah, a player are you, Esteban? Esteban Pablo, unusual name for a blond-haired, blue-eyed American—assuming you're American."

"Well, Dom, if I may be so bold to call you Dom, Esteban is what I go by south of the equator and I've been known to knock the balls around some."

Jane, with a sultry look that makes me proud, leans in and begins rubbing my chest.

"He's quite good at a lot of things, Dom. Wouldn't you agree, Candy?"

"That he is, rides them hard and puts them away wet. And, oh, he's definitely American, all right"

Both the girls giggle. Rosanne reddens.

"Yes, God bless America," Dom says with smugness.

Candy leans into me. "Perhaps you're interested in a game. I have a lot of faith in our man."

"Surely you jest. No offense, Esteban, but you still look wet behind the ears."

"A mistake that's brought many a man down from his perch," Candy says.

"A passionate woman, I see. I like that trait in a woman. Perhaps we can make the game interesting—a gentlemen's wager?" He smiles with self-assurance. "Perhaps $20 per game is not too rich for your blood, Esteban?"

I laugh and mimic his voice. "Surely you jest. That sounds more like tip money at the local titty bar."

The girls giggle. Rosanne cracks a small smile. Dom seems to be unable to reply for a second. He regains some of his composure.

"By all means, then a counter proposal is in order."

I physically brighten. "Now that's the spirit, Dom. What's a friendly wager among good sports? Am I right, Dom? Let's say a C-note is in order."

My own smile of self-assurance broadens.

"By all means."

Our conversation is garnering the attention of others. I now notice one patron that doesn't seem to fit in and is hovering near. He appears fit and capable. Bingo, it registers, this cat is keeping an eye on his boss. I glance around but don't catch the same vibe from any of the others present.

I down my beer and indicate another round. Candy digs into her clutch purse, pulls out one of her own hundreds and waves it in the air. "Taking side bets."

That's my girl. Several take small side bets against her hundred. Andy takes $20. Yep, got to love him—that's my boy.

"Well, Dom, it looks like we have us a game."

I extend my hand now that most of the posturing is behind us. We both try to squeeze the life out of each other's hand. I wink, I've got big strong hands for a youngster.

Dom waves his arms expansively. "Pick a table."

I take a sip of my fresh beer. "Your table will service. I suggest 8-ball, call your pockets not your kisses, must drive object ball or cue ball to the rail and all fouls result in ball in hand."

I watch as he runs a finger around his oppressive shirt collar.

"Lag for break?" he asks.

I select a 19-ounce cue from the nearest rack and roll it across the table's felt. The cue tests true and the leather tip is pleasantly rounded and worn.

"By all means, be my guest," I say.

The cue feels like an old friend to the touch. At the ripe old age of 17, I'm no stranger to the game. There're only a few things I do exceedingly well and shooting pool is one of them. This is a secret that I don't share with anyone—being exceedingly good at only a few things, that is.

I watch as Dom dusts his hands on a talc cone. I see his move as a show of nervousness. A good player needs no talc. I take a bill from my pocket and use it to clean my cue's tapered shaft. The cloth in the paper works well at removing the oils. Sorry, Dom, you won't catch me with talc on my hands.

He makes a decent lag. I chalk my stick and feign an attempt to beat his lag. I have no need to break first because I will be breaking from here on out. I'm not playing for the sole purpose of gambling. I decide that my purpose here is to knock the arrogant bastard down a few notches and oh, to ensure that Candy wins all her side bets, including Andy's $20.

If the game was about gambling, I'd string Dom along by barely eking out wins and by keeping my win/loss ratio close enough to keep him in the game and gambling. The secret, my friends, is to always keep your opponent hopeful that his luck will change. For those of you who have never played pool or billiards, the game is more than a game of skill. Even a skilled player can often be brought to his knees by the simple doubling of the bet, or by being talked into spotting you games in a race to ten. The psychological pressure to win will often cause him or her to choke on the money ball.

Here's another useful tip: after casually chalking your stick, set the chalk slightly to either side of the opponent's called pocket. The chalk will subconsciously draw the eye and, nine out of ten times, the object ball will strike the exact spot on the rail where your chalk rests. No, no need to thank me for sharing this stored knowledge. Oh, and always, I mean always, chalk your cue between shots. There's no excuse for ever miscuing and it's a mite embarrassing as well.

Dom lays into his break and jumps the cue ball off the table. What a shame. Two stripes and a solid and I get ball in hand. Jumping the cue ball off the table is a needless mistake and can be avoided by the use of top English on the break. The other beauty is that with top English, after the cue-ball bounces back from the break, it will run back through the rack.

As a true sportsman, I opt for the solids despite the fact there are more stripes on the table. Or maybe I'm taking the solids because they sit in better position on the table?

I place the cue ball on the table to my advantage. I always shoot with at least the next two or three shots in mind and my goal in taking the shot is to make my next shot as easy as possible. I use English on every shot unless I want the cue ball to stop in its tracks on contact with the object ball. And, as pretty as banks look, I prefer to cut a ball when possible and practical.

From the cue's spot, I run the table on Dom and pocket the 8-ball. Running the table on a nine-foot table is actually easier than running the table on a smaller table because the tabled balls are less cluttered. Sure, there is added green, but as you develop your game and confidence, the difference becomes negligible.

I innocently shrug my shoulders. "I must have gotten lucky."

He tosses $100 on the table and mumbles something: "Right, lucky." If I'm not mistaken.

I roll the pocketed and un-pocketed balls to Dom's end of the table, the rack end of the table, that is. In the next few seconds, there's pandemonium. His body guard yells, "He's got a gun!" and draws on me. Andy and Jim draw on him. The bartender pulls a double barrel from under the counter. Felix draws on the bartender and Candy, bless her heart, sticks the 25 in Dom's back.

"Dom, tell your man to set his gun on the table or I'll blow your spine out!" Candy orders.

Dom nods. "Miguel, put the gun on the table."

The bodyguard complies and I retrieve his piece. It's a Taurus 9mm. A decent gun. I drop the clip, eject the chambered round and hand the pieces back to Miguel.

"Can't we all just get along," I say and smile. "Your rack, Dom, I believe."

The guns slowly disappear and the commotion dims.

"Exactly who are you, Esteban?"

"As I told you, Dom I go by Esteban Pablo south of the equator, but you have nothing to fear from me as long as you don't cross me. If I meant you any harm, you would already be dead. Now, as custom dictates, I believe it's your rack."

He looks flustered by the ordeal but sucks it in. He starts to rack. "Very well."

To add insult to injury, I pay for a round with Dom's hundred and instruct the bartender to keep the change. As beads of sweat form on Dom's brow, I quickly relieve him of an additional four bills.

In frustration and embarrassment, Dom lays his cue on the table.

"Well, I can see I've been bested."

I imagine the concession was a difficult one. I give him a small point for that, but at the same time, I'll likely have to kill this man. That's a thought that will give one pause. I decide it's now time to put salve on his wounds. I stick out my hand.

"Good game, Dom. How about you and your lady friend join the girls and me for a round or two of something stronger. Oh, and tell Miguel if it makes him feel any better, he can put the bullets back in his gun." I grin. "I'll buy."

"Well, I suppose that would give me the opportunity to ascertain who you are and what you're up to."

I throw my arm across his shoulders.

"That's the spirit, Dom," I say and steer him toward a lone table. Rosanne and the girls join us.

"Esteban, as a true carioca, I must insist on a pitcher of cachaça," Dom says with a recaptured flair.

Quick to regain his composure, I note.

"So, Jane, how did you manage to tie up with such a young gun-toting group? By the way, Esteban, one needs to watch out for the military and police when unlawfully carrying firearms."

"I'll be sure to pass that tip on to your bodyguard."

Dom attempts to suppress a chuckle. "Touché, Esteban. Jane, forgive me for being so inquisitive, but you were about to say?"

"They're frequent guests on our international flights."

"Intriguing... A group so young yet so worldly. So, Esteban what exactly do you do?"

I throw out one of my favorites. "If I told you, Dom, I'd have to kill you."

The girls giggle. Rosanne stifles one.

"I suppose. Curious, though." He stops in thought. "Ah, our drinks. I'd like to propose a toast."

He pours everyone a glass and raises his.

"To Jane and her young companions. Let the gods watch over you in your travels."

I raise my own glass. "I don't know about the rest of you, but I can drink to that. Well, truth be known, I can drink to almost anything."

I toss back my drink. My girls, I like to think of them as my girls, toss their drinks back as well. Rosanne takes a sip of hers. A hand falls in my lap from each side. Does it get any better than this?

"I must say, Esteban, you have truly piqued my interest. Young, armed, protected, a traveler in the company of a pair of beautiful women and you seemingly have a total disregard for money. Remove young from the equation and it screams drug dealer."

"Close, but no cigar, Dom. Let's call my field of expertise procurements. I'm a capitalist through and through. A believer in the principles of supply and demand. One might even say I'm a commodities broker, so to speak. My help often involves the underdog."

He claps. "I must meet your speech writer. That aside, when I look at you, Esteban, I stumble upon your youth."

"Dom, sometimes the apple doesn't fall far from the tree."

"Ah, perhaps I'm starting to get the picture despite the fact that you like to muddle things with your clichés and riddles." He smiles and refills the glasses around the table. He snaps his fingers for another pitcher.

That I do. I love my clichés and also adages, quotes known and unknown and meaningless phrases and sayings. I have to admit to myself, I love to sling the bullshit.

Dom turns back to Jane. "So, Jane, when do you take to the skies again?"

"Oh, Dom." She stirs her drink with a finger and sucks the sweetness from it. "I'm having so much fun and receiving so much satisfaction, I believe I'll take some leave time."

Hmm, Jane would make for a fine actress. I feel a stirring as I start to believe her myself. The girl's warm hands in my lap doesn't help.

"Esteban, you and your young companions might care to join me at my villa tomorrow. Perhaps, if I'm reading you right, there's an opportunity here to explore a mutual area of interest."

"Perhaps there is, Dom."

"And perhaps you'll give me the opportunity to recoup some of my losses."

"At pool? I'd love to, Dom, but I'm afraid it's not going to happen for you."

"May I suggest some other competition, oh, say... Tennis? You do play tennis don't you, Esteban?"

"Does a bear shit in the woods?"

He smiles.

"I think I'm starting to like you."

Well, tennis is not something I excel at, but I do have a passable game and a serve on which I've worked hard. In addition, I clearly have youth and likely speed on him.

"Well, Dom, it looks like we've got us a game."

"Splendid, splendid, Esteban. Shall we start early? It's a significant ride—an hour and a half out. I'm tucked away slightly east of Ouro Pleto on a rolling hillside overlooking a wonderful valley. Where might you be staying, Esteban?"

"The Palace."

"Shall I send a car?"

"Sure, one to follow."

"Ah, cautious I see. I don't suppose I can talk you into leaving your multiple arms at the Palace?"

"Sorry, no—not a chance."

He laughs. "Fair enough, I suppose. You and your men haven't shot me yet."

"Hey, Dom, I haven't shot you yet either," Candy says with a smile.

"That you haven't, Candy." He rises from the table. "Well, if there's nothing further, will ten-ish be acceptable? Shall I have them ring your room when they arrive?"

"Suite, it's 'suite.' We're staying in suite 704," Jane says as she squeezes my leg.

Do we have a bed-mate? Could one such as I be so fortuitous? Only time will tell.

"Then my lovely companion and I shall be on our way." He bows. "Lovely ladies, Esteban, until tomorrow. It's been a pleasure."

The crew joins us at our table.

"Well, that was interesting," Felix says.

"Steve-O, did you catch his man's voice?"

"Yeah, couldn't miss it. Sounded like an old mafioso, like Wallace described to me, as if he was speaking with mothballs in his mouth."

"Man, there were a lot of wide eyes when all the hardware came out," Felix says.

We all laugh.

"Who do you think was faster on the draw? Andy or Candy?" I ask no one in particular.

"Candy for sure," says Jim.

"Yeah, it was Candy by a mile," says Felix.

"That's the way I saw it," says Jane.

"Whatever," says Andy.

We all laugh, except Andy of course.

"Sorry Andy, I couldn't help myself," Jane says.

"Well, Steve-O, as unlikely as it would seem, you got us an invite to his home. Do you think we will find Melissa there and get a chance to free her?"

"Good question. The answer, of course, is that your guess is as good as mine. If Dom doesn't know about Melissa's disappearance, an unlikely scenario, we know his bodyguard does."

"I say we should have taken both of them hostage," Andy says. I reach over and squeeze his shoulder.

"Let's have another round and head in."

I raise an empty long-neck and signal for another round.

"That was good, Steve-O. Procurements, a commodities broker, underdogs. You come up with some good shit."

We all laugh.

"So, in what kind of commodities are we involved, Esteban?"

"Why, Felix, Dom is a suspected leftist and the country's ruled by a military regime, so quite naturally, we're international arms dealers."

I smile in satisfaction as the rest laugh.

"Fucking international arms dealers. Who would have thought?" Jim says.

We shoot the shit as we drink our final round. Although I'm sure the bartender is happy to have our money, he does seem to be relieved when we settle up and head for the door.

The sun is gone and the air is cool as we step out into the night. The area is more alive now in this early evening hour. I suspect it to be around 8:00 p.m. or so. I take a cautious look around. No one seems to be paying us much mind—no shots ring out. I always take that as a good sign. We load up in the Chevy. She fires right up without a bang, also a good sign. I put her into gear and we're off.

"Honey, where are we going to buy our tennis rackets and gear?"

"Ah, Candy, plan to play some tennis, do you?"

"I plan to look and play the part, so I'll be needing a cute little outfit and tennies. Besides, we might get a doubles game going."

"I plan to play my part as well," Jane says.

I look past Candy to Jane grinning back at me.

"You ladies do know that we're kind of on a mission to rescue someone? That things might turn nasty?"

"Yep, that's why you need us for backup," Candy answers.

"So, I take it you'll be calling in, Jane?" I ask.

"Yeah, I'll get a girlfriend to take my flight."

"Well then, you know we'll be leaving out early. It might be best if you stay over," I manage to say without losing it, but it's a close call.

"That's what we were thinking," Candy says.

Oh, the joy of those words: "That's what we were thinking." But, could it also be a continuation of their earlier plot against me? I hear my dad. "What plot, Son? You're being paranoid. They both want you."

"They do?" Oops, I believe I said that out loud.

"Did you say something, honey?"

"No..."

I realize I've been hearing dad's voice more often lately. I decide to send him a thought back. "I'll try and make you proud, Pa." I don't really call him "Pa," it's something that Chuck Connor's son on The Rifleman would say. But, hey, it was a funny thought, okay?

"I don't know about Andy and Felix, but I'm going back to the Academia da Cachca or whatever you call it, for even just beer" Jim says.

"I'm with you, Jim," Felix says.

"Me too," Andy says.

Candy tugs at my sleeve. "Let's go, too. Jane?"

"Absolutely."

"Well, I guess that's settled, children of the corn. The Chevy is pointing the way." It doesn't take much to make me want to go, but I need to call Wallace. I know he's going mad waiting on some news. "Kids, I have to stop by the Palace and give Wallace a call. It's the right thing to do. Y'all can go on, or wait for me to come back down."

Candy kisses me on the cheek. "We'll wait for you, honey."

I stop at the Palace and make the call. There's more relief in Wallace's voice then one could imagine. I tell him about our invite to Dom's villa in the morning and that we've met the guy with the strange voice. I assure him that we are properly armed and will be exceedingly careful. He thanks me over and over again and asks me to please forward his sentiments to my crew. While in the suite, I also retrieve a message from the desk that Sandra called. I call the number she left and briefly tell her that all is well and to consider herself as good as home. Much like Wallace, I can hear the relief in her voice. She tells me there is something else she needs to tell me, but it has to be in person. I promise her I'll hear her out and see her soon.

It turns out Jim wasn't exaggerating. The indoor-outdoor place is hopping. I soon learn the place serves over 500 varieties of cachaça. Fortunate for me, right? Andy lets me in on the fact they serve traditional Brazilian cooking. I thank him but decline any food recommendations from him, realizing there's a good chance I may never learn the Portuguese word for ketchup.

We take an outdoor table and for symmetry purposes, I evenly space the girls, one to each side of me. The girls are hungry and I'm a mite hungry, too. I tell the crew to order up.

"This one's on Dom Fucking Pedro." I don't say it too loudly for I'm sure Dom is known at this watering hole. The place emits the feel of an upper scale botequim. We all opt for our waitress's recommendation of picanha, a cut of steak, along with all its trimmings.

By the way, our waitress is young and vibrant with a refreshing bounce in her step and the most endearing smile. In other words, she looks like she's going to get a healthy tip. The girls choose a cachaça concoction and the boys and I beer. I'm ever mindful of my tennis match early tomorrow. I rub my hands together in thought and secretly hope the girls don't keep me up too late. Yeah, right.

I ask our waitress to invite a pair of handsome young ladies two tables over to join us to tell them we're celebrating. Dinner and drinks are on us. Candy pinches my thigh under the table before I can complete my request, but I'm one step ahead of her. I'm already expecting something painful and I grin and bear it.

The pair decide to take up the offer and join us at our table. They prove to be good company and their presence at the table sure brightens the crew's day. They appear to be in their late teens and I'm amazed at their capacity to eat and drink. It turns out that they're from Paris and they're having such a fun time in Rio that they will not want to leave when their time is up.

I have to concur—Rio's one hell of a party town. But as much as I hate it, I have important things to do tomorrow. As far as the girls and me, I make the noble decision for us—we need to get back to the suite. The girls are again feeling little pain and are in a giggly mood. I'm right behind them with a decent beer buzz myself and to put it mildly, I'm eager to get back to our suite. I assume you get the picture by now?

I pay our tab, tip our waitress right nicely and leave the boys to fend for themselves. Who knows, perhaps one or more will get lucky. I've clearly upped the odds for them. Hey, I do what I can.

I halfheartedly listen to the girl's chatter on the short drive back to the Palace. My mind is flooded with could-be situations. The outside of the Palace is alive in activity. I park where I can. Passing through the lobby, the girls order up a bucket to "wind down with." I'm not hating on them for it. Coming off the elevator, I stick my arm out to block their exit and signal for quiet. I mouth to them: "We have company."

I pull my Colt and, out of the corner of my eye, catch Candy extracting her 25 from her clutch purse. What a trooper. Don't you love her?

Centered in the hallway and to the right side of our door, stands no other than Miguel himself with his own pistol drawn. Hmm, imagine that. I ease my way toward him as silently as I can and watch him rap on our door a second time. He doesn't sense my approach until the muzzle of my gun is pressed behind his ear. The .45 emits an audible, double click as I cock the hammer.

"Miguel, Miguel. Fancy meeting you here."

"Shit!" he says.

"I reach around and relieve him of his gun.

"I'll be taking that, thank you very much." I drop the suite's key to the floor before him. "If you would be so kind as to unlock the door."

"Shit," he says again. He's clearly not having a good day, I suspect. I cock his Taurus and hand it to Jane.

"Girls, you have my permission to shoot him if he tries anything funny."

I give him a swift kick in the ass despite his intimidating persona. It's easier to do when one holds the gun.

"Hurry up and unlock the fucking door, Miguel."

He's flushed beet red as he retrieves the key from the floor. It takes him several attempts to insert it into the lock. We step through the open door.

"Miguel, Miguel. Now, what do you propose we're to do with you? Your presence sure complicates things here."

"I say we shoot him with my 25. It shouldn't make more than a pop," Candy says with conviction.

"Hold on there, turbo," I tell Candy as I kick the door shut. "But I will take it under advisement. For now, grab something with which to tie his hands."

"How about a robe belt?"

"Perfect. But we need to hurry before the bellhop arrives with our bucket of beer."

"Ten-four, honey."

I bind his hands tight behind his back and cut a section of the belt with my trusty Uncle Henry to gag him. Gagged, I usher him into the bedroom. I shake my head as I look him over.

"If you only knew, Miguel. You could fuck up a wet dream here, you know that?"

It's meant as a rhetorical question, but being gagged and all he's not in much of a position to answer.

"I'll take the gag off in a minute, after the beer arrives. Then we'll have to figure out what you're doing in my upscale neighborhood trying to sneak up on me. And, oh, to be fair, I feel duty bound to inform you that I keep my Uncle Henry honed to a razor's edge."

The awaited knock announces our expected delivery. The girls quickly deal with the bellhop and merrily send him on his way.

"Turn around, Miguel," I order. I untie his gag. "If you'll be so kind as to join us on the terrace."

I pop the cap from three long-necks for the girls and myself. I have Miguel sit and I take a seat opposite of him. The girls maintain a safe distance and vigil over me.

"Feel free to begin any time, but keep this in mind: for every lie I suspect you tell, I remove a finger. And then one of two things will happen. One, you run out of fingers, or two, you run out of blood. Not pleasant by any means. So, let's try not to resort to violence, shall we?"

"I know why you're here, Esteban, or whatever your real name is."

I lean back and steeple my fingers. "Do tell."

"You're here about Mel—the girl from Texas."

I slam my open hand hard on the table, causing everyone to flinch.

"Girl? What fucking girl are you talking about?"

He seems taken back for a second. "The girl from Texas. I answered a call meant for Dom and was told by a reliable source that someone from the states matching your description was asking questions."

I laugh.

"So, what the fuck are you here for, Miguel—to shake me down?"

"Yeah. You give me, say, $50,000 U.S. and I won't tell Dom what you're here for."

I laugh again and lean forward.

"Two slight flaws, Miguel. First and foremost, you're not in any fucking position to shake anyone down and second, I don't know anything about any fucking girl." I lean back again. "So, you see now we really do have a problem."

"But... But if you're not here about the girl, why are you running around town asking about Dom?"

"Didn't this evening kind of spell it out for you?" I stare at him long and hard—he doesn't respond.

"I represent a fucking arms dealer, okay? I was given orders to find Dom. Sell him and your little dissident group some small arms. Shit man, wake up. You're under military rule and have been since '64. Isn't change what you leftists want? Change?"

"Why the charade at the Bilhares Guanabara?"

"Not a subject you breach lightly. So, when I learned he was heading to the pool-hall, I thought I'd a have a little fun with him. Haven't you ever been 17, man? Plus, I've heard things about Dom, that, well, made me want to fuck with him some, Capisce?"

He bangs his head on the table. "Shit, you don't know nothin' about the girl."

"What do I need another fucking girl for. I've got too many as is." And I can't even get them in bed at the same time—yet. I qualify my thought with a smile.

He sighs deeply. "I guess I fucked up, huh?"

I stand, take a deep pull from my beer, step to the railing and stare down at the night's activity below.

"I don't suppose..." Miguel begins.

I raise my hand to silence him, but keep my back turned. Let him stew for a minute, I decide, while I figure out what to do.

"I still say I pop a cap in his ass," Candy says.

"Why don't we keep him tied up until morning and see what his boss thinks about him trying to shake me down?"

"And being disarmed for the second time tonight," Jane adds.

"Aw man, Esteban. Fuckin' let me go, okay? There's nothin' for me to say to Dom anyway."

The girls follow my lead and laugh. I don't believe Miguel finds things so funny for he forgoes joining in.

"How much do you have in your pockets?" I ask.

"What?"

"Your pockets? Your wallet? How much fucking money do you have?"

"What? You going to fuckin' rob me now? You're fuckin' kiddin', right?"

"Let's say I'm thinking about letting you fucking post bond. That, of course, is contingent on how much money you have on you." I grin. "Jane, let me hold his pistol. Miguel, stand up. Girls, empty his pockets."

I watch in amusement as the girls empty his pockets and wallet.

"Count it out."

"Two hundred and forty-two dollars," Candy says and laughs. "Dom must not pay well."

"Split it between you."

"What about the credit cards? We could pay our hotel tab with them," Jane says and manages a grin as wide as mine. That knocks the wind out of Miguel's sails. He collapses back in his seat.

"Aw man, shit," he mutters.

We laugh some more. I slide my open knife across the table.

"We'll let him make it this time. Jane, cut him loose."

Hands free, Miguel wearily stands.

"You're dismissed," I say. "You can leave us now."

"But... But my gun."

"Sorry, Hoss. You forfeit it to the cause. You'll get a chance to buy it back. Here's a parting tip for you: bet on me tomorrow. Now beat it."

I rub the circulation back into my hands.

"Thanks a lot," he says with little enthusiasm.

We listen for the front door to click and burst into laughter. After a while, Jane catches her breath.

"You guys are too much fun. I don't know how I ever made it without you."

I wink. "I propose we take our bucket into the bedroom. Maybe watch some foreign TV or something."

"I'm game... Jane?"

"Wouldn't miss it for the world."

Oh, there is a god, I think, as I gallantly show the way. "I told you so, Son," I hear dad say. I stop in the bathroom first to brush my teeth and when I'm done, I check myself in the mirror and wink at my reflection.

"You are one lucky fucker," I mouth before stepping out. I bow. "All yours, ladies."

I watch as Jane totes her small case into the bathroom. Candy follows with her larger case. I overhear the sound of giggles before the door shuts.

I toe my boots off and shuck my clothes down to my boxers as I merrily whistle a Steve Miller tune. I use my Uncle Henry to pop the cap of one of the long-necks, yank the comforter from the massive bed, toss it to the floor and happily take up my position dead-center. I change tunes to "Midnight Rider" by the Allman Brothers.

I pat the mattress on either side and warm up for their highly anticipated arrival.

"Come here sex kittens," I say and crack myself up. I try another: "Now, now, ladies. No fighting. There's plenty of me for both of you."

The bathroom door opens and Candy steps out. Although I've seen her naked a dozen or so times now, she's breathtaking in her lacy azure teddy with matching panties.

She does a spin for me. "What do you think, Big Boy?"

"Beautiful. You're as beautiful as they get."

She playfully jumps into the bed and pulls my boxers down.

"We won't be needing these." She tosses them to the floor. Oh, the joy—music to my ears. She takes a hold of me with a small hand. "Missed me, I see." She strokes me a couple times, looks me deep in the eyes and then passionately kisses me.

"Jane will be right out," she huskily whispers.

I believe I'll never get tired of this. Her Chanel #5 compliments her beauty.

The bathroom door opens, I swallow hard in anticipation as Jane steps out. I do a double take and almost, I stress almost, go soft. There standing in the doorway, makeup free, in sweats, with curlers in her hair, is the second half of my fantasy: Jane.

She smiles. "Well, what were you expecting, Big Boy? To get us both in the bed?"

I manage a feeble "yeaahh."

They both burst into laughter.

I smile. "Okay, good one, Jane. It looks like you girls got me."

Jane returns the smile. "Not yet, Big Boy." She yanks out one curler at a time and tosses them to the floor and then, in one sweeping move, pulls the sweat top over her head and drops it beside her.

Oh, bless her, she's bra-less and she's sporting a pair of most every man's dreams. In short order, she removes her sweat bottoms, too. To my heart-thumping delight, she's pantie-less and beautiful down there too—her bikini trim highlighted by the surrounding tan. The sight of her makes me swallow, for real this time. Patience is a virtue. I smile, life is good.

Jane climbs into the bed on the other side of me. I pull loose the bow-tied lace securing Candy's teddy and she allows it to slip from her shoulders. Although not as big as Jane's, Candy's breasts are equally perfect. I watch as she slips her panties down to a single foot and kicks them to the floor.

"What do you propose, Candy?" Jane asks like they don't already have something planned out.

"Let's have some fun with him."

I'm here to tell you, fun in this past week has taken on a whole new meaning for me.

"I say we take turns with devil boy and see which one of us can make him cum first." Candy continues, "Then five strokes apiece, per turn, and I get to go first since I found him."

"And to make things fair, I'll hold out as long as possible," I add with glee. "Let the games begin!"

Candy pats me on the belly. "I know you will honey. I know you'll do your best. Now if you'll be quiet long enough, I'll get this thing started."

I vigorously nod my assent, keeping as quiet as I can. Candy straddles me and guides me in. With the escape of a single "Oh" she takes all of me.

"That doesn't officially count as a stroke." She informs Jane and giggles again.

"Okay, here we go: One... Two... Three... Four... Five! Six! Seven! Eight! Nine! Ten!"

"Hey, you hussy!" Jane yells and laughs. "That's cheating!"

They begin to laugh and tussle. It takes Jane a few seconds to dislodge Candy. They roll and tumble from the bed, landing with a thud. The end-table lamp goes with them.

"Ow! I friggin' bumped my head," Candy yells. "Slut!"

"Hussy!"

"Slut. Hey, hey no friggin' tickling!... No tickling..."

"It's my turn you little hussy."

"Okay, okay, let me up! Let me up! Stop, let me up!"

"Say uncle."

"Uncle! Uncle! Uncle!"

They giggle climbing back into bed.

"Okay, that was fun," Jane says catching her breath. Without preamble, she mounts me and guides me in. "At least this one is cooperating. Okay, here we go, Big Boy. One... two... three... four... four-and-a-half, four-and-nine-sixteenths, four-and-five-eights..."

"Hey! We're not trying to teach them fractions here," Candy yells as they begin to struggle and giggle again. "My turn again!"

"Okay, okay, Candy. It's your turn again."

Candy remounts. Jane giggles as she moves to straddle my face.

"I'm going to introduce Big Boy to the little man in the boat."

"Hey, I planned to kiss him at least once," Candy says.

"And you still can if you like the taste of raspberries."

Well folks, it's like this: I knew this day would come.

The little man in the boat is prominently displayed before me and I take to this new experience like a fish takes to water. I vary my tongue and lip action and I know things are working when Jane's giggles turn to soft moans. I grab her by each of her firm cheeks to steady her and keep her in place. All I can see of Candy is the tips of her fingers on Jane's arms, but her actions don't go unnoticed. It doesn't get any better than this, my friends.

Only moments elapse before I can feel Jane's increased body tension—deep moans escape her lips before spasms overtake her. As her spasms start to subside, she topples to the mattress.

Ah, now that was fun. Catching her breath once again, Jane turns toward me and gives me a long hard kiss.

"Thanks," she says throatily.

"Roll me over, honey," Candy says. In one swift motion I do and she wraps her legs around me. I can feel Candy's hot quick breath on my neck.

"Now honey, now please," she whispers in my ear before forcing her lips to mine. I feel her body convulse beneath me and I release in a gush. I can feel both our hearts beat as we hold each other tight.

"I think I love you, Steven Paul," Candy intimately whispers.

"And I love you too," I whisper back. We both glance at Jane, she's down for the count, fast asleep.

"Hussy," Candy says and we both laugh. In a state of bliss, I drift off to sleep.

Sometime in the early hours, I groggily open my eyes to find Candy curled almost in a fetal position with her cheek resting on my chest and her hand tucked under her chin.

I turn to what aroused me from sleep, yes, you heard me right: "Aroused me from sleep." Jane, in the semi-darkness, has taken it upon herself—not that I'm complaining mind you—to wake me by giving me head. I run my fingers through her long soft hair and silently encourage her to continue. No longer under the beer buzz, the sensation is overwhelming and it only takes her moments to complete her mission.

I slowly exhale my breath as I watch Jane kiss my belly and, much like Candy, make a comfortable spot in the crook of my arm. One in each arm—got to love it. I rub the back of Jane's neck as I drift back to sleep. My last conscious thought: it doesn't get any better than this.

Chapter 17

I awake to the shrill ring of the bedroom's phone. There're collective moans all around. I painfully smile and smack Candy's bare ass. Misery does love company, you know.

"Ouch! Shit." She rubs her ass. "Honey, don't do that."

The phone pierces the brain once again.

"Argh, aren't you going to get that," Candy says holding her head and covering her ears.

"Jane's closer," I say.

Jane takes a stab at reaching it, but only manages to send the phone clattering to the floor.

"Shit!" she says as she leans over the edge of the bed to retrieve it and moons me in the process. I pinch her on the ass and she slaps at me with her free hand. After a few fumbles, she reels in the phone by its cord.

"Hello... Yeah... Yeah... Give us 30 minutes."

She drops the receiver to the floor, sits up, runs her fingers through her hair and stretches. She turns to look at Candy and I and grins.

"I'd laugh if it wouldn't hurt."

"And you look beautiful this morning yourself," Candy says as she rubs her temples. Candy looks comical with part of her bangs spiked in the air. Comical but loveable.

"Well, my giggling duo, sometimes you pay when you play. I personally feel wonderful."

I manage a grin through the pain and pat each on the leg as I scoot my way down to the edge of the bed.

"Cheerleaders, time to get ready for the big game. To start, I propose a group shower."

I get a pair of thrown pillows in response. As I step into the bathroom, I whistle a lively tune that I make up on the fly. After last night, it will take more than a hangover to dampen my mood.

The shower sparks some life into me. As I step out, the girls step in. I'm tempted to step back in. I don't know if I can trust them in the shower together without me. I chuckle at the thought.

I call the boys and tell them we roll in 20. Since we know that I'm not one to kiss and tell, I hope when they see me, my grin doesn't give me away.

I dress in my usual attire of ostrich and Izod, my new usual attire of one week. I wait on my crew's arrival and for my girls to get ready. I sure like the thought of that: "My girls." With last night's conquest, I feel it's safe to say that my harem's official count now stands at two and several strong possibles. Life is good.

My musing is interrupted by a knock at the door. Ah, the crew's arrived. I open the door for them and right out of the gate, I notice something different about them—different in that they're not grinning from ear-to-ear like myself.

Jim shakes his head. "Of course. Let me guess. You somehow weaseled your way into getting them both in bed at the same time."

"Well, I wouldn't call it 'weaseled,' and not being one to kiss and tell, I can only describe it as unbelievable."

"Esteban, my man, you got my vote," Felix says.

"Vote for what?" Andy asks.

I ignore Andy.

"I take it you boys didn't fare so well last night. Here I invite two cuties to the table, nearly charm them out of their panties and leave them with you." I shake my head in mock disgust. "I'm too disappointed to even talk about it."

"Are we going to eat before we leave?"

I wink. "I ate in the middle of the night, so I'm not hungry."

"You're shitting, Steve-O."

I shrug. "Hey, what can I say? I shit you not. Ah, here comes the pair of sinners now."

"Whatever he's telling you, don't believe him," Jane says.

Candy nods in agreement. "Honey, did you tell them about our visitor last night?"

"Oh shit, I almost forgot. Miguel paid a visit. He tried to shake us down."

"How did you handle it, Esteban?"

"The only way I saw fit. I relieved him of his gun." I smile.

"And we robbed him of $242," Candy says and bestows on us her own special smile.

"Nah, man, you fucking robbed him too?" Felix says laughing.

I shrug again. "It seemed like the right thing to do at the time. Now, if you girls can hold your questions, we can be on our way."

"Fucking unbelievable, Steve-O," Jim says as he shakes his head.

"Hey, I'm still hungry here."

"Well, we're all set then," I say. "Let's roll."

On the elevator down, Jane proudly announces: "I've got Miguel's pistol in my purse, you know, to back you guys up."

We collectively look at her. I didn't realize that she had the pistol, but hey, that's fine with me—she's good at handling pistols. That thought pleasantly takes me back in time, hours back in time, that is.

Miguel and some other Dom crony meet us in the lobby.

"Keeping banker's hours, Miguel?" I ask for no logical reason now that I think about it.

"Yeah, Esteban, something like that. This is Raub. Raub, this is Esteban and his disciples."

Raub, scruffy and about 35, tries to give us a menacing eye. "Has Dom lost his fucking mind? What are we now, fucking babysitters?"

Candy kicks him in the shin and warns him: "Watch it, buster."

"Bitch!" he yells and goes to backhand her.

Miguel catches his arm. I can see he's trying to suppress a smile.

The crew and I openly laugh. Raub's expression indicates he doesn't take too kindly to being laughed at. He's not very friendly, I reason. Not much I can do about that but see if I can push his buttons. Perhaps not one of my better decisions, but I'm starting to feel frisky.

"Raub? Raub? Where have I heard that name before?" I ask myself out loud as we step into the morning sun. "Ah, I remember now..."

Everybody stops to hear what I'm fixing to say. I allow the suspense to drag out for a few seconds.

"Yeah, I remember now—that's the name for the North African Dung Beetle."

Yep, that one struck a nerve. Raub takes a swing at me, which I easily avoid. I counter with a quick left jab, snapping his head back and follow through with an audible straight right to the jaw. I try to punch through him. To my surprise and astonishment, he falls to the pavement. I'm here to tell you, it hurt—my hand that is. It's hurting like hell.

"That's for thinking about smacking my girl," I say as I reach down and remove his concealed weapon from his hidden shoulder holster. I realize that all my fake sparring with my heavy bag paid off. I hand the pistol to Jim. Miguel does nothing to stop me.

"That's my man," Candy says proudly as she hooks her arm through mine.

"Help him up, Andy, so we can get going. Miguel do they have an athletic store at the shopping center near the metro?"

"Yeah."

"Great. We need to stop there and purchase tennis gear."

A few people start to gather with concern for the downed Raub, but Miguel says something in Portuguese that seems to satisfy them.

Raub makes it shakily to his feet. Andy straightens his shirt for him. I stare Raub down.

"Can we try and play nice from here on out," I say but fail at suppressing a grin. I doubt I made a friend here. Well, no need crying over spilled milk, right?

He rubs his jaw. "I want my fucking pistol back."

"Take it up with Dom," Miguel says with amusement. I think Miguel suddenly feels better about losing his own pistol. He points to an older Cadillac. "We're in that olive Coupe de Ville."

"Nice ride," I say. "'66, is it not? With that rare 429?"

He simply nods before heading toward it, leaving Raub to follow. We pile into the Chevy.

"The way you're acquiring free guns, Steve-O, we sure wasted a bundle buying the others," Jim says.

"Man, Esteban, you almost took that dude's head off. You got my vote again."

"How did you know about the North African Dung Beetle?" Jane asks.

"I didn't. I made it up."

Jane looks across Candy at me and smiles. "I think I'm starting to see a pattern."

"Yeah, that he's full of shit. When are we going to eat?"

"Andy, I suggest that you find something to eat while we purchase our tennis gear."

"What's your plan for the day, Steve-O?"

"Quite naturally, I plan to win."

"Not that plan."

"We'll strategize on the way out."

I crank our car, back out and pull in behind the waiting Caddy. We follow Miguel and Raub the short ride to the shopping center and pull into a parking slot several cars over. Before us, there is a small athletic store. Inside, the tennis racket selection is slim, but they do have the racket of my choice, the Wilson Pro Staff "Stan Smith." My two-fold disappointment, however, is that it's pre-strung with a thick 15-gauge nylon and that it's strung at what feels to be about 55 pounds. I prefer a thinner and tighter string for the bite and the action. Oh well, that's life. As I mentioned, my game is passable. My favorite shot: a looping heavy topspin forehand. I use a full half-turn grip to maximize the spin and place the ball accurately on an inside or outside shot. My backhand, well now, that's a different story. A straight up and down grip and usually a slice, unless one sets up right and then I'll go quarter-turn and hit a topspin. I hate to admit it, but I run around a lot of the backhands.

The girls pick their rackets based on color. Not all girls mind you, but these pair do. Well, at least the place doesn't sell pink balls. I get a couple cans of Wilsons.

I'm a firm believer in practicing and playing with new balls.

I watch the girls try on their tennis attire and I highly concur on their selection. A healthy woman in any kind of short skirt does it for me. I think you get the picture by now. They pay for their own purchases and I remind them to thank Miguel. Despite Miguel's loss, I'm sure he'll approve of how his money has been spent.

We're soon on our way again and winding through the hillsides leading out of Rio. Ultimately, we hit Interstate 040 and head west.

"Esteban, what do you think?" Felix says.

"I believe we need to play it by ear. By the way, girls, do either of you have aspirin?"

"Aw, my poor baby, is your hangover hurting you?" Candy asks.

"Actually no, my fucking hand is killing me. Anyway, let's play it by ear. If we find Melissa and get a chance, we'll take her. What we're not going to do is get any of us shot. If we find her and can't grab her outright, we'll case the joint the best we can and regroup to form a plan."

"Here you go, honey," Candy says. "Sorry we don't have anything to wash them down with."

I dry swallow a couple and look in the rearview at my crew.

"I think it best if each of you stand apart as much as possible. That way you have more angles and it makes it harder to be taken if Dom gets any funny ideas."

"That makes sense, Steve-O," Jim says.

We pass through a small town named Juiz de Fora. According to the map in the Brazil book, we're at the third mark.

"What kind of tennis shoes did you buy, Steve?" Jane asks.

"Wilson Pro Staff, of course. I like the fact they're all leather and all white."

"I think our Converses are cute," Candy says.

Andy chuckles. "Too bad, Steve—you're not part of that Wilson family."

"Yeah and it's too bad that you drive a Pinto," I say.

"That's a pretty low blow, Steve-O."

"Isn't it, though," Felix says.

That should shut the peanut gallery up for a few, I think. We drive in silence. The hills we pass through are semi-tropical and I occasionally spot a parrot which I can't name and, for a moment, what I believe to be a Scarlet Macaw.

I look at my hand and hope Raub's jaw swells just as much. There's a steady throb and I wonder if the aspirins are going to help. Make no mistake, it hurts when you hit someone. I'll concentrate on kicking more in the future. I realize something funny: I don't recall my heartbeat changing any from the confrontation. I chalk it up to my increased confidence.

Candy turns to look over the seat. "So, what did happen with that cute pair from Paris?"

"Too much cachaça," Jim says. "But we hailed them a cab and made sure they made it back to their hotel. We could have walked, it was so close. 'Maria All Suites.' Nice."

"Well, that was very gentlemen-like of you guys," Candy says. "Steve, maybe you could pick up a few pointers about being a gentleman from these guys."

"Like how not to get the pussy. No thanks. Are you forgetting that I managed to get both you girls back safely and would have safely tucked you in...?"

Candy elbows me in the side.

"Ow. You get the point."

"We should be getting close," Candy says. "The sign we passed said 20 kilometers to Ouro Preto and Dom said it's before you get there."

We ride a few more miles until the Caddy brakes and slows. It turns into a gravel drive flanked by stone structures that stair to the outer grounds and secure the drive with a wrought iron gate. Raub gets out to unlock and open the gate. To my satisfaction, he rubs his chin as we follow the Caddy through. Raub closes the gate behind us. We wind our way a good half mile through the cut foliage before emerging into a clearing where we pass through a pair of concrete lions. Nice touch, Dom. The house, Dom's villa as he calls it, comes into view. The place is quite beautiful. Built in a Brazilian baroque style, it features tall, heavily-crowned and arched windows on the first floor and crowned doors at individual terraces on the upper. The house is a unique plum color trimmed in white and capped in Spanish tile. The grounds resemble a botanical garden with an abundance of palms, ferns, bananas, elephant ears and other tropical flora. The drive turns into pavers and circles around a pissing Cupid fountain. We park before the house. Dom awaits us in front of the house's massive twin doors which are beautifully carved out of oak.

"Ah, Esteban, how nice of you to have made it," Dom cheerfully greets us. He does his now familiar expansive gesture with his arms. "Welcome ladies and gentlemen to my humble abode. Ladies, I love your tennis attire."

To me, Dom looks amusing in his own all white tennis attire with a blue fleece sweater casually tied around his neck. This guy might not be playing with a full deck, I decide.

"Are they here yet?" A recognizable voice reaches us from inside the house and then Rosanne steps into view. She smiles showing perfectly capped white teeth. "Ah, there you kids are. Esteban, Candy, Jane and the entourage."

"Nice to see you again, Rosanne," I say.

The others echo my sentiments.

"Dom was kind enough to provide for some refreshments down by the courts," Rosanne informs us. "You know he's quite the accomplished tennis player."

"If you would be so kind as to follow me," Dom says. "We'll take a slight shortcut through the house."

The interior is eloquently and richly appointed. The place screams money. Dom is blasé in his description of different pieces of art as we pass by them. I have to give it to him with respect to his style.

We step out the back to a patioed area and pool and the place does, as Dom boasted, overlook a valley below. Centered in the larger of the fields is a dirt runway and a hangar.

"Beautiful place you have here, Dom," I say. "Are you a flyer too?"

Dom chuckles. "Too? As in, you're also a pilot, Esteban?"

I chuckle too.

"Quite naturally, cut my teeth on a crop duster, I did," I say reminding myself of a couple brothers from elementary school that we called the 'I did brothers' for everything that they said ended with an "I did."

"What do you have in the hangar?" I ask.

"A 172."

"Cessna, nice single propper, but limited range and non-existent payload." I arch one brow giving Dom my most inquisitive John Belushi impersonation.

"And what do you fly may I dare ask?"

"A Beechcraft Super King Air, of course."

Dom noticeably reddens. "Ah, a turbo prop. They have a civilian version?"

"Since '75." Out of the corner of my eye, I catch movement. Hmm, more security than meets the eye, I conclude. Fifty yards off and cut into the hillside is a pair of tennis courts. I internally cringe at their sight—fucking clay courts. Shit, I've never played on clay, something I should have foreseen. What I do know about clay courts are they're fast. I hope there's not much of a learning curve.

We make our way to the courts. To the left of them is a pair of canvas-covered observation tables, one of which is laden with fruit, finger sandwiches and a couple pitchers of iced tea. Andy eyes the finger sandwiches hard—he's not one into fruit.

"By all means, help yourself," Dom says in his most gracious voice.

"No beer?" I ask.

"Beer and tennis? Surely you jest."

"I jest you not." Remind you of, "I shit you not?"

"Very well. Anyone else care for a beer?"

He makes beer sound disgusting. My whole crew, girls and all, raise their hands. Miguel tentatively raises his, too. Dom scowls at him before pulling a walkie-talkie from his tennis bag and ordering a cooler full. I catch a faint smile on Miguel's face. I believe he's starting to have fun with us as a whole and at the expense of his boss.

I toe off my boots and change into my tennis gear right where I stand. The girls giggle as I tuck my pistol into the waistband of my tennis shorts.

"Seriously, you're not going to play with your weapon, are you?"

"Nope, but I'm going to seriously play with my pistol stuck in my waistband." I wink at him. "Keep you honest. Oh, and it serves as a hell of a tiebreaker as well."

There are plenty more chuckles and giggles to be heard. I pull a banana loose and peel it with fluid confidence. Well, I'm not sure if that's possible, but I'm trying to make up for the clay courts – play with his psyche some.

"One set, two sets, or best out of three?" I ask.

"I think that one set is sufficient and I believe I mentioned that I'm interested in recouping last night's losses."

"That you did. Make it more interesting? Say a thousand?"

That provokes a smile all the around with the exception of Dom and Raub, who is rubbing his jaw again.

"Very well, a thousand it shall be."

I smile. "That's the spirit, Dom."

Jane comes up behind me and begins massaging my neck and shoulders.

"Have to make sure that our man is loose, although, I can't imagine him being tense after last night."

She kisses me behind the ear.

A new face and our beer arrive. Another henchman, I think, as I grab a beer, pull the tab and take a decent pull from it.

"Ah, now that's good. All I need now is a cigarette and I'll be ready."

Dom gives me an incredulous look.

"Only fucking with you, Dom. Lighten up." I down my beer, wipe my mouth with the back of my hand and purposely belch.

"Let the games begin," I say with exuberance.

"Taking all side bets," Candy announces waving a hundred in the air. "Andy? Anyone?"

"I'll take that bet," Raub says.

"Let's see your money," Candy says gleefully.

"I've got the fucking money," Raub snaps.

I wave my racket in the air to get Raub's attention. "It's not nice to talk to your company like that, Raub."

Raub mumbles a barely audible "Fuck you" and Dom scowls at him. Peace and harmony. Don't you love it?

"Up or down?" I ask Dom as I prepare to spin my racket like a coin.

"Up."

I spin the racket in my hand and the W ends upside down.

"Sorry, Dom, I'll opt to serve first." I roll my head and shoulders. "Man, I feel good!"

I take a few warm up serves. Conclusion: not good, not bad, but workable. With the loose springy strings, I'm not able to generate much kick, but flat and down the middle feels decent. My service game goes fast. Dom only manages one return—a short high hopper that I easily put away with a heavy forehand.

I request a beer and a towel as we change sides. There wouldn't be any sweat at all but for the beer and the sun. The beer of the past week, I mean.

The second game proves to be more difficult. I actually get aced once when I get distracted momentarily by what appears to be a woman's face in an upstairs window. For a second, I question myself as to what I really saw. Dom almost wins after a couple of unforced errors. The loose strings cause my returns to go long and I have difficulty adjusting to sliding into the shots. The clay proves a slick and tricky surface. After a couple of long rallies and a few adds, I manage to put him away as my girls cheer me on.

As we start our third game, my service game again, I almost decide to ease off some. I start to feel sorry for the guy, but then I begin to think why feel empathy for someone who may well be holding Melissa against her will. Before I put him away, another thought pops up—if you annihilate Dom, big boy, you may also kill all hope of getting Melissa back. I throw the game without making it obvious. I throw the next two as well. Dom beams as my crowd starts to look dejected.

I rally to win the next two, lose the next and, winded and sweating profusely, I struggle to win the last two and the set.

Dom takes the loss more gracefully than I expected. He congratulates me as we shake across the net. I make it to the table and collapse in a seat. Dom takes the seat across from me.

"Well, Esteban, I underestimated your youth. Raub, go up to the house and bring my wallet." He gets a beer for himself, pulls the tab and takes a big swig. "Maybe I should have drank a beer between each game like you did. Anyhow, now that I feel I have my gambling bug quashed, maybe we can get down to the real reason that brought you and your gang to Rio."

"It's simple, Dom," I say staring him in the eyes. "I'm here to sell you small arms."

"And why the charade?"

"That's simple too... I'm seventeen and can't seem to curtail my desire to have fun."

He laughs. "At my expense."

I shrug.

Raub returns with Dom's wallet. Dom fishes ten crisp bills from within and attempts to pass them over.

I wave him off. "Keep it, Dom."

He shakes his head no. "I must insist, a bet is a bet and a bet must be paid."

I accept it this time.

"So, you believe I'm interested in buying arms?"

"Are you not?"

"And what makes me trust you?"

"I'm young and naïve."

He laughs again. "I'll let you plead your case over a late lunch here."

"Fair enough. I'm interested in seeing more of your fine home anyhow."

He drops his hands to his knees as he goes to stand.

"Then it's settled: over a feast, we shall see if you can win me over and not only win my money. Now, I believe the young ladies have dressed to play."

"That we have," Candy says as she snatches the hundred from Raub's hand. "Jane and I challenge you, Dom and your friend, Rosanne."

"Would you care to make it interesting, Candy?"

"Does a bear shit in the woods?"

Dom laughs. "Esteban must be rubbing off on you. The jury is still out on whether that's a good thing."

"Hey, it works for me. Let's say a hundred for the set, and an additional hundred for every game won."

"Let the chips fall where they may," Dom says. "People we have us a game."

We drink beer and watch the match. The girls have a decent game, as does Rosanne for an older chick. Miguel joins us at the table and begins drinking beer as well. Raub makes an icepack for his jaw and sulks at a distance.

"You know, Miguel, I could have sworn I saw a woman's face watching us from-the corner window on the second floor."

"Probably did—probably Mel. You'll meet her when we eat. She doesn't come out of her room much."

"So, what's her story?"

"Sorry, not for me to say."

I take a swallow of my beer. "Fair enough."

We slip back into silence, drink and watch the match. The teams seem on even keel, nobody's going to come out too far on top. They are clearly having fun on both sides. I applaud the good shots and long points. I enjoy watching the game almost as much as I enjoy playing it.

I change back into my boots and jeans and wipe my .45 clean of sweat. I watch as Miguel eyes my gun.

"Miss your piece?"

He pats his hidden shoulder holster and smiles. "I've another one."

Game over, the laughing foursome join us at the table. The girls won in a tie breaker. Candy earned another hundred. She gives me a kiss.

"How did I do?" Candy asks.

I rub her bare leg. "Beautifully."

"Best hundred I've ever spent," says a smiling Dom as he passes over Candy's winnings.

Dom radios his home to see when chow will be ready. No, he didn't quite use the word "chow." He would probably cringe at the word. He determines the table settings and tells us the meal will be ready to serve in five. The news is music to Andy's ears. He perks right up. Tennis simply is not his cup of tea. Hmm, nor is tea for that matter.

Vertigo

Chapter 18

Dom's dining hall is an expansive affair. Centered in the 30- foot ceiling is a spectacular chandelier featuring hundreds of teardrop crystals. The heavy oaken dining table is set in sterling for 20. The chairs are carved and upholstered in red velvet. Portraits of persons past adorn the walls in gilded frames. Impressive.

"Lovely," Jane says as she's seated by Dom.

Dom seats Candy as well. I find myself content with the seating arrangements—a girl on each side. Dom seats Rosanne in one of the empty seats near his at the head of the table. Two stoic older French-dressed maids await his command.

"Monica, notify Mel to join us. You'll have to excuse Mel. She's been under the weather for the past few days. Well, I hope my guests enjoy seafood. We're having a hearty moquecas bobo, which is a sumptuous stew made with shrimp. Then there's a three-fish carpaccio I think you will find divine. "

"As long as it's boneless and comes in squares or strips, I think we'll be able to work with it. Oh, tell Monica don't forget the ketchup," I say.

"I'm not biting on that one, Esteban." Dom smiles. "Ah, here comes Mel now. Mel, we have guests from the states. This is Esteban and to his left is Candy, to his right is Jane..."

I help him out. I point out each member of my crew: "Jim Andy and Felix."

She demurely nods as she's seated in the other vacant seat next to Dom. Her pictures do not do her justice. Melissa's stunning despite a pixie cut which still happens to work for her. She's wearing a lime-green satin slip of a dress that clings to her upturned breasts and hugs her curves. There's something missing though, something that takes a second to register—her eyes, her eyes are dull and void of life. I instantly suspect she's drugged, or cowed to the point of total despair. I'm suddenly struck by a hot flash and for, a fleeting second, I think that I'm going to pull my pistol and shoot Dom right where he sits. I literally taste blood. Somehow, I've managed to bite the inside of my cheek.

Candy must sense something wrong—she squeezes me hard above the knee, bringing me back around. I internally shake off the thought of action that could erupt the table in gunfire. The sight of Melissa's eyes, however, strengthens my resolve to save her or die trying. This is not the time or place though, I decide. Bide your time, big boy. Bide your time. Dom intrudes on the tense moment shared by me and my crew.

"Shall we decant the wine then?" he says as he begins to uncork one of the chilled bottles before him. "I believe this Brazilian Chablis will be a real treat. Monica, if you would be so kind as to pour for our guests."

The second maid busies herself with setting out baskets of cloth-enclosed breads and ladling out generous portions of the stew. Our salad bowls are soon filled as well.

"A toast to my guests. May you live long and prosper."

Andy downs his wine in one swallow. "Not bad, Dom. The grub smells great, too. Are we waiting on some special signal to start?"

"By all means, my young guest, dig in."

"That sounds like a go to me." I make a big showing of letting a shrimp slide off my spoon and into my mouth. I chew slowly and savor the taste. "Ah, now that's some good shit."

The girls giggle and I briefly catch Melissa's eyes. I nod so slightly that I'm not sure if it registers with her or not.

"Coming from you, Esteban, I'll accept that as a compliment."

You may soon accept a bullet as well, I think.

The fish is served. Crisp and too salty for my taste, but it nevertheless fits the bill. We manage the meal without a ketchup request. A true culinary feat has been pulled off. Andy's palate consistently calls for ketchup, but somehow, he's managed to forgo it this time. Perhaps a medium rare steak is within his horizon, too? I have to remind myself to take things one at a time when it comes to understanding Andy.

"Now that the meal is behind us, let's hear your spiel over a Cuban, shall we, Esteban?"

"Works for me," I say as I take the offered cigar box, remove one and pass it down.

Candy snatches one before it's beyond her reach. Not to be outdone, Jane takes one, too. Those are my girls. Got to love them.

I lick my cigar and bite the end off. Dom clips his. The girls, my crew and Dom's men follow my lead. I fire the girls up, then myself. I blow a thick, blue plume toward the chandelier.

"It's like this, Dom, you order a sufficient number of small arms, at a satisfactory price plus shipping and my crew and I deliver."

"And why would I want to buy arms when, as you can see, I'm living quiet comfortably as is?"

"Comfort doesn't necessarily equate to content, Dom."

"True. True."

"You want to be a leader for your people, bring about change. Correct me if I'm wrong." It even sounds like bullshit to me, but I throw it out there.

"I won't correct you, Esteban. I have ambitions and you're right, I'm not content with the current rule. What's available?"

"AR-15s at $500, AK 47s in .223 at $300, MP-5s at $1200, Smith & Wesson 9s at $375 and Beretta 9s at $400. The ARs and AKs are in semi only. Conversions you'll have to do yourself."

"Negotiable in kilos?'

"U.S. only. I'm not a drug smuggler, Dom."

He laughs. "Morals have you, Esteban?"

"Not as far as drugs are concerned. To each their own."

Candy interrupts, "Dom, can I have Mel show me to the lady's room?"

She leans in and whispers in my ear. "Tell him it's an emergency girl-thing."

"Um, Dom," I say. "It's kind of an emergency girl-thing that's just come up."

Dom looks annoyed but acquiesces. "Very well. Mel dear, please show Candy to the lady's room. Now, where were we?"

"I believe you were about to calculate your order. Might as well make it a sizable amount since shipping to your backdoor will be the same—an even ten grand."

He lets out a soft whistle. "Ten grand seems steep, Esteban. What's the payload on your King Air?"

"Ten grand is a bargain. I'll violate God knows how many countries' air-space, not to mention it's 4,000 miles each way. Shipping at ten grand is a sweet deal."

"I suppose. And the payload? You didn't mention the payload."

"It doesn't matter. We have a retro-fitted DC-3 as well."

"An old school workhorse for sure," Dom says. "I want to see and test samples of your merchandise."

"The privilege will cost you ten grand, Dom—an extra ten grand."

Dom flutters a hand as if the amount is of no consequence.

"I must insist."

"And I must insist on the cash up front."

Candy and Melissa return. Candy squeezes my leg again.

"Esteban, no offense, but I don't know you from Adam. How do I know, to put it bluntly, that you won't fuck me?"

"You don't. It's a chance that you have to take—the same chance I have to take. How do I know you won't try to hijack the load once I've landed? I don't, Dom, but I think that you're too smart of a business man for that. Why burn a bridge and take a chance that someone might come hunting for you? I found you easily enough."

"Good point, good point. I think we can do business. Let me think my order over and get back with you. Meet me here tomorrow at noon. I imagine you can find the place now."

"You imagine correctly."

Dom goes to rise. "It's been fun, but now I believe I need to show Mel back to her room. She tires easily. Ladies and gentlemen, until tomorrow. Miguel will show you out."

I watch as Dom leads Melissa by the elbow from the room.

"Miguel, are there a couple six packs around here that we can take for the road?"

"Monica, if you would, help the gentlemen out."

"What about our tennis gear, honey?" Candy asks.

"Leave it."

With six packs in hand, we follow Miguel out.

"You haven't changed your mind about giving my pistol back, have you, Esteban?"

"Nah, only give my crew weapons. Thinking about switching teams, Miguel?"

"Not yet. Mind locking the gate on the way out?"

I salute him. "Sure, see you around, Miguel."

Miguel salutes me back as he turns for the house.

"You're a strange one, Esteban," he says over his shoulder.

We pile into the Chevy. She fires right up and we're off. Candy's chomping at the bit and we're all eager to hear.

"I told Melissa that her dad sent us—that we're going to figure out how to get her out of here. She seemed dazed, but I'm sure she understood. I gave her my gun."

"Oh shit, I don't know if that was such a good idea," I say.

"I told her to use it only as a last resort. What kind of bird is that?"

"It's an Amazon parrot. Where did she hide the pistol?"

"I hid it for her in the bathroom. There was nowhere to hide it on her. I'm sure she'll remember where it's hidden."

She chews a nail. I pull Candy's hand away from her face.

"It will be fine. You did good."

"So what's the plan now, Steve-O?"

"Jim, I truly don't know at this point. We've found her, she's still alive, but the question does remain as to exactly how we're going to get her out of there."

"We should have taken her right then," Andy says. "He only had two bodyguards."

"Two that you saw, Andy. We were being watched from a distance. I saw movement." I stop past the gate. "Jane, would you get the gate."

"I felt we were being watched, too." Felix says. "I'd bet there were others in the house or near enough to respond if need be."

"I'm sure it's going to come down to force, so we might as well figure out how we are going to make it happen on our terms," Jim says.

Jane gets back in and closes the door. We pull out on 040 and head east.

I open the Chevy up some. I check the rearview, we have the road all to ourselves.

"Let's head back to the Palace and do some brain-storming. Plus, I need to call Wallace and also call and see if Sandra's working tonight."

We ride back in relative silence, each lost in their own thoughts. The most worrisome and prevalent of mine is the thought that I'll get one of my friends hurt or, worse, killed. That's a hard pill to swallow. Even the sight of Candy's firm legs doesn't break my sudden sullen mood. Imagine that?

I take another look, cop a quick feel and decide maybe it helps some. Candy turns toward me, smiles and covers my hand with hers. I reevaluate—maybe it helps a lot.

We arrive back at the Palace to find our original bellhop back on the job. I raise two fingers and he gets the message. On second thought, I have him add five dozen-oysters on the half shell and two kilos of peel and eat shrimp. I remind him not to forget the hot sauce. A youngster in my position can't take the chance of running low on vitamin E, can he?

Back in our suite, the message light on our phone is blinking. I call the desk to retrieve them. Our chum suddenly seems to have churned up a school of hungry fish. Too bad, too sad, too late, I think, for the dozen who have left a message and number. There's also a message from Sandra saying she will be at work and two from Wallace seeking an update.

The food and beer arrive and we all huddle around the table on the terrace.

"Any suggestions, boys and girls?" I ask.

"Pay some others to get shot at," Jim suggests.

"Maybe that's not a bad plan, Esteban—recruit some thugs through Andre."

"You'll still need to get her out of the country. Chances are she's not going to be rescued with her passport," Jane says.

"Good point. Where's the U.S. Embassy, Jane?" I ask.

"São Paulo, I believe."

Felix pops the cap off a beer and takes a swig. "If the Embassy is in São Paulo, that's a good ride and there is only one highway from here to there. Any type of alert and there won't be a chance in hell of making it."

"Not to mention, Steve-O, we don't know how deep or how long Dom's reach is. We're liable to spark an international incident. We get arrested here, we're fucked. Diplomacy didn't work to get Melissa back."

I fork a hot-sauced and well-peppered oyster from its shell and study it before downing it whole.

"So, the Embassy is out."

"That leaves my plane. We'll have to use my plane."

"You have a plane, Candy?" Jane and Felix ask at the same time.

"Yep, it's cute and fast. It's the Beachcraft Steven Paul mentioned. Honey, you think you can find Rio?"

I take a swallow of my beer and wipe my mouth.

"I can find Brazil... I think."

We all laugh.

"I'm not flying with the fucker. I don't even like getting on the back of one of his bikes," Andy says.

"Well, the sissy's got a point," I mockingly concede. "I'm clearly not instrument rated."

"Your nothing rated, you mean," Andy says smugly between shrimps.

"Says he who drives a Pinto," I retort. We all laugh, except Andy of course. Doesn't get much lower than driving a Pinto, except perhaps a Vega.

"Well, it's settled then, Jimbo. It looks like you need to take a crash course in navigation seeing's how you're the navigation officer."

"Navigation officer, right. I'm not sure that will help you much if my feet remain firmly and safely planted on the ground."

"You know, Jimbo, Andy needs his chaperone as well. You know how he's not allowed go anywhere without one. And, I'm sure you'll agree, I'm not parental approved, nor of the right ilk to provide the needed guidance ole Pinto Boy requires."

Jim laughs. "You've got a point there."

"Aw, fuck you guys, I don't need a chaperone."

"I'll learn to navigate," Candy offers. "If I need to."

"Fuck it. I'll do it, Candy. If you're willing to fly with him again, I don't know how I could live with myself if I said no."

"That's the spirit, Jimbo," I say with a smile.

"Careful, don't push it. This is not Andy you're speaking to here, you know."

"What's that supposed to mean, Jim?" Andy snaps.

Jim raises his hands in defense. "Whoa, Andy. I didn't mean it that way."

"Okay, Candy you call your man and authorize the plane's release to Wallace. Then I'll call Wallace and see what he can work out for us. We're going to have to refuel somewhere around the halfway mark—Panama or thereabouts—coming and going."

"What about customs, Steve-O?"

"If we don't disembark and only refuel, there should be no problem. I'm only guessing here though, because I really don't have a clue. We'll get Wallace started on the details. Felix, I propose that you stay here and work with Andre to put together a local crew. You're the logical choice—closest to Portuguese we've got."

"I can do that. Give Dom's boys targets to shoot at other than us."

"Something like that," I say.

"What about Jane?" Candy asks with real concern.

"Well, I'm sorry to say, it's been fun, but now things are starting to get sticky..."

"So, it's wham, bam, thank you, ma'am." Jane says sounding hurt.

"You know it's nothing like that, Jane. You'll be a friend for life now. We'll exchange information with you. It's a smaller world than you might imagine," I say.

"I know. I'm only feeling sorry for myself. I've never lived as much as I have these past couple of days. I feel like I'm part of the team. Knowing how much I will miss you guys, I guess I don't want it to end."

A tear rolls down Candy's cheek. She gets up and wraps her arms around Jane. They hug each other for a long moment.

"We'll miss you too, Jane," Candy tearfully tells her.

Wow, they sure bonded fast. I realize how much I care for Jane, too. She's one cool, older gal.

"You know, Steve-O, we'll need to fuel up on this end as well."

"Shit, I didn't think of that. It will need to be done somewhere nearby. Paraguay would be ideal."

"Bolivia would work too, Esteban."

"Yeah it would," I say. "I guess we'll see what Wallace can come up with."

I fork another oyster and down it. "Damn these things are good."

"You're not going to catch me eating one of them." Andy says. "They look gross."

"They look like and remind you of something, Andy?"

"No."

"Oh, that's right. I remember now. You've never actually seen any real pussy before." I say. We all laugh, except Andy of course.

"Aw, fuck you."

Jane gets her laughter under control. "I assure you, Andy, mine doesn't look anything like that. You'll have to take my word for it."

Jane's remarks start us laughing again.,

"And I'll vouch for—" I catch Candy's elbow in my side. "Ow... Her. Candy, go ahead and call your guy if you would."

"Sure," Candy says as she disappears into the suite.

"Esteban, where did Candy get a plane?" Felix asks.

"Man, it's bad ass. Wait 'till you see her. Her grandfather left it to her."

Felix takes a swallow of his beer. "Cool," is all he says.

Candy bounces back onto the terrace and plops back into her seat. "All set."

I rise to go make my call. Wallace picks up on the second ring. I picture him snatching the receiver off the hook with a callused hand. I can feel his relief through the crackling phone line as I tell him about seeing his daughter. I let him know she's fine. I neglect to tell him that I believe she's being drugged, but I tell him she knows her father is trying to rescue her.

I give him the rundown on what we're up to and what all we need him to do on his end. I get the feeling he's happy to have something to do beside sweating the phone for a call. He assures me he'll take care of everything, one way or another, including getting me an official-looking pilot's license. He profusely thanks me before I'm finally able to get him off the line.

I rejoin everyone on the terrace.

"All set on Wallace's end, too. He assured me he will get everything done, one way of another. Looks like we'll be set to go, I mean fly."

"Why does that still sound scary, Steve-O?"

I shrug and offer my most innocent look. "Beats me, Jimbo."

"Okay, so what now, Steve-O?" Jim asks between shrimps.

"Nothing for us to do until tomorrow. I guess the girls and I are going to head back to the Baronneti and talk to Sandra. She said she had something she needed to talk to me about in person. Plus, I need to find out when she would like to leave. You guys can tag along or do whatever you want."

"What do you think Sandra needs to talk to you in person about?" Candy asks with suspicion.

I flippantly answer to see if I can get a rile out of her. "Who knows? I reckon I'll find out." I like the word 'reckon,' don't you? I reckon you need to be off with them-there britches woman. Haven't you always been wanting to say that? Well, you guys, that is and perhaps a few of you ladies, too. Hey, I'm not hating on you.

Candy waves her hand in front of my eyes. "Earth to Steven Paul. What's that smile about, buster?"

"Oh, thinking about how lucky I am to have you, honey."

"'Good answer," Candy says.

"Good answer," Jane agrees.

"So, what does Sandra look like, Steve-O?"

Vertigo

"Jimbo, I try not to get stuck on such superficial things as looks." Careful, big boy, you don't want the girls to think you're shallow. "But..."

"But what?" Jim urges.

"Well, hmm, if you must know, she's as fine as all get-out in her short-shorts and pushup bra."

"She's cute, is what devil boy here means," Candy says.

"I think I'll tag along with you guys then."

"I'm with you, Jim," Felix says.

"Me too," Andy says.

"Well now, that's settled." I wink at Candy and then wink at Jane and purse my lips in fake contemplation. "I believe I'll go and take a shower and freshen up some." I clear my throat. "Candy? Jane?"

"Yeah, me too," they sound off in tandem.

"Gentlemen, if you will be so kind as to excuse us for a while."

Jim shakes his head, Felix grins and Andy grabs another shrimp. I grin back. I can't be the life of the shower by myself, now can I?

To save you most of the horrid details, the shower, well, let us say, is fun. I have to remind the girls more than once, if they intend to save some of me for later, they might consider washing one particular part of me a little less and a whole lot less vigorously. Candy finds this amusing,

Jane finds it convenient, a convenient place to hang her face towel, that is. I do my duty to make sure the pair and all sets of pairs, are squeaky clean as well. To my adolescent wonderment, I find the occasional moan elicited from each of them gleefully promising. Life is good.

Jane, lacking additional sexy formal wear and Candy being whom she is, the girls are regulated to jeans and blouses. Knowing how much I like them on her, Candy wears her new boots. Candy is considerate in these ways, I'm learning.

I opt for another shade of red Izod. Until proven wrong, I'm going to keep believing in the article I read about women being attracted to men in red shirts. And I'm here to tell you, they seem to be working mighty fine here lately.

I run a wet face cloth over my boots, since I have yet to clean them with the given saddle soap—the saddle soap which I neglected to bring along. I brush my golden locks just so.

"Well, don't you look the spiffy one in another red Izod," Jane says.

See what I mean about red shirts? Draws ladies like flies to honey. Well, maybe I can come up with a better analogy than that: Like stink on... No, that won't do, fuck it, I decide.

Being the gentleman that I am, I go on the terrace to fetch the girls a couple of beers. Their prep time is a little longer, you know. I pop the caps, deliver the beers and return to the terrace.

"Well, boys, I believe you will like the Barronetti and since the girls are not around this sec..." I'm always mindful of their feelings. "I can openly tell you Sandra is hot, but..."

"Alright, Steve-O, I'll bite again, what?"

"I think she really wants me."

Jim laughs. "You think all women want you."

"Nope, only the ones in my desired age range."

Jim laughs again. "Yeah, 15 to 50."

"You have to draw the line in the sand somewhere, Jimbo, my man," I say and laugh with them.

"You forgot crippled and crazy, Jim," Andy says with a smirk.

Candy steps out on the terrace. "Okay, what are you boys laughing about this time... Don't all own up at once."

My crew knows how to clam up when confronted, so I naturally fill the void.

"Honey, did I tell you how nice you look in your jeans and boots?"

Candy steps back into the suite and we all laugh some more.

"Esteban, you sure got my vote, man," Felix says.

"Vote for what?" Andy asks again.

He's answered with laughter. On the upswing, lots of beer equates to lots of laughter, don't you know?

"Aw, fuck y'all. I hope they have food at this joint."

Vertigo

Chapter 19

We step into the Barronetti. Again, the place is hopping. Sandra is on us like stink on shit. Well, again, an analogy that might not be quite appropriate. There's a little work for me to do in the analogy department, I decide.

"Thank God, Steven Paul. I thought for sure you were bullshitting me. I get that a lot around here. Hi, Candy, Jane. So, you guys are for real."

I smile. "Some say it is true, Sandra."

"Too cool."

"Sandra, I want you to meet the boys. This is Jim, Andy and Felix. Boys, the lovely Sandra."

"Hi, boys," Sandra says.

Tongue tied, all but Felix acknowledge Sandra with a nod. Felix wins the introduction, "Nice to meet you, Sandra."

"After I get your 'on the house' drinks, I'm quitting," Sandra says with exuberance. "Fuck this place... Sorry."

No table is available at the moment, so we more or less huddle within the jostling mass. Once again, it crosses my mind that this is the place to come if you're single. Quite the variety from which to choose. I see the girls eyeing one of the dance floors. I'm not two-left-footed by any means, but I do mostly lack rhythm, which perhaps I mentioned before. A thousand years of practice and I'd still not be a Fred Astaire. On the other hand, at a slightly elevated state of inebriation, I'm always game. I shall not balk when the girls request my participation on the dance floor—I'll leave it up to you to draw your own conclusions. I have an evil thought: have one of the girls drag Andy onto the dance floor. Employing the Bell Curve rationale, his presence shall aggrandize all other dancers, including yours truly. And not to mention the potential entertainment value.

Sandra returns with our sugary, but stout drinks.

"I don't want to step on anyone's toes," she says. "But could I talk to Steven Paul a minute in private?"

Both Candy and Jane nod their assent. You caught that did you? Jane nodding her assent, too. It's enough to make a young man proud.

I follow Sandra to the employee's break room. She smiles as the door shuts behind us.

"You like your red shirts, don't you?" she asks.

"Yep and for the opposite sex, let me clarify that: for most of the opposite sex, I'm right keen on short-shorts and pushup bras."

"Thanks," she says taking my words for the compliment intended. "Wearing them gets me groped a lot in here, though."

"I imagine, but it's dress for success in a place like this. I bet you do well."

She nods.

"How come you haven't tried to grope me yet?" she asks playfully.

"Have you ever heard the saying, 'two birds in hand is better than one in the bush?'"

She laughs. "I don't believe it goes like that, but I get your drift. Anyway, what I wanted to talk to you about... Well... It's kinda embarrassing..."

I wait her out.

"Okay, it's like this: I really don't have a place to go back to. Being stuck here so long and all, I lost my apartment in Laredo. I grew up in foster homes and don't have any family." She takes a deep breath and holds it for a few seconds.

"There, I said it. You probably think it's a lame story," she says and averts her eyes.

I let out a short, soft whistle. "Wow, ookaaay."

I think for a second: am I going to swallow this hook, line and sinker? Damn right I am! The story does ring true after all and it naturally has nothing do with the fact that she's easy on the eyes and sexy as hell in her short-shorts and pushup bra. Besides, I realize, Sandra falls into the category of damsels in distress and saving them is what I do—it's who I am. Well, starting a few days back that is.

"Okay, we'll figure out something. My first suggestion is you speak to Candy. Her house in Austin is currently our base of operation. In your favor, Candy has a soft touch with a heart of gold and also she currently has two spare bedrooms."

"I only need a place until I can get back on my feet," she says as she meets my eyes again. Sandra has penetrating brown eyes, I note.

"She won't say no, but if by chance she does, I have you covered, girl."

She hugs me tight with her warm hard body. Along with her scent, I feel a stirring. Hey, I'm only human, okay? Being the gentleman I am, I forgo my impulse, well dammit, to grope her. She did plant the seed, you know.

We rejoin the group. Everyone looks on expectantly, especially Candy.

"Sandra actually needs to talk to you, Candy," I say in a serious voice.

"Me?"

"Yep."

Candy leans in to whisper. "I'm not sharing you with any others."

"Never crossed my mind," I say with a smile.

"Okay, I guess. Lead the way, Sandra."

Out of earshot, Jane has to know. "What was that all about?"

I innocently shrug. "What can I say? The girl wants me."

Jane's mouth drops open, Jim shakes his head, Felix grins and Andy wants to know if they sell any grub in this joint.

"You can't be serious?" Jane says. "She's going to ask Candy for permission?"

I shrug again and examine the nails on my right hand—can't suppress the laughter long, however.

Jane punches me in the shoulder.

"You fucker," she says and laughs.

"Good one, Steve-O. Can't never tell with you. Jane, this guy can piss in the wind and not get wet."

Yeah, Jim likes saying that and well, I don't mind hearing it either. I order another round from a different waitress. I feel eyes on me. I turn to catch Jane staring.

"I'm going to sure miss you and Candy. Actually, the guys, too." Jane sighs. "I'm coming to visit you all," she says with conviction.

Candy and Sandra return. The smile on Sandra's face says it all. She unties and pulls loose the small pocketed apron from around her waist, extracts the bills and tosses the thing over the crowd where it lands behind the counter of the nearest bar. She beams. "I'm officially part of the gang now. I need a drink."

There's no objection from the boys and Jane only looks momentarily stunned.

"Hey! Sandra, what the fuck do you think you're doing?"

We all turn to see the bartender with Sandra's apron in his hand.

"I fucking quit, that's what I'm doing. I'm going back to Texas with my new friends here."

"You can't fucking quit in the middle of your shift."

I decide to intervene. I only have to look up some.

"I think the little lady has made her decision," I say with confidence, believing all is under control, until who, looking larger than life, should appear towering over the bartender's shoulder?

The largest fucking bouncer in Rio, I suspect, perhaps even Brazil. Imagine that? In light of this unforeseen development, only rational thoughts cloud my uncluttered mind like: where in the fuck did they find this guy? And: this is liable to leave a mark, like on me. After managing to swallow a rather large lump, I come up with this: "I feel it prudent we take our leave at this time, dear sir."

It's not that I'm running scared, mind you, we'll call my decision a tactical retreat.

"You may leave anytime you like. Sandra, however, is finishing her shift." The bartender says and pushes me in the chest for emphasis.

I sure wish he hadn't done that, I think. Now I have to make a decision tantamount to purposely stubbing one's own toe. "Go with the plan, Son," I hear my dad say. "Thanks for the encouragement," I radio back.

The bartender goes to push me again. Ever mindful of my previously hurt hand, I go with my, oh so, thought-out plan: I knee him in the groin and elbow him in the nose. Instantly, I recognize, that though my delivery is precise, I've grossly miscalculated the move's effectiveness. He drops from sight making room for the largest fist yet I've ever seen coming in my young and possibly short, life. I dodge it with all my body, but I fail to get my head totally out of the way. Boom, out goes my lights.

 I awake to commotion and a chorus of voices while being stuffed and pulled into the back of the Chevy.

"Get the fucking keys out of his pockets. We've got to get out of here now," Jim yells. I feel a small hand dig in my front pocket and extract the keys.

"I've got them! I've got them! Here! Here!" Candy yells. Still dazed, I hear the slam of the doors, the roar of the engine and the squeal of tires.

"Keep the pressure on him," I hear Jane yell. Through the fog, I also hear the distant sound of a siren.

Tires squealing, we slide hard into a left turn and accelerate up what feels like a hill. We slide and bounce off a curb as the Chevy makes a hard right.

"Okay Jim! Slow down! Slow down! We've gotten away!" I hear Felix yell over the continued commotion.

"Hey! He's coming to. You okay, honey?" I hear Candy ask. I think about it for a long second, if there is such a thing and other than my head being numb and my face feeling sticky with blood, I realize I feel fine.

"Yeah, I hope I broke his fucking hand," I say.

I get a few nervous laughs.

"How the fuck did we get out of there alive?" I ask.

"Candy maced Roger, that giant bouncer," Sandra says.

"You maced him?" I ask.

"Well, kind of. All I had was hairspray, but it blinded him. I didn't think you would approve of me shooting him."

I laugh. "That's my girl. And where were you when I needed you, Andy? Blazing an exit path?"

"Hey, somebody had to take the responsibility," Jim jokes.

"Very funny, Jim," Andy says.

"I don't think I've ever seen anyone hit so hard before," Sandra says.

Seemed pretty hard from my angle, too. I realize now that my head is in Sandra's lap and she's the one applying pressure to my head. I look into Candy's concerned eyes and openly mouth: "Ménage a quarte?"

Candy gives me her version of the evil eye before breaking into a smile.

"He's okay, guys. Steven Paul's screwed up way of thinking has resurfaced." She mouths to me: "No fucking way."

"And he's my hero," Sandra excitedly says. "I'd rather crash headfirst into a brick wall doing 90 than go up against the likes of that brute Roger. Steven Paul sure didn't hesitate to stand up for me."

Well, at least that's what I think I hear her say? What I do know, though, is that I stepped up to the plate before I knew who the relief pitcher would be. Oh well, I'll take it with a grain of salt, I decide. In consolation, I didn't reinjure my hand and I won over a new fan as well. Isn't that something? You can lose and still come out a winner. I'm like a martyr for my cause. Well, okay, almost a martyr. But one can't say my unique eudemonistic system doesn't produce results. I'm as giddy as can be, basking in the warmth of Sandra's crotch. If I'm not mistaken, I believe I can feel the bristle of bikini trim on the back of my neck. Isn't life grand?

"Yep, his smile says Steven Paul is back with us," Candy says.

The car comes to a sudden stop and the engine dies.

"We made it, Steve-O," Jim tells me.

"We need to clean him up some before he passes through the lobby," Jane says.

"I'll go get him another shirt, a wet towel and a cap," Candy says. "I guess I better bring some sweats to cover you up, Sandra. They might mistake you as a working girl dressed like you are."

"A high-class working girl," I assure Sandra. "All the oysters I've been ordering up to our suite, they may very well believe the girls need help, you know, sating me."

"Yeah, I believe Esteban has fully recovered," Felix says. "Sandra, let's see how much damage lover boy sustained."

Sandra removes what I suspect to be a bar towel from my head.

"Ugh. You have a pretty deep gash along your brow," Sandra says. "Looks like it's stopped bleeding though."

Candy gets out to go up to our suite. Jim leans over the back of his seat.

"Yeah, looks nasty. He busted open the same spot Steve-O did when he busted his head on the steering wheel of his Firebird."

"No coincidence, I assure you, Jimbo. It's my strict policy to consolidate my injuries that's working for me. You see, Sandra, for publicity shots I have to maintain a clear right profile," I say followed by a grin.

"Publicity shots?" Sandra questions.

"It means nothing, Sandra. Steve-O simply enjoys filling the voids with his nonsense. Most often, he's trying to get someone out of their panties," Jim says.

"I see. You're one of those," Sandra jokes.

"I do what I can," I say humbly. I sit up and I'm hit by a wave of nausea and lightheadedness. Probably a concussion. The bad feelings quickly pass. I'll live.

I shuck my shirt at Candy's return. She passes a wet towel to Sandra so she can commence with her doctoring. Yeah, I know, too many idle hours spent watching reruns of The Beverly Hillbillies. Sandra goes to scrubbing. I polish up right proper, given enough attention, I'm here to tell you.

"There, that's about as good as it's going to get," Sandra says.

We all join Candy on the outside of our ride. I don my clean shirt and adjust Candy's cap to fit. I find some adjustment necessary to accommodate my big head. Imagine that? What can I say? I was blessed with extra storage capacity.

Sandra slips into the sweats Candy provides and, with the bill of my cap pulled low, I'm told I'm once again presentable. Passing through the lobby, I order up a couple of buckets of beer with a raised peace sign.

We make it to the luxury of our suite. I don't know about the rest of them but, regardless of the early hour, I'm done for the evening. Sandra is in awe of our digs. The boys are in awe of Sandra. Based upon Sandra's arrival, I feel it safe to say the boys won't venture far from the nest. If I were in their shoes, I wouldn't either. Maybe she is a bit crass, but who isn't, right?

We gather on the terrace and await the delivery of our beer. The temperature has dropped to a pleasant 70 degrees or so. The breeze off the ocean is refreshing. I love the combined sound of the wind and surf. Someday, I decide, I'm going to own a beach house. Sun and fun—that's how it's done.

"Wow, this place is nice," Sandra says with nice envy. "You guys know how to live."

Our beer arrives in short order. The gentleman that I am, I pop the cap off enough beers for the girls and me.

"Thanks," Sandra says taking hers then smacking her forehead with a free hand. "My packed suitcase is in the trunk of a friend's car back at the Barronetti. I kinda forgot about it."

"No problem," I say. "We'll send Andy back to fetch it."

"Fuck that! I'm not going back there!"

We all laugh. Jim pops the cap off a beer and takes a long pull from it.

"Yeah, I think we've worn out our welcome there," he says.

"Probably burned our car locally, too." I take a pull of my own beer. "Your friend a he or a she?"

"She. She's another waitress there."

"Can you get the message to her to drop it off here?"

"As long as one of the assholes doesn't answer the phone."

"Try. If not, we'll pick it sometime tomorrow. Jimbo, you guys still have plenty of time to go out—it's early."

"I don't think so, Steve-O. I'll hang here with you guys."

I salute him with my long-neck. "I don't blame you, Jimbo. Let's order non-traditional food like their best cut of steak, corn on the cob and a salad."

"I want a baked potato with all the trimmings, too," Candy says.

"Why don't you order everything up for us then, Candy," I say.

"Okay, sure. Medium rare work for everyone but Andy?"

"I want mine medium rare, too."

I almost spit beer and do manage to knock my nearly empty bottle over. "What?" Am I hearing things? Maybe I suffered a worse concussion than I thought.

"I want mine medium rare, too," Andy says reddening some.

"Wow, I'm at a loss of words Andy... I'm encouraged. Sandra, you witnessed a miracle."

"Miracle?" she questions. I grab another beer from the ice, pull the tab and raise it.

"A toast to my friend Andy—may he finally enjoy his steak."

We all bump bottles. Perhaps there's even oysters in Andy's future. One never knows, does one? We drink our beer and mostly listen to the girls' chatter. I don't mind being a good listener. Being a good listener is important, too. Wow, did I just think that? Maybe Roger, the world's largest bouncer, hit me harder than I realized? Yes, Roger has grown in stature in the last hour. He's become the world's largest to anyone who wants to hear my death-defying story. This has become a matter of necessity for how else will I be able to maintain my modesty?

The beer is cold, the food is good, the company excellent and my mind is abuzz with possibilities. Now, why would Candy be so adamant against the idea of a foursome, I wonder? It really sucks that I should be penalized for her hang-up, don't you think? Maybe she needs to get with the program and join the rest of us in the '70s? I smile to myself over my flawless rationalization.

"When he smiles like that, Sandra, is when you need to watch out," Candy says lacking malice and with a smile of her own.

"I'm still trying to figure out the relationship you guys have. You make for some interesting company. When are we going back to Texas?" she asks no one in particular.

I mentally return to the table. "We'll know more tomorrow. You'll have to entertain yourself here for a short while. Go to the pool or the beach or something."

"Going to visit Dom? Have you found the girl in the picture?"

"Yes to both. We simply can't take you when we go."

"I know. I really do hate the creep, though. I hope you do something to him."

"Like not lead with my chin?" I say.

Sandra laughs. "Yeah."

My head quits hurting as the night winds down. To my dismay, Sandra is destined for the couch despite the ample space available on our oversized bed. Once in the bedroom, however, any disappointment soon turns to rapture. The girls decide to swap positions this time. Candy opts to fertilize the old 'stache and Jane mounts the rocket ride to the moon. Literally muffled, I'm in no position to complain, nor would I if I could. Funny, even though I'm the obvious object of their pleasure, I don't feel cheapened by their actions. Must be a sign of my maturity.

Afterward, snuggled between the warm, lithe bodies, I sleep the sleep of the pure in thought—oh, and perhaps one with a permanently etched grin. However one chooses to look at it, life is good.

Chapter 20

I awake to the drumming of fingers on my chest. Why do women do this? I look upon a smiling face to my right and then a smiling face to my left.

"What?"

"Nothing, only wondering if you plan to sleep all morning?" Candy cheerfully says. "The area around your eye is starting to yellow."

"Thanks for the update, honey."

"Well, since you're up now, we might as well order breakfast. It will be here by the time we get out of the shower," Jane says also very cheerfully.

I give them each a good squeeze on the leg and eye them in turn with suspicion. Their outburst of giggling turns me cautious. I shake it off.

"Well then, girls, up and at it."

I give Candy a resounding smack on the ass before she can scuttle off the bed. Jane doesn't fare much better. I manage to thwart her escape with a quick snag and tug of her foot. Her hand partially blocks the smack to her ass. She tumbles off the bed as I release her foot and hits the floor with a satisfying thud.

"Ouch! Steven Paul!" Jane yells.

Candy examines her ass. "Hey, buster, you left a handprint!"

"Only marking my territory girls. Kind of like you did to my neck, Candy. Remember my neck?" I joke cheerfully. Jane gets to her feet giggling and checking her ass.

"Hey, Big Boy, you only partially marked your territory here."

I feign a move toward her, but she darts out of reach.

"I'm calling in a big breakfast," Candy announces and picks up the phone.

We take our play to the shower and once more end up squeaky clean. I realize I may never be able to shower alone again. A spot check in the mirror reveals a crusty crevice three quarters the length of my brow. I probe the yellowing area surrounding it and it is only mildly tender. I decide the injury doesn't affect my overall aura.

"It shan't leave more than a dubious scar," I tell the mirror. And, as we know, there's a giant story behind it, pun intended.

I slip into a Palace robe. A Cuban would accentuate my ensemble, but I have one not. Sounds funny when thought that way, doesn't it?

I mosey into the living room where I espy the sleeping Sandra. She looks peaceful. I lightly touch the tip of her nose. She swats at my hand but remains asleep. I decide to leave her be for now. Eight seconds elapse before I wonder what Sandra would look like in a teddy. It's inspiring thoughts like this that keep my going.

She must feel my eyes on her—she stirs, wakes, stretches, yawns, smiles and says "Good morning," followed by another yawn. I note that she comes with good teeth. Quite the total package.

Candy joins us. "Is he in here molesting you, Sandra?"

I answer for her. "Only with my eyes."

"No. I'm just waking up," Sandra says.

"Good, the shower's open and breakfast is on the way."

"Thanks."

A knock at the door announces the arrival of our food.

Upon entering, our grinning bellhop gives me the thumbs up as he eyes our newest arrival. It takes him some time to clear away the debris from the previous night. He doesn't bother with the hundreds of beer caps that now litter the terrace's floor. As I watch him set out the new covered dishes, I pick a cap from the floor and with the snap of a thumb and finger send the spinning projectile over the railing and out of sight—another talent I've honed through relentless practice.

I hear Candy in the background calling the boys to join us. Soon everyone has gathered again around the terrace table. Candy ordered up plenty of food and beverages and the piling of plates indicates we have some hungry folks. It doesn't take long to collectively devour it all.

I top off the gullet with a large iced milk which seems to be exactly what the body craved. I hate to admit to myself, I've been somewhat rough on the old physique the past few days and I'm not much pleased with myself for foregoing any type of exercise—albeit the sexual kind, for which I'm highly pleased, of course.

Jane lends Sandra a bikini. The top I imagine will be slightly large, but tops are optional here in Rio. I secretly hope we will be back in time to view Sandra in it. If God willing and the creek don't rise, it shall come to pass.

Back in the Chevy and we're off and en route to Dom "Fucking" Pedro's. No one seems to be paying our ride any attention, which is a good thing after the furor created by the bartender and the giant's transgressions toward the girls, crew and yours truly.

Our trip west on 040 is uneventful. The flora and fauna are interesting. We spot several varieties of parrots along the way, the names I know not. One can only guess at the variety found in the Amazon region of Brazil. It seems like every other day a new species of something or another is found.

Miguel's Caddy awaits us at the entrance to Dom's drive. He waves for us to follow. As we come within sight of the villa, Dom steps out followed by Raub and another man unknown to us. He may be another of Dom's security detail and he looks the part and has a military air about him, sports a crew-cut and a square jaw. Another tell-tale sign: he appears to be standing at attention.

We pile out of our ride and into the significantly hotter noon-hour temperature. Coupled with the high humidity, I'm instantly uncomfortable. Dom greets us with his usual expansiveness.

"Ah, my young friends, so good of you to come once again. You know Raub and this is Roberto, my go-to man, you could say. Roberto, this is Esteban and the ladies are Candy here and Jane over there. Then we have Jim, Felix and Andy if I'm not mistaken. I see you acquired a new flesh wound, Esteban?" He raises an inquiring brow.

"Exacerbating, Dom, I tell you. I failed to adhere to a rule of thumb..."

"Which is?"

"Never step between two females vying for your attention."

He laughs. "A catfight—I suppose that could be dangerous and perhaps agreeably diverting. Well..." He sighs. "If you would please follow me out back once more, I think you will find the credenza catered to your satisfaction. Your iced beer awaits you, ladies and gentlemen." He chuckles. "I felt iced beer would be appropriate for the ladies, as well."

Out back, the credenza is, in fact, loaded with snacks, sandwiches and fruit. I retrieve three beers for the girls and myself and pull the tabs of the girls before joining Dom, Raub and Roberto at a table overlooking the valley. With beers in hand, Jim and Felix also take their seats. Andy opts to hover around the credenza to protect as much of the food as possible by consuming it.

"Esteban, do you ever feed your friend?" Dom jokes.

"Only between meals, I assure you."

That provokes a smile. "I see. Well, down to business, Esteban."

He snaps his fingers and yet another man appears from the house carrying a briefcase which he sets before Dom. Dom unlatches the case and opens it to reveal stacked and bound hundreds. He tosses one at a time to me until he reaches ten. He doesn't introduce the latest guy, another fit and capable-looking fellow.

"I've decided to take a chance on you. Your story is too outrageous not to be true. You're very colorful. I'm paying to see samples of your products. Satisfied with your product, you will be returning in your DC-3 on the next flight." He waves a hand over the remaining stacks. "As you can see, money is not an object."

I immediately think of Wallace using these exact same words. I also think Wallace's deep pockets are to be Dom's downfall.

I reach across and offer my hand, which he shakes.

"It's a done deal then, Dom," I say.

"When can I expect you to return, Esteban?"

"I have to arrange the refueling. It will expedite things if I can refuel here as well."

"Consider it done."

"Then perhaps as quick as two days. I'll leave my man Felix at the Palace. Maintain contact with him and he'll provide you with our ETA."

"Fair enough."

I go to rise.

Dom raises his hand. "Stick around and play a few rounds of poker with my men and me."

I stand. "Perhaps on the rebound, Dom. Business before pleasure."

He chuckles and shakes his head. "Work ethics, too."

"Something like that. A piece of advice, Dom..."

Dom raises an eyebrow.

"Hone up on your card skills before I return."

"A card shark, too?" he says faking surprise.

"Some say it is true, Dom. Girls and boys, if you're ready. Dom, I'm going to take a few beers for the road."

"By all means, help yourself. Fly carefully, my friend. Miguel will show you out."

I turn and catch Melissa in the corner window again looking down on us. I wink before the curtain falls back into place. I hope she understands we are coming for her. There are two new men on the scene today. I don't like it a bit, not a bit.

We're soon in our ride and on 040 heading east.

"Steve-O, did you see Melissa in the window as we were about to leave?"

"Yeah, Jimbo, I saw her."

"Two new men today," Felix comments.

"Well, if we have to raid the place, at least we know what part of the house she'll likely be in," Candy says in all seriousness.

What a trooper—got to love her.

"Sorry, Candy, but there are two people in this car that are not going to be shot at—you're one of them and Jane's the other."

"That sucks," Candy pouts.

"She does have some big cojones," Jane says.

"Cojones?" Andy questions.

"Not literally, thank God," I say.

We all laugh.

We arrive back at the Palace without incident. It would seem that, so far, last night's upheaval hasn't been linked to our ride, or our stay at the Palace. I'll take that as a good sign. As tradition dictates, I order buckets of beer at the desk. With my lively step, I traverse the lobby in record time. I'm eager to get back to the suite in case the phone rings. Okay, maybe that's not the reason.

Anyhow, the elevator is in a cooperative mood and opens before I even have a chance to press the call button. Good luck perhaps? We ride nonstop to the seventh floor. Another sign?

"Daddy's home," I announce as we enter our suite.

"Daddy's home," Candy mimics and smacks me in the back of the head. Feisty thing, isn't she?

"I'm out on the terrace," Sandra calls back. Gravitational pull, can't fight it, steers me in the right direction. The girls and boys follow in my wake. Sandra smiles as we all file out onto the terrace.

"Hi guys," she says. I return the smile. No denying fate this time. Sandra is sunning in Jane's bikini and it's a pleasure to behold. Nice and firm. Yet another ass, I suspect, which one could bounce a quarter off.

Candy smacks me in the back of the head again.

"Getting an eyeful, Steven Paul?" she asks.

"Quite." I wink at Sandra. "Thank you. Now I must call Wallace."

I turn to re-enter our suite. I leave them to decide who I'm thanking. Again, Wallace answers on the second ring. I give him a quick update and I once more assure him I've seen his daughter and she's alright. He informs me the King Air is now at his ranch, my pilot's license needs only my photo and things are progressing as to the refueling stops.

I instruct him to get us on the next available flight out, with the exception of Felix who is staying behind. I call Sandra into the room and pass her information on to Wallace. Wallace doesn't question me about this newest member. He tells me he'll call right back with the flight information.

I notice Sandra does a decent job of filling out Jane's bikini top. I believe I've mentioned this before: I notice things like this. I've trained myself to do so. I maintain my keen eye as I watch her walk barefoot back out onto the terrace. I sigh... To be so young and vulnerable. I'm talking about myself, of course. The thought reminds me of my former petite Debra who said something to the effect: "Somehow, I can't picture you as the victim." I guess she proved herself wrong when she absconded with the bearer bonds. I smile at the thought—chalk it up to the game.

Our beer arrives. I tip our bellhop and send him packing.

"Wallace is going to call back with our flight information," I say.

"There's a flight going out this evening at 8:00," Jane says her voice dripping with sadness. "I was scheduled to work it. Shit, I guess I might as well."

She pulls the 9mm from her purse and sets it on the table.

"And to think I didn't even get to shoot anybody."

Candy gives her a hug. Sandra looks on in confusion.

"Jane works for TWA," I tell her.

"Wow. You guys met on a flight here? Too cool."

"Candy, can you give me a ride to my place to pick up my uniform and overnight bag?" Jane asks.

"Sure," Candy says while giving me the evil eye. "And you, buster, better behave while we're gone."

I give her my most innocent shrug and meekly tell her, "I'll try." Hey, I do what I can and she did fail to specify the type of behavior, good or bad. She literally said I "better behave." Could she mean behave as in "usually behave" or "normally behave?" Confusing, isn't it? I decide I better get clarification before they leave.

"See you, girls, when you get back," is the best I can come up with.

After they leave, I dig a cold one out of the ice, pull the tab and hand it to Sandra. I retrieve another for myself and raise it in salute. "Cheers." Sandra raises her own. "Cheers," she says. Jim shakes his head.

"Oh boy," he says.

Felix laughs. "Esteban, you've got my vote."

And Andy, well Andy says, "What vote?"

We all laugh.

The phone rings and I rush to answer it. It's Wallace as expected. Our flight is on TWA with an 8:00 p.m. departure time, a connecting flight in Miami on Delta to Houston to Austin.

I rejoin the tongue-tied boys and Sandra on the terrace. Sandra has taken a seat on a half-turned chair at the table. With her legs crossed, her abs are ripped. Nice.

"My friend delivered my suitcase while you guys were gone," Sandra informs me.

I look her over appreciatively. It runs through my mind what a shame it is to clothe such a body. I believe the boys are equally impressed. She takes a sip of her beer and continues to smile.

"Ever been to Austin?" I ask.

"Sure, but it's been a while and I was too young to party at the time."

"Well, you sure look old enough now," I say. "I mean that in a nice way."

"I want to go to the Broken Spoke," she says. "Know where it is?"

"Yeah, it's a hole in the wall on South Lamar, but anyone who is anyone in country music passes through there." I take another swallow of beer. "We'll have to take you."

"Cool... As in you and Candy?"

"Yeah, we're pretty tight."

Jim gets up and puts his hand against my forehead. "Yep, running a fever."

We all laugh. We shoot the shit for a while. Candy and Jane return and we drink beer as the afternoon turns to early evening. I give Jane $1,000 from Dom's money, which she refuses up to the point where I threaten to throw it over the railing. I decide to leave the additional $9,000 with Felix should he need it. The boys leave to pack their suitcases and we decide to keep this suite since Dom knows the room number.

We pack up and head out. Felix drops us off at the airport. At the concourse, we have to part company with Jane. It's a tearful moment for Candy and Jane until I remind them Jane is going to be our stewardess. It's a touching moment, to say the least. It's hard to imagine we've only known Jane for such a short time. I've got to give it to her. She's a fun chick and I honestly hope this first leg of our flight won't be the last time we see her. Maybe instead of a final parting kiss, Jane will enroll me in the mile-high club. Wouldn't that be the bomb? I wonder if you get bonus points if two women are involved? Something to ponder? Perhaps I could become the trendsetter for the club?

Our pre-paid tickets and boarding passes await us at the TWA counter. For such a small regional airport, the concourse is abuzz with activity. Quite the diversity of languages being represented here.

With a short time to kill, we pick one of the few watering holes to have a pre-flight drink. We're big on pre-flight drinks. Actually, the drinks are had with Candy in mind—knowing her fear of flying and all. I'm ever mindful of the needs of others. Mindful of being mindful, I tip our captivating and beautifully deserving bartender $20.

Drinks gone, we still manage to make our gate early enough to be among the first boarders. I smack our ticket taker's ass in passing. A gasp of surprise can be heard somewhere behind us. We all laugh. Jane did complain about me not properly marking my territory earlier, remember? Hey, as you know, I do what I can.

An older woman gives me a condescending look—I give her a wink.

"Why I never!" she exclaims and I answer her with, "Now you have."

She scurries toward the back of the plane to be among the commoners. Jane steps onboard and gives me a damn good imitation of Candy's evil eye. We all laugh, including Jane.

"I'm working first class," she informs us with a smile.

"And work it shall be, woman!" I say with exuberance. "Drinks for my crew and oh, a double for the blue-haired lady back in coach. Tell her it's from the young gentleman in first class with his apology."

"Oh her, I know the old pompous hag. She drinks tea, always complains... One time, I caught her saving the teabag."

"Skip the apology then," I say.

We all laugh. Camaraderie sure is a good thing. After a few rounds and tons of laughter, Jane brings us pillows and blankets. I don't know about Jim, Sandra and Andy, but Candy and I are asleep in no time.

I awake to the pilot's announcement that we're on the final approach and all that entails. Needless to say, I wasn't inducted into the mile-high club—unless my pleasant dream counts, that is.

I wake sleeping beauty. From her deep sleep, she has part of my shirt collar imprinted on the side of her face. I un-muss her hair and kiss her forehead. She sleepily rewards me with her smile. No longer tipsy from drink, Candy squeezes the life out of my hand during landing.

Departing is once more an emotional affair. The boys even get a peck on the cheek. Andy reddens when he receives his. His first kiss, I think. Hey, it's a start. Sandra is excited about being back in the States. Her excitement is catchy. She elevates all our moods.

We breeze our way through customs and we're soon among the throngs. The airport is a beehive of activity. Again, I'm amazed— being an international port of entry, it's a people watcher's paradise.

Our layover is short, so we have to make haste. We ride the shuttle to the Delta terminal and then take a moving sidewalk to our gate. We're allowed to board, which means we're able to get right back on the wagon, or is it, "off the wagon?" Whatever, despite the wee hour, we're allowed to order drinks. Candy snickers and elbows me in the ribs when our stewardess turns out to be a steward. What's the fucking world coming to? It sure takes the joy out of ordering, at least for me.

Despite the injustice, I order a Bloody Mary—mostly for the vitamins, you know. Candy opts for the same.

"I think he' s cute," Candy teases.

Women! "Put him in a fio dental and I bet you would reconsider," I counter.

"I bet I would, too."

We both laugh. I realize I've totally forgotten about not using the word "bet" in front of Candy. Whatever negative connotations the word might have once had for her, she seems well beyond it now. I must be therapeutic to one's being.

Crossing the gulf, our flight to Houston is relatively short. By car, it makes for a 24-hour trip. Thus, the advantages of flying. We don't have to change planes so, after 45 minutes on the tarmac, we're airborne once again. Houston to Austin, of course, is only a hop. No sooner do we hit cruising altitude than we're once more on approach.

I crane to look out Candy's window with her. The sun has barely begun to rise, the cars down on the roads look like toys.

I pop my ears and think it's good to be home. We disembark and Jim heads for the long-term parking to retrieve his mighty Buick while we head toward the baggage claim to claim the girl's luggage.

I throw my canvas carry-all over my shoulder and grab Candy's largest suitcase, then relieve Sandra of hers. Despite the fact Sandra's suitcase contains all her worldly belongings, it's surprisingly light. I decide I'll have Candy take her shopping. Perhaps even suggest a stop at Allens. I inwardly smile at the thought. Andy takes Candy's mid-sized case and we all head out front to await Jim.

When we spot Jim, we load all the luggage in the Buick's colossal trunk. The big Buick features front bucket seats. Feeling generous, I cede shotgun to Andy, forcing me to ride in the back with the girls. I endure the discomfort of sitting between them. I'm good at enduring when such unpleasantries call upon me. We take Airport Blvd west to IH-35 North. The traffic is mild for the early hour. The Buick's clock shows it's going on 6:00 a.m. as we take the 38½ Street exit and head west. We soon merge with 35th Street. I point out Guadalupe to Sandra as we pass over and explain the street's significance to Austin. We soon pass Camp Mabry on our right. Having been nabbed in a borrowed jeep with the camp general's German Shepherd, my personal playground privileges have been revoked for life. Imagine that? Can't a kid have any fun? I have Jim weave the back way through the neighborhoods to Candy's place. Sandra is in awe of the magnificent homes of Tarrytown.

We arrive at Candy's, or should I say: "Our house?"

"This is your place, Candy?"

"Yep."

"It's nice. And that's a park next door?"

"Yep."

"Does it have a pool?"

"Yep."

"Cool."

We exit Jim's car and hear barks coming from within the house. The front door opens and the dogs rush out. Candy and I both yell, "Bonnie" at the same time. In her excitement, Bonnie doesn't know what to do or where to go. She's a bundle of nerves and her whole rear-end wags. I try to pet all three dogs at the same time.

"You're some good dogs," I tell them.

I introduce the other two dogs to Sandra. "These two are Andy's. This is Smokey and this is Rosie."

James steps forward.

"And this fellow here is James. James meet Sandra."

They nod at each other. I can see the question in James's eyes: "Where did you find this one?"

"James, do we have breakfast stuff?" I ask.

"Yeah, John called and said to expect you early. I went to Safeway last night and bought some good junk. You busted your eye again."

"Candy kicked me in her sleep. Do you think you can whip us up a big breakfast?"

"Candy kicks pretty hard, huh? You know I'm not a very good cook, but I'll try."

"Don't let him bullshit you, James. He ran into a large fist," Candy says.

I put my arm across James's shoulder and steer him toward the front door.

"That's the spirit, James, always willing to try. Andy, bring the luggage in," I call out over my shoulder.

Inside, we gather around the dining table while James cooks.

"Any calls, James?" I ask.

"Only death threats and hang-ups. Candy, your husband has been calling at all hours and oh, Steve, I'm supposed to give you the message he's going to kill you." He adds the "kill" part with his back turned from me.

"Nice," I say. "I don't suppose you know how he got my name, do you?"

"I think I might have let it slip out when he threatened to kill me too. I've been sleeping with all three dogs and my pistol."

Jim and I laugh. Sandra looks confused and mouths: "Husband?"

"I don't think he has the balls to confront anyone in person," Candy says. "Besides, Steven Paul will pistol whip him if he comes around. Won't you, honey?"

"Absolutely, I think I'll hunt him down right after breakfast." I wink at Candy. "Or perhaps right after a power nap, you know."

"Sandra, you can have the back bedroom next to ours," Candy says.

"If you hear moans and things through the thin walls, it's probably only the wind or the house settling," I say and smile.

Candy pinches me in the side.

"Ow! Dammit, girl."

"Those are the sounds that you'll likely hear, Sandra," Candy says and we all laugh. We devour our simple but hearty meal of scrambled eggs, bacon, toast and milk and juice. The heavy breakfast plus the long flight brings on a protracted yawn.

"Come on, Big Boy, let's go take your nap now. Sandra, follow me..."

"Sandra, follow me?" I perk right up with the news.

"I'll show you to your room," Candy says.

I noticeably deflate. Jim and James laugh. Rome wasn't built in a day, I have to remind myself, but I am eternally hopeful.

I unplug the bedroom phone and I forego tapping the moose, opting for some sleep instead. I'm comfortable in our ever-budding relationship and don't have to get some every time. One to five times a day will suffice.

I pull her warm, hard lithe body in close and shut my eyes. Sleep is quick to arrive.

Chapter 21

I awaken to a lick to the face. "Bonnie, what are you doing, girl?" I put up a defensive hand. "Okay, okay, okay that's enough, girl."

"Huh, who you talking to?" A groggy Candy asks. "Oh, it's you, Bonnie. How did you get in here?"

I point. Our bedroom door stands wide open.

"Looks like she decided to join us." Candy leans over me to pet Bonnie. "I wonder what time it is?"

"Who knows, but it's pretty bright outside." I yank the sheet off and kiss Candy on the flat of her belly. "I'm going to work out some. You can inspire me by holding my feet."

She blows the bangs out of her eyes. "I like being an inspiration."

And inspiration she is, in only bra and panties. The way she holds my feet, she manages to playfully push her breasts together making them appear larger. I wish we had a simple trick like that—make our girls wear a pair of 350 reading glasses to bed, perhaps?

I truly hate sit-ups and crunches and that's the reason I usually do them first. One big set of 300. Bonnie watches me like, "what's this fool doing?" I finish my set, kiss my inspiration and embark on five quick sets of 50 pushups with my feet elevated on the bed. I'm amazed at how rapidly short of breath I become. Candy laughs and roots me on. Beads of sweat soon drip from the tip of my nose. I do the last set level with Candy sitting on my back. She adds a big 100 pounds or so of bulk. Hey, it's true, I'm now a believer: "dynamite comes in small packages" or however the saying goes. Candy's living proof. I know one thing, too, I wouldn't trade her for two 200 pounders.

"Come on, Big Boy, let's take a shower."

I realize she's the third woman to call me a big boy this week. Could I be causing a national fad? A new women's movement? Wouldn't that be the shit?

I follow Candy's firm little ass into the bathroom and then into the shower. I come out smiling, squeaky clean once more and 300 calories lighter. I may not be in the mile-high club yet, but I can now add a new notch to my pistol to represent some unique shower-time action. Man, life is good.

We dress which reminds me I need to drive by the real home—to gather up some additional clothes, preferably while dodging Mother Dearest. She's currently freaked out about the recent shootout I was in. It's not every day there's a shootout in Tarrytown. The last, I believe, dates back to the 1800s and didn't involve automatic gunfire, so I guess she's within her rights. I almost feel for Andy, too, seeing how it was their home that was shot up. His parents were out of town when we burned off to the south of the border, so Andy has yet to be confronted. I promised I'd help him explain, but he's pretty sure I won't. Sometimes we're on the same wave-length. Hey, I do what I can.

We join James in the living room. "Where is everyone?" I ask.

"Jim took Andy by his house so Andy can try to sneak in and bring the guns and ammo from there and Sandra put on a bathing suit and went down to the pool."

"Bathing suit or bikini?" I ask.

James reddens. "Uh... Bikini."

"How did she look?"

"Okay... I guess."

Candy and I laugh. She elbows me in the side. If she keeps it up, I muse, she's going to end up with calluses on her elbows.

I call Wallace to see how things are progressing. He tells me things are going better than expected. He's lined up refueling in Panama City coming and going, for a bribe, of course, and refueling in Paraguay, for another bribe, of course.

The good news, he tells me, is we'll only be violating Colombian and Brazilian airspace on the way down, but it's Paraguay, Bolivia, Brazil and Colombia on the way back. He assures me none of them have much of an air force.

Wow, that's a relief, I tell myself. Yeah, right.

Wallace suggests we leave "early, early," so most of our flying will be done in the daylight. Finally, he tells me he has all the topographical maps we will need, a portable potty and his own pilot to give us a crash course on navigation and, most importantly, the King Air's onboard avionics.

I next call the Palace but get no answer. I leave the message to either call me or Wallace. Candy and James have been watching and waiting.

"How did the call to Wallace go, honey?"

"Everything seems to be set."

"So, when are we leaving?"

I feel this is not going to go over well. "We're not, Candy. We're not going to be able to take you."

"What? What do you mean we're not going to be able to take me?" she says sounding hurt and angry. I sigh.

"Listen, Candy, you have a heart of gold and are as game as anyone I've ever met, but I can't take the chance of something happening to you..."

"But it's my plane."

"You mean too much to me."

Her shoulders slump in disappointment and defeat.

"We can take Wallace's plane," I say. "But it's not as agile or as fast as yours. Look, Candy, I'm not even a real pilot."

She wipes a tear and lets out a sigh of her own.

"No, you guys can take mine. I knew I wouldn't be able to go," she says so sadly, it's heart-wrenching.

I pull her in close and kiss her forehead. Nope, I think, I can't let anything happen to this one. I realize again how crazy I am about Candy.

The moment's interrupted by the phone. It's Felix and he has just returned from meeting with Andre. He tells me Andre has some recruitable guys in mind if the cash is right. According to Felix, the guy seems a lot braver since I'm not there. We share a laugh. I tell him to expect us sometime in the early afternoon tomorrow.

"Be careful, Esteban," Felix says before he hangs up.

Not for the first time, I realize my friend Felix is a standup kind of guy. To think the relationship formed over an initial purchase of a single joint is pretty amazing.

I hear the slam of car doors out front. Jim and Andy have returned. They find us in the living room. Andy carries his AK and Mossberg and wears his Ruger on his side. Jim carries his Mossberg, the case of ammo and wears his shoulder holstered Taurus 9.

Andy smiles. "We made a successful daylight raid. It was pretty hairy because both my parents were there. Hey, Steve, you're still going to help me explain what happened to our house, aren't you?"

"Absolutely."

Jim and James laugh.

"Anything new, Steve-O?"

"We roll early. Our refueling stops are lined up."

"Are you going with us, James?" Jim asks.

"Uhm... Oh, I wish I could."

"How much?" Andy says and we all laugh.

"Not bad, Andy," I say throwing him a rare bone. You know how I feel about being overly-generous with complimenting the boy.

"Where's Sandra, Steve-O?"

"James says she put on a bikini and headed to the pool."

"Oh yeah, how does she look in a bikini, James?" Jim asks despite knowing how she looks.

"Uhm... Okay, I guess," James says and reddens once again.

"I believe he's a little sweet on her, Jimbo," I say.

"So, what if I am?"

"Wow, James, the meek shall inherit the earth. That's the spirit, stand up for yourself. Hey, speak of the devil, here she is." Sandra steps into the living room. "We've been talking about you, especially James. We think he might be sweet on you."

"Aww... James."

James reddens even more.

"He was just telling us how hot you are in your bikini, or was that Andy?"

"Hey, I didn't say that," Andy says. We laugh at Andy. He didn't score any points there.

"Candy, I need to swing by the house and pick up some more clothes. Then I'm going to go by the gun store on South Congress. Want to ride along?"

"Sure. Sandra, do you want to ride with us?"

"Let me change."

"What are you going to get at the gun store, Steve-O?"

"Another shoulder holster and some .45 clips. Need anything?"

"Nah, but I think I'm going to shoot by the Holiday House and get us something to eat."

"Ready," Sandra announces.

We load up in the old Bonneville. I point out for Sandra a few things along the way. She's surprised to learn I'm to be a senior at the start of the school year. She gives Candy an incredulous look when she learns I just turned 17. Candy merely shrugs and we all get a good laugh out of it.

We park in front of the gun store and all go in. The owner greets us with a smile and me with a firm shake.

"Steven Paul, running low on NRA bumper stickers?" he jokes. "Quite the news sensation here lately."

"I do what I can," I say modestly. He laughs.

"What can I do you for?"

"I need a left-handed shoulder holster for a 9, a half dozen Colt 1911 clips and, for my friend Candy here, four boxes of .45s and four boxes of 9s."

"I won't ask you what you're up to." He winks. "I'll wait and catch it on the news. Hey, I hear you buzzed Tarrytown and Westlake in a Super King Air?"

"That would be me."

He laughs as he stacks ammo on the counter. He forages through the bin to pick out 1911 clips.

Candy looks in awe at all the available guns. "I want one of the Colt ARs like you have, honey, or even better, one of the machine guns."

I pat her on the shoulder.

"That's nice, honey," I say and then to the owner, with a little shake to my head, "Women," I add as if it explains it all.

"That's supposed to placate me?"

I imitate her earlier shrug and look. "Lunch at Guerro's?"

"Well..."

"Plus a stop at Allens?"

"Deal."

"What's Allens?" Sandra asks.

Candy nods in my direction. "Lover boy's favorite western-wear store."

"Oh, I'm not much into western wear."

"That's okay, girl," Candy assures her. "Welcome to Steven Paul's world."

"I'm right partial to ladies in high-heel cowboy boots and short denim skirts," I add for clarification.

"I see... I guess."

"Anything else for you today, Steven Paul?"

"No sir."

"Well then, this only sets you back $220."

"Perfect."

I pay up and gather the heavy bag to leave. I open the door for the ladies.

"We'll walk since it's so close."

I dump our purchases in the Bonneville's trunk and we cross the street to walk the short distance to Guerro's which is a popular

Tex-Mex joint that serves a good margarita. I usually sit at one of the few tables fronting the place to eat, drink and people watch. Due to the high temperature, we opt for an indoor table. The place is brick, narrow and deep, with lazy ceiling fans spinning overhead.

The waitress lights up when she spots me. She's pretty, but pregnant and has served me here before. Don't get me wrong, I don't have anything against pregnant gals unless they're attired in bikinis and searching for the daddy. She sets us at a small side table for four and hands us each a menu. My opening gambit is a neatly folded $20, a move I've perfected in the past week.

"Margaritas?" our waitress asks.

"Frozen."

"This is a pretty cool place," Sandra comments. "I guess they don't card you here, huh?"

"My credentials override most management concerns."

"Credentials?"

"The folded $20."

"Oh," Sandra says and we all laugh. "You're crazy, aren't you?"

"Some say it is true. But what do doctors really know?"

I believe Willie summed it up nicely: "There are more old drunks than there are old doctors." Sorry, Willie, if I got that wrong.

"What do you recommend, Steven Paul?" Sandra asks.

"I'm going with the beef fajitas."

"And you, Candy?"

"That sounds good to me."

"Okay, that's good enough for me, too, then."

We order our food and another round of drinks. The drinks have some kick here. Some places cut their tequila with Everclear, but I'm not about to suggest that this place does. I decide to be mindful of the fact I'm flying in the early morning hours and only have a few. That makes sense, doesn't it? With another refreshing swallow, it makes sense to me.

The food is good—the company better. I enjoy the crowded atmosphere and the girls' chatter. They seem to be bonding nicely. Wouldn't that be nice? Never mind, lightning doesn't strike twice in the same place, or does it? Well, no point in not wishing.

"Now take that look, for example," Candy says. "When he looks like that, his little mind is up to something."

They both laugh and I salute them with my drink and order another round. Life is good. We finish our latest round in time. Things are starting to get fuzzy around the edges. The noise of the patrons sound like one. Candy hiccups and they both giggle. That, my friends, is an indication it's time to roll on.

"Well ladies, as much as I've loved this two-hour lunch in your company, all good things must come to an end."

They merely look at me and giggle some more. I pay our bill and tip our waitress another $20. I have to tug each by the hand to get them up and going. Nobody seems to notice or care.

We step out into the blinding glare of the afternoon heat. A leashed chow stops to sniff my pant leg before its owner gently pulls on the leash and gets him moving again.

I eye the girls and shake my head. "See how easy that was for his owner to get him going?"

Candy scrunches her face and gives me the evil eye before both of them burst into giggles again. I think to myself, "I bet they won't be giggling so much when the tequila wears off." I put my arms across both of their shoulders to steady them, or is it to steady me? I guess that's not the point. The point is, we manage to walk the short distance to Allens Boots and step inside the cool interior. I always love the smell of new leather. I inhale a deep breath. Sobering? Nah.

The owner greets us and instantly notices I've yet to clean my boots. He shakes his head but smiles.

"Steven Paul, back so soon? How can I help you folks today?"

"I believe the girls want to do some shopping," I say as Candy takes Sandra by the hand and pulls her toward the back of the store.

"Hi," Candy says in passing.

"Candy, nice seeing you again."

"The other one is Sandra."

"New recruit?"

"Something like that."

"Any pointers for an older gentleman?"

"Women love shopping and oh, ply them with lots of tequila."

"Long lunch at Guerro's?"

"You guessed it."

"I believe the little ladies will be feeling remorse when the tequila wears off. I received another call from Cheryl. She asked about you again. I told her I gave you the number—she sounded disappointed you haven't called."

"I've been out of the country. Rio."

He smiles. "So that explains why you haven't been in the news lately. You're right comfortable in front of the camera."

"Thanks." That throws him off. "Maybe we should check on the ladies. The giggling has stopped."

I follow him to the back. The girls have amassed a pile of jeans, skirts and shirts and Candy is struggling to pull a boot off Sandra's foot. As we watch, the boot pulls loose and Candy topples off the stool and onto the floor. They resume their giggling. I shake my head in amusement and the owner chuckles.

I pull Candy to her feet. She hiccups.

"I couldn't get the freakin' boot off," she tells me.

"I'll take over for you, young lady," the owner says. "I believe a size seven will work and I have just the boot in python. Would you like to try them on, Sandra?"

She wiggles the toes of her outstretched socked foot. He takes that for a yes and retrieves the pair, helps her put them on, helps her stand and guides her to the mirror.

"What do you think, young lady? They sure look good on you."

"We'll take them and a matching belt," I say looking around at the mess the girls have made. "And, hell, the rest of this stuff, too."

I help him carry everything upfront.

"You must have a good-paying job," he comments.

The haul comes in at $500. My wad takes a hit. Oh well, easy come, easy go. I pay the gentleman with a wink.

"Could you entertain the girls for a minute while I get the car?"

"Sure you going to be all right, Steven Paul?"

I salute him before stepping back outside and into the glare and heat. I jog across the street and open the door to a furnace. We left all the windows rolled up. "Smart, big boy," I tell myself. I crank the car and let the AC run for a minute before climbing in. I'm careful not to touch any of the vinyl.

I like the big Pontiac. I rev the motor one good time. I love the way she sounds. She's a boat, but she's got some muscle. I back out and cross the street where I park at a slant in front of Allens.

I help the giggling girls into the car and the owner helps me with our purchases. He discreetly hands me another card with Cheryl's number on it. I give him the thumbs up and we're out of there.

Candy throws her arms across both of us, puts her feet up on the dash, changes her mind, puts her feet back down, removes her arm from Sandra and turns the stereo on. Texas's very own ZZ Top, "Cheap Sunglasses," pumps through the speakers. Candy cranks it up, returns to her original feet and arms plan and cheerfully joins Sandra in the song. I can't sing worth a shit, but I join in as well.

The music—or maybe the tequila—makes me get in the throttle, that's the way us motocross riders say it. ZZ fades to Heart's "Barracuda." The song gets us home.

The dogs greet us enthusiastically. The boys are in the living room watching the Price is Right. Jim notes Sandra's new boots and shakes his head.

"I'm glad I'm not your accountant," he says.

"Me too," I say. "I'd probably never get any pussy."

"Not everything revolves around pussy," Jim says.

"In my world, it does," I say.

The giggling girls plop down on either side of Andy and he noticeably reddens.

"Did you miss us, Andy?" Candy teases.

"Long lunch?" Jim guesses correctly. Andy remains mute.

"How about you, James?" Sandra asks. James likewise reddens.

"Gosh, the guys aren't much fun," Sandra teases.

"How much did you guys drink, Steve-O? You do remember you have to fly early—I'm not really secure in that thought as is."

"Relax, I'll sleep some first and we'll take a little cocaine with us."

"Cocaine? You guys have cocaine?" Sandra asks.

"For medicinal purposes only, I assure you," I say. You may recall me mentioning I'm no expert on cocaine, but the cocaine we relieved from the mob pair seemed like some pretty strong stuff. The crew's 'testing' of the stuff turned into an all-night, jaw-clenching, teeth-grinding binge. It took a number of valiums to bring us back to earth. I'm not eager to get back on that horse, but there is no denying it will spark some life into you. So that being the case, if need be, I'll do it for the 'cause.' I'm all about causes, you know.

"There's a lot of cheap cocaine in Rio," Sandra comments. I ignore her.

"Jimbo, let's grill some ribs before we head out this evening."

"Pork or Beef?"

"Candy?" I ask. She hiccups and shrugs. "James, why don't you get Candy a spoonful of sugar for her hiccups. Sandra, any preference?"

"I like to snort my coke." Okay, maybe she is slightly crasser than I realized.

"Not that. On the ribs—pork or beef?"

"Oh, I don't care," she slurs, nods and snaps back. "Any tequila around this joint?"

Reminds me of Andy asking about food.

"We'll send for some, but girls maybe we should go lie down for a while first." James returns as Sandra's chin hits her chest once more.

I pull Candy to her feet. "Take a spoonful of sugar first and then help me with Sandra."

Candy readily agrees. I spoon feed her the sugar, steady her and then walk around the table to rouse Sandra and pull her to her feet.

I lead them both to our bedroom. They take a nosedive when we make it to the bed. Not exactly what I had in mind. Oh well, there's always another day. Both are down for the count. I pull

Candy's boots loose and then Sandra's. I toe mine off and crawl in beside Candy. It doesn't take me long in joining them in sleep.

I dream I'm flying the big DC-3 and we're hitting turbulence. Beads of sweat form on my forehead. The needle on the altimeter is bouncing—the clouds are so thick and dark I can no longer see anything beyond the windshield. I suddenly feel my stomach drop and look over at my co-pilot.

"Candy, I don't know if we're level or not. I think we're fucked."

"Don't look at me, I'm not a pilot either. Besides, you told me I couldn't come along."

I look back at my dials. "But Candy, you're right here."

I turn back to look at my co-pilot. There's no one there. I wake with a jerk. I'm lathered in sweat.

"Oh shit, big boy, what did you get yourself into?" I ask myself out loud. My heart's racing as I climb out of bed without disturbing the girls. I peer into the bedroom mirror. The whole area around my eye looks worse. Even the corner of the eye itself is now red with blood. My mouth feels like cotton—I need a beer. "Well, big boy, I hope your vertigo dream wasn't a premonition," I tell the guy in the mirror. I pull off my damp shirt, wipe the sweat from my face and toss it to the floor. I take a few deep breaths to compose myself. "Forgot to stop by the house and pick up clothes too, didn't you?" Yep. I sure did.

I stop by the fridge to get myself a beer. Jim is outside starting the fire. I pull the aluminum foil cover from a large baking sheet. Slabs of seasoned pork ribs are piled high. It looks like Jim has things under control. I pull the tab on a cold Tecate and take a large refreshing swallow.

Jim steps back into the kitchen. "I see you lived. How are the girls?"

"When I left them a minute ago, they were still down for the count. The margaritas at Guerro's had some kick to them today."

"You really want to take some cocaine with us?"

I take another swallow of my beer as I think about it.

"Sure, why the fuck not?"

"I also got us baked beans and Safeway potato salad and coleslaw," Jim says.

I down the rest of my beer and wipe my mouth with the back of my hand. "Works for me. I'll wake the girls when everything is about ready."

I grab each of us a beer from the fridge and hand Jim his. I roll the can across my forehead. My head feels surprisingly well. We join Andy and James in the living room. The 5:00 p.m. news is on. My favorite news lady is working the desk today.

"Ah, Stacey Keys, aren't you looking fine." I salute her with my beer. A gesture that is somehow second nature to me. "Someday, you will be all mine," I tell her image.

Andy snorts. "She's at least 30."

"Stranger things have happened. We need her off the desk and back on the scene," I say.

"I think she's only filling in," James says. "Man, she's a fox."

"Give it time. She's just playing hard to get," I say. "But believe me, she's coming around."

"Don't you wish? You've only met her twice and probably got her in trouble the first time."

"Hey, I didn't make the FCC's arcane rules. Where's our First Amendment right to free speech?" I say and take a good swallow of my beer. "You know how big I am on Constitutional Rights."

"Right, Steve-O, as in 'hopefully get you out of trouble Constitutional Rights.'"

"Are there any others I'm not aware of?" We all laugh.

Jim takes a swallow of his beer. "Anyway, Steve-O, I hope we don't make the news anytime soon. Like: 'Private twin-engine goes down. No pilot found among the dead.'"

"Yeah, that would be a bummer," Andy says.

"Steve-O, I hope we don't get lost."

"I promise you, I'll find Brazil."

"That's comforting."

"Thanks, Jimbo. You know me—I do what I can."

Sanford & Son follows the news. That Redd Foxx is one funny fucker. During the commercials, I bring in the girl's purchases. I'll make a cowgirl and a lady out of Sandra, too. What exactly qualifies me to do so, I know not. My vivid imagination? I work with what I have.

Rockford Files follows Sanford & Son. I wonder why he doesn't drive anything better than a plain Firebird? Perhaps the same reason he lives in a trailer.

Jim indicates the ribs are near perfection. I go and rouse the girls. I endure the moans and hand slapping in doing so, but ultimately my will wins out. I inform Sandra that we picked up the tequila she requested. She makes a dash for the bathroom. Candy rubs her temples and stares at me. I reward her with my boyish grin and tell her, "I thought you said I'd never get the two of you in the bed together at the same time?"

"I faintly recall going to Allens. What do they put in their drinks at Guerro's? Not painkillers, that's for sure."

"I hope you girls are hungry. Jim grilled pork ribs and bought some other stuff to go with them."

"Maybe it will help. Oh shit, my head hurts."

"Go check on your sidekick—see if she's going to live."

She trips on her boots. I keep her from falling. The girls finally join us at the table. I have to give it to Jim—the ribs are cooked to perfection. The girls pick at their food. There will be some leftovers. I give each of the dogs a meaty rib, rewarding them for their big-eyed patience. Bonnie is so delicate in taking her rib she almost lets it drop to the floor. She is a timid thing.

After we finish eating, we load the additional firearms in the big Bonneville's trunk. We also decide to take Big Blue, my cooler, with us and stop along the way to pick up sodas and snacks to supplement our beer. Man can't live on beer alone, you know. And, just in case, I have Jim go ahead and cut us out a few grams of coke to take with us. With nothing left to do, I pet the dogs for a minute, hug and kiss Candy, wink at Sandra, nod at James and promise all I'll be careful and limit my aerial displays. I suspect the porta potty will check my desire to do any stunts such as rollovers. It makes sense to me.

Loaded for bear, we head out. A quick stop at Safeway provides us with plenty of sustenance: more beer, soda and about 20 pounds of beef jerky. Wallace's ranch is only an hour away. Not much to see en route. Not to mention it's getting dark, but should you ever travel this way, one can stop to take a dip in the Guadalupe in San Marcus and then knock down some suds at the Cheatham Street Saloon, or you can mosey on down to New Braunfels and tube the river and then kick up your boots to live music at the famous Gruene Dance Hall.

We have time to think on the drive and as quiet as Andy and Jim are, I imagine they are lost in deep thoughts. Personally, I'm having a hard time getting beyond the thought of: "What the fuck did I get myself and the boys into?" Oh well, it is what it is and I'm always mindful of Robert W. Service's saying: "A promise made is a debt unpaid." Of course, Robert W. Service never had the pleasure of making Andy's acquaintance or there would be an exception clause stuck in there somewhere. But I did make the promise, so live with it, big boy, I tell myself.

I pull the tab on a can of liquid courage, or is it perhaps liquid stupidity? Anyhow, I take a big swallow and realize whichever one it is, it's mighty refreshing.

"We're almost there, boys," I say. "We take the upcoming FM exit and then Wallace said we would find his place two miles up on the right. Look for an iron-arched entrance which says quite aptly 'Wallace Ranch.'"

Everyone perks up as I take the exit. It's still many hours until we take off, but that fact doesn't make the situation comforting, at least not for me. I can relate to what an astronaut must feel prior to being blasted into space: excited, but anxious.

Finding the entrance is easy. Wallace's home turns out to be a sprawling stone and rough-hewn lumber affair. An antler chandelier illuminates the heavily carved double doors. The ranch style home features four separate stone chimneys. A rearing bronze bronco centers the circular drive. Overall picture: rustic and impressive.

We park and exit the Pontiac.

"Man, this place is badass," Andy says.

"No doubt," Jim concurs.

"It looks like a hunting lodge, almost," I say.

The door opens and Wallace steps out. "You boys made it, I see."

A thin slightly stooped lady joins Wallace under the entrance lights.

"This little lady here is Martha, my better half and Melissa's mother. Martha, I want you to meet Steven Paul, Jim and Andy."

"Nice to meet you, ma'am."

"Bless you, young men, for what you're doing. You will be in my prayers tonight and every night. Please bring my baby home."

"Yes ma'am," I answer for us all. "We'll do our best."

"God bless you. That's all anyone could ask."

"Boys come on in. I've set things up in the dining area. My pilot is there sorting maps and he'll be able to give you a quick course on the plane's instruments."

We follow Wallace to the dining area. Wood, stone, antiques and mounts—a prevailing theme throughout. Someday, I would love to own a place like this. Aerial maps cover the long wooden table. Andy is good with maps, so I decide to put him in charge of this.

"Marty, I would like you to meet Steven Paul, Jim and Andy, the young men I've told you about."

Marty sticks out his hand and we all shake it in turn. "Nice to meet you. I confess I was expecting you guys to be significantly older. That's a lot of plane out there, boys."

"Yes sir, she is," I say. "I've flown her and she's a beauty."

"Rio is a far piece," Marty says.

"Yes it is, and you're here to teach us enough to make it there and back safely."

He sighs. "Let's start with the maps. I have coverage here for everything you will fly over and more. Melissa's like a daughter to me, so listen and listen well."

The maps are made for flying. Essentially, they highlight landmarks, objects you can spot from the air to keep you on course. Naturally, this means that if you intend to fly VFR, you need to do so on days where the ground is visible. Also, one must keep in mind there are few points of reference when flying over open water.

Having stacked and wrapped the maps, we take them and go down to where the King Air sits. She's a beautiful plane but is dwarfed by the old workhorse DC-3 parked beside her.

The avionics are straight forward. One simply dials in the beacon when in range of the desired airport. A beacon is a radio transmitter that emits a characteristic signal for aircraft. King Air also happens to have auto-pilot which is a nice and expensive feature. For the airport's benefit, the plane squawks its own signal to identify it on tower radar. Marty points out this identifying signal can be disabled.

Well, that's it for our little introduction to the plane's avionics and navigation system. Short and sweet, I think we should be alright. I call that a positive thought.

Marty concludes things by giving us a list of airports, their signals and some alternatives should we get in trouble.

"Well, that's pretty much it, boys. Get Melissa back." With that admonishment, we rejoin Wallace and Martha in the kitchen.

"Can I get you young men some tea?" Martha asks.

"No thank you, ma'am," I say.

"Mother, us men are going to take things to my study to talk turkey and smoke cigars."

She seems flustered, her hands are nervous. "Okay dear, I'll be in the den should you need anything." She pauses for a long second. "I'll make sandwiches and goodies for your trip, boys."

"Thank you, ma'am," I say. "That would be right nice of you."

We follow Wallace to his study. The aroma speaks of a thousand cigars, not an unpleasant smell by any means. The furniture within is thick and heavily upholstered in soft, Italian leather. Actually, I don't know where the leather is from, but you get my drift. This whole house spells money.

Wallace takes a seat before a Western-era desk and removes from the top drawer an etched silver flask. He uncaps it and takes a swig before recapping it and returning it to the drawer.

"Sorry boys, I'd offer you some, but in not so many hours you will be airborne. Andy, the panel behind you slides open."

Andy slides it open to reveal a hidden fridge within.

"There's beer, though. Help yourself and take a seat."

Andy hands Jim and I a Bud in a can and takes one for himself.

"This is the place I come to do a lot of soul searching and take a nip or two, or drink an occasional beer. I try to keep it from Melissa's mother as much as possible. She worries about my blood pressure and my heart." He sighs. "She doesn't realize I'm still a tough old mule... Bless her heart."

I pull the tab and raise my beer. "Here's to getting your daughter back, Wallace."

"John."

"John, here's to getting your daughter back."

"I believe in you boys, despite your age. Like the first well I wildcatted—I believed in her and she came in big for me. My gut has not steered me wrong often." He sighs. "Anyway, I feel the best time for you to head out is 3:00 a.m. or so. The sun will be up by the time you hit Panama City. We have plenty of extra rooms here and I believe it's advisable to catch a few hours sleep before you head out. That's up to you. I would like to say it would make mother happy to prepare you boys a big breakfast before you left. She needs to feel she's contributing. She's lost without her daughter."

He pauses long enough to retrieve a cigar from the box on his desk.

"Would you boys care for a cigar?"

"No thanks, John."

Jim and Andy demure as well.

"John, I think rest is a good suggestion and we'll take you up on the breakfast offer," I answer for all.

"Before I forget..."

Wallace opens a bottom drawer and removes three bank bags, two of which have taped-on labels.

"A money bag for each potential stop. Included are fuel payments plus gratuities or grafts or bribes or however you want to view them. It's the way it's done down there. The universal language. Finish your beers, get you another one and I'll show you to your rooms."

We each grab another beer and follow Williams to the left-wing of his home. The rooms are spacious and inviting. The beds are thick and covered with down comforters. Piled at the head of each, four fluffy down pillows. Each room has its own full bathroom. The bathrooms feature restored claw-foot tubs and porcelain pedestal sinks. Each room also features a 25-inch console Curtis Mathis TV with a satellite connection. Wow, satellite connection, I think. It must be nice.

John leaves us to our thoughts. I hear the TV volume from Andy's room right away. I turn my TV on as well. With so many channels from which to choose, I still opt for Channel 7 to catch Austin's news despite the fact Stacey Keys doesn't ever appear on the late edition. I like to stay current. According to the news, Jimmy Carter is gaining in the polls. What're the odds of a Georgia peanut farmer becoming President. If it's up to Texas, I imagine it's a pretty good chance. I wonder if my mother has discovered I've covered her Vote Carter bumper sticker with one of my own that reads: "You can have my guns when you can pry them from my cold, dead fingers." I smile at the thought. Hey, you might recall I do what I can. I've read about Billy Carter as well. A colorful character. I'd like to sit down with him, have a beer or two and see where he stands on foreign affairs. A shot in the dark here but I imagine it's somewhere along the lines of: "Nuke them all, let God sort them out." He'd make a good vice president—not.

Nothing much else interesting on the news. The economy is still in a dump and the GDP is expected to grow at a flat two percent throughout the remainder of the year. Oh well, it doesn't seem to be affecting my purse strings. I snicker at the thought. I kill the TV and close my eyes. I picture Candy in her short skirt and boots and I realize I miss her already. Now that I think about it, I miss Debra too and Cheryl and Jane, but not quite like I miss Candy.

Have to make it back safe to her, I decide.

I drift off to sleep. I look over at my co-pilot, Jim. He's saying something I can't quite understand. He's tapping on one of the gauges.

"What?" I ask.

"We're losing manifold pressure on our number two engine."

"What the fuck does that mean, Jimbo?"

"How the fuck should I know, you're the pilot."

"Jimbo, I'm not really a pilot. Check the owner's manual. Jimbo. Jimbo?"

I look over—Jim is gone. I feel a heavy wind whip my hair. I look toward the back of the plane. The loading door is open, everyone is gone. "What the fuck?"

Vertigo

Chapter 22

I awake with a start and jerk to an upright position. I'm
momentarily confused by my surroundings. Shit, I've been
dreaming again. I wipe a sheen of sweat from my forehead.
"What a fucking dream!" I say to the room. The TV screen has
turned to static. Channel 7 is off the air. "Whoa big boy, get a
grip." My heart's still thumping. My subconscious must have
recalled seeing manifold pressure gauges.

What a stupid dream—my boys would never abandon me. We've
been through some wild shit this past week. Even the timid James
came through when he was asked to. I think back to when we
tried to blow up the mob pair's car and James, because of his
diminutive size, was elected to plant the IED, or improvised
explosive device, which was of my own unique design and which,
in theory, would blow the pair to smithereens. "Smithereens."
Not a word you get to use every day. Needless to say, the bomb
did not go off without a hitch, as masterminded. What did ensue,
however, was a spectacular fireball which momentarily engulfed
the pair's big Buick. I chuckle at the memory. I'm here to tell you,
it was hell on the paint. Their rear bumper caved in when Tony C,
in a state of panic, threw the big car into reverse and accelerated
into a telephone pole. Oh, to be young, six-foot-tall and bulletproof. The point I'm trying to convince myself here is—my crew
would never abandon me, even if scared shitless.

I undress and draw myself a hot bath. Normally, I'm the shower
type and baths are reserved for the morning after a night of over-
imbibing. The kind of morning where you're close to swearing off

drinking for life. Ever been there? Despite deciding to take a bath at the moment, I feel fine, albeit somewhat anxious. The two recent dreams didn't help matters much, but the quick lessons on the avionics and navigation allay my fears some. For the benefit of my peers, I like to bottle up my fears. Something you probably never expect of me, right? Then there's the fact that I've proven to myself I can fly the plane and that should be worth something, right?

The bath is relaxing beyond words. I catch myself nodding several times. I add a little hot water when the temperature drops. Bath behind me, I dry and dress. I realize, looking back now, Wallace didn't comment on my latest battle wound. It looks pretty bad— there's no telling how long the discoloration will last.

I step from the room into the hall, where I'm greeted by the mouth-watering scent of bacon. I could eat bacon with every breakfast. I follow my nose and locate the kitchen, John and Martha. The clock on the oven reads 2:30.

"Ah, there you are, Steven Paul. I was fixing to go wake you boys," Wallace says.

"Good morning," Martha says.

"Good morning, ma'am."

"Please, call me Martha."

"Martha, that bacon sure smells fine. I'm amazed Andy hasn't caught the spoor yet."

"Well, you growing boys need to eat. Coffee?"

I go wake the boys, inform them we're at roughly T-minus 30 to lift-off. I inspire confidence in the boys when I talk all official-like. I bet you can feel it, too? Just kidding.

It doesn't take Andy long to dress—he simply puts his tennis shoes on. Jim tells us he'll catch up with us in the kitchen. Andy seems to be in a good mood. He always is prior to a feeding.

"Good morning, Andy. Care for some coffee?"

"Yes, ma'am."

"You boys and your 'yes, ma'ams,' make me feel old. Please call me Martha."

"Yes, ma'am."

Wallace chuckles. "I pulled the cart around to your car. I suspect you have some gear to load up?"

"Yes, sir—Wallace—John, I mean."

Martha watches Jim enter. "Coffee, Jim?"

"Yes, ma'am, please."

She overlooks Jim's 'ma'am' and wipes her forehead with a small cloth. She fills our cups with a rich-smelling brew. Like a diner, centered in the table are sugar, a dispenser for creamers and a napkin holder. Andy pours sugar in his cup until coffee runs over onto the saucer. Wallace's eyes speak amusement. Andy's antics are comical at times. Being a semi-formal breakfast and having not smoked one this morning, Jim and I let Andy have his breakfast. Usual feedings are rife in entertainment value when it comes to Andy. He rarely gets a bye.

Martha piles on the food and we dig in. I imagine she was quite the looker in her day. I can see some of Melissa's features in her. At the moment, she looks refined but beaten. The current ordeal has taken its toll. Watching Martha nervously busy herself around the kitchen strengthens my resolve to bring her daughter back. Even if it means taking it to the ultimate level—an assault of Dom's villa.

We finish up. The time of reckoning is at hand. It's time to roll. Martha clumsily hugs us each but, try as she may, she's unable to contain her emotions. Wallace is forced to lead her away so she can get some "rest."

I retrieve the money bags from the bedroom and meet everyone out front. The temperature hovers around 70. A cloud briefly obscures the full moon. A gust of wind rips my cap from my head and sends it tumbling. It takes quick strides and several attempts before I secure it underfoot.

We load the cart with our weapons. Wallace is impressed by the amount of hardware we're carrying. With Big Blue aboard, we take the short ride to the awaiting King Air in silence. A windsock near Wallace's hangar is in constant inflation toward the south. The moon breaks back through.

With nothing left to be said, Wallace shakes each of our hands in turn with his callused grip, bids us farewell and good luck. Everything stowed, Jim and I take our spots in the cockpit. I instinctively buckle up, Jim follows suit. I do it because I know I'm the pilot. Jim does it because he knows I'm not a pilot. Or could it be that we're simply safety conscious? Not likely.

"Steve-O, the winds kicking up some," Jim says with concern etched in his voice. "It won't affect us, will it?"

"Not really, unless it stays constant, then it could really shorten the first leg of our trip."

I bump the throttles as a gust of wind buffets the plane. The engines fire and purr. The airstrip runs from north to south, meaning I'll need that much less runway taking off into the wind. I bump the throttles some more. The hum of the perfectly tuned engines is rewarding. The back-lit gauges are all in the green.

"Well, Jimbo? You ready, Big Boy?"

"Fuck it. Let's do it."

"Andy, ready for your maiden flight?"

"Fuck it. Let's go for it."

Another gust buffets the plane as I throttle her up some and adjust the pitch. She strains against the brakes. I deploy the flaps. Wouldn't do to forget them, would it? With a deep breath, I push the throttles forward and release the brakes. Pinned to our seats, we streak down the grass runway. She's an exhilarating ride. I ease the yolk toward me and we take to the air. I bank hard and buzz the waving Wallace and then bank slightly to the east so as to skirt San Antonio. I level her at 1,000 feet, retract the flaps and landing gear, ease back on the throttle and max the pitch. She evens out at the desired 240 knots. With the strong tailwind, I estimate our ground speed to be significantly greater.

"Steve-O, fucking awesome, man. This is a fucking nice plane," says Jim.

"This is your pilot speaking, the no-smoking lights have been extinguished, feel free to move about the cabin," I yell over the hum of the engines.

We all laugh in jubilation. What a natural high. Almost as good as pussy and beer—not.

"Andy, check the map, see where we are."

"What?"

"Hey, I'm fucking kidding."

I adjust our flight path until our compass pegs northeast. I believe if we maintain this direction, we'll catch a corner of Mexico once we're across the gulf and then I'll correct our flight path from there. I'm not worried about violating Mexico's airspace, but I'd sure hate to get too far off course and violate Cuba's. They have Migs, wouldn't you know. I believe, the operative word being 'believe,' we'll be just fine on this current flight path.

"On the way back, Steve-O, let's stop in Jamaica and pick up some ganja, mon," Jim says in a Jamaican accent.

"I brought some pot," Andy says.

I ignore him. That's the last thing I need right now. If I get stoned, we may end up back in the U.S.

"That's probably Beaumont to our left. We'll be hitting open water any time now," I inform my flight crew. You like that, don't you—my flight crew. "I will take a beer though, Andy."

I know it's a little early, but it's to calm my nerves. I put the plane on auto-pilot, get up and stretch.

"Andy, take over for me, I've got to take a shit."

"I'm the map guy," Andy says as I take the beer from him. "Jim, you take over for him."

"Relax Andy, she's on auto-pilot." I fake a yawn. "I think I'll close my eyes for a couple of hours."

Andy bites again. "Do you think that's a good idea?"

I pull the tab on my beer, take a sip and retake the pilot's seat. We hit open water. A few lit-up offshore rigs are all that can be seen. The moonlit water below looks gray and deep.

"Steve-O, why are we flying so low?"

I set the barometric pressure at 30 on our altimeter. The adjustment doesn't affect our altitude reading.

"Unlikely to encounter any other aircraft at this altitude."

"How long before we cross land?"

"If we hit land at all, I suspect in about two hours or so. If we don't, after three hours, I'll correct our course to the south."

"You're a hell of a navigator, Steve-O."

"Thanks. Map boy, a second opinion?"

"All I see is water."

"Well then, I think we should make it to Panama City within seven hours. I'm not sure how close we need to be before we pick up their beacon. I guess we forgot to ask that question." I love the word "we." There's no better way to share the credit when things go wrong.

"Damn, we should have known better." I silently practice the phrase.

I sip my beer and think of Candy. Man, I'm crazy about the girl. Wonder what Debra is up to? Cheryl? Brandy? Yeah, Brandy. Then there's "anyone for a game of tennis?" Jennifer. Her dad forbids her to see me. Must be narrow-minded. She said she would see me on her 18th birthday. Wow, they must be all thinking of me because my ears are ringing. Oops, almost forget Sandra. She sure looks good in her short-shorts and pushup bra.

"What are you thinking about, Steve-O?"

"Women," I say followed by a dreamy smile.

"Figures. So, what's Candy like? She's some spunky gal."

"Now, you know my policy about kissing and telling, Jimbo," I say in all seriousness.

"Yeah, that's why I'm asking."

"Okay, okay, you're twisting my arm. She's one hot firecracker. She's the best, Jimbo. I think I'm in love."

Jim laughs. "Yeah, right. You'll chase anything in a skirt."

"Not true, Jimbo. For example: put Andy in a dress and I'd run like hell."

Jim and I laugh.

"Hey, I'm not even part of you guys' conversation," Andy complains. "Besides, I wouldn't be caught dead in a dress."

"Sayeth the man who douches," I say.

"Aw, fuck you. Hey, this beef jerky's good."

"Jimbo, you better put some of that up here with us."

Jim salutes me. "Ten-four, Captain. Give me your can and I'll get you another beer, too."

"You make for a hell of a co-pilot, Jimbo."

We fly on in silence for a while. Not much to do when the plane flies itself. I should have brought a crossword or two. I'm right partial to a good crossword. Can't spell worth a shit, but I can't read braille either. Somehow, I manage to get by. If one could only bottle charm and sell it—wouldn't that be the shit?

"Is that little extra voice in your head acting up today, Steve-O?" Jim asks laughing.

"Noooo... Don't know what you mean."

"The one that keeps you in trouble," Andy chimes in from the back.

"Save the comments from the peanut gallery, Andy."

"You probably don't even know what that means."

"Well, gallery refers to a theater's upper balcony where, historically, people like you, vulgar and with limited means, were relegated. Peanuts, being a favorite snack of the old days, were used to pelt the performers."

"Oh."

"Hey, Andy." Jim turns to look at him. "Remember that time we left you asleep in the theater during the last show and they were closing up?"

Jim and I laugh. It was funny as shit. When Andy was the last one in the theater, we had the usher go and wake him while we all hid. You should have been there to see Andy's reaction when he found himself all alone. It's friendships like these you don't see every day. One must start with a firm foundation. That, my friends, is the secret.

The sky starts to lighten in anticipation of a rising sun. Jim checks his watch.

"Steve-O, we've been in the air for almost four hours and all I can see is endless water."

Funny he should put it that way: "endless water." Makes one grasp the enormity of the ocean, or should I say "the enormity of our situation?"

"Is that an official request to change course from our navigation, officer Jimbo?" I ask.

"Maybe not a bad plan, Steve-O. Man, if we were to somehow miss South America, that wouldn't be good."

"Fair enough," I say. "Andy, pick a number between 20 and 30."

"Twenty-five."

"Unoriginal, but fair. We'll adjust our flight path 25 degrees to the south." I make the adjustment and reset the autopilot. "That should get us there."

"Or somewhere," Jim mutters.

"Is there discontent amongst the lower ranks?" I ask.

"Note, Steve-O, your navigation techniques are suspect."

"But hopefully effective. Ah, check it out Jimbo—aircraft at two o'clock."

"Damn sure is. Wonder where he's going?"

"West and, quite naturally, toward land." I turn the plane's radio on to sporadic Spanish. I turn the King Air toward the west. "It looks like he's descending. Must be on approach."

I don't understand much of what is being said over the radio, but one word I easily pick up: "Cancun." And we can see the peninsula and the distant city taking shape ahead. I alter our course again to due south.

"Fucking Cancun, Jimbo. Who would have guessed?" I say and smile. "Right on fucking course, Jimbo. I threaded the needle, I did."

"I'll be goddamned if you didn't, Steve-O. You must have a rabbit's foot stuck up your ass or something."

I join Jim in laughter. "I sure fucking hope not."

I hear Andy excitedly shuffling papers in the background.

"Yep, here we are on the map. That's Cancun, all right. Maybe someday if you're ever really a pilot we can go there. Look at this, Jim. We squeezed right between Mexico and Cuba."

I have to admit, I amaze myself at times.

"We could almost take her due east from here and hit Montego Bay. Wouldn't that be the shit? Drink some Red Stripe, man."

We all share the laugh. Andy digs in the cooler and hands Jim and me another beer. I'm starting to believe there is a good chance we'll find Rio and Dom's airfield. Stranger things have happened.

I retake the controls, put us into a dive and pull her out to skim the water. We buzz a shrimp boat heading into port. Man, I love this plane.

"Hell yeah," Jim yells.

"Shit, lost my stomach there for a second," Andy says.

I take her back up to a thousand and level her off again, reset the autopilot.

"Hold her steady for a minute, I need to take a piss," Andy says.

"Andy, we could hit some turbulence... It's better if you sit down to piss."

"No, I don't think so."

I wag the rudder causing Andy to stumble. "See what I mean, Andy? If you piss on the rim, we're going to be mad. Jim, tell him."

"Damn, Andy, that's how they do it on these small planes."

"I guess... I don't know though."

"Andy, now you're being ridiculous." I wag the rudder again.

"Oh, okay, but you guys better not say anything stupid."

I give him a minute to take a seat. "Jimbo, look at the little sissy boy squat to piss."

Jim joins me in laughter. "Look at the little sissy boy squat to piss," he echoes.

"You fuckers—I knew it. I'm going to stop listening to you guys altogether."

"Andy, you've been promising that for years."

We fly on. We seem to be doing well on fuel—over half a tank remaining. I try and dial in Panama City's beacon—nothing yet. I decide I'll try every 30 minutes or so. We settle down to our thoughts once more. I realize I forgot all about Stacey Keys earlier. How in the world could I have done that? Sorry, Stacey, didn't mean to leave you out. I wonder what she looks like in a bikini? Pretty awesome no doubt.

The sun comes up in full force. The clouds are now all but gone. The water has taken on a bluer hue—lost its menacing feel. The whitecaps are barely visible at our altitude.

Andy breaks the silence. "Are we there yet?"

I've been wondering when that question would be asked.

"Consult your maps," I say.

"We're over the ocean."

"Jimbo, remind me next time to bring crayons and coloring books." I try the beacon again. It's there and we lock on. I allow the plane to correct its own course. The correction goes virtually unnoticed.

"Well, we're close enough to pick up the beacon, so at least we know we won't get lost on this leg of the trip."

"Yeah, Steve-O, but you still have to land this thing."

"Jimbo, as Doctor Anthony Storr once said: 'One man's faith is another man's delusion.'"

"Meaning?" Jim asks.

"No meaning. I simply like the way it sounds. What do you think, Andy?"

"I have faith that you're delusional."

"Not bad, Pinto boy."

"Look, Steve-O, jet stream at 12 o'clock. They must be at 25,000 feet or better."

"And they're headed in the same direction. Inspiring wouldn't you say, Jimbo?"

Jim takes a drink of his beer. "Yeah, yeah it is."

"He's probably lost, too," Andy says and laughs at his own wit. Wit that is lost on me. No pun intended. Besides, I'm confident I don't know where I'm going. I'm relying on divine intervention to get us there. Kids, don't try this at home. You know the drill: do as I say, not as I do.

The radio begins to pick up random air traffic, most of it in Spanish. This fazes me not, for I know there are English speaking air traffic controllers all over the world.

"How do we know if we're getting close, Steve-O?"

"Good question. Another question we forgot to ask. I suspect seeing land will be a pretty good indication."

"I've got the map right here," Andy says. "The airport looks small, only one runway, but there's a control tower."

We lapse back into silence. It's long moments like this that make me realize we have little in common outside beer, food and weed. How our little quartet formed now eludes me. I'm here to tell you though, they're a great group of guys.

"Land ahoy," Jim yells causing me to jerk awake. I grab the mike and key it.

"This is King Air GNN 224 to air traffic control, do you copy? Over."

"Tower here, go ahead King Air."

"On approach from the south at 1,000, request permission to land."

"Roger that, permission granted to land from south approach."

"Wow, that was easy enough," I say as I throttle her back and we slowly lose altitude. "If you've never prayed before boys, now's the time."

"Steve-O, Candy said you landed okay the other day."

"Yep, so far I'm batting a thousand."

Jim downs his beer and buckles himself in. I laugh. I mean, I laugh and buckle myself in as well. You remember that mantra of mine? "Safety first."

I throttle her back some more to hasten our descent. I remember to lower the landing gear—pretty useful when landing—and give her full flaps. She takes a hop before she slows.

"You see it, Steve-O? You see it?"

"Relax, I got her Jimbo."

I line her up dead-on, bump the throttle up and decrease the prop's pitch. In theory, you do this so you have the RPMs to abort if need be. Hey, it's not my theory. Our glide path seems perfect, our airspeed down to 110. As we meet our shadow, I cut the power, the stall speed indicator shrieks and we smoothly touch down. I retract the flaps and brake as we near the end of the runway. A fuel truck with a flashing yellow light meets us at the end of the runway and motions us to follow with a wave. Must be expecting a pretty good bribe, I imagine.

"Sure eager to please aren't they, Steve-O? Nice landing by the way."

We come to a stop near an empty hangar. I cut the engines and grab one of the money bags labeled Panama City. "Una momenta boys, I shall return." I exit the plane.

"Esteban Pablo, si?"

"Si."

"Buenos días. Como esta?"

"Muy bien. Hablo poquito español." I indicate my limited Spanish with a narrow gap between thumb and finger. He winks.

"Petrol si?"

I nod and toss him the money bag. "Si."

He opens the bag and thumbs through it. A big smile creases his face.

"Muchas gracias. Me salunda Wallace si."

I nod again.

"Buen viaje." He winks again. "Have a nice trip, Steven Paul," he says in clipped but decent English.

"Ojalá. I hope so," I say and climb back into the plane. I grab a beer on my way to my seat to drink and await refueling."

"That seemed to go over well, Steve-O."

"Not bad, Jimbo, my friend." I pull the tab on my beer and take a drink. "All about the dinero, amigo."

"Speaking of which, how much do you think we'll get paid?" Andy asks.

I shrug my shoulders. "Don't know, but I'll put you in for a bonus for not pissing on the seat."

Jim and I laugh. I hear the crunch of a can and the pssst of another being opened. "Fucker," Andy mutters.

There's a tap on the fuselage and I lean to look out. The fueler steps back and waves as he allows the fueling hose to rewind on its wheel. I hit the ignition—the fuel hand pings full. I salute him and mouth "adios."

Fueled up, we're soon back in the air and back on course. On course to violate some more airspace, that is. If I haven't mentioned it before, my pappy once told me: "It's only cheating if you get caught, Son." Just kidding. In all seriousness, he'd likely draw the line in the sand at violating foreign airspace, seeing as how he's retired, Air Force.

We're truly flying VFR now. I'm holding her steady at 2,000 and assigned Andy to spot, being good with maps and all. A couple of hours in, we cross over into Brazil. The Amazon in all its vastness is an awesome sight from the air. It's a hell of a lot more interesting flying over land and in the daylight. Even the beer tastes fresher, crisper. Well, maybe that's stretching things a mite. We'll just call it refreshing, shall we? So, I have a fancy for beer. I think George Bernard Shaw said this: "I'm only a beer teetotaler, not a champagne teetotaler." Hey, it worked for him. Oh, wait here's something that really rings true: "There is wan thing an' only wan thing to be said in favour iv dhrink, an' that is that it has caused manny a lady to be loved that othewise might've died single." Finley Peter Dunne said that. I believe he was English. Sounds English, doesn't it. I personally frown upon such a tactic as it applies to me, of course. However, I'm a firm believer in plying them with drink. I have my standards, you know.

"Steve-O, what the fuck you grinning about now?"

"Silently rehearsing some pick-up lines."

He smiles. "An array, no doubt. Seems to be working better than average lately."

"Stop, you're going to make me blush. Andy, how we looking?"

"Keep it on the same course. We'll miss the City of Brasília by a good piece and then we'll be maybe an hour out."

"See, Jimbo, that's why I pay him the big money. All I have to do is steer this thing."

"And drink beer," Jim notes. "And hopefully land it, too."

"Duly noted, Jimbo."

"Plane, five o'clock, Steve-O. Not interested in us—they're heading in the wrong direction."

We pass Brasília on our port side and 45 minutes later, we begin to look for Dom's villa and airstrip. Andy informs us that if we hit Rio we've gone too far. I kind of deduced that myself, but can't think of anything witty to say so I keep my conclusion to myself and spare his feelings. I'm big on sparing feelings.

"Look, look, Steve-O, four o'clock. I can't fucking believe it! We actually found the fucking place."

I put her in a steep bank and dive. In screams and laughter, we buzz the shit out of Dom's villa. It becomes "buzz the shit out of" after about twelve beers or so. The Monte Carlo sets in the circular drive, so Felix is there. I bank her hard again and line up on the runway. Landing has become second nature to me now and I unconsciously go through the necessary steps to put her down nice and soft. Three landings under my belt now and I'm giddy with joy. I feel like a real pilot.

The villa has come alive. A '40s-era Jeep makes its way down the winding dirt lane from the house above. The Chevy follows, a good indication to me that Felix has not been taken hostage. Miguel and Raub accompany Dom, both wearing exposed shoulder holsters. I put my pair on as well. The .45 for a right-hand draw, the 9 for a left. Beside me, Jim straps on his Taurus 9. Behind me, Andy threads his 22 Ruger through his belt and buckles it to his side.

We grab fresh beers and exit the plane.

Dom smiles and sticks out his hand.

"Esteban Pablo, a man of his word, I see." We shake. "I cannot help but notice you didn't bring your lady bodyguards. I hear Candy is quite handy with a can of hair-spray."

"True, true, news travels fast. She's quick on the draw as well," I add with my dazzling smile.

"Yes, quite the lady."

Felix grins. "Nice landing, Esteban." His eyes say "nice come back."

I nod in Miguel and Raub's direction. Miguel is having a hard time containing his grin. I'm tempted to believe he's coming around to my way of thinking. And, if not, he's clearly amused at the expense of his employer. We're gathered around like one big, suspicious happy family.

"Esteban, let's see what we're working with and then I have quality Brazilian beef smoking for us to whittle on. Plus, for your distinguished taste, a complement of iced beer."

He looks at the beer in my hand and frowns. "Sorry, no Tecate."

"Andy, hop up in the plane and pass out the firearms and ammo."

Andy passes out the AR-15 first. I drop the clip and pass the rifle to Dom.

"One fine U.S. assault rifle." I toss the clip to Felix and take the offered AK-47. "Chinese made AK, like promised."

I drop its double-taped banana clip, pass it to Miguel and toss the clip to Felix again. Andy next passes out one of the Mossbergs. I pump it once to make sure it's empty and pass it to Raub. Finally, Andy passes out the MP-5 with its double-taped straight clip.

"The cream of the crop, Dom. One sweet gun."

Andy hops down with the remaining Mossberg and a case of ammo. Out of caution, the crew and I remain staggered. I'm proud of my crew—they took it upon themselves this time. All those minutes of formal training have paid off, I realize.

We follow Dom to an area where he has targets set up perhaps 100 yards off. Dom shoots each weapon in turn. I save the MP for last. Like a fireworks display, she's the grand finale. Dom's like a kid in a candy store, his excitement evident in the way he shoots the MP-5. Like the first piece of pussy. I openly laugh at him and all but Raub joins in.

"You liked that did you, Dom?" I ask.

He regains his composure and hands it back. Smooths an otherwise unwrinkled shirt.

Andy picks a straw of grass and puts it in the corner of his mouth. I've broken Andy of picking the ones near the base of the trees in the dog-friendly parks of Austin. You put two and two together.

Plus, I'm often guilty of marking my terrain after a number of beers. I guess better put: "I mark my terrain often." Andy looks lost in thought. I believe he's tasting the Brazilian beef now.

I surprise Dom by loading the weapons in the Monte Carlo's trunk and inform him that these are my own personal firearms and are for demonstration purposes only. He didn't pick up the fact that there were two Mossberg 12s. The last thing I want is for him and his men to be further armed with our own weapons. We follow the Jeep back to the rear of the house. Dom, true to his word, has the smoker going and the emanating aroma stirs my neglected gut.

We gather around the table out back as Dom's maids busy themselves ladling out steaming bowls of what looks like and I hope tastes like, New England clam chowder. A fresh salad containing what must be Brazilian greens is served as well, along with a freshly baked bread of sorts. Miguel serves up the beef Brazilian-style, slicing it right off the skewers and on to the plates. The meat is tender and succulent, with the lightest of noticeable spices. The long-neck Devassas, which we're told are brewed in Rio, bob among the ice and water in a large galvanized tub. Dom presides over the affair like he personally smoked the meat, tossed the salad, caught the clams and brewed the beer. I can hardly imagine myself doing the same.

I spot Melissa peering down at us from her window. She is beautiful but still has that distant look. Miguel notices me noticing her but continues to eat like he hasn't. Dom is going on, fork and knife waving in the air. I've tuned him out but occasionally throw in "Yeah" or a nod. What I'm thinking about is who else may be around. Dom wears no apparent weapon so, on the face of things, we outgun them four to two. The half case of beer plus has me leaning not on the side of caution. I'm tempted to draw both guns and end things now.

I casually look around. A hundred yards out, among heavy foliage, a glint of light catches my eye. The reflection of a scope lens perhaps. I haven't smoked any pot, so I'm not being paranoid. In all likelihood, it is the reflection off a scope lens, I decide. We're covered from at least one angle. I think Jim senses what I'm thinking—he barely shakes his head no. I imagine there are one or two more hired guns that would appear, if needed. Now is not the moment to act.

"Cigar, Esteban?" Dom asks as he pushes the box my way.

"Why not?" I extract a Cuban. I decide I'm going to buy a case of these things to take back for Wallace. That won't make me a smuggler, will it? Dom lights his cigar, puffs out a cloud of thick blue smoke and studies his cigar.

"Esteban, I believe we're in business. You seem to be a man of your word. Now, I must confer with my associates to determine type and quantity." He steeples his fingers. "Esteban, a question has crossed my mind: Why are the ARs and AKs not available in full-auto?"

I ape him and steeple my own fingers. "Our rifles are purchased domestically through straw buyers at gun shows and whatnot. Domestically, full-autos are virtually impossible to buy in any quantity. Besides, they're not hard to convert. I believe Paladin Press sells conversion how-to books. I'm sure you can arrange for someone in Rio to machine the parts."

He nods his head in understanding or acceptance. "I believe the order will be sizable. By the way, the fuel truck will be here later."

"Fine. I'll fill any order. I'll require the ten grand delivery fee again, minus the cost of this fueling of course, plus a 20 percent, non-refundable deposit—a restocking fee, so to speak. The balance I'll expect C.O.D."

He takes a moment to size things up. He sighs and puts his hands on his knees.

"Deal. Well, now that that's settled, how about that belated poker game?"

I shake my head and smile. "Dom, Dom, persistent fellow, aren't you?"

"I'm looking for your Achilles heel."

"Won't find it in cards, Dom," I pronounce with confidence.

"One can only see, I suppose. I believe Miguel and Raub are eager to play as well. Jim, Felix, Andy?"

Jim and Felix decide to play. Andy opts for his own skewer of meat and a ringside seat. The maids hurriedly clear the table. Miguel steps inside and returns with a thick green felt to cover the table and a rack of red, white and blue poker chips. We decide on five dollars for the white, ten dollars for the red and $25 for the blue chips. The game is dealer's choice and a $1,000 per bet limit.

I wring my hands in mock anticipation. I realize this sure is a step up from my last game of nickels, dimes, quarters and one-dollar bills. Well, a man has to take the plunge and step up his game at some point.

It's Dom's turn to ape me. He wrings his hands in anticipation.

"Let the cards fall where they may," he says.

I'm not sure, but it seems like that's one of my sayings. Even if it's not, it reminds me of Samuel Butler's written words: "Man is the only animal that can remain on friendly terms with the victims he intends to eat until he eats them." Of course, Dom's not really a victim, but you get the point, right? His days are numbered, his time is almost up, sayeth he who intends to rescue the damsel in distress. I smile at my own dumb thought.

Miguel starts the deal. We each toss in our five-dollar ante. He opts for Texas Hold'em. He doesn't realize we are from Texas. I guess it matters not, for he ends up winning a sizable pot.

It's my deal followed by Raub's. I'm picking up some bad vibes from him. I play my hunch and choose seven-card, roll-your-own. As expected, Raub folds on the first three and collects the folds as the hands play out. Felix wins a decent hand. I watch Raub out of the corner of my eye as he fast shuffles and then crimps the cards. He's playing us for a fool. It kind of pisses me off. I play along as I grit my teeth and cut the cards on his desired crimp.

I allow him to deal them out before I snatch my .45 and backhand him in the forehead, knocking him from his chair and sending him sprawling and spewing blood. It's pandemonium time. Everyone who can draw does so. I jump from my chair and stuff my cocked pistol under the jaw of the moaning Raub.

Through the fog, I hear Dom yelling. "Esteban! Stop! Stop! What the hell are you doing?"

I snag the dazed Raub's pistol. Someone new joins us, screaming, "Drop it!" I assume he's yelling at me, but I'm not sure. I pick up the thrashing sound of someone advancing toward us through the thick foliage. I slowly raise and turn to see what appears to be a

Mexican stand-off. Dom is ashen and waving his hands frantically in the air.

"Everybody calm down. Put the guns down, please. Please put the guns down."

I smile at Dom and allow the clip from Raub's piece to fall and bounce off the chest of the stricken man. From the whack to Raub's head, a nasty slab of skin has been peeled back and he's bleeding like a stuck hog. I slide Raub's weapon across the table to Dom as a panting man in camouflage breaks from the thicket and pulls up short with a scoped, bolt-action rifle. In one slick move, I've exposed Dom's hand. And you thought I was seeing red, I bet. It's called winging it. Don't you know that by now? It's becoming my signature move. I drop the hammer on my piece and re-holster it, right my chair and calmly sit back at the table.

The tension begins to ebb and guns slowly return to their holsters. Dom looks perplexed as he shakily takes his seat.

 "What... What the hell's gotten into you, Esteban?"

"Can't stand for anyone to play me for a fool. He's lucky he's not dead."

My crew looks on stunned. Miguel looks relieved and amused. The newcomers, dumbfounded.

"What... What in the world are you talking about?" Dom asks as a bead of sweat runs down his temple.

"Check your hand, Dom," I calmly say. "You'll find the two red kings and the king of clubs plus two discards. I, on the other hand, will find three queens and two discards."

He flips his cards to reveal the three kings. I take the edge of one card and flip the rest of mine, exposing three queens.

"You see, Dom, from the bottom of the deck you would have filled out with a pair of tens. I, on the other hand, would have filled out with a pair on nines. Read into it what you may."

I deal him the tens from the bottom of the deck and then deal myself the nines. There's a collective gasp around the table.

Another bead joins the first one on Dom's head. "Esteban, I swear, I knew nothing of it. "

I stare him down with my most intimidating stare. I know, I'm only 17. How intimidating can I be? My opinion: decent. I've practiced it enough in the mirror. Bet you would have never guessed that?

"Prove it. Make it right, Dom," I say.

He stands and picks up Raub's pistol, cocks the hammer and walks over to stand above the groggy Raub.

"You fucking incompetent fool," he says. He pulls the trigger—the boom's deafening. The top of Raub's head disappears in a spray of mist and matter.

Damn, now there's something I didn't see coming. I guess Raub had a round chambered.

"Miguel, clean up this mess and dispose of the body."

I shrug and look up at Miguel. "Sorry for the mess, Miguel."

And it is a hell of a mess. Blood, bone and gray matter extend ten yards beyond the remains of Raub's head. I look up to see Melissa peering down at us. She nods briefly and lets the curtains fall back into place. One less man to contend with and I never even fired a shot.

A contrite and still somewhat nervous Dom pleads once more. "Esteban, I swear I didn't know."

I may not appear overly intimidating to him, but I have a suspicion Dom hasn't completely ruled out crazy. Heck, I haven't completely ruled it out myself. Just kidding, only bipolar in a good sort of way. Hey, you might not appreciate my methods, but you can't knock my results, albeit the one where I got slightly knocked out by the world's largest bouncer. I like to believe there's a method to my madness and, no, I don't know who said that. I'll probably remember after another beer or two. Dom interrupts my musing. He's regained some of his color.

"I trust we can still do business. I offer my most humble and sincerest apologies for what transpired."

I take my time, sip my beer, tap my fingers on the table and finally smile.

"Sure. What's a little misunderstanding between friends."

Dom lets out a long-held breath. "Thanks, Esteban. I'll get the order worked out, ready the cash and have your plane refueled. I suppose that's enough poker for one day. Esteban, you boys split Raub's chips and we'll cash out."

He blesses us with a wan smile.

I stand, stretch and throw in a fake yawn. "I'd like to head out at 3:00 a.m. your time."

I'm dictating now. I'm running the show. I'm good at both. Reminds me of when James chimes in with: "you're a legend in your own mind." I'm always quick to remind him: "a legend that gets the pussy." Maybe I'm the one that's a little crass at times. Nah. I come to this conclusion by not considering it very hard.

I watch as Miguel and a new crony of Dom's roll Raub up in a blue tarp.

"Couldn't spare a rug, Miguel?" I ask.

"Right, that's only in the movies."

"Would you like us to drop Raub off somewhere for you?" I ask with my best poker face.

"Sure, you'd do that for me?"

"Just fucking with you, Miguel." I make my hand into a pistol and point at him. "Gotcha."

He grins. "Fucking Americans."

I pat him on the back and grab a couple of beers from the tub.

"Ain't that the truth. Dom, if you don't mind, have someone restock the plane's cooler. A couple of wrapped skewers of meat would be nice, too."

Relief washes over Dom. Perhaps because we're fixing to roll out, or perhaps, I surmise, because Dom has already promised someone the impending arms shipment.

"The plane will be fueled and the beer iced. And I'll throw in a couple of skewers of meat as requested," he says. Dom turns into the gracious host he's good at pretending to be. "You sure you wouldn't like to stay for dessert?"

"Good one, Dom, but we're out of here." I wink. "Later."

We load up and hit the road for the Palace. Felix turns the AC to high.

"Esteban, I almost shit when you slapped Raub with your pistol. I was sure there was going to be gunplay."

"I figured it for a Mexican stand-off and I was counting on the one Mexican I invited to the party. Things played out as I imagined," I say.

"How, I can't imagine. Scared the shit out of me too, Steve-O."

"I skewered myself in the thigh when I tried to ditch the meat and draw my Ruger," Andy says.

We all laugh at that one. I turn to look at Andy in the back. He's sporting a shit-eating grin and wears part of his meal on his shirt. He causes me to crack up again.

"I brought them out of the woodwork, didn't I," I say. "Plus, now we know there is one less of them around."

"True," Felix says. "But I'm sure he'll be replaced. Well, at least we have an idea of how many are usually around the hen house."

"Steve-O, when did you actually come up with the brilliant plan?"

"Thanks. Genius, wasn't it? Oh, about three seconds after my last sip of beer. I have a hunch Miguel wants to change teams."

"You're an inspiration to us all, Steve-O." Jim shakes his head. "Sometimes I truly am being facetious, you know?"

"I know, but I don't want to ruin things for Andy. He really looks up to me."

"Since when?" Andy says.

"Well, ever since I taught you to change channels with your toes."

"That has saved me from getting up a lot to channel surf," he concedes and we all laugh.

"Now what, Esteban?"

"We've run out of options. How's your recruiting going?"

"Slowly, I've hired on three extras so far."

"That's a start. Keep it up. How many can you recruit from Austin to join us?"

Andy interrupts. "We going to finally storm the place?"

"I'll call my uncle when we get to the Palace. Maybe a half a dozen or so"

"Why wait?" Andy asks.

I turn toward him. "Andy, we're going to overwhelm the place. And, have our escape plane fueled, running and protected from the ground. The more firepower we have, the less likely you'll get shot. Plus, there's Melissa to consider—you may have to carry her."

"Are we going to bring James?"

"Andy, are you going to start lifting the lid when you piss?"

"Steve-O, in Andy's defense, I believe he started to lift the lid when his mama told him he was old enough to hold it and aim it himself."

"Aw, fuck you, Jim. When did your mama quit holding it for you?"

"When the cold water no longer bothered me."

"What?" Andy asks and we all laugh.

"Never mind, Andy," I say. "Let's finish our planning at the Palace over a bucket or two of beer."

"Some of your better planning has been over buckets of beer, Steve-O."

"Thanks, Jimbo."

We all laugh, including Andy.

As we enter Rio, still relatively early, I'm amazed at all the activity. "What the fuck's going on, Felix?"

"One of their many festivals. Today they're celebrating throughout the city. It's Dia de Santo Antoñio."

"Who the fuck is that, Felix?" Jim asks.

"Fuck if I know. I imagine some saint or something. Do I look Catholic?"

"Damn," I say. "I'll have to come up with something other than rosary beads this year for Christmas for you."

"My grandmother thought them very thoughtful," Felix says and we all laugh.

"What did Steve-O get you for Christmas last year, Andy?"

"A box of condoms."

"About as useful," Felix notes and we all laugh at Andy's expense.

"That's where you're mistaken, Felix," I say. "I invited him to a water balloon fight."

"He did not. I still have them all."

"Risqué in the lone safe sex department are you, Andy?" I ask.

"Nooo."

We all laugh as we turn into the Palace's parking area. With my cap pulled down along with my shades, I order the customary two buckets as we pass through the lobby. I bet the bellhops will miss us when we're gone. I'm going to kind of miss the place, too, I think. Of course, without the girls, the suite doesn't hold the same allure for me. I especially miss Candy and hope she knows I'm thinking about her. The elevator opens and a tall one, scantily clad for the festival, exits. I take in an eyeful as I run into Jim, who apparently got stuck in his tracks. Felix ends up bumping into me and Andy gets on the elevator. I think, for the thousandth time: "You can lead a horse to water, but you can't make him drink."

We find our way to our round table on the terrace. I notice the beer caps have all been cleared away. If I'm not mistaken, I smell a trace of perfume as I pass through the suite.

"Get lucky Felix, did you?" I ask.

Felix smiles. "The maid returned after she finished her shift. Brought her overnight bag with her."

I smile as well. "The hired help, huh? Well, it's nice to see someone besides me getting some. How did you manage it?"

"She thinks I'm a rich Mexican from the states."

"And what gave her that impression?" I probe.

"Well, the suite, a fat money bag and lavishing her with food and wine, I suppose."

"Impressive," I say. "False impressions do serve their purposes at times, although I tend to shy away from such a policy."

The operative word being "tend."

Jim laughs. "Yeah, right, Steve-O. Since when?"

"Since I learned an outright lie works better," I say.

We all laugh. I'm not really into lying, but I've been guilty of such a time or two—mostly to spare the other person's feelings. I'm sensitive to other people's feelings, you know. Well, with the exception of Andy, of course, for whom I'm still trying to build character. Like earlier, I was so close to telling him he did a fine job with the maps. Slap me if I repeat myself too often.

Our beer arrives right on time. Too much introspection gives me a headache. Or could it be that sobering up gives me a headache? Whatever the reason, I'm glad the beer has arrived. Andy can use some to wash the stain out of his shirt.

I tip the bellhop, pop the cap off a beer and take it to the railing so I can view the activity below. No sign of the woman from the elevator. Other feathered specimens, however, of indeterminate gender can be seen roaming around. Maybe I should send Andy down there to sort them out, I muse. Not.

I step in to phone Candy. She answers right away. She's been waiting to hear from me. I assure her all is well, everything went down without a hitch, but we're going to have to resort to plan B—an assault on the villa. With that, I promise to fly safely and vow I shall return tomorrow afternoon.

I call Wallace next and give him our progress report. Explain we're going to have to resort to an attack on the villa. I reassure him Melissa is still fine, that I saw her again today. Finally, I run down our needs for the assault. The DC-3 fueled and ready, ten AR-15s with plenty of extra clips and ammo and eleven parachutes in case of an emergency. I'm not as trusting in the old bird. With that settled, I only hope I can fly the old gal. One thing I do know, she's capable of short takeoffs and landings, which means she has a slow stall speed. I rejoin the boys on the terrace.

"Felix, Candy says to congratulate you on your maid conquest."

Jim laughs. "He wants to bring you down to his level."

I laugh. "Felix, my man, I'm only fucking with you."

"Whoa. Shit. That's cool man. She's a nice chick."

"Hey, call your uncle," I say. "We'll need a total of at least six recruits. Tell your uncle we'll supply the weapons. All they need are camo and some cojones, los huevos."

"They'll be fine. And the rest of the plan, Esteban?"

"You need at least five on the ground with you here. Outfit them with the weapons we have and walkie-talkies. You take the MP-5. Part of the deal is they get to keep the weapons plus whatever they can loot. Don't tell them about the cash we're expecting for the arms."

"That goes without saying," Felix says.

"Naturally," I continue. "We're going to try and take that for ourselves. Oh, and when the assault is underway, we'll need to be able to identify ourselves so we don't get caught up in friendly fire."

"How about white armbands, Steve-O."

"That will work, Jimbo," I say. "When the firefight is on, assuming one ensues, everyone will don white armbands."

"Let me make the call, Esteban."

"So, are we going to order room service or are we going to eat out?"

"Andy, why don't you run yourself through the carwash first, then we'll consider taking you out in public with us. Personally, I'm going to rest until at least dark."

"I'm with you on that, Steve-O."

"Not literally, Jimbo. You get the couch."

Jim laughs. "That's what I meant."

I take my act to the bedroom where I do one grueling combo set of sit-ups and crunches, followed by three elevated sets of pushups. Well, at least everything combined is enough to get the old beer sweat flowing and the heart pumping.

I cool down with a long refreshing shower. Unfortunately, I'm unable to exfoliate for a lack of a damn loofah. Right, I believe in that about as much as I believe in a man's pedicure or manicure. A real man, you know, harvests his fingernails as needed for toothpicks. The toenails, however, I deal with as nature intended—I use nail-clippers. After a long shower is the best time to clip those sturdy manly toenails. No need to thank me for sharing that piece of wisdom.

I wrap in a Palace robe and dive onto the oversized bed. It's what the doctor ordered. I'm down and out as soon as my head touches the fluffy down pillow. I sleep the sleep of one truly exhausted for once... A deep, dreamless sleep.

Vertigo

Chapter 23

The ringing phone brings me back to the present. I groggily answer with a protracted "Hello."

"Hi, honey, it's me," Candy says cheerfully "What are you doing?"

I stifle a yawn. "Sleeping."

"Alone?"

"Of course. My baby's not here."

"That's sweet. Miss me?"

"More than you can imagine."

"Okay, just checking on you. James is cooking for us girls."

"He'll make somebody a fine wife."

"Hey, he's sweet. He's nice."

"I thought you said I was sweet?"

"You're sweet in a different kind of way. Anyway, fly safe and hurry home. I have something hot waiting for you."

I'm tempted to say, "What, Sandra?" to see what kind of reaction I can get out of her, but settle for something safe that won't risk knocking me out of the saddle.

"Is it edible?"

She giggles.

"You know it, that and then some. See ya, honey."

"Bye, Candy."

I ditch the robe and pull on a pair of jeans. I find Jim asleep on the couch, Andy asleep on a lounger and Felix entertaining who I believe must be the maid. The sun is mostly down and the terrace is in the shadows but what I can see of the maid, she's nice. She's wearing a flowery sundress, sandals and no jewelry. She looks to have a hard, lithe body beneath.

"There's my rich Mexican friend from the states. So generous to invite us up. This must be the lovely young law student you told me about."

Felix laughs. "Nice try, Esteban. She doesn't understand English."

The maid smiles, at least understanding that much.

"Well then," I say. "She looks like she has some good pussy."

I smile in her direction. He laughs and she continues to smile.

"Actually, Felix, she looks nice and has an endearing smile. Are you two going to come with us for a couple of hours of festivities?"

Felix asks her in Spanish and she answers with another smile: "Seem."

I point to the sleeping Andy. "Well, with that settled, I shall roust the demon here... And Jimbo, too."

I politely bow to the pretty maid. I kick the lounger causing Andy to jerk awake and nearly fall out of his chair.

"Up and at it, private. I see Felix lent you a shirt. Somewhat tight, but perhaps it will help you meet that someone special. Oh, and sometimes the color of the feather plume is telling."

"What the fuck..." He stops in mid-sentence as he spots Felix's friend. "Umm... What are you talking about?"

"Food, Andy. We're going to go to eat."

That lights a fire under his ass. He jumps to his feet. I'm surprised he doesn't pop a button. I wake Jim a little more gently considering he's bigger than me—I snatch the pillow from under his head.

Jim comes awake. "What?"

"Andy says 'wake your ass up,' because we're going to go eat and check out the festival. Hey, let's check out the Via Sete in Ipanema. It's a high-end place to eat and the front patio is supposed to be a prime, people-watching spot."

"That will work for me. I'm getting hungry."

I step back out onto the terrace and say to the maid, "Via Sete seem?" She smiles and shakes her head yes.

"Felix, it's an upscale eating joint in Ipanema. To maintain your facade, I'll even allow you to pay—and not out of the big bag."

"Thanks, Esteban. You sure know how to look out for a guy."

I smile. "I do what I can."

One of the pleasures of being young and irresponsible is the many smiles it produces, not that I'm necessarily irresponsible, mind you.

The temperature has dropped to a tolerable 80 or so and we opt to walk among the party-goers to the Via Sete. The crowd is colorful and the atmosphere electrifying—makes me almost wish we didn't have an early flight. With that early flight in mind, I decide that I'm going to keep my beer consumption to a minimum. It's the responsible thing to do. There's that root word "responsible" again. Can't seem to shake it, being a born leader and all.

The patio tables are all taken, so I do what any well-rounded responsible born leader would do in my situation: I pay $100 to a group for them to relinquish their table.

The food turns out to be fabulous, the variety of party-goers beyond entertaining and the company better. Well, with the exception of missing Candy, et al. Sorry, that's a Latin abbreviation for et alia, or "and others." Latin sure comes in useful at times, doesn't it?

Well, all good things, at some point, must come to an end so remaining true to my word, I allow Felix to pay. I'm also still mindful of the fact we're all in this together, so we all need to limit our imbibing. You see "we" as I commonly use it means "those who are vicariously liable for my actions." That's consistent with my belief in sharing responsibility. I'm just that kind of guy. I'm sure you understand. We all have our tenets.

We work our way back through the crowd. I choose the path of least resistance—I follow in the wake Andy has plowed for us. I've only seen him more determined when foraging for food. Translation: cutting in line at the nearest fast food joint. Needless to say, we make it back to the Palace in decent time. The two love birds will soon have to part company, at least long enough for Felix to run us out to Dom's. I have to admit they make a handsome couple. The chaperone in me, however, keeps their parting kiss tactful. My oversight is done sua sponte. Oops, more Latin. "On my own accord" is what I mean. No cheap thrills on my watch.

The night is clear, the air is still as we take our leave. That, my friends, makes for optimum flying conditions. I re-strap my shoulder holsters in preparation for our arrival at Dom's. Have to stay on top of my game, you know.

We arrive to find the gates open. I remind everyone to be on alert. Never can know what will go down, but I'm of the belief that Dom has no desire to fuck us over. The memory of my intimidating stare should keep him in check. Yeah, right. On the other hand, the memory of me unexpectedly pistol-whipping Raub out of his chair, well, that might keep him toeing the straight and narrow.

The villa is lit up. We're expected, of course. Dom and Miguel greet us at the door. Felix is quick to burn off. Can't much blame him, having a consuelo sexual in the works. That means 'booty call' for those of you who want to hone your Spanish.

"Esteban, made it back safely, I see. Didn't shoot anyone on the way over, did you?" Dom jokes.

"Nah, everything set?"

"Absolutely. If you gentlemen will be so kind as to follow me to my study, we can finish up this end of the business."

"Heard you're hiring, Dom," I say.

"What? Oh, good one, Esteban. You mean to replace Raub. Well, he wore out his usefulness, didn't he?"

"I imagine it will take two to replace that one."

He leaves that one alone. We follow him into his study, a room of dark wood paneling and bookshelves. The universal rich man's study. Much like the large carved double-door entrances, a rich man's must. Personally, I'd rather have a mirrored canopy bed. I imagine being in it would be much like starring in one's own movie if you get my drift? Now that to me seems like the ultimate rich man's must.

"Take a seat, gentlemen. My organization and I have decided on the following: One thousand AKs..."

"Three hundred grand," I instantly say.

"One hundred MPs."

"Hundred and 20 grand."

"Two hundred Berettas."

"Eighty grand. That's a half a mil so far. At 20 percent, that's a hundred grand—plus the ten grand, minus today's fuel."

"Well, quite the mathematician, I see."

"I watch a lot of Beverly Hillbillies."

"What?"

"I'm good at ciphering."

"I'll take your word on that."

He pulls a briefcase from under his desk, clicks the double clasps open, opens the case and turns it to me for my viewing pleasure.

"One hundred thousand U.S. A 'hundred grand' in your words. However, you neglected to quote ammo prices and I neglected to inquire."

"Chinese .223s a hundred a thousand. Remingtons or Winchester 9s, three hundred a thousand."

"Sounds fair. Firearms without ammo, no bueno. Very well, then. One hundred thousand .223s and 50,000 9s."

"Fifteen grand."

"Shouldn't you be writing this down, Esteban?"

"No need. Another three grand and your deposit will be covered."

He taps his fingers on his desk and stares at me. He's first to blink and break eye contact.

"If you fuck me, Esteban, I'll send someone to find you."

"That's a two-way street, Dom."

He rises from his seat and goes to a hidden safe where he merely turns the handle to open it. From within, he tosses me three, individually-wrapped $1,000 stacks. I neatly stack them in the case among the other cash.

"What's the combo? I'll return the case."

"It's still set on zeros."

I close it and snap it shut.

"Well, Dom, my friend, it looks like we're off. See you in a couple of days or so. You can check in with Felix if need be."

"Fly safely, Esteban. You can take the Jeep down."

We follow him out back, where he and Miguel bid us farewell. What I perceive to be a knowing smile slightly creases Miguel's face. He's clearly enjoying himself. We take the Jeep down and board the plane. I go through my pre-flight checklist. We're good to go. Both the ice chest and the fuel tank appear to be full. I know, I may be skimping a little here, but I doubt Andy could find the dipstick anyhow.

We roar down the grass airstrip and take to the air before we all burst into laughter.

"We're fucking rich, Steve-O. I can't believe he bought your shit." I bank to the northwest.

"Hook, line and sinker," I say bringing a fresh round of laughter. Life is good, my friends. Andy squeezes between Jim and I with a shit-eating grin.

"That's a lot of fucking money. How are we going to split it?"

"Equitably, Andy."

"I don't know. That doesn't sound too fair."

"Okay then, we'll base it on merits, or in your case demerits."

"You going to still help me explain all the bullet holes in our house?" He asks moving onto a new subject.

"You know it, Andy." I reach across and pat him on the shoulder. "What are friends for?"   Jim chuckles and stares off into the night. I put her on auto-pilot and close my eyes.

"Jimbo, wake me in a few hours or if we need to make an emergency landing or something."

"Sure. Why not. Get you some beauty rest."

The drone of the engines is relaxing. It's no time before I nod off. I don't know how long I've slept and it takes me a second to get my bearings. I quickly ascertain everyone else is asleep. We've been in the air some time—I can tell by the slowly rising sun to the east. Below, the ground is one vast-looking grey jungle. Shit, I realize, if you were to crash here and survive, you would likely never be found.

I step over Andy's outstretched legs to get something out of Big Blue to kill my cottonmouth. Of course, all the sodas are buried in the freezing ice. I opt for a beer, being ever mindful of the dangers of frostbite, or even worse, hypothermia. It wouldn't do to have something happen to the pilot, now would it?

I open my beer on the end of the cooler and take a long pull from it before smacking myself in the forehead—I forgot about picking up some Cubans for Wallace. Another thought crosses my mind: wouldn't it be cool if I could hide somewhere in the plane and then when Andy and Jim wake up there would seem to be no pilot? I chuckle when I realize that's true whether I hide or not.

I retake my seat and turn the plane's radio on. No air traffic as of yet. I try the Panama City beacon: nada.

Nothing much to do but stare out the window and let the plane fly itself. I do what I do best in situations like this and say, situations like being in the classroom and finishing my test long before the others—I fantasize. And fantasize I do well. Jim finally wakes and joins the living.

"Shit, Steve-O, we've been in the air for six hours," he says after consulting his watch.

I try the airport's beacon again. This time she locks on and the plane corrects its course.

417

"We're good to go, Jimbo."

"That's always reassuring to hear," he says.

Andy soon joins the living as well. "Where are we?"

"Check your maps, Andy," I say. "We're getting close."

It's not long before we start seeing signs of civilization. Andy actually determines where we are on this leg of the journey. The radio chatter has picked up as well. I mentally prepare for the final approach by opening another long-neck and taking a drink.

Without a hitch, we land, bribe, refuel and take to the air. Isn't life grand? Out above open water, I wonder out loud: "Why didn't what's his name give us the beacon for Cancun? Lock on it when we can and we'd miss Cuba altogether and not violate their airspace."

"They do have the Russian Migs," Andy says. I hear the rustling of maps. "Hey, here it is, right on this map."

"See, Jimbo, once again I must remind you this is why he gets the big bucks."

"Your blind luck system of navigation, Steve-O, seems to work pretty well, too."

"Ain't that the truth," I say. "Nothing better than flying blind."

"I used to close my eyes on my bicycle," Andy comments.

"You daredevil, you," I say.

"You go, girl," Jim says.

"Aw, fuck you, Jim."

We all laugh.

I'm guilty of doing the same on my motorcycles. Dare myself to see how long I can keep my eyes shut. It's a trip and not recommended. Something else I'm still guilty of doing is getting my bike going as fast as I can and then standing on the seat and riding it like it was a skateboard. Also not recommended. It didn't work out for me one time. I ended up crashing and wedging my Yamaha 100 under the rear bumper of a parked Jaguar, which was witnessed by a number of my neighbors. Not one of my better exhibitions. But other than a rock buried in my knee, I came out mostly unscathed.

Flying is fun, but out over the open water, there's nothing to see. I can't even think of anything about which to rag Andy. That sucks, too. Well, maybe not for Andy.

"Steve-O, what's going to happen when we enter U.S. airspace?"

"I hope we go undetected. We're going to come in low and fast. Interdiction levels are at about ten percent."

"So, we have a 90 percent chance of going unnoticed," Andy says.

"It would seem so," Jim says. "Andy, hand us a beer and a pack of the beef."

I use my trusty Uncle Henry to whittle off some beef. Even cold, the stuff is good. In time, we lock on and eventually pass Cancun. Knowing now that we'll have plenty of fuel, I bank hard to the west for an hour and 30 minutes before taking us north again. I decide this approach will likely be less monitored. I admit, a pure hunch.

I turn toward the back. "Andy, when we spot land, it will be up to you to figure out where we are. Here's a clue: we'll be way west of Galveston, I suspect."

I throw in a little disclaimer should I be off a state or two.

A couple of hours later, we begin to pick up air traffic. An occasional plane can be spotted thousands of feet above us. I take over control and bring us down to skim the water. I wag our wings as we buzz a shrimper. The men on the deck wave. A couple of oil platforms can be seen in the distance. When I spot a seagull, I know we'll soon hit land. My calculations turn out to be correct. We come in just west of Houston and manage, it seems, to go undetected.

We yell in unison as we buzz a crowded beach and wag our wings again for the pleasure of waving to our fans. Well, maybe the fan part is a stretch, but if they knew who we were and our mission, I bet they would-be fans. Everyone loves a hero, right?

I take her back up to 1,000 and soon we take in the skyline of Houston. I bank her to the west to follow I-10 for a while. We're in a jubilant mood, sensing we've made it yet again. The relief is palatable.

In what seems like no time, we zero in on Wallace's ranch and I execute another flawless landing. I feel like I have become one with the plane. Yeah, I know, I've watched too many episodes of Kung Fu on TV, but it's either that or I've developed a decent beer buzz.

The relief is evident in the smiles of John and Martha as they greet us.

Martha is first to speak as we exit the plane. She grabs her heart.

"My goodness, I'm glad to see you boys. John tells me Melissa is fine," she excitedly says. "And that you're going to bring her back."

"Yes ma'am," I say. "We're bringing her back on the next trip."

Wallace throws a heavy arm across my shoulder and shakes my entire body. "If I harbored any doubts in you boys, they're gone now. Nice landing."

"Hell, it must be true. I've been hearing it a lot lately," I say. I would pat myself on the back but Wallace's arm is in the way. Just kidding, but everyone likes compliments, right?

Small talk gets us back to the house. The aroma of fresh hot food gets us to the kitchen. Martha has been busy. Jim and I are happy. Andy is overjoyed.

Post-meal, we take things to Wallace's study where we go over our final plans to free his daughter. Everything has been taken care of on his end. A call to Felix confirms his uncle has come through and he also has Andre and five others on his end. The consensus: refueling at the airport in Asunción, Paraguay and an early nighttime landing and assault on Dom's villa. We close the call on that note.

A planned nighttime landing gives me pause, but I'll have two landings with big bird under my belt at that time and that should count for something. Well, assuming those landings are a success. We should be alright, though.

Our goodbyes said, we load the cooler and the briefcase of cash into my big Bonneville and we're en route to Candy's. Our intended departure for the mission is 5:00 a.m., which would make the estimated time of the assault 8:00 p.m. their time.

I love driving the big boat. The ride is smooth and she's got the power. I turn the stereo on and even at almost an hour out of Austin, KLBJ comes in loud and clear. A Led Zeppelin tune pumps through the speakers. I don't know the name of the song, but Robert Plant sings about a girl that wants to ball all day. Maybe the name of it is "My Street Corner Girl?" Whatever it is, I love the song.

Time flies when you're floating along and jamming to good music. My thoughts bounce from the planned assault to Candy and how I look forward to seeing her again. She's one special woman and I feel fortunate to have her in my life. I know, I'm getting soft, but to quote mother dearest again. "It is what it is."

We arrive at Candy's and I hear the dogs bark as we exit the car. The front door flies open and the three streak out. Bonnie leads the pack. She bounces off me and does a comic spin around the front yard before bouncing off me again. Candy, Sandra and James join the commotion. Candy jumps on me and wraps her legs around me, almost causing me to fall. It makes me think, "wouldn't it be nice to be greeted like this every day." It's good to be home. Funny how I'm already thinking of Candy's home as my own.

"I sure missed you, honey," Candy whispers in my ear as I set her back on the ground and give her a big smack on the lips.

Sandra gives me a basic hug. It still feels good. "I'm glad you boys made it back, Steven Paul, I was worried about you."

I try to pet all three dogs at once. "And I missed all you kids, too," I tell them, despite the fact that Smokey is getting on up in age.

I spot James. "James, I've heard you've taken over the cooking and cleaning since we've been gone."

James actually reddens, or should I say blushes?

"I hope you have something good planned for later," I finish.

"Yeah, James," Andy says.

Candy looks me over. "No new contusions, lacerations, or bullet-holes, I see. Too bad, I was intending to apply some TLC."

"I could still slip in the shower," I tell her and we both laugh.

We take things to the living room where I run down the brilliant plan we've come up with. Note again how quick I am to share culpability. Reminds me of the commercial where the kid is asked, "What did you learn at school today?" to which the kid answers, "sharing." I believe that school lesson stuck with me. Of course, Candy wants to go along this time as well and I have to reiterate why she can't, namely, I can't allow anything to happen to her.

Felix's uncle calls and we go over the basics and agree we'll meet at Candy's at 3:30 a.m. Again, things look to be all set. Nothing to worry about except worry itself. Setting worries aside, we decide to send James to the Holiday House for our standard fare, including three doggie burgers. What I'm really waiting on is a reasonable time in which to tell everyone goodnight and discover what Candy has in store for me. Although I'm enjoying everybody's company, it seems like 7:30 takes forever to arrive. See, I can be reasonable.

I pick up the giggling Candy, toss her over my shoulder and salute the others good night. Still giggling, Candy looks at Sandra and tells her: "We'll try and not make too much noise."

With my free hand, I grab two long-necks from the cooler to take along. Nothing wrong with a nightcap, is there? Being the gentleman that I am, I flop Candy on the bed and dive in after her. Not one to kiss and tell, but Candy caps off a perfect day. And when she curls in next to me, sleep comes swiftly. I'm crazy about this girl.

Chapter 24

The next thing I realize is someone shaking me awake. I open my eyes to find the grinning Sandra staring at me.

"You have visitors, Steven Paul."

"What time is it?" I groggily ask.

"Three fifteen," she says laughing.

"You find that funny, do you?"

Candy stirs. "What's funny?"

"You are, honey," I say and tickle her.

Candy giggles as she tries to fend me off. "Hey, quit! Quit it! You better quit!"

I relent and hop out of bed before remembering I'm missing my boxers. Funny how things such as that slip your mind.

"We have company, honey. Up and at it, girl."

Candy wags her finger at me before chasing me nude into the bathroom.

"At least she didn't see much," she says once again finding something humorous.

"Yeah, I'm sure she's seen smaller breasts in her high school P.E. class."

She frowns and punches me in the arm.

"That's not what I was talking about, buster."

She takes a hold of my member and pulls me toward the shower. I grow hard in her hand.

"Now that's a little better," she says as she stares down at me.

"You better change that to a lot better or I might forgo pleasuring you."

"Okay, lots better! Lots better! Lots better!"

I join her in the shower where it's soap and suds and lots better. I dress in my camos, strap on my holsters and join the crowd in the living room. It's a comical scene with everyone dressed in camo. I'm self-conscious of my ostriches. They could use a cleaning.

"Juan, my man," I say and stick out my hand to shake with Felix's cousin.

"Esteban!" He laughs. "I hope you don't plan to get us shot."

I laugh with him. "Never part of my plan."

"But inevitable," he finishes for me.

I shrug. "I hope your men remembered their green cards in case we get stopped at the border."

"Good one, Esteban. About the pay?"

"The woman's father is loaded and he's a damn good person. Everyone will be taken care of."

"That's what Felix tells me. He doesn't know much about your flying history, though."

"I was born to fly. So, let's roll. Jimbo, let's take your ride. Juan, you can follow us. We'll learn everybody's name on the flight. Andy, you grab the cooler. Add a bag of ice."

"Works for me, man," Juan says.

I decided we'd take Jim's car since the briefcase of cash is still in the Bonneville. That cash is on a need-to-know basis only, so I'll tell Candy and James about it upon our return. I give Candy a long kiss goodbye and promise I'll be extra careful. I guess she forgot my middle name should be "careful."

Jim's ride is also a boat, but a fun ride. With its big block, she'll get up and on down the road, too. I have to remind Jim a couple of times that Juan is following us. To the motorists we pass, we probably look like we're being chased by a carload of Mexicans in camo. It's an amusing thought.

We arrive at Wallace's ranch—the place is lit once again. No doubt Martha intends to send us on our way with a full stomach. No complaints on this end. They both greet us at the door and after brief introductions, we're led into the main dining hall where Martha has once again outdone herself. She's cooked for a small army. No pun intended. We're more like saviors, doers of good deeds, avenging angels. Well, maybe 'avenging angels' is a slight stretch of the imagination, but you get the point. We're just down-right good people.

Sated once again, we head down toward the plane. I help Andy with the heavy cooler load—I lessen the weight by one can. I do what I can.

Martha has to hug and bless each of us in turn. The ARs and ammo are already on board. Up close, the old bird is daunting compared to the smaller and more agile King Air. I unconsciously swallow as I look upon her. Hmm, I must have had something caught in my throat, I decide.

We load up. Wallace has thought of everything, it would seem. Beyond what I requested is a large box full of everything from duct tape to bandages. The only thing that seems to be missing is a can of WD-40. I decide not to get on Wallace for this oversight. I'm big on forgiving.

Loaded, nothing left to do but a silent prayer and for Juan's recruits, the sign of the cross. I do one myself. No sense in not hedging my bet. My pre-flight check routine includes the downing of my first morning's beer. You know the routine by now.

She fires right off. The big engines rumble—not quite the hum I've grown used to. Man, she is a big bird. I take a moment to familiarize myself with her controls. As Wallace mentioned, she's been retro-fitted with turboprop engines. To instill confidence in my crew, I make a big showing of buckling up. This provokes a fresh round of prayers and signs of the cross.

I salute them before throttling up a bit. The windsock lays dead on its pole. What a break. I don't have to figure in the crosswind or figure out how to figure in the crosswind. Wouldn't that have been a quagmire? I adjust the pitch and throttle her up. She lumbers down the airstrip but picks up speed. Nearing the end of the strip, I ease back on her yoke and she lifts into the sky. There's a round of cheers and olés. I bank to the southeast and take her up to 10,000 feet—enough to avoid most all light aircraft and all pressurized craft. I put her on auto-pilot and join everyone in the back of the plane for a round of cervezas. In fear we'll run out of beer, I'm quick to remind everyone that we're on a mission and we need to go easy. You see, I readily express my insecurities, especially when it comes to running out of beer. It's best to confront phobias head-on. That's my policy.

One of Juan's recruits, Jessie—I know, not much of a Mexican name—brought along a deck of cards and we soon get into a poker game. It takes me less than two hours to clean everyone out. I wish they would have brought more money. Bored now, I go back to flying. Nothing to see, but the sky is starting to lighten and I can now make out the water far below. Just for the heck of it, I check out one of three money bags that were waiting for me in the pilot's seat. Each contains five grand. I'm not sure of the price of fuel, but I'm sure that a majority of the money goes toward each bribe.

A couple more hours of twiddling my thumbs and I'm able to lock on to Cancun's beacon. The big bird barely corrects course. It makes me wonder why commercial pilots make so much? Of course, I've yet to land her.

Juan joins me upfront and hands me a fresh beer. "Well, it looks like you know what you're doing, Esteban. How long of a flight is it?"

"Around 4,000 miles total. We'll be refueling a few hours beyond Cancun." I turn on the radio and we pick up some air traffic. I point to a plane at one o'clock. "They're probably headed to Cancun, which means it's about time we head some to the east. We need to skirt Cancun, stay out of their way."

"Where did you learn to navigate?"

"Between you and me, I didn't."

"But you know where we are?"

"Sure, look to your right. That's Cancun down there."

"Cool, man."

I take a sip of my beer, correct our course to the west and reset the autopilot. I note we seem to be doing well on fuel. Juan and I rejoin the rest in the cabin where we spend 30 minutes loading clips for the ARs and going over our assault plan. It's pretty basic: we'll hit the place from all four sides. Hopefully, we'll catch most of them outside and off guard. It's unfortunate that it has to come down to this. I'm starting to feel for Miguel. I believe given time, he'd change teams. Well, that's the way it goes. Sometimes collateral damage simply can't be avoided.

I kick back and close my eyes after instructing Jimbo to wake me in a couple of hours. I go through several rescue scenarios where I heroically save Melissa and she's forever grateful. Yes, I think I like my new career. I drift off to the drone of the big engines.

"Wake up, Steve-O. It's been two hours."

I snap right awake. I dial in Panama City's beacon and the plane adjusts its course. Radio traffic has picked up, we're not far out. I spot a plane above us going in the opposite direction. I announce to my enlarged crew that we're on the final approach and to "extinguish all reefer."

The landing goes without a hitch and we do a splash and dash. It was the same grinning fueler and he instructs me to "please hurry back." Naturally, he would.

I was pleasantly surprised at how easy the DC-3 was to land. She's a fine craft. We're soon flying over Colombia and I keep Bogota far to the right. We cross several large rivers which allows Andy to keep us in the know. I'm reminded of the time when we got our hands on some Columbian Gold weed. The stuff was kick ass and tasted like hash. It was a slow-burning, resin-filled reefer. We're all amazed at how vast and lush the land is below. It truly is an awesome sight.

I ask Andy if he remembered the black, shoe polish since this is a night mission and, then to Andy's dismay, tell our new members about our recent night's mission and its aftermath. The part about the aborted Safeway douche run has everyone rolling, except Andy, of course. Life is good.

We spend the next few hours exhausting everyone's jokes. I didn't realize I knew so many Mexican jokes. I try to remember all I hear for my friend Felix's sake. I'm always sensitive to my friend's needs, wouldn't you be?

Finally, I'm able to dial in and receive Asunción's beacon as the sun begins to set. The time is near. D-Day is almost upon us.

Upon successful landing and refueling at Asunción, I estimate the final leg of our flight to be around an hour. Looking at the appropriate map, it looks like a direct flight path to Rio will take us right over Dom's place. If not, short of Rio, I can turn back and follow 040 back to Dom's.

With a few minutes to kill, I bribe the fueler into buying us five cases of beer and two bags of ice. He assures me, "No problema." I think the sight of dos pistolas will keep him on the up-and-up.

Beer iced, I pop the cap on one for the cause. I take a moment to give the crew a pep talk now that the battle is imminent. I'm good at prep talks. I throw in a quote from the colorful Al Capone. "You can get much farther with a kind word and a gun than you can with a kind word alone." Man, Capone must have been one complex dude to impart such wise words.

We take to the air, Rio's beacon dials right in. We're on our way. Andy paces the length of the plane deep in thought. This must be like a dream come true for him—going into battle, storming the hill. It seems like the next passing hour is the quickest in history.

Wonder why that is? Nevertheless, we've bullshitted around enough, I decide, and spent a shit-load of money—some of it frivolously. It's time to do or die, unfortunately.

I take her down to 1,000 feet and have everyone looking out the window to help spot what should be a semi-lit and distinguishable airstrip and villa. No luck, Rio's fast approaching, the glow of the distant city becoming more pronounced. I spot what must be 040 and do a turn-a-round. In moments, we spot Dom's place. I look across my shoulder.

"Andy, hand me a walkie-talkie. Let's see if we can make contact with Felix." Andy hurries forward and hands me one of the radios. I key it as I buzz the villa. "Felix, do you copy?"

I hear our plane's engines as he keys the mike.

"Roger that, Esteban, we read you loud and clear. We're all in place and ready to go."

I reduce the airspeed and lazily circle back. "Felix, any unusual activity to report?"

"Some activity," he radios back. "But it doesn't look like a setup."

"Ten-four. Lock and load—we're coming in."

As we slowly approach the airfield, bright lights from the Jeep come on illuminating the far end of the strip. Two people can be seen running along the strip dropping flares every 20 yards or so.

"Get ready, boys. I'm circling around one last time and taking her in. Stay in pairs and share a radio."

The plane comes alive in nervous activity. I drop the landing gear, deploy the flaps and reduce the prop pitch to where it's worked for me before. I can hear my heart in my ears as I line up on the distant airstrip. I'll have to drop her in right past the heavy foliage to take full advantage of the short strip.

"Here we go boys, showtime!" I yell. My glide path narrowly misses the dense flora, but I believe our landing gear takes out some. I cut back the power some, the stall indicator screeches and the big bird drops from the sky. We hit the ground with a jolting, resounding bang. The impact causes both my pistols to fly out of their holsters and my forehead to bounce off the yoke. We make contact with the ground again and she starts to vibrate and pull hard to the right. Over the clamor, my instincts take over and I give her some hard-left rudder, throttle up the port engine while completely cutting the starboard engine. To my relief, I wrestle her under control and she straightens out.

I slam the yoke with my hand. "Shit! We blew a fucking tire or I fucked the landing gear."

I bring her almost to a standstill as I regain my composure. Thirty yards out, two of Dom's men stand outside the Jeep. These are new faces. I don't recognize them.

"Steve-O, what the fuck happened?" Jim asks his voice thick.

I glance at the altimeter, which I relied upon because of the lack of proper lighting.

"I didn't calibrate the fucking altimeter. The barometric pressure must be way fucking off."

"Shit, Steve-O, do you think you'll be able to get her back in the air?"

"Have to, Jimbo." I key the mike. "Felix, I have two at the Jeep. When I secure those two, move in."

"Ten-four, Esteban. We're getting into position now."

"Ten-four!" I say. "Andy, you, Jim and I will exit first. Juan, the rest of you get ready to move fast."

I gather up my two pistols from the floor and re-holster them. I pat my fatigues to make sure my extra clips are still in place.

"Jimbo..."

I'm interrupted by a big bright flash 75 yards south of the villa followed by a boom that rocks our plane.

"Fuck!" I key the mike as I watch the two Jeep guys pull their weapons. "Felix, what the fuck was that?"

Floodlights surrounding the villa blast us.

"Fucking trip-wire, Esteban! Must have been a fucking trip-wire attached to a claymore! Shit, we lost a man!"

I key the mike again as I rev the port engine and spin the plane in its spot.

"Take the two out now," I yell into the radio.

I cut the engine and can no longer see the pair, but the sound of automatic gunfire fills the air. I jump up.

"Listen up, men." I pull a boot, yank off a white sock and cut an armband from it with my Uncle Henry. "We forgot our white arm-bands. Hurry, those of you who can, make some now."

I cut two more, tossing one to Andy and then one to Jim.

"Listen up. Avoid shooting at the back upper corner room there—that's where Melissa stays. Okay, let's move out."

I grab an AR and a couple of double clips, open the cabin door, jump and roll. I regain my footing and scramble for cover behind the Jeep. Both of Dom's men lay dead in the dirt. The Jeep is riddled with bullet holes. Both driver's side tires are flat. As I look on, gunfire spews from the upper windows of the villa.

I glance back at the big bird as our men scatter and advance on the villa. The landing gear looks intact, but the port side tire is obviously down. It sounds like the Fourth of July.

"Jim, Andy, move out. I'm going to bring up the rear in the Jeep."

With a war cry and pot-shots at the villa, Andy is first out of the gate. Jim shakes his head and takes off after him. A bullet whizzes by my ear, reminding me a battle is underway. I'm a good 300 yards or better from the house, but I squeeze off half a clip anyway, targeting the windows that seem to be unleashing the most gunfire. I love my AR.

I key the mike. "Good work, Felix. I'm taking the Jeep and moving in. Tell your men to watch for crossfire."

"Roger that, Esteban."

I watch for a minute and occasionally catch sight of a white armband as the wearer slowly advances on their target. I toss the AR in the passenger seat, spin the Jeep around and push it, flats and all, for all its worth. Several rounds ping off the hood. A round takes out a headlight. The villa slowly starts to fall into darkness as the floodlights are extinguished one-by-one by our gunfire.

Just shy of the back entrance and right below Melissa's window, I slam on the brakes, throw the Jeep into neutral and bail out. I do another roll and come up fast on my feet and find temporary sanctuary under the house's eaves. The Jeep rolls to a stop 20 feet to my right. I catch my breath and key the mike.

"Felix, everyone, I'm at the back entrance. I'm going in. I'm going in after her. Try not to shoot me."

"Roger that, Esteban," Felix radios. "Several of us are at the front entrance and fixing to enter."

My adrenaline has me pumped. I take several, deep breaths in an attempt to gain some composure. I draw my pieces, hold my breath and burst through the rear entrance. I sweep the large room and let out my breath. All clear.

I yell out. "Dom, I'm fucking coming for you. Let the woman loose and the rest of you and your men can live to fight another day— otherwise, I'll fucking kill you and torch your fucking house."

I hear a struggle ahead. Dom pops through the foyer door shielded by the struggling Melissa. He has what appears to be a small-caliber pistol to her head.

"Fuck you, Esteban. Now you're going to listen to me or Mel dies. Radio your men to retreat. NOW, you sonofabitch!"

"Poor choice of words, Dom, but you got me between a rock and a hard place. I'm going to lower my guns."

He's not giving me much choice. Feet spaced, Dom is maintaining his grip on the still struggling Melissa. I slowly lower my pistols, but in doing so, I hear my daddy's voice. "His feet, Son." What? "His feet are exposed." Thanks, Dad.

I squeeze off two thundering rounds from my big Colt. The second-round scores—Dom's right foot disintegrates. His leg kicks out from beneath him and he and Melissa go down—hit the polished floor. Dom lets out a hair-curling scream that must resonate throughout his entire home. Still, he manages to keep Melissa between him and me. The stump of his foot is bleeding profusely, I can see the bone. He's quickly taking on an ashen pallor.

"You fucking bastard! I'll kill you!" Dom screams.

He drops his arm to shoot but exposes his right shoulder. We both squeeze off a shot. I feel a tug at my side. In that same instant, the top of his shoulder is reduced to bloody gore. The impact of the .45 round sends him sprawling and renders his gun arm useless. He stares up at me in disbelief.

Melissa, slipping in the blood, struggles to her feet. Her slip of a dress is torn, exposing a breast. In a panic, she traverses the space between us and almost knocks me down as we make contact and she locks her arms around me. Hysterical sobs escape her lips as she squeezes the breath out of me.

I whisper in her ear. "You're going to be alright now. Your mom and dad sent me."

Still gripping my pistols, I hold on the best I can. The dying Dom looks on in puzzlement.

"Who the fuck are you?" he mumbles.

"Well, Dom, funny you should ask this late in the game. Back in Texas, some call me Steven Paul. Sorry to shoot and run, but our chariot awaits."

With Melissa still clinging tight, I turn my back on him and maneuver Melissa toward the rear door. Before we can exit, Melissa increases her grip and lets out a wail of anguish. Over the renewed sobs, I hear the distinctive click of a hammer and then one of Dom's last orders: "Shoot Him! Kill him now!"

I slowly turn to face an armed and grinning Miguel.

"Ah. Esteban, you crazy rascal." He shakes his head in disbelief and amusement. "You fucking had me going. Good one."

"Shoot him, dammit! Now! What are you waiting for you imbecile?"

Miguel looks down on the dying Dom. "Would you mind shutting your pie hole. You know, on second thought, I think you've worn out your usefulness."

With that Miguel caps him between the eyes. The spent shell pings off the hard tile. My ears ring from the multiple gunshots. A stab of pain in my side hits me.

"You're bleeding, Esteban," Miguel comments.

I can feel the heat in my side and smell copper.

"What can I say? The shit got off a lucky shot."

Miguel laughs.

"Whatcha got in that-there satchel, Miguel?"

He smiles. "Oh, about $300,000 reasons to bum a ride out of this dump."

I give him the John Belushi one-brow lift. "Oh yeah, and what's in it for me?"

"I don't shoot you." He smiles.

"Works for me. Would you hold one of these guns for a second?"

He walks over and takes my .45 so I can use the walkie-talkie.

"Felix, men, I have Melissa. We'll be exiting the rear with Miguel, yes Miguel." I repeat. "He changed teams. Converge on the rear and cover us. Then everyone to the plane who's going."

I get several "Roger that."

"Miguel if you would turn the Jeep around so I can load Melissa, then we can bee-line it to the plane. You know, I'm kind of glad I didn't have to kill you."

"Thanks," he says. "I'm kinda glad about that myself."

I stroke Melissa's hair with my now free hand. "You're going to be fine, Melissa. We're taking you home."

I feel a quiver run through her, but her sobs are slowly subsiding. Some gunfire can still be heard.

"Okay, listen, I'm going to need your help a little. I need you to get in the Jeep with me as fast as possible so we can get to the plane. Do you understand?"

She nods and her chest heaves as she suppresses a sob.

"Okay, you got to let go of me now. Hold on a sec, let me get this for you." I quickly tie, the best I can, her torn strap. "Okay."

Miguel has the Jeep backed almost to the door. Nobody is shooting at him. They must not realize yet he's changed sides. I hurry her the short distance, shielding her with my own body. Miguel tosses my AR into the back and I pull Melissa onto my lap to protect her the best I can. Miguel guns the Jeep and we're out of there as fast as the crippled vehicle will carry us. We seem not to be drawing any fire from the waning battle. Contrary to popular belief, drawing fire is not a pleasant experience. Firing on others seems more rewarding.

Miguel slides the Jeep to a stop near the big plane. A frown creases his face when he spots the plane's blown tire.

"Esteban, you going to be able to get this craft back in the air?"

I shrug. "Let's get Melissa on board. We'll sweat the small stuff later."

He shakes his head but then smiles. "You're the man, Esteban."

Together we hustle Melissa on board. Miguel disembarks the plane to cover our returning crew. I buckle Melissa into a mid-row seat and find an old cargo blanket to throw over her still shivering body. Cried out, her red, round eyes watch me. Another stab of pain hits me. I look down to find my shirt saturated in blood. I tentatively raise my shirt to view the damage. The sight of the oozing wounds makes me light-headed and somewhat nauseated. I swallow back a mouthful of bile. There are entry and exit holes— right through the old love handle. Who said love handles serve no purpose? This one clearly did, it caught a round. I smile at the absurdity of my thoughts. At least the bleeding has mostly stopped. I take a seat next to Melissa as the returning begin to board the plane.

One by one, all are slowly accounted for. Only one of my crew managed to get shot—me. Ain't that some shit? As far as anyone can tell, only one of Andre's recruits died. The one that found the tripwire. At least that was instant, I think.

The gunfire has all but ceased. Nothing but lively chatter about our success. What lingers and goes mostly unsaid, is whether I'll be able to get the old girl back in the air.

I stand. "Jim, take my seat, watch over Melissa." I give her a reassuring squeeze on the shoulder before stepping out of Jim's way.

"Everybody take a seat and buckle up."

"Esteban, you've lost a lot of blood," Felix says. "Maybe we should tend to your wound first."

"All in good time. First, we've got to get this bird in the air. No telling who has been called and is on the way as we speak."

"Esteban, I left a man behind to cut the phone lines as soon as the gunfire started."

"Good, join me up front," I feel like saying, "If you believe in prayers, now is a good time to use one." Of course, I don't. Not something John, John Wayne that is, or I would say. We just don't go there.

The windsock indicates a decent southerly wind, I take that as a good sign. We'll need less ground speed and less runway to take to the air.

"What do you think, Esteban?" Felix asks sensing my obvious concern.

"Shit Felix, the wind is in our favor, but getting into the air is one thing, landing is another. My guess: I think we'll be fine," says he, the only one who managed to get shot.

To compensate for the pull, I decide on giving the starboard prop more bite and hope the added rudder will be enough to keep us from veering off the strip which is still lit up with flares. Nothing to do but test my theory—I put the throttles to her. As before, she lumbers down the strip but despite the intense vibration, she picks up speed. Just shy of do or die, at the end of the strip, I ease back on the yoke. To my utter relief, she takes to the air, narrowly avoiding the dense foliage and hillside that threatened us.

There's a chorus of cheers and olés. Felix backhands me on the shoulder in excitement and relief.

"Fucking A, man!" I wince at the pain in my side.

"Sorry, man," he says. I optimize the prop's pitch and throttles as we arrive at the desired cruising altitude. I wince again. A bead of sweat runs down from my temple.

"Felix, man, I think I might need to be patched up now and I definitely need a beer or two." I stand. "I'll start with the beer," I say as I step into the cabin.

I receive a round of cheers and a mock standing ovation. Not dying, I realize, motivates people to express themselves more openly. Who would have guessed?

Juan hands me an uncapped iced one. I greedily suck down its contents and then roll the chilled bottled across my forehead.

"Esteban, you don't look so good," he tells me. He digs out another beer after relieving me of my empty. "You going to be alright, man?"

"Yeah." I qualify, "I think."

I watch as Felix rummages through the box of emergency items Wallace put together for us. To my dismay, he sets a small propane torch to the side. He adds to this a tube of salve, some white gauze and a roll of duct tape. I'm not crazy about what he's thinking.

"Esteban, we're going to have to cauterize that wound."

I manage a squeaky, "You think?" Of course, I'm being facetious. I rate cauterizing one's own wounds right up there with purposely doing a head dive off of one's own two-story house. I guess I'll have to bite the bullet. Literally, bite the bullet, that is. Well, that and I hope I don't pass out like some sissy.

"Lay on your side and hand me your knife, Esteban," Felix says as he sparks and adjusts the flame.

"The bullet went straight through, Felix, I don't think you need to operate." I weakly joke. I hand him my knife. He takes it and flicks it open.

"A few of you hold him down. I imagine this is going to hurt."

I know he doesn't mean 'this is going to hurt me more than you.' You know the drill—that youthful speech we sometimes got before a justified whuppin'. It makes me wonder what kind of demented psychologist or psychiatrist came up with that bullshit? Well, I guess that's not really the point, is it? The point, I believe, is that this is going to fucking hurt.

A good inch of blade glows red. I'm having some serious second thoughts. The hiss upon contact and the excruciating pain is enough to curl my toes in my boots. With that in mind, I do what any equally situated brave man would do—I squeeze as many expletives as I can into one continuous sentence and broadcast it as loud as humanly possible. For an encore, I repeat my performance as the exit wound is seared. Hey, I do what I can.

I realize in many ways, I was lucky the shot went straight through. It was a small caliber, it missed vital organs and Dom was using a steel jacket as opposed to a hollow point—which would have made for a messy exit wound. My lucky streak continues.

Someone dashes my face with ice water to bring me back around. I wasn't really out of it, you know. I was just checking the opaqueness of my eyelids. Always a good policy to check for opaqueness now and then.

I'm helped to a sitting position. Felix applies the salve and gauze and then wraps me in duct tape. I spot Andy and think: "I'd rather be duct-taped than douched." I smile—as you know, I amuse myself easily. I'm helped to my feet. I pull the rest of my shirt off and toss it to the floor. Juan hands me another pain killer and I gulp down half of the crisp brew. Felix discovers some overlooked aspirin and hands me four of them. I eat them all. Jim vacates his seat and I ease down next to Melissa. Her tears are gone and she manages a weak smile.

"You can curse pretty loud when you need to," she says. "Does it hurt?"

I laugh. "Only when I laugh." For emphasis, I involuntarily wince, but I believe I scored a painful point with her. She blesses me with a more pronounced smile.

"Are you crazy?" she asks. "I watched you several times from the window."

"Nah, quite a performance, huh?"

"Yeah, who's flying the plane?"

"I am."

"I was kind of afraid of that," she says but smiles again.

I naturally instill confidence in people, I kid myself.

"Speaking of which, perhaps I should get back to, umm, you know..."

"Flying the plane," she finishes for me.

"Yeah, flying." I ruffle her hair and wink at her. "Here's looking at you kid," I say for no particular reason. I say many things for this same reason. I can't say I'm not consistent. I ease myself back out of the seat.

"Can I get you anything before I go back to, umm, you know..."

She giggles slightly. "Flying."

"Yeah, flying."

"Could I have a beer?"

"At your service, my lady," I say and painfully bow for her.

The things I put myself through for a pretty face amazes even me at times. I fetch, uncap and hand her a beer. I attentively watch over her as she takes her first sip. Her smiles are coming quicker. I think she's going to make a rapid recovery from her ordeal. I now notice her eyes no longer have that drugged look like they did the first time I saw her.

"Shouldn't you be flying the plane?"

"Oh yeah, right you are. Jimbo, come and keep Melissa entertained while I go fly the plane."

Felix joins me in the cockpit and hands me another beer. The night is clear, the sky brilliant with stars, the vastness below a blanket of darkness. Between swallows, I drift off into a fitful sleep, often brought close to the surface by tangled thoughts.

"Wake up, Esteban," registers through the fog.

I force my eyes open. "What is it, Felix?"

"Man, you've been out for a long time. You've been mumbling and you're sweating hard. It's hot up here, but not that hot. I think you're getting a fever, man. Here, take some more aspirin."

Felix tries to hand me six this time. He hands me a coke this time.

"And wash them down with coke. The caffeine and the sugar might help."

I dutifully do so. The soda is actually quenching. "So, this is what these things taste like—I've always wondered."

"Right," Felix says. "I've only spotted one plane so far and an occasional cluster of lights on the ground."

"Meaning we're still right-side up, absent vertigo. You'll make a fine copilot someday, Felix."

"Thanks."

I dial in Panama City's beacon. The plane makes a major adjustment to the west. Probably a good thing Felix woke me up, I think to myself. I make radio contact with the tower and explain that we have a tire down. They have me on their radar and I'm 30 minutes out. The tower informs me they'll have fire trucks on scene. I suggest they foam the runway, too. They inform me they don't have foam and it's only used when there's a landing gear problem. Hey, it was worth a shot anyway, right?

I do remember to calibrate the altimeter with the current barometric pressure. I'm a quick study—sometimes. I send Felix back to inform our passengers that we're soon to be on the final approach and that now might be a good time to say a few words and buckle up. Note: I didn't say "last words."

Our fears turn out to be unfounded. I set the big girl down lightly and the only excitement is the shower of sparks we trail until I manage to bring her to a stop. To say the least, everyone is now jubilant once more. Surviving does that for you—like totally losing control of your ride and not hitting a thing. Someday I hope to experience that 'not hitting a thing' part of my analogy. I'm big on new experiences.

Four hours later and $2,000 additional dollars lighter, we have a used wheel and tire and we're once again in the air. Fortunately, we were allowed to make another beer purchase and I also was able to score a popular recreational drug here, a bottle of penicillin—or morning-after pill for this neck of the woods. Safe sex in a bottle. Perhaps a new marketing approach I've stumbled upon? It's all about marketing, you know. I decide to retrace the path we took on our last return trip. I'm really picking up on the art of navigation. Perhaps my next feat will be crossing the Atlantic solo in a single prop Cessna. Nah, I decide, I believe something similar has already been done. How about this? Have Andy stand on the wing of the plane for the crossing. Now, that has kind of a neat ring to it, don't you think?

"Esteban, you have that scheming look again."

"Oh yeah? What gives me away, Felix?"

"You're not talking. Your mouth's not moving."

"And all this time I thought that indicated I wasn't lying."

We laugh before I go relieve Jim of his seat next to Melissa. She briefly smiles before turning back to stare out her window. Again, it crosses my mind that she is already on her way to healing. We fucking did it, I realize. Our methods were unorthodox and we still fucking made it. I can only come to one conclusion: I'm a natural at this. I bet you already beat me to that conclusion, though, didn't you? You slick devil.

Made a nice little lick off the deal, too. 'To the victor goes the spoils.' Isn't that how that goes? A nice briefcase bonus.

Miguel takes the aisle seat across from me. "You know, Esteban, it's been fun, but I might better get off in Mexico somewhere. This plane may very well be intercepted crossing back into the U.S. and I have $300,000 reasons not to be caught there."

I laugh. "Speaking of which, how again is it that you ended up with my money?"

"I promised I wouldn't shoot you," he says and smiles.

I return the smile. "Ah, yes you did, my friend. Unfortunately, we shan't be making any stops in Mexico. Sorry, I can't help you there. For what it's worth, I would if I could."

"Somehow, I believe you, Esteban. I noticed some parachutes. I could parachute out just west of Cancun."

"True, true, Miguel, but unfortunately you don't own any of them-there parachutes," I say with a southern twang.

He laughs. "Can't get one past you, can I? Let's see, I suppose one could be purchased if the price was right, eh Esteban?"

"You know the parachutes in question were hand stitched by the finest artisans of the craft in the choicest of silk and then lovingly hand packed."

"They look like surplus World War II 'chutes to me."

"To an untrained eye, I suppose. Did I mention they were antiques as well?" I say and smile.

"How much?"

"You do know they come in sets?"

"But I only need one."

I shrug. "I'll tether the other one to you."

"Gee, you would do that for me? Okay, look, you win," he says sounding exasperated. "Ten thousand."

"A piece."

He lets out a heavy sigh.

"Fuck it, ten apiece and you even get to keep the extra 'chute."

"Well then, let's see, at 10,000 feet with a decent westward breeze, you should drift sufficiently inland."

"But, of course, we don't know which way the wind is blowing, eh Esteban?"

I rub my chin. "Hmm, I kind of see your dilemma there, but still feel there's a good chance the air current is moving inland."

"Right, Esteban and what are the odds?"

"Oh, I'd say at least 25 percent."

"I was being facetious."

"And I'm only guessing."

"Okay, I'll bite again, Esteban. How much to increase my odds to 100 percent?"

"And have me blatantly flaunt international law by violating foreign airspace. To jeopardize crew and plane. Surely you jest? By the way, I picked up the 'surely you jest' jargon from your former boss."

"Commendable. Okay, another $20,000."

"Deal!" I blurt out.

"What! Deal? No more haggling, Esteban?"

"Why? What's money between friends?"

He sighs again as he digs in his satchel, produces four banded $10,000 stacks and drops them one at a time in my lap.

"Thanks, I say. "You do realize I was only joking and would have done it for free."

"You're all heart, Esteban."

"Thanks, that means a lot coming from you. Well, plenty of parachutes—pick your poison."

Miguel returns a minute later with parachute in hand. "Esteban, there's no back up 'chute."

"Yep, that's the problem with vintage World War II parachutes. Look, only one in a thousand traditionally fail, but that's why I'm so keen on selling them in sets."

"Again, you're all heart, Esteban!" He squeezes my shoulder." You're alright for an American and a white guy."

I can't see, but I can feel Melissa's smile beside me.

"Miguel, you get bored someday, look me up. Come to Austin, Texas and ask around for Steven Paul. I shouldn't be hard to find."

I stick out my hand and we shake.

"Sure, Steven Paul, why the hell not?"

We end up skirting Cancun by a good margin, say our goodbyes and watch Miguel disappear out the cabin door into the awaiting darkness. He turned out to be alright, I decide. All he needed was the proper guidance and a role model, right? As a born leader, my guidance comes with the package. I dish it out for free.

Chapter 25

The Gulf is rife with boats below, we're coming up fast on what I believe will be the Texas coast. We have also, I am sure, entered U.S. airspace. I drop us to 1,000 feet. Our shadow parallels us on our port side. It's going to be a bright, hot, cloudless June day. Our shadow crosses a platform. Workers on the top wave at us. It's looking more and more likely we're going to make it. Felix rejoins me in the cockpit and hands me an open long-neck. We bump bottles.

"Well, Esteban, I can't believe it, but it looks like we've made it."

"I wish I had Andy up here so that I could knock on wood," I say and we both laugh.

Andy pops his head into the cockpit. "Did I hear my name?"

"Yeah," I say and point to one of the dials. "You see this little spot of the dial?"

"No."

"Look closer."

He leans in and I rap my knuckles on his head.

"Ouch, fucker," Andy says. Felix and I laugh. A moment later Andy joins in.

"Hey, just fucking with you about the dial," I say. "But get the maps out, we should be spotting land any time now."

A shadow passes us on the water and the roar of jet engines rattle our big bird. We watch as a jet streaks by us from above. I look over at Felix.

"I think we have company."

"Shit!" Felix yells.

Jim steps into the cockpit. "Steve-O, what the fuck was that?"

"Fucking fighter jet." I reach over and turn on the radio, as I watch, in the distance, the jet circles back. "I suppose we better see what he wants."

"This is Captain T.F. Riley with the United States Air Force to DC-3, you have entered and are now violating U.S. airspace. Alter flight path and proceed to Hobby Airport. This is an order."

"Fuck, Steve-O, what are we going to do?"

I pick up the mike and key it. "Sorry Charlie, only the best tasting tuna gets to be Starkist."

"Steve-O, what the fuck was that?"

"Land ahoy boys, we're going to make a run for it." I drop her down to skim the water. "Andy! Give me San Antonio's beacon and hurry."

Crumpled map in hand, Andy squeezes by Jim and points it out on the map. I dial her in and manually correct our course.

The jet buzzes us again. "I repeat this is the United States Air Force, you are ordered to proceed directly to Hobby Airport."

"Juan," I yell. "New plan, when I set her down at Wallace's, you and your boys bail first, get in your ride, haul ass to San Antonio and get lost. We'll hook up later. We'll leave out moments behind you and head to Austin."

"I hear you, man," Juan replies.

"Jimbo, Felix, gather up all our weapons, we'll dump them in your trunk and we're out of there once we give Juan a couple of minutes head start."

"What if the jet shoots us down, Steve?" Andy asks sounding pumped up.

"He won't now. He can't put the public in danger." I turn the radio off. "Well, boys, I guess Andy's head isn't made out of wood after all."

I'm joined by a couple of nervous laughs. Shit, I think, so fucking close to making it. Well, I can only hope for the best now.

Short of San Antonio, I veer to the south as I pick up I-35.

"Get ready, boys and girls! We're fixing to be on final approach."

I spot Wallace's place to the west and bank hard as I simultaneously lower the landing gear, deploy the flaps and cut our airspeed. With a sharp bank to the north, I line her up with the grass strip and gently set her down. I kill her engines and momentarily forget my wound as I jump to my feet. A stab of pain slows me down as I step into the cabin. I watch as the cabin door is pushed open and Juan's men bound from the plane one at a time. I snatch my two holsters from the floor where I had dropped them, sling them over a shoulder and reach for Melissa's nervous hand.

"Come on, Melissa, I think you have some people here eager to see you," I say and smile at her reassuringly.

We're last to exit the plane and I lead her down the steps. She maintains her grip on my hand until we round the tail of the plane and spot John and Martha hurrying the best they can across the open pasture. She releases her hold and dashes off in their direction. The reunion makes for a touching scene. Above us, the jet roars past. I watch as Juan's ride tears around the corner of Wallace's home and disappears from sight.

I amble over, not wanting to spoil the moment as my boys load the trunk of Jim's big Buick. John and Martha finally look over. Tears stream down Martha and Melissa's faces. John's face is flushed.

"Sorry to have to eat and run," I joke. "But I fear the authorities will be descending on this place shortly."

Martha, for the first time, notices the duct tape and my blood-stained jeans and boots.

"Oh my God! You're hurt!" she screams.

I hold up my hands. "I'm fine, but we're out of here."

"Bless you—bless all you boys," the emotion-filled Martha manages. Wallace steps forward and offers his big callused hand.

We shake. "Thank you, Son. I'll handle things on this end. My daughter is more important than any storm I could possibly have to weather. You and your boys get on out of here. I'll get with you as soon as I can. You can count on me taking care of you all." He wraps his arms around me and gives me a brief bearhug. "Thanks, Son."

Jim honks the horn.

"See you folks around," I say before taking shotgun in Jim's waiting Riviera and pulling the door shut.

Jim puts his foot in the throttle and we're out of there, kicking up grass and rock. Jim doesn't back off until we hit I-35 and are northbound. He wipes his face on his sleeve as we fall in line with a pack of cars heading our way.

"Shit, Steve-O, what do you think will happen now?"

"Oh, I imagine there will be a hell of an investigation. The law will, of course, suspect smuggling of some sort, but I think Wallace will protect our identity if at all possible. For now, when we hit Austin, I think it best we split up and lay low for a few days. John will get with us when he can."

"Umm, Steve, what about my parents and my house? You said you'd help me explain things to them," Andy says.

"Right, I do vaguely recall saying something to that effect. I tell you what, you head on over, sneak in and I'll catch up with you later."

"Okay, I guess."

I dig in my boots and start pulling the banded cash that I had stashed within. I hand each a $10,000 bundle, all the while maintaining a shit-eating grin.

"A dividend, boys," I say.

"Where in the hell did you get that, Esteban?" Felix says.

Jim laughs. "He sold Miguel a parachute and a drop zone."

"No shit?"

"I shit you not," Jim says and we all laugh.

"We've another hundred grand to split at the house," I say.

"A hundred and four, Steve-O," Jim corrects with a smile.

"That can go toward expenses. You forget, Jimbo, I had to pay two grand out of my pocket for the wheel and tire. Plus, I want to give the girls and James a little something out of the four."

We continue on in silence and thought. As we hit the southern limits of Austin, I'm feeling much better about the situation. I've almost convinced myself we'll come out of this unscathed, other than my gunshot wound and busted eye.

We stop along the way to load up on beer. My heart starts to beat faster in anticipation of seeing Candy. I'm eager to tell her how things played out. I realize I'm also eager to see the dogs and others, as well. Other than the looming threat of legal woes, I decide life is good.

Jim pulls in beside the big Bonneville. I'm quick to make it out of the car and to the door. The dogs are sounding off within. I open the door to wagging tails and hyperactivity.

"Okay, okay, down Bonnie Girl." I try and stop her from hitting my wounded side. "That's a good girl. Okay, calm down. You guys, too, Rosie and Smokey."

I straighten back up.

"Daddy's home!" I loudly announce. I wonder where everyone is? I move on to the kitchen where I find James sitting at the table and drinking a beer.

"James, my man, where's everyone?" I ask. He remains silent.

"James, where is Candy?" I ask more forcibly. He points to the kitchen counter. It takes a second to register. On the counter sits an envelope. Butterflies hit me as I take a tentative step forward.

"No," I moan out loud. "Not fucking again."

I retrieve the envelope. For some reason, it feels heavy in my hand. I remove the single sheet of paper within.

"Dear Steven Paul, if you're reading this now you must have made it back. This is a hard letter for me to write. Please don't take it wrong. This is not a Dear John in the true sense. I will return someday to fight the other women off. For now, I hope you understand, knowing my family situation, I have left again for Rio. Because of you, I now have found the sister I never had and that I've always wanted and dreamed of. Jane has decided to take a leave of absence and we plan to travel around some. John was kind enough to float me a loan until I can decide what I want to do with the plane and my life. For now, I hope you know how much I've come to care for you. I'm leaving and entrusting you with my most valued possession: Bonnie. I know you will love and care for her as I do. Fear not, I shall return, buster. I think you'll fare okay. I sense you have a lot more oats to sow. Not to mention there's the beautiful Brandy to pursue. I think she likes you and I know Sandra has her eyes on you. For now, you're welcome to use the house as long as you like. I only ask that you keep the lights and power current. Well, I guess I better close. There are still some hours until my flight leaves. I think I'll spend the time constructively crying. Love you, Candy.

PS: If you see my sorry husband, kick his ass for me. xoxo."

I re-read the letter before returning it to its envelope. Well, if that ain't the shit, I think to myself.

"Sorry, Steve, I tried to talk her out of it," James says.

"Appreciate it, James, but it's okay. Shit happens."

He stares down at the table.

"Yeah, I guess so. Hey, I'm going to catch a ride with Jim and them."

"Sure," I say as I take a beer from the fridge and take a seat at the table. Andy enters the kitchen carrying a couple cases of beer and sets them on the table near me.

"Can you watch my dogs?"

"Sure, Andy, why not."

"Cool. You still going to show up at my house later?"

"Sure, why not."

Jim and Felix step into the kitchen.

"Steve-O, we're out of here. You have a safety deposit box now, don't you?"

"Yeah."

"Put our share of the cash in it. We'll sort things out later."

"Sure, Jimbo."

"We're out of here, Esteban. Hey man, you okay?"

"Yeah, I'll be fine. Get on out of here. Lay low for a day or two."

"See you then, man," Felix says.

I pull the tab on my Bud, take a long drink and then stare at the can for a moment. I turn the chair sideways to the table so Bonnie can put her paws in my lap and I can scratch her behind her ears.

"It looks like it's just me and you again, kid. Still feel like that trip to Georgia to visit dad? Oh, does that tail wag mean a yes? You know, he came through a time or two when things got hairy. Said, 'Son, stick with the plan.' Funny, huh girl?" I take another long pull from my beer. "Yep, you and me against the world."

I become aware of the scent of coconut. I turn to see a bikini-clad Sandra staring at me. She comes over, gently pushes Bonnie to the side and straddles me to sit in my lap.

"Hey, what about me, Steven Paul? You still have me."

"I suppose," I emote.

"You're crazy about the girl, right."

"Yeaahhh." I draw it out.

She lifts my chin. "Ah, cheer up. I think I can lift your spirits."

"Really?" I brighten somewhat.

"Yeah, really."

"Well, your tan is coming along really nicely and your breasts are glistening with perspiration." I pull the bow tie holding her top up and it falls loose before me. I take an involuntary gulp. They're... Well, they're very nice. "You smell like coconut. Life does go on, right?"

She wiggles provocatively in my lap. "Life goes on."

"And didn't Ewell Gibbons say 'some parts of the coconut are edible?'"

"Something like that," she says and smiles.

I return her smile. "Count me in, girl."

We both laugh as she pulls me to my feet.

"It was the duct tape that did it for you, right?" I joke.

"That and your big guns."

"Naturally."

"Oh, and I went ahead and took the liberty to put the few things of mine in our bedroom."

She pulls me toward the bathroom.

"I wouldn't have it any other way," I say and we both laugh.

"Let's clean you up some," she says.

"Okay and while we do that, I can tell you about the mission. Man, you should have seen me—gunfire everywhere..."

Chapter 26

Well, what do you think? Crazy, huh? Not me, the story, I mean. I only cop to being bipolar, sometimes. Oh, by the way, no animals were hurt during the sharing of this tale. You're probably wondering if I embellished some. Nah, I say, I may have taken a few liberties and perhaps I might be remembering things in the light most favorable to me, but, in my defense, it was a long time ago and I was only a teen at the time.

Anyhow, back to the present. The present sucks. Prison sucks. With that in mind, I appreciate you getting me mentally out of my cell for a while and allowing me to share part of the summer with you. Some of my antics still bring me smiles and I truly do enjoy sharing them. Maybe I got a laugh or two out of you, too? Or maybe even a smile? Perhaps, eh? If so, I've accomplished something.

In some ways, I'm still that 17-year-old. Still have hopes and dreams and I'm still optimistic that I'll be free again. Some days, however, the reality of the situation takes the wind out of my sails—like the fact that the wheels of justice turn so slowly. Contrary to public belief, the cards are stacked against the accused. One only needs to look at the rash of recent exonerations, some taking up to 20 or 25 years, to know the truth of this statement. Well, that's neither here nor there. Or like the fact that other inmates call me "school." Short for "old school." Or like when I look into the fiberglass mirror to shave and the reflection is someone I hardly recognize anymore.

Long gone is the thick, sun-lightened mane of my youth and the stubble on my chin has now begun to turn white. Can't turn back the clock, though, can we?

Physically, I guess, I'm okay despite living hard, the resulting broken bones, the necessary pins and plates and multiple operations. Also long gone are the abs and the motivation to maintain them. Still, ladies, I polish up right nicely.

Could I snap back? Sure, the right news from the lawyers, or the right inspiration via snail mail and accompanied by the photo of a scantily clad woman. Yes, I'm still big on scantily clad women. Who would have ever thought?

For now, I can be found at the Wynne Unit and my prisoner number is 1638937. Yep, that's my number, I shit you not. Or if that should fail, check for my current contact information at stevenpaulwilson.com. Beyond my hopes of freedom, my aspirations include the conversion of the family ranch in Lexington, Texas to an animal sanctuary, the whiling away of my remaining years with family and friends and then passing the ranch and the torch to someone young and enthusiastic. Oh, and I'd like to go snowboarding a few more times, too. And just to see the current Bonnie, my Texas Dingo, again would mean the world to me.

So, was that summer of '76 the beginning of a long downward spiral for me? Maybe, maybe not—the jury's still out. No doubt the introduction of easy money and all that entails played some part. The drugs, the booze and the flagrant disregard for the law weigh in as well. Well, it is what it is.

For those of you who missed the proceeding four-and-a-half days leading into this story, check it out. I wrote it all down and titled it

Hindsight. That summer of '76 didn't end with the heartbreaking loss of Candy. Oh yeah, the summer continued on and I'm soon to chronicle a few more days and title it "Wayward." To say the least, my life took some surprising twists. Some wild challenges for the crew and me which we tackled mostly head-on in our customary fashion—we winged it. A vicariously liable "we." I'm quick to share the spotlight. Just kidding. Those who know me, know I always have their back.

In closing, ladies and gentlemen, boys and girls, I hope you join me again, get some laughs from my antics, but learn from my mistakes. In all seriousness, if it's within your power, go out and adopt a cat/kitten, pup or dog today. The world will be a better place for it. If you're not in such a position, sponsor some hard-to-adopt animal. Unconditional love is there for the adopting.

For now, take care and I hope to see you out there someday.

Sincerely, Steven Paul

About the Author

Steven Paul Wilson is the author of six novels in the Steven Paul Series and two in The Eddie Winston Series. He was raised in Austin, Texas and considers it and Lexington, Texas home. He currently writes from his prison cell in the Texas Department of Criminal Justice where he's currently working on his ninth novel. He's an avid reader and animal rights advocate who hopes to someday be freed and to convert the family ranch into an animal sanctuary. He also hopes his colorful life translates into good reading. To learn more about the author, visit him at stevenpaulwilson.com.

Steven Paul Wilson

Donations: Please scan this QR Code to donate to this Indie author. Thank you for your generosity!

www.ingramcontent.com/pod-product-compliance
Lightning Source LLC
Chambersburg PA
CBHW051939020726
47501CB00001B/196